DEATH AT A HIGHLAND WEDDING

Also by Kelley Armstrong

Rip Through Time

Haven's Rock

Rockton

Cainsville

Age of Legends

The Blackwell Pages (co-written with Melissa Marr)

Otherworld

Darkest Powers & Darkness Rising

Nadia Stafford

Standalone novels

DEATH AT A HIGHLAND WEDDING

A Rip Through Time Novel

KELLEY ARMSTRONG

MINOTAUR BOOKS
NEW YORK

First published in the United States by Minotaur Books, an imprint of St. Martin's Publishing Group

DEATH AT A HIGHLAND WEDDING. Copyright © 2025 by KLA Fricke Inc. All rights reserved. Printed in the United States of America. For information, address St. Martin's Publishing Group, 120 Broadway, New York, NY 10271.

www.minotaurbooks.com

The Library of Congress Cataloging-in-Publication Data is available upon request.

ISBN 978-1-250-32131-2 (hardcover)
ISBN 978-1-250-40887-7 (Canadian edition)
ISBN 978-1-259-32132-9 (ebook)

Our books may be purchased in bulk for promotional, educational, or business use. Please contact your local bookseller or the Macmillan Corporate and Premium Sales Department at 1-800-221-7945, extension 5442, or by email at MacmillanSpecialMarkets@macmillan.com.

First U.S. Edition: 2025
First International Edition: 2025

10 9 8 7 6 5 4 3 2 1

INTRODUCTION

Welcome to 1870 Scotland. If you're new to the Rip Through Time series, here's a little intro to get you up to date. It might also be helpful if it's been a while since you've read the previous books. If you're caught up, just skip this and dive into chapter one.

Our tour guide on this journey is Mallory Atkinson, Vancouver police detective. In 2019, Mallory was visiting her dying grandmother in Edinburgh when a midnight jog took her into an Old Town alley. She saw what seemed to be a glitching haunted-tour hologram—a young blond in period dress being strangled by a shadowy figure. At that same moment, Mallory was attacked. When she woke up, she found herself in the body of that young woman she'd seen: Catriona Mitchell, nineteen-year-old housemaid . . . in 1869 Edinburgh.

Soon Mallory was living Catriona's life, working for Duncan Gray, a doctor and surgeon forced to take over his family's undertaking business after his father's death. Gray's about as suited to undertaking as Mallory is to housekeeping. Luckily Gray has a side gig—as an early forensic scientist helping his childhood best friend, Detective Hugh McCreadie of the Edinburgh police. Mallory soon proved that "Catriona" had a hitherto undiscovered talent for detective work along with a keen interest in forensics, and so she became Gray's assistant.

As the former housemaid, Mallory lives in Gray's town house, along with his older sister, Isla. The Gray family is a little . . . eccentric. Gray has his forensics. Isla is a talented chemist. Formidable eldest sister Annis is all about business. There's also Lachlan, the older brother who dumped the family business in Gray's lap. Mallory hasn't met him. Nor has she met their mother, who cheerfully lives abroad, seeing the world after her husband's death.

The household also includes thirteen-year-old parlormaid Alice (former pickpocket), groom Simon (formerly accused of a double murder), housekeeper Mrs. Wallace (former con artist), and the new maid Jack (former . . . something). Yes, Isla has very odd hiring practices.

Gray, McCreadie, and Isla all know Mallory's time-traveling secret, which makes life much easier. So does Mrs. Wallace, which doesn't change the fact that she's sure Mallory is going to murder her darling Isla and Gray in their sleep.

This particular adventure is going to see Gray, Isla, McCreadie, and Mallory off to a Highland wedding, accompanied by Alice and Simon. We're leaving Edinburgh and the larger cast of characters behind, so that's all you should need to know to get caught up. On to our story . . .

DEATH AT A HIGHLAND WEDDING

ONE

There's nothing quite like a Highland wedding. I say this as if I've been to dozens. I've gone to two, both times as my grandmother's plus-one, attending the weddings of happy couples I'd never actually met and had to keep checking a note on my phone to remember who they were.

This time it's different. Okay, I'm still a plus-one. And I still don't know the happy couple. But instead of keeping notes on my phone, I have them written on a piece of paper, stuffed deep into the voluminous pockets of my equally voluminous layers of Victorian dress.

The last wedding I went to in the Scottish Highlands was June 2016. This one is also taking place in June . . . 1870.

There's a story there. A long one. The short version is that I passed through time at the fickle whim of some unknown cosmic force. My nan named that force Fate and said I am exactly where I was always supposed to be. Which is apparently in the body of a buxom blond twenty-year-old housemaid instead of an athletic brunette thirty-one-year-old police detective.

I have yet to appreciate *that* part of the switch, but I must appreciate where else I landed—in the household of a chemist and her doctor-turned-undertaker brother, who works in early forensic science. Along with their police-detective friend, they know my story, so I'm no longer scrubbing chamber pots. I'm the assistant to that forensic scientist, Dr. Duncan Gray.

I'm also, apparently, his plus-one for this wedding, which is for Detective Hugh McCreadie's younger sister . . . Iona? Fiona? It's in my notes.

At the moment, we're in a coach, heading into the countryside. For propriety's sake, Gray should sit beside his sister, but since no one can see us in here, we've maneuvered McCreadie to sit beside Isla instead. He's across from me—to make room for both Isla's skirts and mine—and Gray is beside me, separated by a decorous handspan gap between my skirts and his thighs.

I'm wearing a traveling dress, which means shorter skirts and extra petticoats for warmth. My bustle pad makes the jostling journey more comfortable. I'm warm and snug, and it would be lovely, if not for the atmosphere.

Any other time, we'd be chattering away, excited about a rare country holiday. Instead, it feels as if we're going to a funeral, everyone somber and staring out windows, with Isla occasionally casting anxious glances at McCreadie.

This is not four friends off to a rousing Highland wedding. It's three friends going along to support the fourth—McCreadie—who looks like he'd rather be at work.

I don't know why McCreadie is estranged from his family. Now that we've all become friends, I think I could get that information easily, but they seem to have forgotten that I don't know, and it's awkward to ask. So I've been playing detective, putting together the puzzle pieces.

I know McCreadie's family is well-to-do. Upper middle class, like the Grays. That's how the boys became friends—they attended the same school. Despite the estrangement, McCreadie is still well-off for a police detective—criminal officer, as they're called in Victorian Scotland. I suspect he receives some family money. I know the break happened when he'd been in his early twenties, around the time he became a police officer, which is also around the time he'd broken off an engagement. I don't know how these three things—the law-enforcement career, the broken engagement, and the familial estrangement—are connected, but I suspect they are.

As for his family, he has one sibling—the sister getting married, who is significantly younger. Like Gray, McCreadie is thirty-one, and his sister seems to be about twenty-one. In the modern world, we sometimes get the impression that Victorian women were all married off at eighteen. In reality, McCreadie's sister is marrying at what's considered the perfect age, as it was for most of the twentieth century.

Any ill blood between McCreadie and his family doesn't extend to his sister, which is why we're here. She asked—begged—him to come, and so he has, for her.

Now we're rumbling along in this coach with our groom, Simon, driving and the thirteen-year-old parlormaid, Alice, riding beside him, having been invited ostensibly as Isla's lady's maid, but really to give the girl a holiday in the countryside.

When Isla casts yet another anxious glance McCreadie's way, I decide it's up to me to break this ice, which I do in the most time-honored of road-trip ways.

"Are we there yet?" I say, peering through the dusty window. "It's so much faster with the bridge."

That gets McCreadie's attention. There are people who are good at long, morose silences—such as the guy sitting beside me—but McCreadie fairly leaps on this excuse, his handsome face lightening in a smile.

"Bridge?" he says. "Over the Forth?"

"Yep."

"How is that even possible?"

"I'm not an engineer," I say. "But there's also a railroad bridge that I'm pretty sure gets built in this century."

"They are starting one next year," rumbles a voice beside me.

I glance over to see Gray, relaxing with his eyes still shut.

I elbow him. "Tell us more."

He sighs. "I do not know more. I only heard that they are beginning a suspended bridge for trains."

I frown. "Are you sure? I don't think they start construction until near the end of this century." I pause, thinking hard. "No, they did build another one, but it coll—" I snap my mouth shut. "Never mind."

Isla's brows rise. "Are you suggesting that if another bridge is built first, we should not use it?"

"Er, probably not."

"Well, I for one might be willing to play the odds, if such a thing comes about," McCreadie says. "Taking the ferry really does make this an interminable trip. Dare I ask how long it would take in your day, Mallory?"

"With bridges and motor cars? An hour to Stirling Castle. So probably two hours to where we're going."

Isla sighs. "I was born in the wrong century."

"What is going on out there?" McCreadie says, opening his window to poke his head through. "I swear we have slowed."

"See what you have done?" Gray says to me. "A few moments ago, we were all perfectly content with our eight-hour coach ride, and now everyone is complaining."

"*You* spent all of yesterday moaning about spending all of today in a coach."

His eyes narrow. "I mentioned it once."

"Once at breakfast, once while we were dissecting that liver, once while—"

"I had resigned myself to the journey," he says. "And now you have spoiled it. Remember whose coach this is. It will be a much longer trip if you walk."

"Can I walk?" I say. "Please?" I lean toward McCreadie's open window. "I'm sure I can move faster than this."

"There does appear to be some sort of slowdown," McCreadie says, still looking out the window.

"See what you did?" Gray aims a mock glare my way. "You complain about our speed, and the universe takes umbrage."

"Can you tell what's going on up there?" I ask McCreadie.

His smile sparks. "No, which means we ought to investigate."

McCreadie raps on the roof for Simon to stop the carriage. As I gather my skirts, Gray rises and reaches for the door handle.

"Opening the door for us?" McCreadie says. "Very kind, but unnecessary. Stay right there and nap—"

Gray is already out of the coach. Then McCreadie holds the door as I descend.

"Not joining us?" I say to Isla.

"I deem this particular mystery too minor to deserve my attention. I will stay here, and absolutely will not stretch my legs onto the other seat in a most unladylike fashion. Nor will I sneak anything from the picnic basket in your absence."

Gray slowly turns around.

She rolls her eyes. "Do not worry, Duncan. If I open the basket, I shall take only a sandwich. Sometimes I think I would *prefer* a brother who worried instead about me behaving in an unladylike fashion. Now go. Your beloved pastries are safe."

As soon as we're out of the coach, the problem is evident: it's a traffic jam. The road curves ahead, but there are three coaches between us and that curve. Simon had discussed the route with Gray, and they'd decided to avoid the major road and take a side one. Seems everyone else did the same, and now it's like leaving modern-day Vancouver on a Friday, heading up to the lakes and mountains and fresh air of the Okanagan.

I'm guessing it will get better the farther we travel from Edinburgh, but for now, this really is like those weekend traffic snarls—city folk trying to get a bit of time away on a gorgeous June day.

It's *not* the weekend here. In fact, it's Monday. Weekends aren't a thing yet, at least not in the sense of getting time off. If you're nobility, you have all the time off you want. Middle class? Depends on where you fall on that scale. Gray runs his family's lucrative business and can take time off whenever he pleases. McCreadie cannot.

As for the people who *really* need time off to rest? Those working in factories and shops and domestic service? A good employer will give you Sunday morning for church, and there's been a move toward making it a full day, but two entire days off? How would the world function?

In modern times, we look back at that with equal parts horror and superiority. Horror at the long hours, and superiority at the thought that no one realized people are more productive with time off to rest and enjoy themselves. And yet the forty-hour work week has been a thing for a century, despite studies proving that employees can do as much by working less. Don't tell that to corporations, though. A four-day work week? How would the world function?

The people in the coaches ahead will *not* be working class. The carriages are all as fine as—if not finer than—Gray's. While the "less fortunate" might get into the Highlands to visit relatives, they'll take the train. The well-to-do want the privacy and convenience of their own conveyances. Like private jets that move really, really slowly.

I don't grumble for long. It's too nice a day, and walking under the shade of oaks and willows, I'm reminded of how much I love country getaways. Oh, I'm a city girl. No doubt about that. But there is much to be said for walking along a sun-dappled dirt road, a light breeze smelling of grass and loam and lifting the heat, birdsong filling the air. No stink of coal fires. No clatter of hooves. The only familiar smell is . . .

Gray takes my elbow to sidestep me past a pile of steaming horse dung. Yep, there's always that.

As we walk, coach doors and windows open, with people calling out to ask what's going on, as if we can see better than their high-perched drivers. We keep walking. When we reach the corner, I let out a groan.

It's not a "volume of traffic"–style jam. It's the kind caused by a disabled vehicle. Just around the corner, a single coach has stopped. Two well-dressed men stand back, eyeing the coach as if waiting for it to levitate, lifted by a hand from the heavens above.

McCreadie sighs. "Looks as if we will get our jackets dirty, Duncan. These fellows are going to need some help."

Gray only grunts. If the problem is a stuck coach or broken wheel— which happens as often as flat tires—neither of them will stand by waiting for divine intervention. They'll take off their coats, roll up their sleeves, and get to work.

"Trouble with the coach?" McCreadie calls as we draw near.

The two men turn, and McCreadie's gait slows. They're about our age. Both are dressed as if heading to a formal event, wearing silk cravats and top hats. Even McCreadie—usually a total fashion plate—is dressed for travel.

One of the men is tall and broad-shouldered, with light brown hair. The other has medium brown hair and is more compact. When they see us, the darker-haired one's frown lifts in a welcoming grin. He opens his mouth to speak, but before he can, his companion steps forward.

"Duncan Gray," the bigger man says. "Thank God you are here. We are in most urgent need of your very special skills."

Something in his tone grates down my spine, and I find myself hoping he's in need of a doctor . . . to treat some terribly embarrassing rash.

"Cranston," Gray says, his tone managing to be both cool and cordial at the same time. "What seems to be the trouble?"

"I have lost my lapel pin." He motions to his cravat. "We stopped to take . . . a brief jaunt into the woods, and when I climbed back into the carriage, I realized it was gone."

McCreadie's eyes narrow. "You are holding up an entire line of coaches because you lost a stickpin, Archie?"

"It is a very expensive pin."

The darker-haired man murmurs, "I did mention that we ought to pull over up ahead and walk back."

"Nonsense, Sinclair." Cranston claps the other man on the back. "They can wait. We shall be moving soon, now that we have Detective Duncan Gray on the job."

"Hugh is the—" Gray begins.

"Yes, yes, but Hugh is a *police* detective." Cranston gives the word a derisive twist that has my hackles practically vibrating. "Gray here is the celebrity. Even has books written about his adventures. Well, children's books, but still."

Yes, someone is chronicling Gray's investigations. No, they are not children's books—they are detective serials. Victorians may be a prudish lot, but they make up for it with a thirst for blood and guts, and a good mystery provides that.

We are seeing the start of the detective novel, with Sherlock Holmes still nearly twenty years away. The primary market for such work, especially true crime, is women, just as it is in the modern world. Such an interest, though, could be concerning in a woman, and so these stories are shared with children, as cautionary tales.

Crime doesn't pay, lass.

The detective will find you out, lad.

Seeing a market, someone leapt on Gray's adventures. Since then, they've been shut down and replaced with our own scribe—and new housemaid— Jack, who is far less inclined to make me look like a simpering magician's assistant and McCreadie look like a bumbling police detective.

But it's still Gray who gets the limelight. People prefer heroes to ensemble casts, and that's fine for McCreadie and me, who like to stay out of the limelight. Not quite so fine for Gray, who would really rather join us in the shadows.

"Dr. Gray's specialty is forensic pathology," I say.

Both men turn my way, as if the trees spoke.

"My assistant, Miss Mitchell," Gray says. "Who is correct. Unless you have a body that requires dissection, I cannot help solve your mystery."

"As for the stickpin," I say, "it's right there. Caught on your pocket."

Cranston looks down, and McCreadie barely suppresses a snicker as he sees the jeweled pin, half caught on the edge of Cranston's pocket.

"The mystery is solved," McCreadie says. "We will take our leave. Good day, gentlemen."

"Wait. You cannot leave before saying hello to Violet. She would be most offended."

Something spasms in McCreadie's face, but he quickly schools his features and gives a stiff nod of his head.

"Violet!" Cranston bellows, as if the coach isn't six inches away. He throws open the door. "Look who we have met on the road. Hugh McCreadie. You remember Hugh. Your former fiancé."

I tense, and my gaze swings to that open door. A small hand grasps it. Then a woman looks out. She's tiny, with perfect features, milky skin, and raven-black hair. Her gaze is shuttered until it falls on Gray, and then she smiles.

"Duncan," she says. "It is good to see you."

She visibly braces as she turns to look past the door. She doesn't try to keep the smile, just fixes on a placidly empty look as she turns to McCreadie.

"Hugh," she says.

He dips his chin. "Violet. I hope you are well."

"Oh!" Violet says, as her gaze lands on me. "Miss Mitchell?"

I nod and smile as I move away from McCreadie, and Violet gratefully follows me with her gaze.

"Our housekeeper adores the stories of your adventures with Duncan," she says. "She is most enamored with your character." Her cheeks pink. "With you, I mean."

I smile. "It's half me and half a character. I'm glad your housekeeper is enjoying the stories."

"She truly is. I shall have to read them. I keep meaning to but . . ." She trails off, and I can imagine why she doesn't read them. I'm not sure what I expected of McCreadie's ex-fiancée, but it wasn't a woman who—a decade later—still needed to brace herself before looking his way.

Violet clears her throat. "I *will* read them. They sound most delightful. And I am pleased to make your acquaintance. I am sorry for the delay. My brother . . ." Her gaze slants his way, with the faintest eye roll. "I do apologize, and we will not delay you any longer. It is good to see you, Duncan. And . . ." That hitch, as she braces. "Hugh."

They both tip their hats as Violet withdraws into the coach.

"We will see you all again soon enough," Cranston says as Sinclair climbs in after Violet. "A race to the castle."

"You are attending the wedding?" I say, in what I hope is a neutral tone.

Cranston grins over at me. "I should certainly hope so," he says as he swings into the coach. "They would have a hard time holding the wedding without the groom."

TWO

When we return to the coach, Gray speaks to Simon and suggests we find another route, even if it takes longer. That removes us from the line of traffic heading into the Highlands, and soon we're stopping for a picnic lunch along a loch, where we relax on the shore to eat. After lunch, Isla, Alice, and I take off our boots and stockings and wade into the lake, and our excruciating journey finally becomes a fun adventure in the countryside.

By the time we're approaching the estate, it's early evening. That doesn't mean it's getting dark. We're even farther north now and nearing the summer solstice, meaning it's full sunlight, and I squint as I try to see the house. Instead, I spot two baby deer sprinting away from the coach.

"Fawns!" I say as I point.

"Deer," Gray says.

I give him a look. "Yes, fawns are baby deer."

"No, I mean those are full-grown deer."

I peer at him and then at the others. Sometimes it's fun to tease the time traveler. It's like telling a child that "house hippos" are a thing, except without the guilt of, you know, lying to a child.

"Duncan is right," Isla says. "That is a roe deer. Likely full grown."

"Let me guess," McCreadie says. "They're bigger in your time."

"Nah, they're just bigger in Canada. They start a little smaller than your red deer and go up to . . ." I crane my neck skyward. "As tall as this coach."

Gray snorts. McCreadie and Isla eye me skeptically. Yep, this game works both ways.

"I'm serious," I say. "Look up moose. They have them in Europe, too. Poland, maybe? Definitely Russia." I catch sight of a white tower ahead, and I'm diverted by that until the full building comes into view. "Holy crap. It really is a castle."

"Hunting lodge," Gray says.

I lean out the window. In the distance, tucked down in the valley, is a white three-story building with towers and turrets. "It *looks* like a castle."

"That is intentional," Isla says. "It is an inhabitable folly."

"Ah." I know about follies. Victorians are fond of them. Or rich Victorians are, because you need money to build them and space to showcase them. A folly is a miniature version of some grand—and usually exotic—structure like a Greek temple or Egyptian pyramid. Most are purely for show, but some are large enough to inhabit.

I'd love to roll my eyes and mock the ridiculousness—and extravagance—of building a miniature colosseum in your yard, but I have to admit, follies are kind of cool.

"You said it's a hunting lodge?" I ask. "Please don't tell me Archie Cranston is hunting those tiny deer."

"Then I will not tell you," McCreadie says. "You may close your eyes and pretend he is hunting man-eating tigers."

"Mmm, not sure that's much better. I'm kinda on the man-eating tigers' side. They get hungry, and people are right there, slow and defenseless." I keep watching the estate as it comes into better view. "Did Mr. Cranston inherit it?"

"If I recall," Isla says, "and correct me if I am wrong, Hugh, but I believe the lodge is a fairly recent construction. By the same man who designed Balmoral Castle, in fact." She turns to McCreadie. "Did Archie buy the land?"

Her use of the familiar address tells me she knows Cranston as more than the groom of McCreadie's little sister. Since all four men seem to be about the same age, and refer to each other by both first and last names, I'm going to guess they went to school together. McCreadie and Gray didn't attend the same college, so that would make it high school. Yes, it's actually called high school—the Royal High School, to be exact—a term Americans will later adopt.

"The previous owner bought the land and built the lodge," McCreadie says. "But it is still recent and, as I understand, a point of some contention."

"The sale?" I say.

"No, the original build. There were people living on the land, who were turned out of their homes to make way for pleasure hunting."

"Ouch."

"Hmm. I understand there is some animosity locally. If you see anyone on your rambles, I would suggest you tell them you are staying at an inn."

"Taking that further," Gray says, "I would ask that, given the state of affairs, no one goes for rambles alone."

"It's that bad?" I say.

"I fear it is."

Well, this is shaping up to be quite the holiday.

As we approached the estate house, I itched to get inside and see it. Once we're there, though, everything passes in a blur of chaos. Two other coaches arrived just before us, and everyone needs their baggage unloaded and taken to their rooms. That becomes the priority. No one has time to show us around—they just want to get us inside and parceled out to our assigned rooms.

A maid whisks us up one flight of stairs, where she is met by the house-keeper, who has just finished escorting other guests to their chambers. She tells the maid to show Gray and McCreadie to their quarters, and she will take "the ladies."

I struggle to understand the housekeeper, Mrs. Hall. The Victorian Scottish accent is not exactly the same as the one I knew from holidays with my grandmother. There are also levels of strength, just like there are now, and the more "country" one is, the stronger the accent—and the more of the Scots language used. All that means the speech takes a little longer to run through my mental translator.

As for myself, being in Catriona's body means I have her voice and also—less explicably but very conveniently—her accent. It's the Scots that I've needed to learn, and by now *dinnae* and *aye* and *ken* come naturally, though in my head, I still hear "did not," "yes," and "know."

"Mrs. Ballantyne will stay in the small balcony room." She opens a door. "The young ladies will be two flights up."

I quickly calculate what I'd seen from the outside.

Isla beats me to it. "The attic?"

"Yes, all the maids will be up there."

Isla glances at me. "Miss Mitchell is my companion, not a maid. I hoped she would stay with me, and Alice would be happy to find a place in my—"

"There is no room. As I said, you are in the small balcony chamber."

Ah, housekeepers. They are an imperious bunch, rulers of their domain. Even guests are intrusions, disrupting the clockwork flow of the household.

Isla meets the woman's gaze with the equally imperious stare of a fellow female professional. "Then Miss Mitchell and I will share the bed."

"The attic is fine," I cut in. I catch Isla's eye and jerk my chin toward Alice. Our young parlormaid won't know anyone here, and she'll already feel out of place.

Isla nods. "You may show the young ladies to their quarters." Then, to us, "Come see me when you are settled in, and we will take a ramble through the grounds."

"That is not possible," Mrs. Hall says.

Isla raises her brows.

"Mr. Cranston's orders," Mrs. Hall says. "All guests are restricted to the house and gardens. For their own safety."

"That sounds ominous," I murmur.

The woman turns her steely gaze on me.

"Any particular safety concern?" I ask. "Killer deer? Man-eating tigers? Well-armed former tenants?"

"Mr. Cranston requests guests stay within the house and gardens. For their own safety. Now, please come with me."

"You must be more careful," Alice hisses as we climb the endless stairs to the attic. "Mrs. Ballantyne might be amused, but your sharp tongue reflects poorly on her and Dr. Gray."

Being schooled in manners by a parlormaid is a hard blow, but she's right. It's not my manners that are the problem. I'm Canadian. I say please when making automated phone selections. But in the modern world, my smart-assed comments haven't reflected badly on anyone else since I was old enough for people to stop blaming my poor parents. Now I'm in a world where someone else will always be blamed. I am a woman, after all.

When we reach the attic, Mrs. Hall ushers us into a small room, and I smile. It's a perfect little attic garret, complete with sloping wood-beamed ceilings and dormer windows. It's also a whole lot warmer than downstairs. Castles—even replicas of them—are drafty.

The best part, though, is the tiny door in the corner, where someone has posted a handwritten sign reading, in all caps, "DANGER!!! DO NOT OPEN!!!" Yes, there are three exclamation marks both times.

Seeing the sign, I laugh. Then I look at Mrs. Hall, who peers at me suspiciously, as if wondering whether I might be touched.

I point at the sign. I'm presuming it's a joke. I mean, it's a small door in an attic marked with dire warnings. Of course anyone staying in this room is going to open it, if only out of pure curiosity.

But from the look the housekeeper gives me, it's not a joke.

"So we . . . should not open the door?" I say.

Alice suppresses a snicker.

"No," Mrs. Hall intones. "That is what the sign says, in case you cannot read."

I look from her to the door. "May I ask—?"

"No."

The housekeeper turns on her heel and leaves. I walk over and close the door behind her. Then I turn and Alice has already sprinted to the tiny marked door. I do the same, but she beats me there.

"Wait!" I whisper. "That could be where they keep the inconvenient relatives."

She rolls her eyes skyward. "Then it would be locked."

"Ah, but that would be illegal. You can hide your embarrassing relatives in secret attic rooms as long as the door isn't locked. That's the law."

She eyes me, uncertain.

"I'm joking," I say. "Although, if it is Mr. Cranston's mad former wife, she might be fine company. All right, open the door so we can meet her."

Alice turns the handle. When the door sticks, I reach over to help and we yank . . . and it flies open with a wall of spare pillows and blankets tumbling onto us, knocking her down and me back onto the bed. We look at each other, covered in blankets, and start to laugh.

"I told you not to open the door," a distant voice calls. "Now mind you put all those back before you come down."

THREE

While Alice repacks the linen closet, I go to help Isla change and settle in, as her "companion." As soon as she releases me, I go in search of Gray. I have questions. Time to stop detecting and start asking.

I'm lucky enough to find Gray and McCreadie in the hall. Lucky because my only other option would have been to casually hang out until I heard one of their voices. I'm thinking of an excuse to speak to Gray alone when McCreadie saves me from the lie by saying he needs something from his room, and we can meet downstairs later.

"I need to speak to you," I say. "In private . . . but not too private."

He gives a soft sigh. A year ago, I'd have thought he was annoyed by the request. Now I understand it's the "not too private" part that annoys him—the fact that we can't even talk without risking scandal.

Both Gray and Isla chafe at the restrictions of their world, and while it's tempting to enable that, I've learned that wouldn't help them in the long run. Social rules are so much more rigid here—especially for their station—and rebelling against them risks ostracism.

The Gray family is known to be eccentric, and that's tolerated as long as it's tempered with era-appropriate manners and mores. Yes, you can raise your husband's illegitimate son. Yes, you can educate your daughters. You can even let those daughters "dabble" in chemistry and business. But you must otherwise acquit yourselves in a proper fashion, raising that brown-skinned boy to be a perfect Scottish gentleman and those girls to make good matches and be good hostesses and engage in all charity work expected of their social standing.

For Gray to take on a female assistant raises brows in a world where even secretaries are men. But he is eccentric, so it's allowed. However, when that assistant turns out to be young and pretty? Of course everyone thinks that's why he hired me, which means that outside the town house, we can't be shutting ourselves up together in private conversation.

"I hear there are gardens," I say. "Shall we find them?"

He waves me toward the stairs. As we descend, he says, "We could take a ramble."

"Not allowed."

He gives me a hard look. "Yes, I realize I said we must be careful. As long as we stick to the paths, we should be fine."

"The housekeeper said guests are restricted to the gardens. For our own safety."

He grumbles under his breath.

"Agreed," I say.

There is a door right at the foot of the steps, and we duck out that one, avoiding what sounds like Cranston's booming voice in the next room. Once on the drive, Gray shades his eyes and then points.

We make our way to a kitchen garden. Even Edinburgh's far enough north to limit the sort of produce one can find in the market. A kitchen garden helps. Also, there's little need for flowers when they bloom all around us, the rhododendron bushes loaded in riots of color from red to purple to white. They're gorgeous, and I feel a pang of guilt thinking that, because from our gardener—Mr. Tull—I know they're invasive. He rightly refuses to plant them at the town house.

I make sure no one else is around. Then I say, "I have a question about something that's none of my business."

Gray's lips twitch as he relaxes. "The best sort of question."

"No, the most awkward sort because, until now, it really has been none of my business. But now I need to know at least the basics, so I don't make a mistake and offend someone I care about."

His brows rise. "Now *I* am curious."

"It's about Hugh's family situation. I'm not fishing for gossip. Just the essentials are fine. Whatever will keep me from saying or doing something that might embarrass him."

"It is hardly a secret. How much do you know already?"

"Uh, nothing."

He glances over, frowning.

I push aside a hanging tendril of beans. "I've gathered a few clues. I know he's estranged from his family. I know he's still fond of his sister—the bride—and she's fond of him. I know he was engaged, and now I've met his former fiancée. I wonder whether the estrangement has anything to do with that, but I don't want to presume."

"Then I must apologize for not being forthcoming about the situation. I suppose I presumed Isla would have said more, but now I realize that, unless it came up in conversation, she would not."

He glances at the house and then lowers his voice. "Hugh will not mind me discussing it. He would rather you knew than be wondering whether he did something heinous to deserve the estrangement."

"I find it hard to imagine Hugh doing anything heinous."

Gray gives a soft laugh. "Do not tell him that, or he would be quite insulted. Yes, Hugh is one of the few people who I can say, without hesitation, would not have done anything so scandalous or abhorrent that it deserves banishment from his family. Except . . . he did."

"What?"

When Gray glances over, his face is impassive but his eyes glitter in amusement. "Yes, I fear our Hugh was a right cad, thoroughly humiliating his family not once, but twice. They forgave him, grudgingly, for the first. But the second offense was too great." He lowers his voice. "Do you want to know what he did?"

"Used the wrong fork at dinner?"

Gray's brows shoot up. "Certainly not. Hugh knows exactly which fork to use, and to insinuate otherwise is most offensive, Miss Mitchell."

"Yeah, yeah, get on with it."

"The first offense was . . ." He leans to my ear. "He became a policeman."

"Okay. That makes sense. I've gotten the impression his family is well-to-do."

"They are indeed. His father is the third son of an earl, which means while Hugh carries no title, he is, point of fact, nobility. At least by blood."

"Seriously?"

Gray waves us down a side row. "Moreover, his mother comes from a wealthy shipping family, which means when my father became friends with Hugh's father, my father was the one climbing the social ladder. For me to go into medicine was perfectly respectable for my family and my situation. If Hugh had done the same, his family would have been less pleased, but they would have tolerated it. A police officer, though? He might as well have said he was joining the night-soil collectors."

"Night soil" is a euphemism for sewage, particularly the solid-waste component that can't just be dumped out onto the ground.

"But they didn't disown him," I say.

"No, in that case, he was saved by the fact that his future father-in-law did not object."

"Hugh was already engaged?"

Gray plucks two pea pods and hands me one. "Hugh had been engaged for most of his life. To Violet Cranston. They were betrothed as children."

"That's still a thing among the nobility?"

"Mmm, actually, it's more a thing among those who *model* themselves after the nobility."

"The upper middle class."

"Yes. Hugh is the eldest son of a family with both noble blood and vast business interests. The Cranstons also have noble blood and vast business interests. The two families are close, and they saw this as a mutually beneficial union."

"Beneficial to *them*. How did Hugh feel about it?"

Gray sobers as he waves me to a bench near the rear of the garden. We sit facing outward, looking across the lawn abutting the forest.

"To be honest," Gray says, "Hugh did not think much of it either way. It was a fact of his life from an early age. He would marry Violet who is, like Hugh himself, sweet-natured and kind."

"Also gorgeous."

"Is she?" He tilts his head. "I suppose so. We grew up together, so it is hard to see her impartially. But yes, there was nothing objectionable in the match. So Hugh did not object."

"Wait." I twist to face him. "Isla said he proposed to *her* once. She wanted to learn under a famous chemist in Yorkshire, and she couldn't do that on her own, so he offered to marry her and accompany her."

"Ah. That. Hugh, as you may have noticed, can be impetuous. If Isla had accepted, it would have been a terrible scandal, with Hugh already being engaged. But Isla presumed the proposal was merely a kind but foolhardy offer."

I meet his gaze. "And was it?"

"Of course not."

We sit in silence for a few moments. Gray and I both know how McCreadie feels about Isla, and I'd suspected that the proposal was, yes, impetuous and foolhardy, but also honest.

When Gray speaks again, his words come slow. "I do not think Hugh truly realized how he felt about Isla until . . ." His gaze fixes on those distant trees. "Until it was too late. Or, I should say, on the cusp of being too late. Had I known it myself, I would have acted. But I was absorbed in my studies. Young and self-absorbed and, as you would say, clueless."

"I can see that." When he looks over sharply, I smile. "Sorry. I mean that in that situation, I can understand a person not noticing that two people had feelings for each other, especially when they didn't seem to realize it themselves."

"Yes, well, things came to a head with Lawrence."

"The asshole husband. Your college friend."

"*Not* my friend," he says with a hard look. "Classmate and acquaintance only. But, yes, Isla met Lawrence through me, and I did not mind sharing a pint with the man, but I absolutely did not want him marrying my sister. Hugh hated him. He saw dangers that even I missed. But, of course, Hugh was betrothed to Violet, and as Isla grew older, she had begun treating Hugh more as her brother's friend than her own."

"Distancing herself."

"Perhaps. She asked for our parents' permission to marry Lawrence. Our father was fine with the union, but our mother was not. That was when Hugh broke off his engagement. Again, it was typical Hugh, which means he led with his heart rather than his mind, and he made a hash of it, unintentionally humiliating Violet. Isla had already gone to the coast with a friend, and when she returned . . . we discovered she had not only been with a friend."

"She'd eloped with Lawrence."

"Yes. That left Hugh with a rather spectacularly broken engagement, furious parents, and furious future in-laws. Still, the Cranstons—and Violet—were fond of him. They had overlooked his career choice and they would have overlooked this, too, if he had reversed his decision."

"He didn't."

"Another man would have. After all, Isla was married and beyond his reach. But Hugh is damnably honorable, and I believe he'd realized he could not offer Violet a proper marriage, and so he refused to mend the rift. His parents disowned him. He is not welcome in their home. He has money from his grandfather, who left him a sizable inheritance. Fiona—the bride—still adores him. His parents will not even be staying here because Fiona insisted on inviting Hugh. They will come for the wedding only."

"And the Cranstons?"

Gray sighs. "While Violet's parents were fine with a policeman for a son-in-law, after the broken engagement, they tried to use their political leverage to have Hugh removed from his position. You will meet them, unfortunately."

"And we can run interference between them and Hugh?"

"That is the plan. Isla will want to help, but it's best if she does not. While Hugh has never said anything about Isla—not even to me—I believe his feelings for her are obvious."

"To Violet as well?"

He stretches his long legs. "I do not know what Violet suspects, but while I sympathize with Hugh, his treatment of Violet was . . . unfortunate. He was kind, of course, but she cared for him and expected to marry, and while it has been ten years, she is still hurt by his actions."

"I could tell."

His shoulders slump, as if he'd hoped he was mistaken. In a situation like this, the best everyone could hope for is that Violet would emerge better than ever. Find a wonderful man, if that's what she wanted. Or simply move on and realize she'd dodged a bullet, not spending her life wed to a man who didn't want her.

I clear my throat. "What about Archie Cranston? I can tell you and Hugh know—" I stop as movement catches my eye. Then, seeing what it is, I smile. "Seems the estate has kitties."

Gray follows my gaze. Right at the edge of the forest is a brown tabby. I walk to the edge of the garden and crouch lower, carefully with my corset, as I drop my fingers and *psp psp* at the cat, who stares in wary confusion.

"Careful," Gray says, coming up behind me. "You could lose those fingers. That is a Highland tiger."

My lips twitch. "A man-eating one?"

"Probably not," he says. "But nor is it a domestic feline. It's a Scottish wildcat. Otherwise known as a Highland tiger."

I blink at the cat as I remember a trip north with my nan, when she'd talked about seeing Scottish wildcats as a girl. Hunting and habitat loss had nearly wiped them out, the remaining wildcats interbreeding with domestic ones until, in my time, they're considered functionally extinct.

If I'd ever seen a photo of a Scottish wildcat, I don't remember it, and even if I had, I'd pictured something the size of a lynx. This isn't much bigger than a house cat, with slightly longer limbs and a bigger head.

"*That's* a Scottish wildcat?" I say.

"It is."

"A young one?"

"No, full grown, I would say."

"Huh." I maneuver in my skirts to get lower for a better look. "Smaller than I expected, and it really does look like a—Oh!"

Two small heads peek up from the grass.

"Babies!" I say.

"In Scotland, we call them kittens."

I ignore him and creep forward. The mother disappears, the kittens vanishing before I can get a good look at them.

I sag. "Damn it. I wanted to see them."

"Well, then, I believe we have a perfectly valid excuse for venturing into the wilds."

I look up to see whether he's serious. Of course he is. We've been here less than an hour and already found an excuse to break the rules.

I should be the responsible one and say no. But there are kittens. Adorable wildcat kittens.

I glance toward the house. Everyone is inside and the blinds are drawn on this side of the house, where the sun beats down. We won't go far enough to get into trouble.

"Are you offering me a tiger hunt, Dr. Gray?"

He smiles. "I am."

FOUR

The "forest" turns out to be only a strip of trees maybe ten feet wide. Beyond that is rocky open land dotted with purple thistles. In the distance, a lake shimmers under the early-evening sun, and to our left are a crumbling stone wall and a dilapidated shack. Seeing that vista, I can imagine I'm back in my time, where everything would look exactly like this—the hills and dales undulating into the distance, dotted with stands of trees and maybe a sheep or two.

The wildcat and her kittens have scampered off, and I'm not inclined to freak out Momma Cat by giving chase. We slow and tramp through the field as I inhale the scents of a Highland moor—heather and damp earth and blooming flowers. When I glimpse a heap of rusty red fur in the distance, I let out a gasp of delight, not unlike the one I gave seeing the kittens.

"Coos!" I say, using the Scots word. "Highland coos!"

"Yes, those are cows. They do not have those either in your time?"

I sock his arm. "Yes, we have cows. Even Highland ones—at least, in the Highlands. But I haven't seen one in years. When I was a kid, my parents had to drive me out of the city just to see them. I had two stuffed ones. A red and a black."

His brows rise. "You had stuffed *cows*? And you roll your eyes at people with stuffed tigers in their homes."

"*Toy* cows. Like teddy bears."

When he gives me a blank look, I say, "You don't have teddy bears yet?

So, I'm guessing Teddy Roosevelt hasn't been the American president." At his look, I throw up my hands. "I suck at history, remember? I only remember the interesting bits, which includes the origin of teddy bears. Teddy Roosevelt—"

"Future American president."

"Er, yes, but forget I mentioned that part."

"Oh, I shall not forget it. When he is nominated I shall place a very large wager on his election. I will finally follow in my father's footsteps, as a seemingly prescient investor."

"Except you actually will be prescient. Thanks to your assistant-from-the-future."

"Sadly, she is not very helpful, having mostly forgotten her history lessons." He mock glowers at me. "You could have made me a very rich man, Mallory. It was most shortsighted of you."

"Hey, I gave you the DNA tip. That's gold. Now do you want to hear about the origin of teddy bears or not?"

"Yes, though I will take it with a grain of salt, considering the source and her very poor memory."

I shake my head. "Okay, well, Roosevelt went on a hunting trip, and wanting to impress the president, his hosts tied a black bear to a tree for him to shoot. He refused, and the papers printed a cartoon mocking him for it."

"Mocking him for refusing to kill a creature trapped for his amusement? I rather like Theodore Roosevelt."

"He also believes in a natural hierarchy based on skin color."

"I am not at the top of that, am I?"

"The United States was originally a British colony. That will always answer your question."

He sighs.

I continue, "From what I remember, Roosevelt believed in the natural superiority of whites. He was also vehemently against slavery as well as being an environmentalist responsible for creating America's National Park system. Which doesn't cancel out the racism. Nothing ever does. But back to the cute bear story. After the press roasted Roosevelt, someone decided to present him with a small stuffed bear. They became known as teddy bears, and pretty much every North American kid will have one at some point."

"Stuffed bears?" Gray eyes the distant coos. "I suppose that makes more sense than stuffed cows."

"Hey, don't mock my childhood tastes. I love coos. They're so big and fluffy." I veer in their direction. "I'm going to say hello—"

"Stop right there," says a male voice, and I literally halt with my boot in the air. I twist to see two figures stepping from a stand of trees. They're to the west, and I'm partly blinded by the setting sun, but I can see one holds something long and slender, pointed straight at us.

I lift my hands, only to realize that might not be a thing yet. "We are wedding guests at the house."

"Mallory?" Gray murmurs. "I do not think that is the problem."

He points at something ahead, and I lower my foot to move closer, but he grabs my arm.

"Careful, miss," another voice says, this one feminine. "Listen to your fellow there."

I lean forward to see what they do . . . and as I move, my perspective shifts and the sun glints off metal nestled in the long grass.

"Is that a . . . bear trap?"

"No bears here, miss," the feminine voice says. "That one's for people."

"Holy—" I cut off the curse.

Then I turn to face the duo. They're a young couple, maybe in their late teens. What I'd thought was a rifle is a walking stick. She must have been pointing it at the trap.

Both are wearing the rough-spun clothing of country laborers. Both are dark-haired, with tanned skin that speaks to a life spent largely out of doors. The girl looks slightly older, maybe eighteen or nineteen. There's enough similarity in their coloring and facial structure that I'm going to guess they're closely related, possibly siblings. As for the walking stick, I can make out the young woman's boots peeking from under her long skirts. One boot has a thick heel and twists inward.

"Thank you for the warning," I say. "We were told it wasn't safe to wander, but I did not expect . . ." I shudder as I look toward the trap, a big and ugly piece of metal with wicked jaws. "Do you work on the estate?"

The young man's face darkens. "We are allowed to be here."

"I never said you weren't. I was making conversation." I remember what the others said about the land, and I realize this would be a contentious issue.

"Ignore my brother," the young woman says. "He is still testy. We used to live on the property but . . ." She shrugs. "We were taking the public foot-path, which even His Lordship does not dare scatter with those things." The twist she gives to "Lordship" says it's mockery, not Cranston's actual title.

"They really are for people then?" I move closer to the trap, ducking Gray's restraining hand.

"They are," Gray says, with a rumbling note of deep disapproval. "They are utterly inhumane, capable of killing a man if the jaws cut deeply enough. At the very least, it will break the bone."

My gaze shoots to the young woman's walking stick, and she shakes her head. "No, miss. I have had this bad leg since birth. A clubfoot." She grins, a wicked glint in her eye. "A sign of the devil, don't you know."

Her brother elbows her. "One day you will say that to the wrong person and find yourself in trouble, Len."

"A clubfoot is a birth defect," Gray says. "Caused by short tendons, not the devil."

"A doctor, are you?" the girl says.

I nod toward him. "Dr. Duncan Gray. I am his assistant, Mallory Mitchell."

"I'm Lenore, and that lout is my brother, Gavin. As I said, we were on the public footpath, which is open to all, but I would ask you not to tell His Lordship you saw us. It could cause trouble for our mother. She's the housekeeper on the estate."

"Ah. I have . . . met her."

Lenore's grin grows. "Yes, that is our dear mama."

"And you used to live on the estate?"

Her brother answers, "Our father was the gamekeeper until Mr. Crans-ton decided to bring in some foreign fellow who worked at . . ." A dismis-sive wave. "Some castle on the Continent. The man does not know the first thing about Scottish game."

"We should let you be on your way," Lenore says. "We only wished to warn you of the traps. If you want to walk the grounds, I would suggest you stay on the roads or the right-of-way. His Lordship has not trapped those."

"Yet," her brother mutters.

They lift a hand in farewell and return to the strip of trees, the public path being presumably on the other side. I remember those from my times in the Highlands. In Britain, there are very old laws requiring that properties have a path through them that anyone can use. That path might lead you through a cow field, complete with bulls, but the law doesn't say that the path needs to be safe. Just that the owner can't legally prevent you from using it.

Once they're gone, I sweep my skirts aside to bend by the trap, ignoring Gray's noise of protest.

"I'm not going to touch it," I say. "But this really does look like an old-fashioned bear trap. Setting these out for bears is bad enough. For people?"

"Unconscionable," Gray says curtly. "I will speak to Archie. Whatever concerns he has about the locals, they do not warrant this."

"You think they're for poachers?"

Gray sniffs. "Likely. He is a new landowner, accustomed to the city. He came into his own wealth—through the opening of the whisky trade—and he seems to fashion himself some sort of country gentleman." He pauses. "That is impolite of me."

"Mmm, anyone who lays human traps on their lands doesn't deserve civility."

"I will speak to him and hope it is a misunderstanding. What he sees as poaching has long been the way of things in the country. The locals will hardly strip the land of game—they understand how to conserve it better than most gentry. The proper thing to do is to speak to them and come to an understanding."

He looks over at that dilapidated shack. "Or that used to be the way of things. These days, it seems those with money wish to keep their land entirely for themselves, driving everyone else off it, as if they could possibly use all this land and its resources." He looks at the trap and shakes his head. "I will speak to Archie."

When we reach the house, I hear voices, and I slow, not sure I'm ready to be civil to Cranston after seeing that trap. But the voice I hear is McCreadie's and the tone makes me smile. He's obviously telling a story, relaxed and among people he feels comfortable with. Then I draw closer to see him beside the garden, with a young woman practically hanging off his arm.

My hackles rise. But as soon as we approach, I can better see the young woman—pretty with honey-brown hair and laughing hazel eyes—and the resemblance to McCreadie is so obvious that I know this must be his sister. I also see Isla with them, equally relaxed and enjoying McCreadie's story as she sips her lemonade.

"Duncan!" the young woman cries, dropping her brother's arm as we approach.

Gray smiles with genuine affection. "Fiona, it is good to see you. Congratulations on your nuptials."

She comes forward to greet us. "Is this Miss Mallory? Please tell me it is. I have been *dying* to meet you. I have read all the stories of your adventures, and I must say I prefer the new ones, though the old ones were amusing."

"With me always bending over to examine nonexistent evidence?" I say.

She laughs, and it's a very pretty laugh. She's twenty-one, but she seems so much younger. Young and sheltered, as she would be. Straight from her father's guardianship to her husband's. The thought of her marrying the jackass we met earlier . . .

None of my business. Though I do wonder whether, like Hugh and Violet, this is an arranged marriage and if so—

No, I'm not thinking of that. Again, none of my business.

"I am very jealous of your adventures," Fiona says. "It all sounds so exciting. I do wish there was more science in the stories, though Hugh says that is not what most people read them for."

"And now you have Duncan here to answer all your science questions." McCreadie winks at Gray, as if telling him to prepare for an enthusiastic onslaught.

"What area of science are you interested in?" I ask.

Fiona's expression freezes, the youthful joy in it extinguished before she plasters it back on. "All of it," she says, "but it is purely an amateur's interest. I . . . have not received any formal schooling in the sciences."

"Nor have I," I say. "But there are many ways to learn, for those who are interested."

That genuine enthusiasm surges anew. "There is. I have books, and I have even snuck into a lecture or two, but do not tell Mama or Papa. I would love to hear more of the science behind your investigations, both Duncan's and Mrs. Ballantyne's." She turns to Isla. "The chemistry is fascinating. I wish there was also more of *it* in the stories."

Isla smiles. "There is as much as there needs to be. I leave most of the investigating to my brother, though I will squeeze myself in if the case seems interesting."

"I would squeeze myself into them all." Fiona turns to Gray and me. "Remember, I am at your disposal should you ever need my specific talents. I am very adept at needlepoint and perfectly adequate on the pianoforte."

She says it lightly, but the note of bitterness cuts through me. This isn't Annis or Isla, encouraged to pursue whatever interests them, provided with all the resources and private tutors they needed. This is an average Victorian girl of their class, raised to be proficient in the womanly arts and no more.

"You joke," I say, "but we might actually take you up on that, Miss Mc-Creadie. We had someone last month who contacted us to find a pianoforte that had somehow been stolen from their home."

"Oh, I would be no help at all there," she says. "I would pay someone to steal mine. *Oh, no, it has been taken! Whatever shall I do? I fear I can no longer practice, Mama.*"

We all laugh, and McCreadie is about to reply when someone appears from around the house, stopping short as she sees us.

"Violet!" Fiona exclaims. "My soon-to-be sister-in-law. We were just going for a walk about the gardens. Will you join us? Please say yes."

Violet's gaze shoots to McCreadie.

McCreadie clears his throat. "Violet may take my place. I really ought to unpack."

"No," Violet says, her voice soft, barely audible. "Please come along, Hugh."

McCreadie shoots her a look that clearly says he will stay behind if she prefers, but she firmly takes Fiona's arm and says, "Into the gardens. Quickly, though. I have heard we might spot the wildcat and her kits, but if my brother joins us, his voice alone will surely scare them off."

"We actually saw them," I say. "A wildcat and two or three kittens."

Fiona's face lights in pure joy. "Did you truly? Archie said they are about, and I am dearly hoping to see them."

"Fiona adores animals," McCreadie says. "She may have joked about the needlepoint and pianoforte, but her true passion is caring for God's creatures, particularly those in need. She set the wing on a songbird just last month and released it back to the wild."

I look at her. "That is amazing."

Fiona blushes. "My brother makes it sound far more impressive than it is. I dabble, that is all." She clears her throat and takes my arm. "Now, tell me all about the wildcats you saw."

FIVE

The garden walk is actually very lovely. McCreadie gives Violet her space, and she relaxes. It's impossible not to relax around Fiona. She really is delightful. I get the sense there's more sadness to her than meets the eye, but there's also obviously more depth, and with depth comes sadness sometimes. She's not an empty-headed girl, content with her role in life. She sees more and wants more and . . .

And she's marrying Archie Cranston, a wealthy asshole who sets out bear traps for poachers.

Which doesn't matter as much as it might seem. If this marriage is meant to merge the two families, it isn't intended to be a love match. They will lead their separate lives and pursue their separate interests, and I will try very hard not to patronize Fiona McCreadie by pitying her.

She certainly doesn't seem like a reluctant bride. Not an excited one, either. In fact, she seems far less like a bride than a guest enjoying a holiday with family and friends. But, again, none of my business.

We enjoy our walk in the gardens. Between Isla and Violet, they are able to identify most of the plants, even some of the rarer herbs. We take our time wandering the gardens before heading back to the house.

"Dinner ought to be ready by now," Fiona says. "I wanted to wait until everyone had arrived, so I apologize for the lateness of the hour."

"It has given us all time to relax and refresh after our journey," Isla says.

We reach the house, and McCreadie holds the door as we enter. Fiona leads us through to a large sitting room. Cranston is on his feet, regaling Sinclair and another man with some story. As he spots us, his gaze passes right over his bride and lands on Gray.

"Gray!" he says, coming forward. "Impeccable timing, old chap. We were just talking about you."

Gray slows, and the pit bull in me starts to growl.

"I told them how you solved the mystery of my missing stickpin," Cranston says.

"That was Miss—" Gray begins.

"And James here—you remember James Frye, from school?—he said he seems to have misplaced his pocket watch. He had it in the coach, and now it is gone. You can find that for him, can't you?"

Gray opens his mouth, but Cranston only claps him on the back. "Good chap. Now, who else has a mystery they need the famous detective to solve?"

"How about your missing manners," a voice says archly, and I'm surprised to see it's Violet.

To my surprise, Cranston actually seems to hesitate at that, and then offers his sister what looks like a nod of acknowledgment.

"Dinner is ready," Fiona says. "Please follow me to the dining room, and make yourselves comfortable. The first course will be served promptly."

If the walk through the gardens was surprisingly pleasant, dinner is unsurprisingly awful. Oh, the food is excellent. And I give Fiona full props for playing the perfect hostess, deftly but politely cutting off her groom when he gets out of hand. Except, even with help from his best man—Sinclair—they can only mitigate the worst of it.

I'll admit to being baffled by Sinclair, increasingly so as the meal continues. He seems like a genuinely nice guy. He clearly recognizes that Cranston is an ass, which makes me wonder how the hell the two men are such good friends.

Cranston has chosen Gray as his primary target. He finds Gray's detective work hilarious, as if it's an amateur hobby. I suspect he also uses it to insult McCreadie. McCreadie is the professional detective, and yet Gray is the one Cranston zeroes in on, with endless suggestions of silly mysteries he can solve.

Even Cranston soon tires of the "fun" and turns to more normal conversation. If I'm interpreting correctly, the other guest—James Frye—was another classmate of the groom's, along with Gray, McCreadie, and Sinclair. Frye is here with his wife, who is apparently too exhausted from the trip to join us for dinner. As Gray said, McCreadie's parents will be staying elsewhere, and they have not yet arrived. Nor have Cranston's parents.

For now, it's just the younger generation, their pasts intertwined in ways that have me suspecting this is why Frye's wife bowed out of dinner. When Cranston isn't mocking Gray, he's making inside jokes that I need to smile at awkwardly. Isla joins me in that. She knows everyone here, but she doesn't know them well. Fortunately, the two of us are seated beside each other and when the conversation trips too far down memory lane, we talk together, with Fiona sometimes joining in.

When dinner ends, Isla invites me to a "turn about the gardens." I have a feeling we'll be making very good use of those gardens.

"It is past dark," Cranston says when he overhears us talking.

"We will take a lantern," Isla says, her tone gentle but firm.

"Might I join?" Fiona says. "I have a lantern we can—"

"Absolutely not," Cranston says. "The grounds are far too dangerous for you ladies to be traipsing about in the dark."

I want to make some sharp comment about the bear traps, but I keep my mouth shut. Let Gray handle that. I only say, smoothly, "We will take care, sir, and—"

"And no," he says. "I am the host, and I have spoken. There will be no leaving the house past dark. Now, who is up for charades?"

I skip charades. So do Isla and Gray. McCreadie obviously felt obligated to join in, but the rest of us beg off after our long trip. Unfortunately, that means we really do need to retire, and Gray can't join us in Isla's room to chat. Isla and I stay up for a while, but soon she's yawning, so I head up to my attic quarters to find Alice sound asleep.

While it has been a long day—starting at dawn and ending past midnight—I dozed on the coach ride and now I can't sleep. At first, I'm chilly, so I pull out an extra blanket. Then I'm overheated, so I crack open the window next to me. Is that my stomach growling? I should have snuck food up for later. My throat feels parched. Why didn't I bring up a glass of water? Do I need to use the chamber pot?

I'm not really hot or cold or hungry or thirsty or in need of the bathroom. I'm fussing, attributing my sleeplessness to everything except the two actual causes. One, I'm not tired. Two, I'm worrying about everyone else.

How torturous is this trip for McCreadie? Is Cranston really just poking at Gray, or is it outright bullying? Isla seems tense—is that just empathy for McCreadie or is she uncomfortable being among people she doesn't know well? Is she uncomfortable being around Violet and the reminder of how McCreadie hurt her? Is Alice okay? I should have made sure she wasn't having any problems with the other staff. What about Simon? I should have checked in on him at least once this evening.

I'm in that kind of mood where, once I start worrying about people I care for, that worry seeps out to those I just met. How awkward is this for Violet? She seems fragile, and being here with McCreadie must be hell, especially with her asshole brother around. And speaking of Cranston, is Fiona ready to be married to him? She's so young, and I can tell myself she understands the way of things, but *does* she?

Yep, I'm fretting. It's dark and quiet and I have nothing to do but churn through other people's problems, as if they're mysteries that I need to solve.

I know things have gone too far when I start peeking at that closed door with its warning signs. I've already investigated it. I know what's in there. But in the cold dark of night, my mind starts playing tricks, whispering there could be something behind those stacks of linens.

Finally, I give up on sleeping. I know that's the best thing. Get up and do something instead of lying there, letting my brain spin. But where do I go? I'm not at home. Alice is sleeping right beside me. I can't light the lamp and read. I can't wander the house either. While Gray considers me his guest, my attic bed says that, to everyone else, I'm a servant. I can't curl up with a book in the library. I can't even go out for a walk with those damned traps everywhere.

I catch a voice that sounds like McCreadie's, and that has me rolling out of bed. He's speaking to someone, and it sounds like Fiona, which would be perfect. No one would think it improper if I was up at night talking with McCreadie and his sister.

I pull on my wrapper over my nightgown. It's a full wrapper, with a night corset underneath. Wearing that, I'm not exactly "dressed" but it's considered appropriate enough to be seen in, covering everything that needs to be covered. Soled house slippers complete the outfit.

When I reach the stairs, though, the male voice comes clearer, and I realize it's Sinclair, whispering with Fiona on the next level down. That gives me pause—and ignites a spark of concern. The two of them being up together *would* be improper, especially when he'll be best man at her wedding in two days.

Then I hear what they're saying.

"You are concerned about her," Fiona whispers. "You may always speak to me about such things, Ezra. I am happy to help. I have heard her pacing, and I was concerned myself."

"It is nerves," Sinclair says. "Having her here with—" He clears his throat. "She will be fine."

"Having her here with Hugh." Fiona sighs. "I have made a mess of things, haven't I?"

"Of course not. You want your brother at your wedding. That is natural."

"I truly did not think it would be a problem," Fiona says. "It has been nearly ten years and . . ." She sighs again. "I have made a dreadful mess and upset two people I care about very dearly."

"No, you have not. It is past time for Violet to move on, and I know that sounds harsh, but I have known her most of my life. I care for her very deeply, and moving on is the best she can do. This gives her the chance to remember who Hugh really is—not an ogre who abandoned her but a good man who did what he thought was right."

"He really did," Fiona says.

"I know, and he is being a gentleman, properly considerate of Violet's feelings. Hugh is a good man."

"He is. Thank you for seeing that."

"I have always seen that. Just as I have always seen you, Fiona. His kindhearted and clever sister. I hope Archie appreciates what he has won."

"You are very sweet. You are also very sweet to care about how Violet is feeling. You have always been good to her. You have looked after her when Archie . . ." Fiona trails off. "I know Archie cares very much for his sister, and he would do anything for her, but he can be . . . less than observant when it comes to how others are feeling."

"He can be, and so I have always tried to help, which is why I am concerned about Violet. I will take extra care to watch where her brother does not. He does not deserve you, you know." The words come teasingly, and Fiona laughs softly.

"You are sweet to say so, even if I disagree. Now, I shall take tea for Violet and sit with her until she is settled."

"I will help you get it. And remember, Fiona, I am here for whatever you require."

"That is very kind."

They continue down the stairs. I hesitate at the top. It doesn't feel right to join them and get a tea for myself. It might even be awkward, "discovering" the bride-to-be and best man together at night, even if there is a perfectly innocent explanation.

In the end, I go back to my room and try sleeping again. The second time is not the charm, and I toss and turn for the next hour. Then something outside makes a noise—just some distant animal—and I find myself at the window, listening with far too much interest.

Time to give up on sleep entirely and get out of this bedroom. I don't know where I'm going, but I really need to go somewhere—anywhere—that isn't this dark and damp attic.

On go the wrapper and slippers again. There's a portable oil lamp on the bedroom table, and I take it, but I don't light it yet. Enough moonlight pours through the windows to let me see where I'm going. And once I reach the next floor down, I start wishing for less light and more shadows to hide the ghastly decor.

It's not the usual kind of ghastly Victorian decor, with its riot of clashing colors and patterns. I've gotten used to that, and if I'm honest, there'd always been part of me that delighted in the visual assault, the young Mallory who'd wanted *all* the colors.

This isn't an overstuffed Victorian manor. It's a hunting lodge, and it's the worst possible stereotype. The wallpaper and carpets are actually quite muted by the standards of the time, but that's just to highlight the art. I'm being generous calling it art, especially when it comes to the endless dead critters lining the walls. Or, more specifically, the heads of dead critters.

Earlier today, I'd said I really hoped Cranston didn't hunt the little roe deer. He most certainly does, and not just to provide venison steaks for dinner. He's trophy-hunting them. The horned heads of the stags are displayed along with the hunter's initials and the date, as if killing a deer the size of a dog wins the same bragging rights as bringing down a lion on safari.

There are also paintings, mostly of hunts, with dogs ripping into deer still alive and rolling their eyes in agony. Partway down the stairs, there's a painting where the canines are ripping into each other, fighting over a kill. As I cross to the next set of stairs, I spot a painting that breaks free of the hunting-lodge motif to show a dog with an androgynously gowned toddler, which would be a lot more heartwarming if the child wasn't lying on the ground with their eyes closed.

Is that child dead? I should laugh at the thought. Clearly they're only resting, right? Nope. These are Victorians, and if this painting has a name, I suspect it's "Loyal Dog Mourns His Best Friend" or some such, meant to make the viewer pause and wipe a tear for the grieving dog and its tiny dead master.

As we'd approached the house earlier, I'd temporarily mistaken the estate for a castle. Now that I've been inside, I couldn't make that error. I've been in castles. They're massive walled fortifications that sprawl over acres. This is just a very large house, and not even massive by historical standards.

Being a hunting lodge, it is mostly bedrooms. In fact, they fill three of the four levels. The servants' quarters are in the attic. The next level is guest rooms, as is the level below it, and it feels a bit like being in Gray's town house, endlessly tramping down stairs. Finally, I'm on the main level, which consists of a library, a dining room, a kitchen, one large sitting room, and two smaller sitting rooms. Yes, Victorians love their sitting rooms.

Can I get away with hiding out in the library and reading? It might be scandalous if I'm caught, but it's past two, and everyone's sound asleep. I'm not going to be caught if I shut the door before lighting my lantern. I might not even need to light it. I peer at the nearest window, and the moonlight seems to be coming from the direction the library faces. I can—

Something moves outside the window, and I fall back, biting off a gasp at what looks like some monstrous bird, flapping huge black wings. The creature quickly resolves itself into a person with a long black coat flapping in the wind. I inch toward the window until I make out light hair under a hat.

Cranston.

That's the last person I want catching me poking around down here. I should retreat, but he's heading in the opposite direction, going out toward the fields. Curiosity compels me closer.

The window is open, alleviating some of the stuffiness from the warm day. I can hear Cranston's boots on the gravel drive. He strides up it and I withdraw, ready to scamper upstairs, but he reaches the house and stalks back the other way.

Pacing, it seems, and I remember those traps. Gray spoke to him, but I haven't had a chance to hear what Cranston said about them, and now, seeing that angry patrolling, I start to wonder whether this is more than typical aristocratic arrogance, the outrage at having to deal with people on "your" land. Could it be paranoia? Those traps suggest as much, as does pacing like a guard dog at two A.M.

"There you are," Cranston says, and I jump, but he's looking in the other direction. A figure emerges from the stand of trees.

"What the bloody hell are you doing out here?" Cranston snaps.

Sinclair's voice drifts back, his tone light. "Planning my assault on your castle. I have joined the locals in their fight to see you evicted. If we win, they have promised me the house. I hope you do not mind. All is fair in love and the war for excellent hunting property."

Cranston snorts. "I know you adore your moonlit walks, but I told you to stick to the road."

"I know the property, Archie. I have been here even more than you have. As for staying on the road, I intended to, but then I heard the wildcat yowling."

"Is that what I heard? Damnable beast. It has developed a taste for eggs, and now it will not stop stealing them from the coop."

"At least it is not eating the chickens."

"Oh, I am sure it will."

"Eventually one of those traps will rid you of it."

"Do not start in on me about the traps." Cranston stalks back toward the house. "They were Müller's idea, and Duncan has already lectured me about them. Sanctimonious . . ." I don't catch the next word, but it's clearly not complimentary. "Remind me again why he is at my wedding?"

Sinclair falls in step beside him. "Because he is a good friend of your future brother-in-law, and your future bride wished him to come."

Cranston grumbles under his breath. "The man is insufferable. Always has been. He has too high an opinion of himself and absolutely no sense of humor. I do not know what Hugh sees in him."

"Hmm. A perfectly pleasant and good-natured fellow whose best chum is a horse's ass. I have never heard of such a thing myself."

Cranston makes what I presume is a rude gesture.

Sinclair laughs and then says, "There is nothing wrong with Duncan. You do not like him because you do not understand him. Science was never your strong suit, and you have little patience with serious fellows. If you have forgotten the lesson you learned in school, Archie, let me refresh your memory. Leave Duncan Gray alone. Cease poking and jabbing at him, or you will regret it. Also, steer clear of his little assistant. I have not determined the relationship there, but it is clear he will tolerate *that* far less than he tolerates you poking at him."

"Do you think I have missed the way he tenses every time another man looks at her?" Cranston adjusts his long coat. "I am almost tempted to leer, just to annoy him. But I would not make the girl uncomfortable. Nor would I have any interest in her. First, I am about to be married. Second, she is a child."

"The assistant or your bride?" Sinclair teases.

Cranston stops sharply enough to make Sinclair fall back. "They both are, and if you expect me to say differently, I will not. Gray's chit is a child. My bride is a child."

"Fiona is twenty-one. More than old enough to wed. No one thinks her a child."

"Well, I do. She is clever and witty, but still barely more than a girl."

Sinclair chuckles. "Remember that on your wedding night."

Now Cranston spins, and his friend backs up fast, hands raised.

"I was joking, Archie," Sinclair says.

"It is not a joke. It is a travesty, wedding a girl of twenty-one to a man of thirty-two. I understand it is commonly done, but I find it appalling. I will care for her, as she deserves to be cared for, and if she eventually comes to care for me in another way, that would be ideal, but for now, she is a child moving into my guardianship."

I don't hear Sinclair's response. I'm too busy wondering whether I heard right. I'd decided I knew exactly what sort of man Archie Cranston is, and I feel as if I'm listening to his twin brother.

First, he said he wouldn't leer at me to annoy Gray because that would make *me* uncomfortable. As for Fiona, when we hear of young women being married off to older men, I think we presume the men never have an issue with it. Who wouldn't want a twenty-one-year-old bride? Well, maybe a mature man hoping for an equally mature wife. A man looking for a partner.

Fiona is more than old enough to wed and, in this era, Cranston is actually a "young" groom for her—better than a fifty-year-old widower. If Cranston sees a problem with the practice, then that is more enlightened a viewpoint than I would have imagined from the man I met.

When Sinclair speaks again, his voice is almost too low for me to hear. "I apologize, old chap. I was only teasing. You have not spoken much of the marriage, and I made the mistake of presuming all was well."

"All *is* well," Cranston says firmly.

"I know it cannot be easy. If only Hugh had married Violet, you would not need to wed Fiona."

"I said it is fine. Fiona is lovely, and I will . . ." Cranston clears his throat. "Endeavor to be a good husband. For now, that means looking after her, which I will do. Mark my words. However our marriage plays out, she is under my protection, and I will see that no harm befalls her."

"Good." Sinclair slaps Cranston on the back. "There is a very fine chap hidden under that rough exterior, Archie."

Cranston snorts. "Do not mistake it for weakness. It is late, and I am tired and maudlin. Let us get inside and have a whisky before we trundle you off to bed."

I backtrack fast and hurry up the stairs, and I'm gone before the door opens.

SIX

The problem with not sleeping at night? You really want to sleep in the morning. All morning if possible. Since I'm here as Isla's companion, and she said she wouldn't need me until later, I beg off breakfast to get more shut-eye. But then, of course, everyone starts wondering whether I'm unwell or maybe just having such a shitty time that I'd rather stay in bed. First it's Isla checking on me in person. Then it's Alice coming up on Gray's behalf, and finally, McCreadie sneaks up to rap on my attic door.

Apparently, "I didn't sleep well and I'm just tired" isn't a valid excuse, at least not with friends who worry that the "not sleeping well" part means you're either sick or unhappy.

So I drag my ass out of bed after about three hours of sleep. The truth is that I'm not sure how much of it is that I'm tired, and how much is that I'm kinda dreading the day. I'd envisioned a fun trip to the Highlands with friends, and I've been thrown into far more interpersonal drama than I like. Except that drama *involves* my friends—as the targets, not the instigators—and so I really shouldn't be hiding in bed, hoping the day goes by faster. Nope, I need to bear witness, while unable to run interference because it's not my place to do so.

My first thought is *maybe we can go for a walk*. Then I remember the traps. But if the road is clear, we could walk along it. Would it be rude to tell our hosts we're slipping out in the coach for a tour of the countryside?

I arrive downstairs just as Gray walks out of the dining room. Seeing me, he fairly exhales with relief, and guilt darts through me.

"Sorry," I say. "I didn't mean to throw you to the wolves."

He frowns. Then his gaze swings back to the dining room, where Cranston's voice booms. "Ah. No." He lowers his voice. "Archie fancies himself a wolf, but he has more in common with the smaller canines, the sort who yap and bite at ankles."

Gray smiles when he says it, and I'm supposed to laugh, but I think of the Cranston I saw last night, who'd actually seemed like a decent guy.

Gray continues, "I was concerned about you. Isla said you are quartered in the attic, with the servants, which is—"

"Fine," I say. "It is fine. I just didn't sleep well after napping on the drive, which means I didn't want to get up this morning. But now I have and—"

"Duncan," a voice says. It's Sinclair, leaning out from the dining room. "You would like to join us for a walk, yes? You and Miss Mitchell."

"No one is going for any walks," Cranston booms from the dining room. "Stop that nonsense or—"

"Help me out, Gray," Sinclair mock whispers. "Tell Archie that Miss Mitchell is unwell and needs fresh air."

"We are going out, Archie." It's Fiona's voice. "I understand you are concerned, but you cannot keep us indoors in such fine weather. We will stay on the road, and you may remain behind if you like. But we are going for a walk."

Cranston grumbles something I can't make out. Then he says, "Fine. We shall all go for a walk. I know where Müller laid the bloody traps, and we can avoid them."

"Does that mean we get to leave the road?" Fiona says. "I would love to see the lochs. I could spot one from my window, and it looked lovely."

"Fine, fine. Yes, you shall see a loch, ma'am."

"Ezra mentioned a rowboat." she says. "I would dearly like to go out in a rowboat."

"Anything else, m'lady?" Cranston says with a low grumble.

"Perhaps. I shall let you know."

"I'm sure you will."

Like with any large group walk, we gradually diverge into smaller parties. Cranston insists on being up front to scout the way. He's on his own, marching along like he's leading us into battle. Sinclair walks behind with Fiona, the two of them deep in conversation. Violet stayed behind at the house, along with James Frye and his as-yet-unseen wife. McCreadie and Isla start off with us, but then they get into a conversation about mushrooms, and Gray and I ease back into the rear.

"It really is a beautiful day," I say. "I was thinking earlier that I'd like to walk along the roads. This is even better."

"We can certainly walk along the roads later," Gray says. "I suspect we will need regular escapes—I mean outings. The gardens, the roads, possibly a coach ride to see the countryside."

I smile. "I was thinking exactly that. I just wasn't sure whether it'd be rude to leave the estate."

"Oh, it certainly is rude, but I believe we could manage it. I . . ." He trails off, frowning as he looks to our left. "Do you hear that?"

I hadn't until he stopped talking. Ahead of us, everyone is hiking along, immersed in their various conversations. No one notices when we stop to listen.

I'm not sure what I'm hearing at first. It's faint, and I need to concentrate to pick it up.

"Whining?" I say. "Some kind of animal?"

"Hmm." Gray strides off the path to the left.

"Duncan . . ." I warn.

"I have seen the traps, and I know what to watch for. Wait there."

I snort. "Yeah, no." I hurry after him while scanning the ground. The grass here is short, and a crumbling cow patty suggests it's used for grazing. The shorter grass means we can see there aren't any traps.

We're skirting the edge of the largest of three lakes I'd spotted yesterday. In the distance, there's a dock and a rowboat, which I presume is our eventual destination.

The whining gets louder for the first few steps. Then it stops altogether, as if whatever is out there heard us coming. Gray slows, one hand out to warn me back. I ignore the hand. I'm following in his footsteps, as any smart person would do when traversing a field covered in bear traps.

When something moves in the grass, I'm the one grabbing his coat and holding him back . . . and the one getting the dirty look that says he wasn't going to rush forward. I still hold on to his coat as he resumes a slow walk, scanning the grass until he stops short.

Gray mutters an oath under his breath. When I go to peek around him, his hand shoots up. Then he thinks better of it and lowers his arm, letting me inch forward until I'm echoing his curse and pairing it with an exhale of disappointment.

Ahead is a trap. And caught in that trap? A wildcat, very clearly dead.

I know we'd heard whining, but looking at the poor beast, with the tip of its tongue protruding, I can't imagine it was alive ten seconds ago.

The grass whispers again. Something's moving on the other side of the cat. A tiny head pops up.

"Shi—" I stop myself before finishing the profanity. After a year, I no longer slip up in front of outsiders, but my next goal is not to do it when I'm startled.

I step forward. Gray's arm shoots out again, but only hovers there before he fists his hand, as if he was just stretching. I take another step, being more careful than I need to be, considering that the trap has been sprung.

I bend before the kitten. It glances about uncertainly, as if ready to take off. Then I see why it doesn't. One of its back legs is bloody and bent, badly broken. Seeing that, I do let out a full stream of twenty-first-century profanity under my breath.

A hiss sounds to my left, and I glance to see two other kittens watching me from the long grass. When I inch in their direction, they tumble over themselves to get away, and I stop.

"They seem fine," I say. "But this one . . ."

"Yes," Gray says, his expression grim, anger flashing in his eyes. "I told Archie—"

"Told me what?" a voice says, and we both look over to see Cranston striding through the long grass. Fiona is right behind him. Seeing that, I leap forward with, "Don't—"

"Oh!" she says.

She doesn't fall back or let out a shriek. Just that one startled word, and then she's hurrying forward. Cranston grabs her arm so fast she practically slingshots back.

"Apologies," he says, quickly releasing her. "But there is a trap."

"Which has already sprung," I grind out. "Robbing three kittens of their mother."

"Good lord." Sinclair comes up behind Fiona. He pales, and then reaches as if to lead her away from the grisly sight, but she ducks his grasp.

"Where are the kittens?" she says. Then she sees the one nearest me and sucks in a breath. "It has been injured."

"These damnable traps were not my idea," Cranston says. "Müller promised they would only frighten off poachers and the animals were clever enough to avoid them."

"If animals are clever enough to avoid them," I snap, "then please explain the purpose of traps."

I expect Cranston to snap something back. Instead, he just says "I . . ." and trails off, his cheeks coloring.

"This is unconscionable," Sinclair says, his face hard with anger. "I am so sorry, Fiona. Your groom really must do something about this. If he does not, I will."

"You're the one who recommended hiring—" Cranston begins. Then he spots someone out in the field. "Müller! Over here! Now!"

I turn to see a figure out past McCreadie and Isla, who hang back as if they saw enough to know what's going on . . . and don't need to see more. McCreadie is whispering something to Isla, who looks as upset as I feel. Then he starts leading Isla back in the direction of the house. She doesn't argue. She knows she has a weak stomach, as much as that annoys her.

The other figure watches them leave as he trudges over. He's a man of about forty, dressed in a heavy coat and thick boots, with a long, lean, and weathered face that turns our way with such a look of contempt that I blink, taken aback. His features rearrange themselves into an empty mask, though his eyes still ooze disdain.

The man says something I don't understand—it sounds Germanic.

"Speak English, man," Cranston snaps. He points at the trap. "Explain that."

The man—Müller, the gamekeeper—ambles over, and I swear he moves even slower after his employer's irritated snap.

When Müller speaks, his English is perfect, though heavily accented. "It is a wildcat."

"I mean what happened here?"

"It appears that the trap caught it about the neck, which caused—"

"Stop." Cranston seems ready to start foaming at the mouth, but the person he snaps at next is Sinclair. "Tell me again why I let you talk me into hiring this impertinent wretch."

"Mr. Müller," Sinclair says, his tone conciliatory. "The ladies are obviously distraught at coming upon this, and that has upset Mr. Cranston. You apparently told him this could not happen."

Müller gives an insolent shrug. "The cats should have known better. Apparently, they are not as intelligent as those in my country. Which comes as no surprise." His look says that's aimed at all inhabitants of this country, animal and human. "I am sorry the ladies are distraught."

Müller doesn't even try to sound apologetic. In fact, there's a sneer in those words and in the look he aims at Fiona and me. I think I'm imagining it until Gray rocks forward, his mouth opening.

"The ladies are not distraught," I cut in. "The ladies—and the men—are upset to find such a thing. This is a nursing mother. She has kittens." I wave at the two hiding in the grass and then at the third. "One of which was injured badly by the trap. Now we have a dead wildcat and three kittens too young to survive on their own. That is what the *ladies* are concerned about."

Müller doesn't even look my way. "Four cats caught with one trap. That is not a tragedy. It is efficiency."

"See here—" Cranston says, stepping forward.

"You did not intend to trap the cat," Müller says. "But you were concerned about it eating the eggs, and now you do not have to be. As for the kittens . . ." He gives an exaggerated bow in the direction of me and Fiona, without bothering to look at us. "The ladies need not worry about that. I will handle them."

"You will not," Fiona says. "The kittens are mine."

Now he does look at her, his lip curling. "They are not pets, girl."

"Girl?" Cranston bears down on Müller, who has the sense to back up.

"That is my bride and *your* future employer. You may speak to me however you wish, but you will show her respect."

Sinclair clears his throat. "If Fiona wants the kittens, she should have them, Archie. She is experienced at—"

"They are hers," Cranston says, and Sinclair stops, midstep, mouth open as if he'd expected Cranston to argue.

"Good," Sinclair says finally, collecting himself. "I will help her—"

"I will ensure Fiona has everything she needs." Cranston turns to Gray. "How badly is the little one injured? Can it be helped?"

Gray murmurs that he has not taken a good look, and he does that now, bending before the kitten. When it shrinks back, hissing, Fiona expertly lowers herself to the ground and holds the kitten in a firm grip, ignoring its protests.

"The leg is badly broken and that gash is deep," Gray says.

"Can you fix it?" Cranston says. Then before Gray can answer, he waves a hand. "*Will* you fix it? That is what I mean. Can it be done and will you do it?"

"I . . . can try." Gray glances my way, and I know what he's thinking. He's not a veterinarian, and this is a wild animal. As much as he might want to help, it's a very unusual request.

When Fiona speaks, her voice is soft. "I would appreciate it if you tried, Duncan, but I will understand if you would rather not. I can care for these kittens and return them to the wild. At least, I can for the other two, and I will do my best for this one."

"Return them to the wild?" Müller says.

"Yes," Fiona says evenly. "Scottish wildcats are at risk of extinction, and we must do what we can to save them."

"Save pests?" Müller throws up his hands. "Your groom has been complaining about one cat stealing his eggs, and now he is going to allow three more to grow up and do the same?"

"I only grumbled," Cranston says. "If I were truly angry, I would have asked for the cats to be relocated."

"Relocated?" Müller shakes his head and then stomps off, muttering in his own language.

When he's gone, Cranston spins on Sinclair. "I agreed to six months with him, and I will keep my word, but when it is done, he is gone."

"He seems very unpleasant," Fiona says. "I know you recommended him, Ezra, but . . ."

Sinclair sighs. "I recommended him for his skill as a gamekeeper, and he is very good at that, but there is evidently a conflict of personalities. You do bring that out in some people, Archie."

Sinclair says it lightly, but this is obviously awkward for him. He suggested Müller, and yes, there's a serious personality—and ideology—clash. That isn't Sinclair's fault, but he'll feel bad about it.

"It will be resolved," Fiona says. "For now . . ." She looks down at the dead wildcat, and her shoulders fall.

"I will handle this," Sinclair says. "I take full responsibility for this tragedy, and I will deal with the mother and help you with the kittens."

"You deal with the mother," Cranston says. "Bury her, please. Fiona and I will gather the uninjured kittens and take them to the house. Duncan? Can you and Miss Mitchell bring the injured one?"

"We will," Gray says. "When you reach the house, could you ask Hugh to deliver my bag? I will need to medicate the kitten before it can be moved, and I do not dare leave it." He peers into the sky. "It seems we already have a very interested hawk watching us."

"I will have Hugh bring your things," Sinclair says. "And I will return myself with a shovel to bury the cat."

He hurries off, and then Gray and I help Cranston and Fiona capture the two uninjured kittens. Fiona does most of the work. When McCreadie said she helped animals, I presumed it was . . . well, like the average well-to-do Victorian woman helps the poor. Charitable hobbyist work.

I had pictured Fiona instructing her maid on how to feed motherless kittens and then popping in now and then to give them a cuddle. I should have known better. She may be as kindhearted as her brother, but she's obviously as competent as him, too. She spoke of returning animals to the wild, and I'm not sure how much of a thing wildlife rehabilitation is in this world, but she captures those kittens like a seasoned pro. There are no cuddles or baby talk. She firmly scoops them up and then speaks to them in a reassuring tone before plunking one into Cranston's big hands and telling him how to hold it properly so it won't escape or shred him. And the whole time, he does as he's told and watches her work, looking a little awestruck.

Then they are off, kittens in hand. I wait until they're out of earshot before turning to Gray, who is hunkered down, examining his future patient as the injured kitten spits and hisses.

"Duncan?" I say.

"Hmm?" He doesn't look over, just keeps trying to get a better view of the kitten's injured leg without touching it.

"About the wildcat . . ." I say. "I think we need to discuss how it died."

"Hmm?" He looks up now, gaze still unfocused, trying to show me the respect of giving me his attention . . . but not really able to give it.

"That trap isn't what killed it."

Now those dark eyes focus on me as he frowns. "The trap . . ." He looks at the dead mother wildcat. Really looks at it. And then he lets out a curse.

SEVEN

A few more curses follow the first, these ones aimed at himself for not seeing the problem. I don't blame him, of course. Technically, this isn't a crime scene, and since the wildcat was obviously dead, he didn't need to take a closer look. But once he did, the problem became clear.

The jaws of the trap had snapped around the cat's neck, and that *would* have killed it—either with the force or those serrated edges. Except something is missing.

"Blood," Gray mutters as he kneels beside the dead wildcat. "There is no blood."

"Which could mean the trap only snapped her neck. Except . . ."

He grunts. "The edges have clearly broken the skin, and if she was alive when that happened, there would be blood." He exhales and leans back on his haunches. "She was placed there, already dead, and the trap sprung, to make it appear as if she died that way." He glances over at the injured kitten, who seems to think itself well-hidden and has stopped hissing. "That little one must have been too close when the trap was sprung."

Gray examines the trap, finds the release, and opens the jaws. Then he takes a closer look.

"The wound is clearly postmortem," he says. "Inflicted not long after she died, given that there is some blood on the tines. As for how she *did* die . . ." He looks at the cat. "Perhaps we ought not to have told Archie that I require a dead body for a proper mystery."

"Did someone say mystery?"

We look to see McCreadie striding over, Gray's black bag in hand. He's smiling until he sees the mother wildcat. Then he starts to glance away before stopping.

"Did the trap not kill her?" he says. "If it did, there ought to be more blood."

Gray sighs. "And you see it immediately as well. Clearly I should surrender any claim to the title of detective."

McCreadie claps him on the back. "Do not be so hard on yourself. You are only an amateur, after all. Still learning and all that."

As Gray grumbles, McCreadie says to me, "You saw it as well then. That is what you were discussing. The mystery of who killed the wildcat, because if there is so little blood, she was killed and posed here, which makes it a homicide." He purses his lips. "Caticide? Felicide?"

Whatever this is, it's not our concern. That isn't because the victim is a wild animal, but because no one will thank us for solving this mystery. It's Cranston's land, and his right to rid it of so-called pests. But it's not as if we have anything else to do, and also not as if we wouldn't welcome the distraction. So I zip my lips and adjust my skirts to lower myself and examine the cat.

"It could have been better staged," I say. "Just add more blood, and no one would question it. Meaning the killer either doesn't know better . . . or they presumed no one would care enough to look closer. I—"

"The shovel has been obtained." Sinclair's voice rings out over the field, and the men both straighten quickly as he approaches. I rise slower.

"I will tend to the cat," Sinclair says. "The kittens are up at the house."

"We will handle this," McCreadie says, reaching for the shovel.

Sinclair frowns and keeps his grip on it.

"We will bury the beast," McCreadie says.

"No need. I have done far too much hunting to be squeamish, and you need to work on that injured one there."

"The kitten should rest for a few minutes," Gray says. "As for the cat here, I was going to use it as a demonstration for Miss Mitchell. She has been learning basic anatomy."

"Can't let a good corpse go to waste," McCreadie says cheerfully. "They are bloody expensive."

"Er . . ." Sinclair looks from Gray to me to McCreadie, obviously trying not to judge our hobbies. "I suppose there is no harm . . ."

"There is not," Gray says firmly. "It is a lesson for Miss Mitchell, after which we shall bury the beast, and then I will do what I can for the kitten."

Sinclair shrugs and holds out the shovel. "All right then. I cannot say I mind being relieved of the task. Enjoy . . ." He trails off, as if realizing that might not be the right word. He clears his throat. "Have a good lesson, and I will see you up at the house." He starts to leave and then turns. "Follow the same direction back, and you will be fine. There are no other traps between here and the house."

Gray uses a bit of morphine on the kitten. He has some in his bag—in this era, leaving that out would be like leaving out aspirin or acetaminophen. Once the kitten is woozy, we wrap her leg pending closer examination and we put her aside to rest while we autopsy the wildcat. Or, more correctly, necropsy the cat, that being the word used for an internal postmortem on a nonhuman.

It doesn't take a complete dissection to realize what killed her, but we want to give the kitten time to fall asleep. Gray wasn't lying about teaching me anatomy, and we really have only worked on humans, so this is a teaching moment.

As for what killed her . . .

"Poison!" I say, shouting like it'll win me a quiz-show jackpot.

"I was going to say that," McCreadie grumbles. "I was literally opening my mouth to do so, and then I saw you opening yours, and being a gentleman, I let you go first."

"Of course you did."

Gray looks heavenward in an expression familiar to any teacher who has had to deal with two very competitive keeners.

"Fine," I say, moving back on my heels. "Giving you the benefit of the doubt, Hugh, I will let you point out the signs."

His eyes narrow. "Giving me the benefit of the doubt? Or calling my bluff?"

I smile, showing my teeth. "Either. Both."

"Fine. There are signs of hemorrhaging in the eyes and vomit in the fur."

"Correct," Gray says. "Of course, were this a human patient, I would then be passing on tissue to Isla for confirmation and to narrow down the list of possible toxins. However, as she is here for a holiday and a wedding, that hardly seems appropriate."

McCreadie snorts. "If you think your sister would rather play whist with Archie, James, and that wife of his, you do not know her very well. The only thing stopping her from helping would be a lack of equipment."

"So someone poisoned the cat," I say. "Likely in meat, which we'll see when we open her stomach. Ezra did say he thought he heard her last night. I did, too, now that I think of it. I was drifting off when I heard something outside."

Gray idly taps his probe. "What sort of noise?"

"Hard to say. A yowl maybe? A sound of some distress, but it's the forest at night. Critters are hunting and being hunted. It didn't last long enough to do more than catch my attention."

"What time was that?" McCreadie asks.

"Around two?" I explain how I came down after that and heard Cranston outside.

"I thought he was patrolling," I say. "Guarding his property. But then Ezra showed up, and Archie said something about Ezra roaming about, so I think he realized Ezra was gone and was concerned."

"As he should be," McCreadie mutters. "What the bloody hell is Archie thinking, laying those traps about? And blaming the gamekeeper. That was obviously to appease Fiona."

"Was it?" I say. "Archie grumbled about the traps last night, too, and seemed genuinely annoyed." I glance at Gray. "You spoke to him about them."

Gray nods. "He did not appreciate that, however politely I worded it. We have never got along."

McCreadie makes a noise that says this is an understatement, but Gray only continues, "My interpretation would agree with yours. That the traps are not Archie's idea. If they were, he would have had no issue with saying so to me. Yes, he might blame Müller in front of Fiona, but not to me or Ezra."

I shift to get more comfortable. "But knowing his bride would be horrified if he killed the wildcat for stealing eggs, might he have poisoned the cat and then made it look like the trap killed her?"

Gray looks to McCreadie, as if lobbing the question his way.

"I cannot say for certain either way." McCreadie seems to choose his words with care. "Archie denied that he wanted the cat dead, but that could indeed be bluster for Fiona's sake. My impression there . . ." He pauses and then speaks even slower. "I am not comfortable assessing their relationship, as I fear I am inclined to be too hopeful, for my sister's sake. Archie has his faults—many, many faults—but I would like to think he is genuinely fond of Fiona. Not necessarily in the way a groom should be fond of his bride but . . ."

"Last night, when I overheard him speaking to Ezra, that was the impression I got. He recognizes how young she is, and intends to . . . Well, he seems to see it more as a transfer of guardianship, and he also seems very willing to take on that responsibility. He does seem fond of her. Very fond. Just more as a friend's young sister than as a bride."

McCreadie exhales in obvious relief. "Good. It is not the marriage I would wish for my sister, and I fear I might be responsible, our families still wishing to be joined after I ended my engagement with Violet . . ."

"I've heard nothing like that," I say, managing Oscar-worthy sincerity. "But even acknowledging that Archie cares for Fiona only means that if he did want the wildcat dead, this might have been his way of doing that without incurring her wrath."

"The other primary suspect would be Müller."

I must make a face, because McCreadie shoots me a look.

"He is rather unpleasant, isn't he?" McCreadie says. "However, Europeans often see the British as unsophisticated, particularly those living in the 'wilds' of Scotland."

"It's not only Europeans," Gray says. "The English love to mock us with political cartoons portraying Scots as bumbling and idiotic primitives. Despite the fact, as Isla would point out, that our literacy rates significantly exceed theirs. As for Müller, he will not last. Archie is a man of his word, and he will honor the terms of their agreement and then release him. As for whether he makes a valid suspect? Yes. If Archie did not want the wildcat killed, it is obvious from our encounter with Müller that the gamekeeper would see that as interference. The cat is a pest, and pests are to be eliminated. But to keep the peace, he might poison it and then make it look as if it wandered into the trap."

"Either way," McCreadie says, "it is not as if we can charge the killer with anything. Or even accuse them without causing trouble." He seems to consider the injustice of this, only to shake it off and say, more brightly, "But we can perform the autopsy."

"Necropsy," Gray corrects.

"Yes, yes. On with it then. Your eager students await."

We confirm undigested meat in the cat's stomach, but there's no point in collecting it. This is a mental exercise only, a diversion and to satisfy our own curiosity. While the murder of an animal deserves better, even in the modern day, this wouldn't be considered animal cruelty. Considering she's an endangered species, there'd be some law against killing her, but that doesn't apply here. This was just a landowner getting rid of a pest that broke into his chicken coop. So while it seems disrespectful to use her death as an exercise for bored minds, it's better than realizing she'd been murdered, dumping her into a hole, and walking away.

When we reach the house, Cranston and Sinclair are outside with Frye, and Sinclair calls Gray and McCreadie over. That invitation will not include me. So I continue on to the house. I poke my head into the first of the sitting rooms to find Violet with an unfamiliar woman.

I murmur an apology and start to retreat, but Violet calls me in.

"Miss Mitchell," she says, rising. "This is Mrs. Edith Frye, James's wife. Edith, this is Miss Mallory Mitchell."

Edith Frye is a pinch-faced woman of about thirty. Or so she seems until I realize the pinched-face part is only her expression as she peers at me. "Who? Oh. Some friend of Fiona's, I presume."

"No, Miss Mitchell is here with Dr. Gray."

That look again. "Who?"

"Duncan Gray," Violet says, with great patience. "He went to school with James, Ezra, and Archie. He is a dear friend of Hugh's."

"Oh. The dark one."

Violet responds with perfect equanimity. "Yes, he has dark hair and I believe, dark eyes as well. Miss Mitchell is his assistant."

Edith's gaze rakes up and down me, and she gives the most unladylike snort. "Assistant, you say."

"The Grays have always been . . ." Violet seems to search for a word. "Broad-minded. Have you met his sister, Isla Ballantyne? She is here as well. She is a chemist, and the most fascinating—"

"Is this not a wedding party? Someone's sister. Someone's assistant. It is most irregular."

"It is Fiona's wedding, and she invited her brother and his friends, whose company she enjoys. Just as Archie invited his friends, including your husband, whose company he enjoys. Now, why don't we all go and see whether we can find Fiona and Isla and play a game until lunch."

I open my mouth to excuse myself, but then I catch Violet's expression, a silent scream that begs not to be left alone with Edith.

"That is an excellent idea," I say. "If you can find Miss McCreadie, I will find Mrs. Ballantyne."

I manage to duck out of the game, as does Fiona. We have an excuse— Gray wants to work on that wildcat. I am his assistant, and Fiona asks to watch. Sinclair takes the fourth place for whist, and we leave them to it.

The question becomes where to operate on the kitten. The obvious place is the kitchen . . . if we want the cook quitting in protest. The only animals allowed in a kitchen are the ones served on the table.

We end up in the stable, which is possibly the worst place, between the noise and the manure and the poor lighting. After trying to fix the lighting problem, Gray gives up and has a couple of the grooms carry a barn table outdoors. I scrub it down as best I can, and Fiona helps, ignoring my protests. She is indeed McCreadie's sister, rolling up her sleeves and diving in. I may hate their parents for what they've done to both of them—disowning McCreadie and forcing Fiona into an arranged marriage—but I must give them credit for raising two lovely humans.

Once the table is washed, Fiona disappears into the house and reappears with a bundle of sheets that Mrs. Hall is surprisingly letting her use. They're old bedding, relegated to servants' quarters, but in this world, they would have been recycled until they were threadbare rags.

Gray nails down one sheet as the most sterile table topper we can hope for. We've reached a time when doctors are starting to understand that infection comes from dirty conditions, though cleanliness is still not common practice. While Gray believes in the new science, this insistence on a clean operating theater is in deference to his assistant, who could confirm that yes, dear God, you don't slice into a living body without first boiling your instruments.

Once all that is done, Fiona lifts the kitten onto the cloth. Gray had been adjusting the dosage of the painkiller until the kitten was sleeping but still had a strong heartbeat. Now he conducts a thorough examination of the unconscious creature. Fiona and I silently stand by as he pokes and prods and, finally, exhales.

"I cannot save the leg," he says. "I am truly sorry, Fiona. I thought I could, but I can see now that it is mangled beyond my skill to repair."

"Can you amputate it?" I ask.

He goes quiet, and I glance at Fiona, who nibbles her lower lip.

"That is . . . not usually done with an animal," she says. "I have treated a dog that lost a leg in an accident, and it went on to a good home with lovely people, but I would not ask Duncan to perform such a surgery on a mere wildcat."

There's a note in her voice that has me looking at Gray. It's a note that says she's being polite while hoping he'll agree to the surgery.

"Dr. Gray?" I say.

"I certainly *can* do it," he says slowly, "but a three-legged wildcat is, I believe, unlikely to be returned to the wild. Of course, Fiona is the expert at that."

"You are correct," she says. "However, a Highland tiger is not truly a tiger. She could be kept as a pet, and I would be happy to do so."

We could mention that, in a few days, that won't necessarily be her choice. She'll need to ask her husband's permission to keep the kitten. But neither of us is saying that. Either she's forgotten her upcoming change in status or she believes she can win Cranston's approval for a three-legged wild pet cat.

"I also cannot guarantee the cat would survive the surgery," Gray says. He quickly adds, "I am happy to attempt it, to the best of my ability, but I have only performed amputation on humans, and mostly as a surgical assistant."

"I will understand if she does not survive it," Fiona says. "And even if she does, and the pain or shock is too great, I will not see her suffer."

"All right then. Let us begin."

And so, I witness my first—and hopefully last—amputation. I'm not squeamish, but this is hard to watch.

I believe amputation is far more common in this era than my own. Of course, I can't say that without access to a computer and research stats. But I know a bit about it in this time from my medical reading and conversations with Gray, who believes that amputation rates are already dropping. Chalk that up to the discovery of ether and the ability to knock a patient out and perform proper surgery.

Before that was possible, if the affected area was a limb, it was easiest to just remove it. However, please note the "no anesthetic" part. Yep, speed was of the essence, and speed of amputation was a key surgical skill. How fast could you saw off a leg and cauterize the stump? I believe the record was a couple of minutes. Then you had the risk of shock and, later, infection, which meant you didn't take off a limb unless it was the only way to save someone's life. But, often, it was indeed the only way, as with this kitten.

While Gray doesn't need to perform an Olympic-speed amputation, he does have to work fast, because the kitten won't stay asleep. Again, we lack the necessary ingredient, in this case ether.

We'd asked around. That might seem odd—who the hell brings ether to a wedding party? The answer is "more people than you might think."

Throughout history, every time humans discover a new substance, I'm pretty sure their first question is whether they can eat it. Their second? Whether they can get high from it. In the case of ether, the answer to the second is yes. It's even, apparently, becoming available in some pubs, as an alternative to alcohol for those taking "the pledge."

No one brought party ether to the wedding, sadly . . . and yes, I can't believe I'm adding "sadly" to that statement. For the kitten's sake, though, it would have been helpful. As it is, the painkillers help keep the kitten from completely freaking out, though the poor thing does wake up to a bit of a shock. Fiona and I hold her down while staying out of Gray's way, and in a rather astonishingly short amount of time, the leg is off and the kitten is sutured.

EIGHT

We missed lunch with our kitten surgery. Isla assures us we dodged a bullet there—apparently Edith decided it was appropriate to start critiquing Fiona's menu choices, under the guise of "advising" a new bride and future lady of the house . . . even though the target of her advice wasn't even present. Violet and Cranston jointly put her in her place, and I kinda regret missing that part. But I am glad that Fiona also missed it, and I enjoy a quiet lunch with her and Gray on the back patio, as she peppers him with questions about his work.

The afternoon is supposed to be devoted to wedding preparation, but then someone brings a message that both the bride's and groom's parents are delayed. They're traveling together, and their coach broke a wheel along the road, so they decided to call it a day and spend the night at an inn. Fiona frets about that, and McCreadie and Sinclair both reassure her as Cranston takes action, sending his coach to be doubly sure they can depart in the morning.

The afternoon passes both quickly and slowly, if that's possible. Slowly in the sense that we don't have much to do, but quickly in the sense that we aren't trapped in the house playing charades and waiting for the bride's and groom's parents to arrive.

Edith doesn't join us for dinner, and not even her husband seems disappointed by that. Afterward, we do that thing I've only ever seen in novels, where the men retire to one room and the "ladies" to another. In books, we'd be sipping port, which always sounded very posh until I actually tried it. I can barely hide my relief when Fiona produces a bottle of whisky instead.

In fact, she produces three bottles.

"I propose a sampling party," she says. "There must be some advantage to marrying a man who has chosen whisky as his trade, and I declare this will be it. No port for us." She pauses. "Unless anyone wants that, of course."

We all demur, and she takes glasses from the side table and explains what we're about to taste. I've learned a bit about the history of scotch. While there has always been whisky in Scotland, we're in the era where it begins to be refined and industrialized, slowly spreading beyond Britain's borders. In other words, Cranston has gotten into it at exactly the right time.

"I take it Mr. Cranston is doing well with his business," I say, waving at the house.

"Well enough to be able to fashion himself a country gentleman," Violet says. "Really, I can imagine a hundred better ways to spend his money, but apparently, a hunting lodge is his choice." She glances at Fiona. "And that was sharp-tongued of me. I apologize."

Fiona only laughs. "As his sister, you are permitted to be as sharp-tongued about Archie as you like. I certainly needle Hugh enough. As for the house . . ." She glances around. "I rather like it. It will be drafty in the fall, but I am not certain I would join him for hunting season even if it were warm." She glances at a mounted deer head and shudders. "I will enjoy it in the spring and summer, though. Once we have resolved the matter of those ridiculous traps, of course."

"Resolved the matter of the gamekeeper, you mean," Violet says, sipping her whisky.

"Hmm. He is unpleasant, is he not? I have a list then." Fiona clicks her glass down. "Get rid of the traps. Get rid of the gamekeeper. Convince Archie that a wildlife preserve would be far better than a hunting one."

Violet smiles. "I suspect you will win easily on the first two, but I wish you luck with the last. Now, how about that housekeeper?"

"Mrs. Hall? I do not mind her at all. Mother always says that if a housekeeper keeps the home and staff in line, then the lady of the house does not need to. Mrs. Hall is polite and respectful, which is more than I expected, given my youth. Also given the fact that Archie fired her husband."

"Mr. Hall was the former gamekeeper," I say. "I heard that. I met their children heading home. Well, not exactly children. Teen—Young adults."

"Oh! I have not met them. I must do that. I cannot believe Archie fired their father while keeping their mother in charge of his house. I despair of men sometimes. Even a decent person would be tempted to take small revenges. Extra starch in the sheets. Extra salt in the stew. Perhaps a dead rat, decaying under the floorboards beside his bed."

Isla laughs. "I was with you until that last one, Fiona."

I say, "The trick would be to leave the rat in exactly the right spot, so the person you are angry with only catches a whiff of it now and then."

"You are all wicked," Violet announces. "I would do none of those things." She sips her whisky. "I would water down his whisky and then serve it to guests as if that is what he is bottling."

After we all laugh, Isla says, more seriously, "As for Mrs. Hall, the sad truth is that if her husband has been let go then she cannot afford to do anything that might earn her the same fate."

Fiona sobers. "Indeed. I had not thought of that. I hope that is not what Archie is thinking—that he does not need to worry about consequences because she cannot afford to deliver any."

"He is not," Violet says firmly. "My brother is not the sort to be cruel. He is also not the sort to consider such things, I fear. He decided having a European gamekeeper is fashionable and did not work through the ramifications."

"Then that will be my job," Fiona says. "I will see that Mr. Hall is hired back once this Müller fellow is let go. I believe Archie fails to understand the depth of the locals' rancor and the reasons for it."

"The clearances," Isla murmurs.

She means the displacement of tenant farmers. While this was perfectly legal—the tenants didn't own the land—it violated a very old principle that said clan members had the right to rent land on clan territory. The first round of clearances, in the mid-eighteenth century, had been mostly about profit. The second one, in the middle of this century, had been partly profit-driven but also partly due to overcrowding and famine, as landowners selectively evicted tenants.

Fiona nods. "People still remember being driven from land they had lived on for generations. They lost everything."

"Including their culture," I say, taking a quick drink of my whisky and murmuring, "Outlawing tartan, bagpipes, Gaelic. The death of Highland culture after Culloden."

Fiona grows animated, pleased to find a receptive audience. "I have no idea how much that affected people here. I shall have to find out. But the scars run deep, and now a southerner built a house on land they hunted and told them they cannot even walk across it? That was not Archie, but he needs to understand he is making the situation worse, maintaining the former owner's rules and bringing in foreign help." She takes a deep breath. "Enough of that. I will handle it. Back to the sampling. Now this next bottle we shall sample is—"

"Then when *is* it the proper time to discuss this?" It's James Frye's voice, coming through the wall between us and the men. "Not while you were buying this place. Not while you were planning your wedding. Not while you are here for your nuptials. Not afterward either, I presume, as you will be occupied with taking your bride to France. By the time you are free to discuss this, Cranston, all my money will be gone. Or is that your intention?"

"You are free to withdraw your investment at any time." Cranston's voice is pure ice. "I will refund it in full. Down to the pence."

"Keeping the profits?"

"Good God, man, make up your mind. One minute you accuse me of losing your investment, and the next you accuse me of keeping your profits. Which is it?"

"This house proves there are profits. Whether we investors ever see them is another matter. How exactly did you pay for this?"

"With my share of those profits." Cranston seems to be speaking through clenched teeth now. "Plus my bride's dowry, and yes, Fiona knows I used it for this and approved. As for the whisky business, I provided you with a statement last month, which showed that you have indeed made money."

"Not enough, as I realize after seeing this house."

"You mean not after Edith saw it," Cranston shoots back.

"My wife has an excellent head for business."

"No, she has an excellent head for causing mischief. For sowing seeds of discord. You *have* made money. You will make *more*. If you wish to withdraw your funds and profits, tell me, and I will send a letter to my notary tomorrow. Tonight if you insist. Now, if you wish to discuss this further, might I suggest we go outside. Our friends hardly need to witness our business squabble."

"Indeed," Violet murmurs. "This is rather awkward for us as well." She turns to Fiona. "Please pay no heed to James. The business is doing well, and James will be repaid. This is Edith's doing."

"Oh, I have no doubt of it," Fiona says lightly. "Some people are simply not happy unless they are causing trouble. I have a friend or two like that."

"Reminds me of my sister," Isla says.

"Lady Leslie?" Fiona smiles. "I have heard a great deal about her. She sounds like a very interesting person."

Isla and I snort in unison.

"She sounds like a very *formidable* person," Violet says. "I would not wish to cross her."

"True," Fiona says. "However, I also would not turn down an invitation to one of her soirees. I hear they are perfectly delightful, with all the most scandalous people." She leans toward Isla. "Yes, I am hinting for an invitation."

Isla smiles. "Then you shall have one. I suspect she would find you very interesting as well."

Fiona's brows rise. "I am not sure that is a compliment."

"She finds Mallory *most* interesting."

"Ah." Fiona reaches her glass to clink with mine. "Then it is indeed a compliment. Now, let us finish these and try the third, and then we will pretend to discuss the merits of each, while needing to sample them all again. Oh, and to liven up the conversation, have you ever heard the story of the women of Coigach and how they resisted the clearances? It was around 1852, I believe."

Isla has heard the story apparently. Violet has not. I settle in, thinking I am about to hear some tale from the distant past . . . when I realize it was less than twenty years ago. A reminder that the clearances can be very recent history up here.

Fiona pours us all a third sample and then launches into the story.

By the time we've finished the tasting, we're all a little tipsy. Maybe more than a little. But there's a sense of silly fun about it that I haven't had since barhopping in my university years.

Earlier, I'd reflected on how Fiona was a typical Victorian woman, more than most in my life. Maybe it should seem as if my opinion has changed. She clearly knows her own mind and, in some ways, she's more mature than I was at that age, ready to take on the running of a house when I was barely able to keep up with my coursework. In the makeshift surgery with the kitten, she proved she was capable and intelligent despite a lack of rigid formal education. So does that make her different? "Not like other girls"? I don't think so. I suspect she really is relatively typical for her age and generation. She knows what is expected of her and chafes against it but has found ways to make her life her own. As women always have.

Once Violet is away from the men, she reveals herself to be more than she seemed as well. She relaxes, and that makes all the difference. I'm reminded of my mother, who'd gone to an all-girls school for a few years, and she'd always said it had changed her. She'd felt freer, more confident, and there, she'd discovered her voice. That's Violet, between the lack of men and the addition of scotch. Her tongue sharpens with incisive wit and she shows full confidence in her opinions, as her anxieties and self-consciousness ebb.

I could never have imagined the other Violet with McCreadie. Could I imagine this one with him? Yes, but only in the sense that it wouldn't have been a completely awful match. Except it would have been, because if you're in love with one person, it doesn't matter who else you marry—it will be awful.

McCreadie belongs with Isla, and I will admit, my little matchmaking heart had pitter-pattered at the thought of them spending this week together. Weddings are great for breaking through repressed romances. But when your former fiancée—whom you jilted, presumably on account of this other woman—is also in attendance? Yeah, I'm not going to be finding ways to nudge McCreadie and Isla together on this trip.

Dinner had been at eight, which means that by the time we've spent a couple of hours drinking and talking, we're ready to retire. Tomorrow, the bride's and groom's parents will arrive, and then serious wedding preparations will commence, with the ceremony the day after tomorrow. Then it'll be done, and we'll be on our way home, and I will be able to declare—I think—that as terrible as this trip had looked yesterday, it might actually not be so bad.

And, as if to reward me for my positive thinking, I'm walking down the hall when Gray is passing the other way—deep in conversation with Sinclair—and slips me a note. I need to stifle my grin at that, while I continue on as if I hadn't even noticed him. Then I duck into the spot under the stairs and open the note.

If you anticipate trouble sleeping, meet me at midnight by the sundial, and we shall slip out for a clandestine visit to your coos.

I smile, read it again, and roll my eyes. Gray really needs to be more careful about things like this. I know that he doesn't mean anything "clandestine" in *that* way—only that we aren't supposed to be walking around the grounds. Someone reading it, though, and wanting to see scandal, would find it in that note. Even the part about visiting the "coos" could be seen as . . . Well, I don't know what, but when people want to read something dirty into a word, they have no problem using their imaginations.

Between the whisky and my lack of sleep, I don't anticipate trouble drifting off. But am I going to tell Gray that? Hell no. And since I can't set an alarm, I'll be staying awake. Why? Because I'd hate to miss a chance to see the cows, obviously.

No, I'll be staying awake because I'd hate to miss the chance for a moonlit walk with Gray. I don't expect anything "clandestine." I'm honestly not sure what I'd do if the outing turned in that direction. It won't, and so I'm safe. Disappointed? Sure. I no longer lie to myself about that.

I have feelings for Duncan Gray that go well beyond friendship, but it's not the sort of situation where I'm only accepting friendship in hopes of it developing into more. I've had enough guys pull that bullshit with me in my time. I acknowledge that I have feelings that aren't reciprocated, and I deal with that, which means I expect nothing from this walk except his company, and I will jump at the chance for that.

I spend a bit of time chatting with Alice in our room. She's been doing fine. She's the youngest of the servants, but she's been hanging out alternately with Simon—in the stable with the other grooms—and one of the older maids who seems to have taken Alice under her wing.

Soon Alice is asleep, and I'm lying in bed, pretending that I plan to do the same while keeping my eyes open so I don't drift off. I have my pocket watch clutched under my pillow, and when it hits eleven thirty, I'm up and changing.

I can't just wear my wrapper to walk with Gray. I wear my petticoats instead of my crinoline, but I still have all the layers. I pull the corset stays just tight enough to get into my dress.

I started thirty minutes pre–meet time because it takes so damned long to get dressed, especially while trying to be quiet. It's nearly five to midnight when I arrive downstairs. I peep in all the rooms as I pass. It's not late enough to guarantee that everyone has gone to bed, but they seem to have. I poke my head in the cloakroom and then slip outside.

Gray waits by the sundial, as promised.

"Cranston is out and about," I whisper as I join him.

His brows rise.

"His coat isn't with the rest," I say.

Gray curses under his breath. "I did not think to check that."

"His is the only one missing. Of course, that only applies to the men—the women have their cloaks and shawls in their rooms. Cranston's coat is very distinctive, though, and it's definitely not there. It was when we went to bed. I checked then, too."

"You were far more thorough than I," he says. "I ought to have been more considerate of your reputation."

It's not *my* reputation I'm concerned about. I wish I knew a way to keep people from presuming Gray has hired a bed-buddy rather than an assistant. Of course, that's particularly awkward when I kinda wish—

Okay, I absolutely do not wish that was why he hired me. I just mean that it insults Gray to presume that. Yes, fine, it probably insults me more—implying that's my only use. But while he worries about my "reputation," I neither have one nor need one. He has one and needs it.

I've considered workarounds. Like a fake boyfriend. I even spent some time working on a story. My beau would be a medical student that I met through Gray. He's working in a London hospital right now, but we are betrothed and will wed someday. Once he has a job and is settled.

I broached the idea with Isla. She rolled her eyes and walked away. I take it that means it wouldn't help. Which I suppose it wouldn't. My fake fiancé would only become some poor besotted lad who thinks my relationship with Gray is platonic. Not only would Gray be sleeping with his assistant, but he'd be cuckolding this innocent young man. And, really, while I hate anyone thinking Gray only hired me for sex, at least half who believe that also commend him for it. Getting a pretty young thing to "help" with his work? The lucky dog.

"What do you want to do?" I ask as we move toward the shadows. "I'd still like that walk, but I really don't want to bump into Cranston and have him needling you about it for the rest of our visit."

Gray tilts his head, considering. "I believe, if I am being perfectly honest, that Archie would be relieved to discover you and I are having an affair. It would knock me off my high horse, as he would say."

True, given what I overheard. But do I want to give Cranston fodder?

Fodder for what? Snide comments and jabs? He already does that to Gray. He's not going to make crass comments in front of the ladies.

"Let's just be careful," I say. "I don't care what he thinks, but I'd prefer to have a quiet walk without his particular brand of bullshit."

Gray's lips twitch. "So what brand of 'bullshit' do you want on your walk?"

"Yours, of course."

"Which is . . . ?"

I shrug. "Surprise me."

"Your challenge is accepted." He reaches down into the shadows under a hedge and takes out a basket. "This is my brand of nonsense. A moonlight picnic. Just the two of us out on the heather."

Good thing it's dark, because my cheeks definitely heat at that.

"And the coos?" I say.

"Tucked under their blankets, sound asleep in the barn."

I peer up at him. "So the coos were a lie?"

He lifts the basket. "Onward. We have a picnic to enjoy."

NINE

We take great care with our route. We stick to an obvious footpath, and when the moon ducks behind cloud cover, we wait until it returns so we can watch for traps. A lantern would have been wise, but anyone spotting lantern light would have been suspicious. I guess it's better to die in a mantrap than get caught sneaking around with an actual man?

I can joke, but it's safe enough. We've seen the traps, and we aren't going to accidentally step in one unless we wander into the long grass, which we do not. We follow the footpath until we're on a small rise near a lake. From here, we have a perfect view of the estate grounds stretching in every direction, rolling hills and stands of trees, with the admittedly impressive house in the backdrop.

Gray opens the basket and pulls out a small bottle of whisky. Seeing it, he hesitates.

"I had this packed earlier," he says. "That was before dinner and before your whisky sampling. Perhaps I ought to have packed something else."

"Like port?"

He smiles. "Except port."

"Whisky is fine. I don't think we tried that one." I examine the label. "Oh, wait. We did, and that was my favorite. Excellent choice."

Gray pours us each a glass and then empties the rest of the basket.

"You went on a pilfering *spree*," I say as he pulls out a veritable midnight buffet of breads and cheeses and meat. "Okay, I forgive you for the lack of coos."

"Cows."

"Coos. That's what I said." I take a bite of bread. "It's the accent."

"We have the same accent, Mallory."

"Bite your tongue. I have the accent of a Scot without your hoity-toity education." I take another bite and swallow. "Can I just tell you how weird it was to wake up and not only have another voice but an accent I can barely understand?"

He purses his lips. "I had not thought of that. Yours is very different then?"

"Very. Wanna hear me do it?"

"Of course."

I clear my throat, drop my voice, and concentrate on hearing a Canadian voice. "The rain in Spain falls mainly on the plain."

"That is . . . interesting."

"Flat, you mean. Compared to yours. It doesn't even sound like the North Americans I've met in this time period. The evolution of language."

"Does mine sound like Scottish people in your time?"

I wrinkle my nose. "Mostly? Catriona's brogue is thicker. Yours sounds about seventy-five percent like a modern city-bred Scottish accent. I could usually understand those, mostly because of my nan. The country ones are tougher. Catriona's sounds like what I'd think of as country. Same as Alice or Simon or Jack. More regional."

"More pure Scot. Less influenced by the English."

"Possibly. I remember watching old movies from the forties and fifties, and the Americans all sounded vaguely British. Turns out that was something actors affected in that period to sound more cultured."

"They sounded English, you mean. Not British."

"Right. Sorry. Someday, I will stop doing that. It's like lumping Canadians in with Americans. Never appreciated." I lift my whisky. "Here's to living in countries annoyingly overshadowed by their more famous neighbors."

He clinks my glass and then pauses. "However, in my case, we are under English rule."

"Well, technically, my country stopped being a colony only a few years ago, and we won't gain our full governing independence for another hundred years. Even then, we're still part of the Commonwealth, which means we recognize an English monarch, at least symbolically." I sigh. "It's taking a very long time to snip those apron strings."

He hefts his class. "To the demise of British colonialism. Which *will* end . . ." He looks at me.

"Uh, someday?"

He sighs, deeply enough to make me laugh.

I take a chunk of roast ham and lean back to stare up at the sky before I surrender and flop onto my back. "So many stars."

"Which is one thing we have that you do not, yes? Well, you have stars. You simply cannot see them."

"Not in the city."

He stretches onto one elbow. The movement is slow enough to make me smile. Not that he minds getting his clothes grass-stained—after all, he isn't the one to clean them. But it's like using muscles creaky from disuse, as if he isn't quite sure how to stretch out on the ground anymore, much less flop down on his back, like I had.

Once he's on his elbow, he shifts before finally easing onto his back.

"They truly are glorious," he says.

"Billions and billions of stars. All light-years away."

"And a light-year is how far?"

I twist to look over at him. "Detective. Not astrophysicist."

He smiles, and we resume our stargazing.

After a few minutes he says, his voice soft, "Are you still happy here, Mallory?"

I don't answer too quickly. That would ring false. Instead, I take a moment to find the sincerity he needs. "I am."

"And you know that if you were not . . ."

I tilt my head his way. "You don't need to keep checking, Duncan. I'm a big girl who wouldn't hesitate to try going back if this wasn't what I wanted. But I haven't questioned it for a moment."

I resist the urge to add in a joke, maybe that I *have* questioned it when I had to peel back a corpse's skin and hold it for an hour. Even joking would make him fret.

"I'm here," I say. "I'm staying here."

He nods and looks up at the sky. More minutes of comfortable silence pass. Then he says, "There is something I wanted to speak to you about."

I glance over, but he's still looking up. "Okay."

"Since you are staying, I wanted to discuss . . . That is, I wanted to ask . . ."

He trails off, and I'm about to nudge when he clears his throat and blurts, "My mother will be home this summer."

That didn't seem like what he was about to say. It's as if he'd had something else on his mind and switched midstream.

Or maybe I'm wrong. Maybe he's just not sure how I'll react to this news. The answer is "delighted."

I haven't met Frances Gray. She lives in Europe. Currently Italy . . . I think. She moves around, and mostly, her children go to her, but she does come for a summer visit. Last year, she hadn't—she'd been volunteering in a community suffering an outbreak of influenza.

"I figured she'd be back," I say, "considering Mrs. Wallace has only told me a million times that I need to be on my best behavior when she arrives." I stop. "Is that the problem? Are you concerned about me?"

"Of course not."

I push onto my elbows. "If you are, you can say so. I'll stay with Annis while your mother is here."

His lips twitch though the smile doesn't reach his eyes. "I would never torture you so."

"I wouldn't mind. I know I struggle to act like a proper Victorian at the town house. I'm home, so I relax. Simon and Alice and Jack accept the 'Catriona head injury' excuse, but your mom might be a lot more suspicious. Like Mrs. Wallace."

"I am not concerned about that."

"I'm serious, Duncan. If you are at all worried about my behavior, I get it. Zero offense taken. When it comes to acting like a proper Victorian lady, I'm a work in progress." I pause. "Or is the issue me being your assistant?"

"Not at all. Isla and I have both spoken of you on our visits, and our mother is only pleased that I have a suitable aide. She knows . . ." He clears his throat. "She knows me well enough to know I would never promote you for untoward reasons."

"Good." I gaze up into the stars and then say, "I've been trying to come up with solutions for that. To keep people from making the wrong presumptions."

I tell him about my fake-boyfriend story, and he laughs softly.

"You . . . put a great deal of thought into that one," he says.

"But it won't work. I know."

A moment of silence, before he says, tentatively, "Does it bother you more than you have let on? That people make that assumption?"

"It pisses me off on your behalf. That's what worries me. I don't have a reputation to protect. You do."

"But anyone who knows me understands I would not take advantage of you. And anyone who comes to know you realizes you are a worthy assistant. Even if strangers draw the wrong conclusions, they do no more than snicker and smirk, which insults you far more than me. That is what concerns me, and I will admit I have been seeking a solution as well."

Silence as we stargaze for a while. Then he says, "If strangers presume you are more than my employee, you fear that damages my reputation because . . . why exactly? Because Catriona is a decade my junior? Or not of my social class?"

"Both."

"While I would never dally with someone who was actually so young, it would be no cause for scandal. At twenty, Catriona would be more than old enough to form a relationship."

"I know."

"And *you* are *not* twenty. Do you feel her age? As if you are so much younger than me?"

I shake my head. "To me, we're the same age. Well, you're nearly a year older, but that's nothing."

"As for social class, we do suspect Catriona came from a middle-class background. Even if she did not, a man of my class wooing a woman of a lower class is only cause for mild scandal. It is not an earl wooing a serving girl. You are a fully independent employee."

"I know."

"So . . . it would not be . . ." He clears his throat. "That is to say, if it is presumed I am wooing you, that is not high scandal."

It would be presumed he's *bedding* me, not wooing, but I don't clarify that. Unless we were caught naked, it *could* be a chaste wooing. He hired a young woman he fancies in hopes of catching her eye and getting to know her better, with an eye toward marriage. As he's said, the difference in our age and social class wouldn't make for a scandalous marriage.

"I worry too much," I say.

"You do, and almost exclusively on behalf of others. If this bothers you and you wish a solution, I will continue to think of one. But please do not be concerned on my behalf." He looks over at me. "I would do nothing to hurt you, Mallory. In any way."

"I know."

Our eyes lock. He seems to hesitate, as if considering something. Then he says, "I do not wish to lose you."

"I'm not going anywhere, Duncan. Like I said, I'm here to stay."

"I mean . . . That is to say . . ."

He glances aside and then stops, eyes narrowing. I turn to see what he does, and a figure moves in the distance.

I instinctively roll over and flatten to the ground, which would be fine if I were wearing jeans and a T-shirt. I can only imagine how I look, flipping over in my skirts, because Gray's eyes widen in alarm and he starts bolting up, as if he might need to save me from a seizure. I frantically motion for him to get down.

"Someone's out there," I say.

I literally just thought that no one can prove anything unless we're found in a compromising position. Lying together on the grass in the middle of the night? Even if we're fully dressed, that's Victorian for "compromising position."

Why the hell did we decide to picnic on a hilltop?

I lift my head. The figure is down by the road, making her way quickly toward the house. It's a woman. I can tell that by the bonnet and shawl. Otherwise . . . ? With the shawl, it could be any of the women in the house with the exception maybe of Alice, who is still too slender to be mistaken for a grown woman.

"Can you tell who it is?" I whisper.

"The shawl is . . ." He squints. "Brown? Blue? I cannot tell. The bonnet looks like Isla's, but I will admit to paying little attention to the other women's headwear."

"It does look like Isla's. Any chance she's slipping out for a romantic assignation with Hugh?" I waggle my brows.

"One could hope," he says. "While I doubt that would be the nature of their foray—sadly—they could be doing as we are. Slipping off for a night walk." He cranes his neck farther. "Blast it, I should be able to tell whether or not that is my own sister, if only by height."

"I was just thinking the same. She's nearly half a head taller than any other woman here, but I don't see anything to judge by."

The figure is a few hundred feet away, hurrying along the moonlit road, with nothing nearby to allow us to determine her height.

She disappears around a bend, and I push up onto my elbows. "You wanted me to meet you at the sundial, which is only twenty feet from the door. Would Hugh let Isla meet him so far from the house?"

"That is an excellent point. No, not at night and certainly not with those traps about."

"No one should be out with those traps about," I mutter. "But first Archie is and now someone else." I pause. "Could whoever that is be meeting Archie?"

"Then it would *not* be Isla. I cannot imagine any reason for Violet to meet him at night, but I suppose they might, if they needed to discuss some family matter in private. That is, as you would say, a stretch."

"Mmm, maybe not? We overheard that fight about the whisky business. Violet assured us everything's fine but . . ." I look at him. "How shady is Archie?"

"Interpreting your word choices in context, I presume 'shady' means someone who is dishonest in business in a fraudulent way. I would not be surprised if Archie was exaggerating his success somewhat. As one must often do in business."

"Pumping it up for investors. If Violet knows, Violet and Archie could be discussing that. It could also be Fiona, but from what he said to Sinclair about her, there's little chance Archie's luring her out for stolen moments together, even if they are marrying in two days."

"Agreed. The most likely suspect is Edith."

"For stolen moments? Or business?"

"The latter." He hesitates and then leans in. "Although, Archie and Edith did have an attachment years ago. Briefly."

"Romantic or intimate?"

"Definitely romantic. Though it might seem hard to believe, Archie is a gentleman in such matters. He seemed to consider her as a potential bride, but then Hugh broke it off with Violet, and Archie and Edith's attachment also ended."

"Because one of them changed their mind? Or because Archie was told not to make any marriage plans, with Fiona in the wings?"

"I cannot say. And thinking more on it, I suppose I should not be so quick to presume Edith would be meeting him for business. That is simply more likely. She could have seen him go out and wish to confront him about her husband's investment. But they do have a history, and while I cannot imagine anything illicit, there might be a personal reason for their meeting."

"Okay, so it could be Violet or Fiona, but it's more likely Edith Frye. And whoever it is, it's none of our business. However . . ." I look at the picnic spread around us. "As much as I hate to say it, we should probably head inside so we aren't spotted."

"Agree, with equal reluctance." His lips tweak in the barest of smiles. "Perhaps we might try again tomorrow night?"

"Definitely." I pop a last morsel of rich cheese into my mouth. "It *was* very nice. I have even forgiven you for the lack of coos."

"I am pleased to hear it." He tucks the whisky bottle and empty glasses into his basket. "Now let us slip back to the house, where you can hopefully get some proper rest."

TEN

I do indeed sleep well. So well that I wake to Alice shaking me. When I open my eyes, her concern hardens into annoyance.

"Finally," she says. "You are making it very hard for Mrs. Ballantyne to get her breakfast on time."

I frown and push up. "Am I supposed to fetch her breakfast?"

"No, I am. Only she asked to have it in her room with you, and I said you were still abed, and she worried that you were sleeping late again and might be ill. So I had to wake you first, which means her breakfast will be cool and mine will be ice cold."

"I am so inconsiderate, sleeping at night."

"It is morning."

I glance toward the windows, with the blinds closed tight. "Are you certain? That is the problem, Alice. The closed blinds and lack of light to wake me."

"Would you like me to open them at four in the morning, when the sun rises?"

I yawn and stretch. "That would be lovely, thank you. Be sure to get up at four and fetch me a coffee, will you?"

She shakes her head, scowling, and then peering at me. "Are you unwell?"

I roll my shoulders. "Not at all."

"You have overslept twice. You are not having headaches, are you?"

I frown as I swing my legs out, flinching as my feet touch the cold floor. "Headaches?"

She crosses her thin arms, setting her jaw in an obvious show of belligerence, which means she's anxious about something. "You changed in personality after striking your head. If you had headaches, that might mean you are changing back. Catriona loved to oversleep."

"Ah."

I roll my neck, getting out the kinks. It also gives me a moment to think. Alice fears the return of Catriona, who'd bullied her. Of course, Alice would never admit that, but the concern lingers and I feel guilty about it. I've mentioned this to Isla, who says, quite rightly, that even the truth wouldn't keep Alice from worrying.

"I haven't been having headaches," I say. "I'm oversleeping because I'm late getting to sleep. This isn't my usual room, and I'm fussing. Late to bed, late to rise. I'll reassure Isla. Any time you're concerned, though, feel free to quiz me. I'll tell you something Catriona wouldn't know. Like that last week, when we went shopping for the trip, you fairly drooled over that boy outside the dress shop."

"I did what?" she squeaks indignantly.

"Salivated."

"I did no such thing. I do not remember any boy, and whatever you are implying—"

"That he had something theft-worthy peeking from his back pocket, and it would have been so easy to nick that you could hardly tear your gaze away."

"Oh. Him." She rocks back onto her heels. "I was hardly *staring*. That would only get me caught. I didn't nick it, though. I don't do that anymore. Though it would have taught him a lesson. *Someone* was going to steal it."

"Agreed. But you were right to refrain. Although . . . given that you are getting older, you might not want to stare so openly at young men's bottoms."

She squawks, and then glowers, turns on her heel, and heads for the door.

"You are welcome for the advice!" I call after her.

* * *

Alice and I both take breakfast with Isla, and it's *not* cold, because Alice would never allow that. The more I see of this get-together, the more I'm glad we don't entertain overnight gatherings at the town house. Glad for the sake of the staff, that is. Not only do they need to worry about keeping track of all the guests and their various needs and wants, but there are also the lady's maids trying to give their mistresses a hot breakfast, even if it's hardly the cook's fault it went cold. There's jostling for position among the staff on behalf of their bosses, without those bosses having a clue what's going on "below stairs."

Our breakfast is hot and delicious, and if Mrs. Hall was at all scandalized by Isla dining with her maid, she didn't comment. Nor would Isla consider whether it might add extra work for the staff. As conscientious as Isla is, she's grown up with servants and, in some ways, they're like fairies, magically getting things done.

The private breakfast does make a relaxing start to my day. The balcony doors are thrown open, and we start eating inside, but after an hour, it's warm enough to tempt us out. After Alice removes our breakfast, we finish our morning tea at a tiny table overlooking the lawn.

When footsteps sound, we look down to see McCreadie rounding the corner of the house. He spots Isla on the balcony, and his face lights up. He swings his hat off with a flourish and holds it to his heart.

"'What light through yonder window breaks,'" he calls.

When he doesn't say anything else, Isla waves. "Well, go on."

"Er . . ."

I lean over and fake hiss, "East! Sun!"

"Uh . . . from the east, hark, it is the sun and . . ."

I groan and slouch dramatically against the railing. Then I spot another figure walking over behind him.

"Duncan!" I call. "Help Hugh! He's trying to do the window soliloquy."

"Window soliloquy?" Gray says.

"*Romeo and Juliet*? Shakespeare?"

Gray moves forward, his arms crossing. "Is that the play where the young woman takes some mysterious potion to make her appear dead? Even if such a thing existed—belladonna perhaps—it would be ridiculously risky. And then the young man himself takes some mysterious poison he just happens to have at hand? She wakes and stabs herself in the heart? Do you know how difficult it is to do that? The stomach, yes, but the heart? How sharp is that dagger? How does she avoid the ribs on her first try?"

"Speaking of soliloquies," I mutter to Isla.

"More like a lecture," she murmurs back. "And not nearly as romantic."

"Wait!" McCreadie says. "'It is the East, and Juliet the sun.' That's it, yes?"

I groan and shake my head. "You've lost the thread, Hugh. Try again tomorrow. Maybe brush up on your Shakespeare first. And whatever you do, don't ask Duncan for advice."

Isla laughs softly.

"You are both out bright and early," I call down.

"It is past ten," Gray says.

"We are looking for Archie," McCreadie says. "For . . ." He lifts a croquet mallet and swings it like a baseball bat.

"You're going to ambush Mr. Cranston and beat him senseless?" I say. "I can understand the impulse, but perhaps your sister would prefer you waited until *after* the wedding."

"He wanted to play this morning. At ten. That is what we agreed. He is nowhere to be found, and his coat is gone."

A chill runs down me. "He was out last night wearing it. Did he not come in?"

McCreadie frowns, as if wondering how I'd know this. He waves his hand—still holding the mallet, which makes Gray take a step back.

"No, no," McCreadie says. "There is no concern. Mrs. Hall saw him this morning."

I exhale. "Good. So Mr. Cranston has gone off on some errand. I could point out that running an estate this large means he has a lot to tend to while he's here. However, if searching for him means I can join you for a walkabout, then I think we really should look for him. Make sure he didn't stumble into one of his own traps."

"Which would serve him right," Isla mutters. Then she says, "I do not mean that, of course."

"Oh, while I wouldn't want him *badly* injured, I'd settle for a near miss that scares him enough to have Mr. Müller immediately round up all the traps."

"We should look for him," Gray says. "To be safe, as you say."

"A fine excuse. Isla? Will you join us?"

"Tramping through trap-ridden fields before the heather is dry? No thank you. I will, however, join you for croquet afterward. For now, Alice and I should pop in to see the kittens."

I call down to the guys, "Give me two minutes."

After we set off, Gray tells McCreadie that we'd had a moonlight picnic. Why mention it? Because I'd suggested I knew Cranston had been out last night, and Gray would feel some obligation to tell McCreadie, in case it came up later. McCreadie would hardly care. The obligation is on Gray's part, just another aspect of their friendship.

We don't mention the woman we saw. That's the thin line where honesty bleeds into troublemaking. McCreadie's sister is about to marry Cranston, and we don't want to suggest her groom was having an illicit assignation, even if Gray is certain that wasn't the case.

Gray mentions us being out, and then talk turns to plans for the day. Once the bride's and groom's parents arrive, it'll be all wedding prep all the time. There's much to be done, preparing the grounds for the wedding, and we'll gladly help with that.

"The wedding is tomorrow at eleven," McCreadie says. "Followed by a luncheon and then dancing and such. The bride and groom will depart later in the afternoon. We will need to spend the night, but how long we stay the following day depends on all of you. I have no obligations here."

"We will leave early," Gray says. "The trip is best made at a leisurely pace. I believe it would be best to depart at dawn, which means we ought to turn in for the night after the bride and groom depart."

McCreadie exhales softly, and I realize why. Because while his parents aren't staying at the lodge, his ex-fiancée's parents are, and that'll be a lot more awkward without wedding preparations to keep everyone busy.

"That is a fine plan," McCreadie says. "I—"

A figure appears on the road. At first, I think it's Cranston. He's tall, with a black coat that billows around him.

The figure raises one long arm, pointing past us, and shouts, "Go back."

I blink, not sure whether to laugh or wonder whether I'm still asleep, lost in some weird dream with a black-clad figure on an empty road pointing a bony finger and intoning, "Go back."

"Go back now or all is lost?" I murmur. "Our poor souls damned for all eternity?"

"No," McCreadie says. "I believe the threat is 'Go back or I will scowl at you very hard and sneer about the uncouthness of the Scottish people.'"

"Müller," I say. It is indeed that gamekeeper. He stands on the rise, pointing and repeating those two words, as if we're children who've wandered from the schoolyard. Except schoolyard monitors don't usually carry rifles.

We keep walking.

"Back to the house," Müller says as we draw closer.

"No," McCreadie says, injecting the single word with such cheerfulness that I have to bite my cheek to keep from laughing.

"No?"

Gray responds, his tone mild as we reach the man. "It is an English word that means we will not do as you say. We are on the road, and our host has said that it is safe, and we are free to traverse it."

"On that note, have you seen our host?" I say.

There's a moment where it seems as if Müller is going to pretend I didn't speak. But then he looks my way, and there's such contempt in his gaze that I almost step back.

Gray moves forward, getting slightly in front of me, confirming I didn't imagine that look. "Miss Mitchell asked you a question."

"I have seen no one except three of Mr. Cranston's guests wandering about where they should not be."

"Huh," I say. "That couldn't be us, as we are allowed to be on this road. Now, if you will allow us to pass, please, we would appreciate it."

Müller lifts the rifle to hold it with both hands. The barrel is angled down, but the message is clear.

"I say, old chap," McCreadie says, affecting the worst English accent ever. "You are not waving that gun at me, are you? That would be a poor choice. Very poor indeed. Being a gamekeeper, I would presume you know that you are far too close to use it effectively. Particularly when one of our party has a proper handgun concealed on their person." He looks at us. "Anyone fancy an American Wild West showdown on this fine morning?"

Müller's eyes narrow.

McCreadie continues in that same cheerful tone, "I do not think we were properly introduced, old chap." He tips his hat. "Detective Hugh McCreadie, of the Edinburgh police. This is Dr. Duncan Gray, who also works for the police, and this is his assistant, Miss Mitchell. You have police in Austria, do you not?"

There's the smallest flicker in Müller's eyes, not anger but surprise, as if he didn't expect McCreadie to guess his origins.

McCreadie continues, "As for which of us has the gun, that answer will be given if you do not lower that rifle, sir."

I hold my expression in place, hoping I don't betray the fact that I'm the one he means . . . and that I don't actually have the derringer. I didn't expect to need it on a morning stroll.

Müller doesn't look away from McCreadie. He's decided the police officer is the one with the gun, and he's contemplating what to do about it. I highly doubt he intends to shoot us, but he doesn't want to back down either.

When he lifts the rifle a scant inch, obstinance more than threat, Gray steps forward and, his gaze locked with Müller's, takes hold of the barrel and moves it aside.

I brace for Müller's response, but he only gives a grunt of something almost like respect and lowers the gun. Then he eyes Gray, as if seeing him with fresh eyes.

"We would like to continue on our way," Gray says. "We will stay on the road, and if we must leave it for any reason, we understand the risks. If you see Mr. Cranston, we would appreciate it if you told him we are looking for him."

"I have not seen him," Müller says. "But if you are going to walk, you had best keep your gun out. I found a stag over the hill." He jerks his chin in that direction. "I was going to the house to tell Mr. Cranston. They grow bolder."

"I presume you do not mean the deer," McCreadie says.

Müller snorts. "The deer I could deal with. I could deal with this, too, if the *master* would let me." He twists the word "master." "The stag is dead. They are usually sneaky about it, taking the whole carcass and leaving me with only bloody traces. This time, they butchered it in place and only took part of the meat. Left the rest to rot."

I have questions. But at best, Müller will ignore my queries, and at worst, he'll decide I'm a fool for asking. If he's thawing toward McCreadie and Gray, I should let them handle this.

"This happens often, I presume?" McCreadie says.

"Birds. Deer. Rabbits. They take what they wish."

"Was this a red deer or roe?" Gray asks.

"Red."

The larger subspecies then. That means the culprit wasn't a wildcat or even a stray dog. It's possible that the stag died of another cause and what seemed like partial butchering was actually scavenging, but no one points that out. If we do, Müller will snap that he knows the difference.

McCreadie, however, finds a way around the question with, "Trapped or shot?"

"Bow and arrows. That is what those children like."

"Children?"

Müller waves a dismissive hand. "The boy and his lame sister. They do not even bother to hide that it is them."

McCreadie nods. "I hope you are able to resolve the issue. I understand it would be very frustrating."

Müller mutters under his breath, but it seems more the awkward mumble of someone who doesn't know how to handle an empathic response.

"We will all be on our way," McCreadie says. "If we see Mr. Cranston, we will tell him you need to speak to him."

ELEVEN

There's no question of what we're going to do as soon as Müller is out of sight. We want to get a look at that deer. Yep, we're that desperate for distraction. First a poisoned wildcat. Now a poached deer. When I say that, McCreadie gently corrects me. "Poached" is a loaded term, especially in areas like this, where people who've hunted for generations are being told that the rich can, apparently, own the game, along with the water, the nuts and berries, and even fallen trees that they'd normally gather for firewood.

In my day, this is normal. My paternal grandparents owned a farm. You wouldn't expect to find someone on your property chopping dead trees or fishing in the stream, no more than you'd expect to find them harvesting your crops to take home. If they tried, my grandfather would have schooled them on the concept of private property.

That concept, however, is relatively recent. While there would always have been places you couldn't hunt or fish, just because someone owned the land didn't automatically mean it was off-limits. The problem only came if you took too much, but if you lived nearby and hunted that forest or fished that stream, you knew better than to empty it and leave nothing for the next year.

This particular land traditionally would have been hunted and fished and managed by tenants. Then the former owner built a hunting lodge and kicked out the tenants. That's not Cranston's fault, but I can understand the awkwardness.

Cranston will resolve that, and the last thing he needs is advice from someone who'd firmly be on the side of the dispossessed. But we *can* examine that dead deer, in case Müller missed anything suspicious.

We find the deer by following the croak of ravens. They're opportunistic scavengers, like most corvids. One thing I love about being in the countryside is that I get to be the expert here. I'm not exactly a forest ranger, but it turns out I've spent a lot more time outside the city than either Gray or McCreadie. When I hear the croaks, I know what that means and divert course.

We don't need to leave the path for long. The stag is maybe fifty feet from the road. As Müller said, it's a red deer. Also very clearly a buck, with an impressive rack of antlers. While those antlers would explain why others might choose the deer, whoever killed this one didn't take them, and as I recall from my hiking days, unless the deer population is too high, taking males is preferred. After all, you only need one of them to keep the fawns coming.

As Müller said, the buck has only been partly butchered. Or so I presume, given that most of it is here. I've never hunted, so I don't know much about this part of the process.

"They were interrupted," Gray says. "They'd bled the beast and started preparing it for butchering." He glances at me. "I went on a few hunts with Lawrence."

The sound McCreadie makes—a grumble deep in his throat—reminds me that Lawrence was Isla's asshole husband. He'd been into hunting, with Gray funding his expeditions to Asia and Africa to keep him away from Isla.

Gray continues, "That was back when I was trying to welcome Lawrence into the family. While I was not fond of hunting, I did note the butchering process with interest." He pauses. "Although my interest in *that* did not endear me to Lawrence . . . or any of the other hunters, who typically left such things for their huntsmen to deal with."

I shake my head. "Rich people."

"Indeed. From what I recall, though, the process begins by moving the beast onto an incline, with the head raised. That directs the flow of blood. Then they remove the entrails to avoid them contaminating the meat. You can see that was done, with the entrails being . . ."

He frowns and looks around.

"Here." McCreadie is a few feet away, pointing at the ground. "They dug a hole for them, though it was not covered."

"Digging a hole suggests they planned to take the rest of the stag," I say. "Like Müller said, they usually leave only blood."

"Yes," Gray says. "Which supports the theory that they were interrupted. After the entrails are removed, the carcass would be drained to make it easier to transport. However, this is a big buck. I believe they were quartering it first."

I nod. "Field-dress it. Quarter it. Bury the entrails. Take the rest. But they were interrupted, as you said. They'd finished enough of the quartering to grab the lower two haunches and go."

"Which means we are likely looking at two hunters," McCreadie says. "I could manage both lower haunches, but they would be heavy, and I would not be able to move quickly."

"Two hunters working on the stag," I say. "They hear or see something that tells them to finish and run."

I stand atop the little rise where the deer's head rests. I scan the horizon. "The obvious answer would be the road. Someone was coming along it last night—maybe Archie. It was quiet enough that the hunters would hear his boots. They realize he'll be able to see them when he gets closer. So they grab part of the deer and take off."

"Possibly," McCreadie says. "Except the footprints indicate they actually went *toward* the road."

I walk over and see what he means. There's a damp patch that the hunters walked through, their deep footprints suggesting they were weighed down by a big piece of deer.

"Two sets of prints," I say. "And the smaller set shows an issue with the right leg. See how it's turned in here?"

"Bloody hell," McCreadie mutters. "It seems Müller was right. It was Mrs. Hall's daughter, and presumably her son."

"Lenore and Gavin," I say. "But since we weren't asked to prove that, I'm going to suggest we never saw these prints."

"Agreed," McCreadie says. "This is not our concern. Duncan? We should get back to the house and pretend we never found—Duncan?"

He turns, looking, and I realize Gray isn't with us. He's striding across the field.

"Watch out for traps!" I call.

His lifted hand says he knows. I still don't like him moving quite so quickly through long grass. McCreadie must not either because we both hurry to catch up, while scanning the ground.

"There is something over that way," Gray says when we reach him. "Behind that stand of trees."

I don't see anything, and I'm about to say so when I spot it. I'd been looking up, and what Gray spotted is on the ground. A dark shape almost hidden by the long grass.

"Another deer?" I murmur. That's what it looks like. A lump about the size of the stag, the grass flattened by it.

I start to pass Gray, but he catches my arm.

"The traps," he murmurs.

I think he's echoing my warning, maybe needling me, but his expression is serious. He means that whatever we're seeing may have been caught by a trap. A deer or some kind of large . . .

I slow as I catch sight of folded fabric. Black, like the wing of a raven. In my mind, I see that fabric flapping in the wind, reminding me of bird's wings.

Cranston, striding out the other night, his distinctive coat flapping behind him. For a moment, I'm hoping it's just the jacket, somehow left behind. Then I see a head protruding over the top of the jacket, facedown in the grass, brown hair bloodied from an ugly gash in the back of his skull.

McCreadie bends and lifts the man's shoulder, and I brace to see Archie Cranston.

But I don't.

I see Ezra Sinclair.

TWELVE

This first thing Gray does is check for signs of life. Yes, Sinclair is cold. Yes, his eyes are open. Yes, he's in rigor. None of that will matter to loved ones who will want to be absolutely certain they didn't miss a chance to save him.

Once that's done, Gray eases back onto his haunches, and McCreadie lays a hand on his shoulder. I let them have a moment of silence before I say, quietly and respectfully, "You'd known him a long time."

"Since we started school," McCreadie says. "Duncan and I were friends with Ezra in those early days. It was often the three of us . . ." He trails off as his throat clogs. He clears it. "That was very long ago. I have known Archie even longer, from our parents' acquaintance, and there was a time when the four of us attempted a rather awkward quartet, before . . ."

"Before Archie and I collided one too many times," Gray says, rising. "We simply could not get on. When the dust settled, Ezra had broken off with Archie." Gray pauses. "That was understandable, I fear. Hugh and I were better friends. Ezra sometimes felt like . . ."

"A third wheel?" I say.

When their brows rise, I say, "I'm guessing that idiom gains popularity with the rise of two-wheeled conveyances, like bicycles."

"Ah," McCreadie says. "Yes. I see. A third wheel on a bicycle is superfluous, and the idiom would apply. Whenever three children are friends, it is likely that two will be closer, and that was myself and Duncan."

McCreadie clears his throat. "And that is a poor eulogy for a good man—reminiscences on his early life as a 'third wheel.' We have not seen much of Ezra since school, but our paths did cross sometimes, and I was always glad of it."

Another moment, and McCreadie shakes himself. "We will need to report this, both to the household and to the authorities, as it is obvious he did not inflict that injury himself." He looks at me. "Could this have been who you saw last night? Ezra in Archie's coat? It is very distinctive, and their hair would appear a similar color in the dark."

"I didn't actually see anyone," I say. "I noticed Archie's coat was gone, so I presumed it was on him, because I'd seen him out wearing it the night before—along with Ezra." I look down at Sinclair's body. "But the mistake would be easy to make." I ease back. "Archie said Ezra was fond of night walks. He goes out last night and takes Archie's warmer coat. Anyone seeing him could, I think, mistake him for Archie. He's a couple of inches shorter and somewhat slighter, but like the difference in hair color, that would have been less obvious at night."

"Also he was attacked from behind," McCreadie says. "His killer did not see his face, and likely mistook him for Archie."

"We *did* see someone last night," I say. "A woman. We couldn't tell who it was. We didn't mention that because, well, we presumed whoever we saw was headed out to meet with your sister's fiancé."

McCreadie nods, looking down at Sinclair, as if deep in thought.

I glance at Gray. "We're going to need to get our story straight, and I suggest we stick with the truth."

Gray frowns. "About noticing the missing jacket and seeing a woman? Certainly."

"She means about you two being out," McCreadie says. "I will not be in charge of the investigation, which means you will be interviewed. In order to say you saw a woman—which you must—you need to explain why you were out. I would strongly suggest, as Mallory implied, that you do not attempt to make up some more comfortable excuse."

I nod toward Sinclair. "This is a murder investigation, and I have no idea what to expect from the local constabulary."

"Not much, I fear," McCreadie mutters. "Even admitting you were out of doors last night will brand you as suspects."

"But we do need to admit it," I say. "Both to mention the woman and to avoid later being caught in a lie."

"All right," Gray says. "So we admit we were out together . . . accepting whatever scandal follows."

"Better scandal than murder charges," I say. "We tell the truth. I didn't sleep well the night before, which multiple people know. You offered a moonlight walk. I have the note, which says exactly that."

Gray glances away, his jaw working.

I lower my voice. "If this would hurt your reputation—"

He looks back sharply. "You know that is not my concern, Mallory. And it will not hurt *mine*."

"It's probably only going to be misinterpreted as wooing."

"It would be highly *inappropriate* wooing, taking you out alone at night." He waves it off with obvious irritation. "But you are correct. Lying would be dangerous. I will do as you say. For now, though, I would like to examine the body, if I may."

There's a moment of silence, before Gray turns to McCreadie with another burst of irritation. "Yes? Or no?"

"Oh, was that an actual question?" McCreadie says. "I took it as annoyed sarcasm."

Gray exhales. "You are right that Mallory and I need to be honest, and I should not blame you both for pointing it out. The question was an honest one. Am I liable to endanger the investigation by examining the body?"

"It will take hours for anyone to arrive," McCreadie says. "And even then, we will be lucky if they know the meaning of 'rigor' or 'time of death.' Go ahead and examine him."

This isn't the first time we've examined the body of someone Gray knew. In this period, most cities are still small, and Edinburgh is no exception, the current population being about two hundred thousand. Gray has conducted postmortem exams on Annis's husband—Lord Leslie—and a former professor, Sir Alastair Christie. This is the first time, though, that I've really seen him struggle.

He needs to take another moment to ready himself before he crouches at Sinclair's head. This is not the brother-in-law Gray had only known as a bullying asshole. Nor is it a professor who was partly responsible for Gray not being allowed to practice medicine. Ezra Sinclair was a childhood friend. Now he's dead in a field and, worse, almost certainly because his killer mistook him for someone else.

Gray takes that moment to collect himself and then clears his throat and gets to work. He begins at the obvious spot—that gash on the back of Sinclair's head. It's more of a bash than a gash. Something struck him hard enough to dent the back of his skull.

"Blunt force trauma," I murmur. "Whatever the killer used, it had an edge or a point that cut open the scalp."

Gray palpates the spot and then moves aside the hair for a better look. "Not an edge. That would leave a cleaner mark. This is more indicative of a blunt object with a protuberance."

"A rock? Ezra was about Hugh's height. If I came up behind Hugh, I might be able to swing a rock high enough to hit him in the back of the head."

"But I would prefer you didn't," McCreadie calls from ten feet away, where he's watching for anyone who might interrupt us.

I continue to Gray, "Would I be able to get up enough force to do it, though? Maybe. A rock could also have the kind of 'protuberance' that would break the skin."

"A rock is a possibility," Gray says. "Though, with a rough-surfaced object, I would expect to see more scraping of the scalp. Also, to inflict this sort of damage, at that angle—swinging up—the rock would need to be fist-sized."

I think that through. "Right. I wouldn't be able to swing a larger rock hard enough to kill Hugh."

"Could you choose another victim for your exemplar, please?" McCreadie calls.

"I'd need a rock I could comfortably and confidently grip. This wound suggests a larger object."

Gray nods. "Also more of an oblong shape. Perhaps six inches by four, with a relatively smooth finish."

I frown. "At that size, it'd be hard to smash it into someone's head while gripping it. That would require swinging it. Something on a rope or—Oh! The shillelaghs."

McCreadie turns. "The what?"

"The walking sticks. There's a collection of them in the cloakroom. They're shillelaghs. Irish cudgels."

Gray looks perplexed.

McCreadie calls over, "They are wicked things. I once took one from a man who'd used it to beat a supposed friend within an inch of his life."

To Gray, I say, "It's a particular type of walking stick with a knobby end. They were—are—used for self-defense. I saw a few of them in the cloakroom."

"Ah," Gray says. "I noticed them. I thought they were simply decorative walking sticks."

"Archie probably thinks the same, which is why he has a small collection, but they are . . ." I look back at Sinclair's body. "Deadly."

"Now that you mention it, I noticed them as well," McCreadie says. "And even though I have seen them used as weapons, I did not consider that. Like Duncan, I presumed they were for jaunting about the estate."

"They are. But they have heavy ends, some with knots. That would be consistent with this wound, wouldn't it?"

"It would," Gray says. "We will need to take a look at them."

"Is this wound the cause of death . . . ?" I trail off. "Sorry. Amateur question."

It's an amateur question, not because it seems the obvious cause, but because Gray isn't going to make that determination without an autopsy. He's not even going to speculate without a full external examination of the body.

He forgives my enthusiasm with, "A blow like this *could* be fatal. I cannot undress him for a thorough look, but we will do what we can."

What we can do is mostly just check Sinclair's face and hands, the only exposed skin. We can also look for damage to his clothing—maybe a bullet hole or knife slice. We find none of that, and no defensive wounds on his hands or anything other than dirt caught under his nails.

McCreadie and Gray roll Sinclair over for a better look at his face. His nose is broken and caked with blood, but it's also caked with dirt, suggesting he fell face-first to the ground without trying to break his fall.

"Could he have died that fast?" Then I again answer my own question. "A blow to the head rarely causes instant death, but it can cause a loss of consciousness. He gets hit and passes out. Smacks facedown into the dirt. Then he either dies of the blow or his killer does something else to him. Suffocation would be most likely." I peer at Sinclair's open eyes. "No petechial hemorrhages."

Gray says nothing. He's letting his student run with this one.

"No marks around the neck or mouth," I say. "I can't tell about the nose until the blood is cleaned, but if anything was held over his mouth and nose, it'd have smeared that blood. The other option would be injection, but we're unlikely to see that through his clothing, and I don't see any marks on the exposed skin."

"Anything else?" Gray says.

His tone tells me I'm missing something. I shift as I think it through and then talk it through. "Hit on the back of the head. Loses consciousness. Falls and breaks his nose. I don't know how long it'd take for the blow to kill him."

I shift my position and ponder more. "The intent wouldn't necessarily be murder. Not with a single blow. If the blow was meant as a warning, the killer might have walked away at that point. If they wanted to be sure their target was dead, suffocation would be easiest. Manual strangulation would work. Injection would require bringing supplies. There's no sign of a knife or bullet wound, but if you had a knife or gun, why bother with the blow to the head?"

I rack my brain. Then I look at Gray. "I give up. How else can you kill an unconscious victim?"

"Breaking his neck," he says. "Which could happen with the blow to the head. Or it could be inflicted after."

"Is that something I can tell without an internal exam?" I ask.

"Sometimes, but I see no sign of it here. Externally, that is. I will need to look closer. There is, however, one more thing that is odd."

I look down at Sinclair. I could just ask for the answer. This isn't a pop quiz. But if I'm given a puzzle, I at least want to try solving it on my own.

Gray says, "He is struck and loses consciousness as he falls. There are no signs of defense."

"Meaning he never regained consciousness."

"Yes."

McCreadie clears his throat. I look over at him. No, I glower at him, because it means he is very politely telling us he knows the answer, and it's like being in school, trying to impress the teacher, and your prime rival indicates he has the answer you don't.

"Fine," I say, ungraciously. "What—? Wait! His eyes are open." I look at Gray. "If he lost consciousness and never regained it, his eyes should be closed, right?"

"There are instances where eyelids remain open—loss of consciousness due to seizures and such—but ruling that out, yes, his eyelids should be closed."

"Opening them should mean he woke up, but if he woke up, we'd expect to see a sign of that. At the very least, the blood on his nose, again, should be smeared. Could that mean he didn't lose consciousness? That the blow killed him instantly?"

"Likely."

"I was going to say that," McCreadie pipes up. "The bit about the eyes, that is."

"We'll split the gold star." I look down at Sinclair. "Anything else we need to examine?"

"No, I believe it is time to notify the household," Gray says.

"Which means it's time for Hugh and me to do our crime-scene detecting, leaving you to run to the house."

Gray's mouth opens. Then his eyes narrow, and I know he wants to say McCreadie or I can handle processing the scene alone, so he can stay and participate. But two sets of professional eyes are better, and we *are* the professionals.

He settles for, "I will not *run*. But yes, I will leave the scene to the two of you." He pauses, and then can't resist adding, "And I will examine it later."

THIRTEEN

McCreadie and I start by cordoning off the scene. Hey, since we aren't in Edinburgh, this seems like the perfect time to demonstrate the concept of crime-scene preservation. Oh, McCreadie gets the idea. He's just a little slow to implement it, which I understand. It's that old "but this is how we've always done it" mentality, and as open-minded as McCreadie is, it can be hard to convey the importance of avoiding contamination when almost nothing from the scene can be used in court.

DNA analysis is a hundred years away, and even fingerprints aren't yet admissible. Most of what Gray does in the realm of forensics only helps McCreadie find the culprit. Then McCreadie has to prove the killer did it without needing to explain hair analysis and wound impressions to a judge or jury.

But here, McCreadie understands the need to protect the scene. We have damp earth, which might contain footprints. We also have a missing murder weapon that the killer may have stashed nearby. With the long grass, we even have a hope of tracking the killer through broken blades. All that will be ruined as soon as the household knows Sinclair is dead and tramps out here for a look.

We mark an area where people will be allowed to enter and leave the scene. Then we make sure there's no obvious evidence in that area. We're also looking for footprints and evidence in general, but the only prints we find are ten feet away, and they belong to Sinclair. As for my hope of tracking the killer through trampled grass . . . that doesn't work out, probably because neither of us has any experience at tracking. Any faint paths we find all lead to the nearby lake, suggesting they're just routes left by deer.

"We're going to need to talk to the housekeeper's kids," I say. "I doubt it's a coincidence that they left half a deer near a dead human body."

McCreadie nods. "They saw or heard something. The problem will be getting them to admit they were out here, given what they were doing."

I let out a long breath. "I know."

"The larger problem, though?"

I glance at him as he surveys the scene, and I say, "The larger problem is the fact this isn't our case at all. From my policing history, I recall that before organized forces, law enforcement was mostly handled by the local lord. We're past that, though not at the stage of a national or regional force. So what should we expect?"

"I wish I knew. The General Police Act requires that each county have its own police force or, if it cannot, that it join with a neighboring county to establish one. However, that legislation is just over a dozen years old. A decade may seem long enough to enact a point of law. However . . ."

I snort. "Yeah, organizations don't move that fast, especially if you're talking about the *creation* of that organization. If they've only been ordered to form local police forces thirteen years ago, I shudder to think what they actually have."

"It will largely depend on whether or not they were establishing a force in expectation of the act. Unless people have been the victims of crime, they are not eager to pay for policing, and local governments are not eager to tighten their belts or to raise local taxes. My hope is that—"

He's cut off by the babble of voices. We look to see Gray coming our way, followed by Cranston . . . and pretty much everyone else staying at the house.

"Whoa, whoa, whoa," I say, my hands flying up.

"I will handle this," McCreadie murmurs.

I bite my tongue and stay where I am, having learned that Victorians look askance at a young woman acting like a cop. Before McCreadie reaches the group, Gray is already stopping them.

"My apologies, Hugh," he says, seemingly through gritted teeth. "I did explain that no one except Archie ought to come, but the only people who listened were our sisters."

Cranston is in the lead. He strides toward the body, his face held tight.

"Did you check for a pulse?" Edith says, moving past her husband.

"Yes," Gray says tightly. "Being a doctor, the first thing I did was confirm that Ezra could not be resuscitated."

Edith and her husband follow right on Cranston's heels. Violet hangs back, blinking and looking about, as if she'd been carried here on the tide and now realizes it is not where she wishes to be. She glances toward the house.

Seeing her distress, McCreadie rocks forward, as if to offer her an escort back. Then he seems to remember he's the last person she'll want. I consider stepping in for him, but as much as I want to help, I do not want to walk away from the scene.

Everyone here is a suspect, and I need to see their reactions. That includes Violet. I don't know which woman was out last night, and if the weapon was indeed a shillelagh, then I can't rule out the women. The cudgel would provide them with the height and force needed to kill Sinclair. That reminds me to make note of the women's outerwear. Both have shawls, neither is wearing a hat, though they wouldn't if they came out quickly.

Violet doesn't notice my scrutiny. Her gaze slips to the house, and then she steels herself, as if retreat would be the coward's way out. She looks toward her brother, and she takes a half step in his direction before stopping herself. She chews her lip as her gaze stays on Cranston, watching him with obvious concern.

Cranston is striding forward like he did yesterday heading for that dead wildcat. The landowner taking charge of the situation. But when he sees Sinclair, he falters. He stares down at his dead friend and swallows hard. His fists clench and unclench. Then he notices me and straightens as if he'd been caught sobbing.

I half turn away, giving him privacy while still watching.

"That is my coat," Cranston says, and he isn't looking at anyone except Sinclair. "He is wearing my coat."

I look over, trying to gauge his meaning.

Cranston says again, "That is my coat," and his tone is . . . Definitely not accusation. Not confusion or irritation either. It's as if his mind has found something to seize on, anything except the fact that his best friend lies dead at his feet.

I move in Cranston's direction. "I noticed it was gone last night."

He blinks at me and frowns. Then he nods. "Yes, I saw it was missing this morning, and I was waiting for Ezra to come back, so I could snap at him for it. He is forever taking it. Teasing me, I think. Saying my coat is warmer than his, saying he could not find his. Always making excuses for borrowing it, and then I will growl and grumble at him and he laughs it off and . . ." Cranston swallows and looks away.

When I passed through time, I thought back over all the final conversations I'd had with people. I'm not what anyone would call difficult. At least, not in the sense of someone like Cranston, who seems to argue and needle and grumble as easily as he breathes. But in our everyday life, we're always butting heads with our nearest and dearest. Inconsequential disagreements we'll resolve later. When I passed through time, one of my worries was that someone's last memory of me would be that everyday head-butting.

It doesn't even need to have been actual friction. We could just have been annoyed with the deceased—like Cranston with that borrowed coat—and then they're gone, and all we can think is that, an hour ago, we'd been ready to give them shit over something so trivial.

"I ought to have gifted him the coat," Cranston says, his voice so low that I don't think I'm supposed to hear it. "He liked it, and I could easily have bought another."

Gray moves up beside me and says, gently, "My condolences, Archie."

Cranston looks up. There's a long pause and then he gives a bitter snort. "I wondered for a moment why you were offering them to me. I am not his brother or his father. But there is no one else, is there? Only distant relatives Ezra has not seen in years."

That isn't what Gray meant. He was offering condolences on the loss of a very dear friend, but he only nods.

"I will handle the arrangements," Cranston says. Then he curses under his breath. "And that is not what I should be thinking at this moment. It is only . . ." He gestures at Gray. "You are an undertaker. You handle such things, and I was thinking that Ezra has no family and . . ."

"It will be handled," Gray says. "You need not concern yourself with that."

A throat clearing behind us, and I look to see McCreadie. "Speaking of things it is awkward to discuss, I must ask that no one leave the estate."

Cranston frowns.

"Everyone will need to be interviewed," McCreadie says.

Cranston blinks. Then he seems to realize what McCreadie means and that lost look vanishes in a flash fire of fury. "Because someone murdered Ezra. Someone came onto my land and killed—" He stops and seems to hang there before he audibly swallows. "Killed Ezra while he was wearing my coat." He wheels on me. "You said it was gone from the cloakroom last night?"

I nod.

"I saw him around eleven, when it was growing dark. He did not say he was going out, or I would have gone with him. So he went out, after dark, wearing my coat and someone hit him . . ." Cranston looks down at Sinclair and his voice lowers. "Hit him from behind. Mistook him for me."

"We do not know that," McCreadie says.

Cranston gives a bitter laugh. "Do we not? You are too kind, Hugh. Always have been. No one had any cause to want Ezra dead. I am the one they hate." He looks over at Edith and James Frye, and then past them and points at Violet.

"There is the only person here who does not have some cause to wish me harm, and I cannot even be sure about that. I have surely done some careless thing to hurt her, as much as I have tried not to." He waves at me. "I do not think I have given Miss Mitchell cause either, but with time, I would have."

"There may be reasons someone might have killed Ezra," McCreadie says softly. "Reasons that have nothing to do with you or even with him. If he saw something or learned something or even simply surprised someone out here."

"Poachers?" Cranston's head lifts. "Müller has been warning me about them, saying I do not fully understand the danger."

"The local constabulary will investigate every avenue."

Cranston frowns. "But you are a detective. Better than any country lump who earns his pay breaking up drunken fights."

"We will . . . see what we are dealing with," McCreadie says cautiously.

"But you will not abandon him, yes?" Cranston looks at Sinclair's body. "Our old friend has been murdered."

"I have sent my groom to the village," Gray says. "We shall see what happens now."

"What happens now" is that we wait nearly two hours for the constable. Literally wait in the field because we can't abandon a body to scavengers or interference.

I don't know what to expect. I'm praying for a miracle straight out of a British cozy, where the local vicar or schoolteacher is actually a professional-grade detective. Okay, I can't imagine that—we'd at least need to get deeper into the age of mystery novels, where someone *could* be an armchair expert. But maybe we'll get a former Edinburgh or Glasgow criminal officer who retired to the country.

The problem with that scenario is that there have only been criminal officers for a few dozen years. The chance of one getting fed up with the city-cop life and moving out here is minimal.

When someone finally does appear, my heart drops—and my annoyance rises—because the guy in charge couldn't even bother coming himself. He's sent some rookie who looks like a freshman dropped off at university for the first time, awestruck and overwhelmed. He wanders over to us, looking left and right and all around.

When McCreadie steps out to greet him, the kid nearly bowls him over in his distracted gaping.

"Oh, my apologies, sir. I was called here. Someone has died?"

"Yes, are you with the local police?"

The young man straightens. "I am indeed. Peter Ross, at your service. Er, Constable Ross." He flashes a grin. "Still getting used to that one."

McCreadie returns the smile. If he's pissed off about this rookie's superiors sending him out, he gives no sign of it.

"New to the business, are you?" McCreadie says.

"Nearly two years now, but I always forget the title. No one calls me Constable in a place so small they've all known you since you were in short pants." He looks around. "I was told there was a murder?"

"There was. Have you ever worked one, Constable Ross?"

"I have not, which means this is very exciting. I don't know that there's been a murder in the county since I was born." He leans past McCreadie. "Is that the fellow there? On the ground?"

I bite my tongue against saying no, that's just someone taking a rest. Having the patience of a saint, McCreadie says, "That is. But it really was murder, and we ought to wait for your supervisor."

"That's me," Ross says brightly. "First Constable Ross. Head of the local constabulary."

There's a long pause, as McCreadie studies the young man, trying to decide whether this is a prank or a misunderstanding.

Gray—not having the patience of a saint—steps forward. "Dr. Duncan Gray. I examined the victim. Are you telling us you are the primary police officer in this county?"

"Yes, sir. It was my grandfather, but he retired last year. I was already working with him, so the other fellows decided I would inherit his position." He lowers his voice, conspiratorial. "In truth, they did not want the title. It is very little extra pay for a great deal of extra work."

"I understand," McCreadie says slowly. "However, as this is a murder, while you would clearly be the primary on the case, you might want one of the more experienced officers helping."

"They said no."

McCreadie blinks. "They said . . ."

"Dougie said they don't pay him enough to solve murders. That's what he said, to the word. And Bill is off."

"Off . . . ? Away?"

"Bill drinks. A great deal, I'm afraid, and sometimes he is on and sometimes he is off. Currently, he is off. He would not be much help, though, even if he were on."

I stare at McCreadie. He doesn't look my way, but I do notice sweat beading at his hairline, and his eyes are just a little bit wider than usual, as if there are things he wants to say—so many things—and he's holding them all back.

Thirteen years. That's what he said earlier. The act that forces all counties to have a police force is barely more than a dozen years old. Some areas will already have the kind of local forces that will one day inspire those

British crime shows. Others will take the option to use the police services of a larger nearby county. Then there will be those that decide they don't need much in the way of policing. Just a few guys to keep the peace.

Gray eases forward again. "How much do you know about the situation here?"

"Not a thing," Ross says brightly. "Oh, except that there is a dead body. Or a body that seems to be dead. I probably should check that first."

"The victim is quite dead," Gray says. "I believe proper introductions are in order, as they may resolve this issue."

Ross frowns as if to say, "What issue?"

"May I introduce Detective Hugh McCreadie," Gray says. "An Edinburgh criminal officer."

Ross's frown grows, and he inches back. "You are a criminal, sir?"

"I am a police officer," McCreadie says, his tone making me decide the guy deserves a Nobel Prize for patience. "City forces are large enough to divide officers into various specialities. There are constables, of course. Then there are criminal officers, which you might also call detectives or, if you were in England, inspectors."

"Criminal officers investigate crimes," I say. "Like murder."

Ross turns and gives a start on seeing me. Then he stares. Just stares until Gray clears his throat.

"That is my assistant, Miss Mitchell," Gray says. "She is correct. Detective McCreadie has investigated . . . How many murders is it now, Hugh? Seven? Eight? With every killer successfully brought to justice."

Ross's eyes boggle, and I'm just about to think he understands what Gray is getting at when he says, "Seven or eight murders? No wonder my mother says Edinburgh is the devil's playground."

"The point," Gray says, teeth snapping, "is that Detective McCreadie is very experienced at this, and will be glad to aid in your investigation. As will Miss Mitchell and I."

"Aren't you a doctor?" Ross says.

"Dr. Gray is a forensic scientist who works with the police," McCreadie says. "He assists in all my cases and has gained great renown for his own detective work."

"Ah." Ross nods. "We all need a little help now and then, as my da always says. I am sure you are a fine . . . criminal officer, sir, but I will not be needing your help. This isn't one of your city murders. Things are different here."

"Which I understand," McCreadie says, and there's an edge to his words that suggests he's finally losing patience. "The case is yours. I am merely offering my services, as I knew the victim, and I do have some experience—"

"No need," Ross says. "I will take it from here. Now, you said that *is* the dead body over there?"

As the young man steps in that direction, Gray gives a rumbling warning growl. McCreadie moves in front of Ross.

"That is the body," McCreadie says. "Can I confirm that you have summoned the doctor?"

Ross frowns. "Why? You said he was dead."

"A dead body requires a doctor to examine it," McCreadie says.

"For what?" Ross sounds genuinely perplexed.

"To determine how the man died. For the investigation."

"Oh, I'm sure I can tell that on my own. I see blood from here."

Ross continues making his way toward the body.

"Call the doctor," I say. "Or let Dr. Gray handle it."

Ross turns and again, he just stares at me. Then he says, "Pardon me, miss?"

I walk over. "You have a dead body. A murder victim who is the dear friend of the man who owns this estate, which I am guessing is one of the biggest in your county."

"Er, yes, the biggest actually, but—"

"The owner of this property will expect a proper investigation. Now, you may do things one way here and we do them another in the city, but if Mr. Cranston"—I nod toward Cranston—"is from the city and a childhood friend of Detective McCreadie's, he will expect things done in a certain way, and if they are not, he will raise a fuss. Do you know what happens when men like Mr. Cranston raise a fuss?"

"Er . . ."

I step closer, and his breathing picks up as I lean in. "People like you and me lose our jobs. Now, if you don't want to bother the local doctor—or pay his fees—then might I suggest you let Dr. Gray help you."

Ross's gaze shoots to Cranston.

I continue, "If you need to confirm this procedure with anyone, that is understandable. I presume you do not, though, as you *are* first constable."

It's a cheap shot, and in the twenty-first century, it'd get me in a heap of trouble. You can't just walk into a small town and suggest the local police chief hire another coroner to investigate your friend's murder. But we're in a time before that system is well established. A time when there obviously is no coroner, just a country doctor who may have never had to deal with homicide before.

Ross straightens. "I do not see any reason to bother Dr. Rendall."

"You should still mention it to him," McCreadie says. "As a courtesy. In fact, you could leave the choice to him."

"It is my case," Ross says, his jaw setting as he looks up at McCreadie. "I don't care if you're some fancy city policeman. You will not take it from me."

"I am not trying to. But will you allow Dr. Gray to conduct the autopsy?"

"The what?"

"The medical examination required to prove cause of death."

Ross looks from McCreadie to Gray. "I cannot do that myself?"

"Have you ever cut a man open and removed his internal organs?" I ask.

He stares at me again, and this time, it's a very different look, his face paling before he shakes his head.

"Then leave it to Dr. Gray," I say. "Who is not only a trained medical doctor but a trained surgeon *and* an undertaker. He will deal with the messy bits and leave you to the much more important police work."

FOURTEEN

Two hours later, McCreadie and I are in the smallest of the castle sitting rooms, nearly passed out on the sofas. I have abandoned all propriety to slouch as best I can. When the doorknob turns, I sit up quickly, before anyone sees me in this even faintly unladylike pose. Seeing it's Isla, I relax again. She closes the door behind her.

"Duncan has not returned?" she says.

"I fear we abandoned him to Constable Ross," McCreadie says. "We are terrible friends."

"He's kidding," I say. "Kind of. Ross really didn't like having Hugh around, and it was clear things would be better for everyone if he left the scene. As for me? I'm just a terrible friend."

"Also untrue," McCreadie says. "Whenever poor Mallory moves or speaks, our young constable stares as if an angel has descended from on high. I would suggest she keep him entranced, like a cobra, while I investigate, but that seemed wrong." He leans his head back to look at me. "Yes?"

I throw a small embroidered pillow at him.

"I fear you are not sufficiently devoted to the cause," McCreadie says.

"Yeah, yeah. I'd do it if it would work. Ross only stares until he remembers he's in charge of the case. Then he's right back to being a—" I decide not to finish that, but the face I make has McCreadie laughing.

Isla walks to the globe, opens it, and takes out whisky. Then she pours us each a glass.

"What exactly seems to be the problem with Constable Ross?" she asks.

"Everything." I pause. "Okay, that's not fair. He's just young. Very young and determined to take his responsibilities seriously even if he has zero experience and, apparently, zero support. Hugh offered to help. *Help*, not take over. Ross will have none of it."

"But you are a criminal officer," Isla says to McCreadie. "That makes you his superior."

McCreadie and I both shake our heads. McCreadie answers for us, "If he were an Edinburgh constable, I could indeed take the case from him. But it is not like the military, where one holds a superior rank in the organization at large. It is like being a doctor and realizing the local physician lacks experience. You cannot simply take over his patient."

"It is not like that at all, though," Isla says. "A patient can choose who he retains as a physician, much the same as one could choose a new grocer. They are customers. And the law is the law, whether here or in Edinburgh."

"The law is a uniform entity," I say. "The police are not."

"But does Constable Ross know that?" Isla says, looking crafty. "If he is so isolated and inexperienced, might you not simply tell him to step aside?"

McCreadie hesitates and then exhales. "I could not sustain such a deceit. I would break down under the weight of it. We have inveigled Duncan into the case, and I will do what I can through that connection. I will not let Ross bungle the investigation completely."

"Maybe he won't bungle it," I say. "Maybe he's just got a Columbo routine going." At their looks, I say, "Columbo is a fictional police detective who acts like he's bumbling along to get people to confess to him. They think he's hopeless, so they discount him."

"I know a criminal officer like that," McCreadie says. "He insists that he behaves that way to disarm the criminals into believing him incompetent. The only problem is . . ."

"He's actually incompetent?"

McCreadie sighs. "I fear so."

Isla sips her whisky. "While I applaud Mallory's optimism, what are the chances that such a young man is, in fact, a genius detective?"

"Hey, look at me." I spread my arms. "Twenty years old, and a damn fine investigator, according to Hugh here. Plus I'm a woman, which makes my competence truly shocking."

McCreadie points his glass at me. "I did not say that last part."

"Also, you are not actually twenty," Isla says.

"Prove it."

She turns to face me. "Prove you are. Show me your certificate of birth."

I don't answer that. Catriona has no ID. That's shocking to me, coming from a world where you don't leave the house without something to prove that you are who you say you are. But here, with no driver's licenses, health cards, credit cards, or even library cards, it's entirely possible that Catriona's lack of ID isn't even suspicious . . . though personally, I think it is.

"We will deal with Ross," McCreadie says. "I am only frustrated that 'dealing' with him is indeed what we shall need to do. I would happily have consigned the investigation to an experienced officer."

Both Isla and I give him a look.

"Fine," he says. "I would not have been *happy* about it, but I would have accepted it."

We keep looking at him.

He throws up his hands. "I would have been disappointed. Is that what you wish me to say? I would have reluctantly—but willingly—consigned the investigation to a more experienced officer while still politely noting my own experience and offering my assistance. I would have even more happily tutored Ross, and I struggle to understand why a young officer would *not* want that. I offered tutelage without the expectation of payment or credit."

"Not everyone jumps at the chance to learn from experts," I say.

"Unfathomable, really."

"Agreed, but we can hope Ross will realize he's in over his head—"

I stop short as the door opens. I sit up and straighten as Gray comes in, closes the door, and turns to me.

"Traitor," he says.

I open my mouth.

"You abandoned me," he says, stalking forward. "Left me in my hour of need to come in here, relax, and, apparently, sip whisky."

My cheeks heat, as I start to rise. "I'm sorry. I—"

He waves me down. "I am teasing, Mallory." He pauses. "Mostly. Seventy-five percent. Perhaps eighty."

I exhale as I drop back to the couch. "You need to work on your poker face. It's too good."

His brows rise.

I continue, "I do feel bad about abandoning you, but every time Ross opened his mouth, I had to bite my tongue so hard that I started to worry about permanent damage. If you needed me, though, I'd have stayed. Seriously. You are my boss, Duncan. You can say no when I ask to leave."

He waves that off and takes my whisky, downing the rest in a gulp before pouring another . . . which he also drinks.

"That bad, huh?" I say.

"You were right to go," he says. "I know how much his cavalier attitude upset you, and your tension fed mine. It might have been easier if I did not know the victim. Know and like him, and . . ."

He shakes his head and reaches for the decanter, only to stop himself. Then he stands there a moment before clearing his throat. "And that is enough of that."

Isla rises. "Hugh? You ought to see what Constable Ross is doing, yes? Even if you cannot intercede, you will want to know how he is conducting himself. Perhaps nudge him gently in the right direction? You are very good at being subtle."

Yep, McCreadie is good at being subtle, far more so than Isla, as she hustles him out of the room. Once they're gone, Gray lowers himself beside me on the settee, still holding his empty glass.

"You were saying?" I prompt, while bracing myself for him to dismiss it and move on. That's what he would have done a year ago, even six months ago, but now, there is a soft exhale, as if in relief before he speaks.

Am I far too pleased with myself for being the person he feels comfortable confessing to? Hell, yes. I can rationalize it and tell myself it's not about me, per se, but more that I'm an outsider and therefore a safe confessor. I don't have any expectations for how a Victorian gentleman is supposed to act. True, but I hope it's also about me—that Gray feels comfortable discussing his feelings with me, knowing I'd never see weakness in them.

"I know people think I am a ghoul," he says. "For what I do, examining and dissecting the dead. Particularly when it is someone I knew. How can I cut open a friend? But as a surgeon, I would never hesitate to operate on someone I knew. To me, cutting them open after death is still helping. I am either finding their killer or I am seeking knowledge to find future killers. I did not look down on my brother-in-law's body and see Gordon Leslie. The man I knew was gone. What remained was only a shell that could help find his killer."

He fingers the empty glass. "That was a bit of a lecture, wasn't it?"

I smile. "As long as the lecture isn't about something I did wrong, you know I appreciate them. You're right. While I've never conducted a post-mortem on someone I know, I've seen most of my loved ones after death. That's what happens after embalming begins. We pay them one final visit."

One brow lifts. "You visit their embalmed corpse?"

"Yep, it's actually called a visitation. But I never see the person I knew lying there. They're gone. What I see is a representation of them that gives me a chance to reflect on our relationship. Also a chance to grumble that they never wore their hair that way, always hated that dress, and so on."

He chuckles softly.

I continue, "My point is that I get it."

"Thank you. And my point, as the long way of getting to it, is that I do not see that body as Ezra Sinclair, my childhood friend. I see it as evidence to catch his killer, and I will have no compunction about cutting into it. But standing out there, watching that young man poke at it and flip it over as if it were cordwood . . . I was offended."

"Because that's disrespect, and you never disrespect the dead."

He sets the glass aside. "I understand this is not our investigation. Not Hugh's and therefore not ours. Yet I cannot abandon Ezra to that fate. Perhaps that is foolish. He will never know whether his killer is caught, and he has no family to care."

"He has friends who care," I say softly. "But even if it's not about avenging the dead or stopping a killer, can we trust Ross not to arrest the wrong man? Can we trust the local judiciary not to execute the wrong man?"

Gray shudders, and I almost regret mentioning it.

"I had not thought of that," he says. "I recall Isla talking about several cases where the person accused of a village murder was an itinerant man or woman, an easy scapegoat. It is spring, meaning there are migratory workers."

Gray looks across the room, his gaze settling on a portrait of Cranston, and at first, it's just where his eye happens to fall, but then he blinks. "You mentioned stopping the killer. We have reason to believe they might strike again."

"Because they killed the wrong person."

"We need to warn Archie," Gray says.

"He already realizes he was likely the intended target, but yes, he may not have extrapolated that to mean he is still in danger. I hate to dump that warning on Hugh, but he's best suited for it. You need to focus on the autopsy."

Gray slumps, and I search my words for what I said wrong.

"Is there a problem?" I say.

"Only everything," he says. "I have my medical bag, but I barely had the tools to operate on that kitten. I do not travel with the equipment for proper surgery much less an autopsy. I was quick to offer my services, but I can hardly open up poor Ezra on the kitchen table with a garden saw."

"There's a local doctor, right? Rendall? You suggested Ross make sure Dr. Rendall is okay with you performing the autopsy, and I know that was mostly protecting yourself, but maybe we should pay this doctor a visit. With the body. So you can ask to use his facilities."

When Gray doesn't answer, I say, "I know that risks Dr. Rendall insisting on doing it himself, but which is better? You only assisting in the autopsy? Or you conducting it yourself on that table behind the stables, with a garden saw?"

He sighs and then rises. "Let me summon Simon, and we will convey the body to the local physician."

FIFTEEN

I feel I must thank you," Gray says as we sit in the coach, looking out at the passing countryside.

"For going on a road trip with you?" I say. "I was actually hoping to see the village, so I appreciate the excuse."

"Not that, though I do appreciate it. I mean I ought to thank you for remaining silent."

My brows shoot high. "If I'm ever too chatty, you know you can just tell me to shut up, right?"

He smiles. "You are always the perfect amount of 'chatty,' Mallory. Right now, I am only grateful that you are quietly enjoying the excursion, rather than reminding me that this is not the way to convey the body of a murder victim."

I glance over at Sinclair, his wrapped body across the opposite seat. "Yeah, I've surrendered my crime-scene sensibilities and given in to the spirit of the age." I look at Sinclair again. "Er, those were clean sheets you guys wrapped him in, right?"

Gray shakes his head, and I decide to take that as a yes. I lean sideways, looking past Sinclair's wrapped feet out the window. "Oh, there's the village. It's so cute."

"A 'cute' seething maelstrom of petty jealousies, festering grudges, and, probably, inbreeding."

"Not a fan of small towns?"

"I spent several months in one during my studies, working with a local doctor. Those from the city often speak of villages as bucolic places, where everyone knows everyone and takes care of them. The city is not perfect, but at least they do not gape at me as if I am some monster come to devour their children." He leans over. "In case you think I am exaggerating, a woman asked me whether I was a cannibal. She had seen something about 'dark savages' boiling people in pots."

"What did you say?"

"That I prefer a good pork roast."

I smile and turn my attention to the passing village. One thing I've always loved about rural Britain is that you can find villages that seem rooted in time, and if you angle your camera to focus past the cars and power lines, you can imagine yourself back hundreds of years . . . until some tourist steps in front of you to get that same shot. That's what this village looks like—a tourist town in the Scottish Highlands, with stone cottages and gardens and a cobbled main road.

Ross has given us directions. I worried about asking him, but going behind the constable's back won't help our cause. To my relief, he gave the directions readily.

Simon stops in front of what might be the most adorable cottage on the main street, with the most perfect garden. I do love a proper English—or Scottish—garden. There is a wild perfection to them that speaks to that wild perfectionist in me, the one torn between craving reckless abandon and wanting perfect order.

To me, the best of those gardens are the lush jungle riots of color. What I see here is a more muted version, but it's still a paradise of grasses and thistles and primrose and flowers I can't name, and I want to tell Gray to go ahead without me. I'll just stretch out in the garden, inhale the spring blooms, and work on my tan. And, yes, working on a tan isn't really a Victorian thing, which is one place where they were a whole lot smarter than us.

After the coach comes to a full stop, Gray opens the door and gets out. He's a third of the way up the walk before he remembers me. Or, at least, remembers that I am a "lady" and therefore he should hold the door and help me down.

I would be flattered that he forgets—thinking of me as a friend and colleague rather than a damsel needing help—except that it's more a sign of his single-mindedness. Most of the time, knowing I can handle it, he doesn't come back. Here, he does, because there are at least a dozen pairs of eyes on us, from up and down the road.

He returns stiffly, his expression blank as he helps me down and then offers his arm. I try not to look about, but I feel those assessing gazes, and I tell myself they'd do the same to any newcomers in a fancy coach, but I'm not sure they would.

We continue through the garden to the front door. The cottage is stone with a thatch roof. In the present day, I'll bet a week's wages that the front door is bright blue or mauve or turquoise. Here, it's plain white with a handwoven wreath of lavender.

Gray raps the knocker. A woman's voice calls from the rear of the house, "I am in the garden!"

We walk around to the back, where a stout white-haired woman weeds a raised vegetable bed of green shoots. As we come into view, her gaze goes first to Gray, and she blinks her surprise, but covers it with a wide smile.

"Good day, sir." She looks at me and smiles again. "Good day to you both."

Gray returns the greeting and then says, "We are looking for Dr. Rendall. Is he at home?"

"Oh. Yes, of course." She cranes to look over the garden. "Clifford? Guests to see you."

There's a grunt from behind a hedge, and an elderly man appears. He isn't much taller than the woman, but moves with the ease of someone half his age. Seeing us, he extends his hand to Gray, notices the gardening glove, and takes it off before shaking Gray's hand.

"You must be from up at the castle," Dr. Rendall says. "I heard there was a wedding. I hope no one has taken ill."

Before we can answer, a boy races around the back, calling, "Dr. Rendall! There's been a murder!" Seeing us, he stops short, staring at Gray. The woman clears her throat, and the boy takes off his cap and bobs his head, before continuing in a brogue thick enough I can barely make it out. "I do not mean to interrupt, but I thought the doctor should know that there has been a murder up at the castle house. His Lordship is dead."

"What?" The woman's eyes round.

Gray clears his throat. "That is what we came to see you about. An . . . accident at the estate."

"I heard it was murder." The boy sounds disappointed.

The woman bustles the boy off, and Gray waits until they're gone before continuing.

"It does appear to be murder," he says to Dr. Rendall. "The deceased is not Mr. Cranston but a guest. I am Dr. Duncan Gray, at the estate with my dear friend—and the brother of the bride—Detective Hugh McCreadie of the Edinburgh police."

The name-dropping is intentional. He's not saying McCreadie is investigating the murder, but if that's what Dr. Rendall interprets, all the better for us. Still, Gray does add for clarity, "While I am a doctor of medicine and surgery, I do not practice either. I am an undertaker who also works with the police in matters of medical science."

"Do you now?" The woman is returning from behind us. "That sounds fascinating."

Gray nods her way. "It is gratifying work. In that capacity, I have asked your First Constable Ross for permission to autopsy the deceased. I am hoping we might do that together."

"Autopsy?" Dr. Rendall blinks. "Oh, dear. I think you had best come inside."

Dr. Rendall shows us to the sitting room while the woman—his wife, as she's now introduced—makes tea.

"I certainly know what an autopsy is," Dr. Rendall says, "and I understand the need for it in such a situation, but I will be honest with you, Dr. Gray. I have never performed one. I am a country doctor, not a surgeon."

"Understood." Gray inclines his head. "I am comfortable taking the lead on this. I am not the police surgeon for Edinburgh. That is Dr. Addington. But I know him well. He performs his autopsies in my laboratory, and he would vouch for my ability to perform this one. My assist—" He stops dead. "I must apologize. I forgot to introduce my assistant. This is Miss Mallory Mitchell."

I smile and incline my head. That really was an oversight—a testament to the fact that Gray is not nearly as calm as he seems. There are so many ways this could go wrong, and the smoother it seems to be going, the more he's bracing for trouble.

"I can assist Dr. Gray in the autopsy," I say. "Of course, if you wished to take my place, Dr. Rendall, you would be very welcome to do so. We understand this is most irregular."

He smiles. "I appreciate the offer, lass, but I would have nothing to offer. I am not even certain I dare watch. There is a reason I went into medicine instead of surgery."

His wife pipes up. "But if you have any need of extra hands, I would be happy to provide them. I would find it most interesting."

"Thank you," Gray says. "We would be happy to have you, either assisting or merely observing. Dr. Rendall, as you are not a surgeon, might I presume you lack a bone saw?"

"He does," Mrs. Rendall says. "However, I have butchering tools, if it is not considered sacrilege to use them. We have our own sheep among the local herds, and I handle all of the butchering." She smiles fondly at her husband. "He really is not a surgeon for a reason."

"We will use whatever you have at hand," Gray says. "As for whether such tools would be considered sacrilegious, I am certain that some of the old ones I handled at the college started life in a butcher shop."

"Finish your tea then," Mrs. Rendall says. "And we will find you a spot to do this."

SIXTEEN

I know it's magical thinking, but I can't help but feel as if the universe likes to keep itself in balance. We drew one of the worst possible cards when it came to local law enforcement . . . and so the universe—or maybe the goddess of luck—balances it with the local physician. Gray keeps waiting for the proverbial other shoe to drop, but it doesn't.

The Rendalls are a lovely old couple, happy to help in our endeavor with absolutely no interest in turning this into a pissing contest. This is as it should be, where if a visiting professional is deferential and understanding about stepping on another's turf, the local pro will recognize their lack of experience and step back.

The only potential issue is, as Dr. Rendall said, he's not a surgeon. That means he has neither surgical implements nor a surgical table. We're performing the autopsy in the shed, on a butchering table currently being used for potting.

Gray doesn't hesitate, even as we move the pots and wipe off the soil and Mrs. Rendall searches for the butchering tools that have been stored for fall. That's one advantage to living in an earlier era, I think. You're more accustomed to making do. I look back on all the times McCreadie or Gray teased me for flinching at the handling of evidence or the treatment of crime scenes, and I realize it wasn't just teasing. They're genuinely amused by my struggle to work in less than ideal circumstances. For them, that's the norm.

If anything, Gray approaches this as an intriguing challenge. He's never conducted an autopsy in a garden shed using saws and knives for butchering sheep. How will that be different? What will he need to do to adapt? Can he learn anything from this for future situations, where he might not have the tools he needs?

I need to learn how to do that myself. To not shudder as someone pockets evidence, but to remind myself that it doesn't matter here—no DNA, no chain-of-evidence rules, not even the possibility of using fingerprints at court. Instead of trying to change their attitudes, change my own. Concentrate on the things that matter and accept a lack of control over the rest.

Here, I do that by focusing on lighting. Forget the dirt and the less-than-sanitary tools. None of that matters with a dead body. Lighting does matter, and it's horrible, with just a swinging overhead lantern. As Gray and Dr. Rendall prepare the table, Mrs. Rendall and I gather more lanterns and lamps and put them on every surface. Then Dr. Rendall retreats to his garden with a hearty "Good luck!" and we begin the autopsy.

While Gray and I have worked on plenty of dead bodies, Addington is the police surgeon, which means he conducts the autopsies. If Gray can, he examines the body first, as he did with Sinclair. Then, because Addington conducted the autopsy in Gray's lab, Gray can check Addington's findings and perform any additional work. So while it *feels* as if I've done autopsies with Gray, I've only been there for the post-autopsy examinations.

Has Gray performed a full autopsy before? I noted that he never actually said that to Dr. Rendall. He said Addington would vouch for his *ability* to perform one. I suspect Gray did one or two in college, but he must know what he's doing, because he'd never imperil a murder investigation.

This isn't the first autopsy I've stood in on. Back home, I witnessed them whenever I had the opportunity. It's different here, and not only because it's hardly a sterile morgue with shiny modern tools. For one thing, there's a cloth over Sinclair's genitals, and it's not a tiny scrap of fabric. Gray has laid a foot-wide swath of cloth over that portion, partly for Mrs. Rendall and me, but also just because it's considered showing proper respect to the deceased.

As with any postmortem exam, the blades don't come out right away. The on-site external exam was done while Sinclair was fully clothed. Now that he is not, step one is to conduct a complete external examination.

Mrs. Rendall holds an oil lamp over his body and adjusts the placement as directed by Gray. Beginning at the top of Sinclair's head, Gray and I move down his body, checking it thoroughly and noting every bug bite and healing bruise and scabbed-over scrape. Almost all of those occurred at least a day before his death, judging by the amount of swelling and healing. There are two exceptions. One is a scrape on one knee, presumably from striking a rock in his fall. The other is his broken nose, again presumably from his fall.

We find nothing on his hands that we'd consider defensive wounds. Dirt under his fingernails makes it difficult to be sure there isn't skin under there, too, but we take scrapings . . . which would be far more useful if Isla's microscope were far more portable. Or if she had any reason to pack it for a wedding getaway. We take combings from Sinclair's hair, but all I see there are flakes of what is likely dried pomade.

Once that's done, we turn Sinclair over. The head wound is the obvious point of interest, but we leave that for now. What catches our attention first is a light bruise between his shoulder blades.

"That's recent, isn't it?" I say. "It hasn't purpled."

Gray nods. "It would have been inflicted either shortly before or after his death."

"Can you bruise after death? I know lividity is an issue—the blood pools, which is why it looked as if his chest was bruised."

"It is an area I have been wanting to study, along with a proper reporting of the stages of bruising. The next time you bash into furniture, rushing off after whatever catches your eye, you really must let me properly chart the progress of the bruising."

I narrow my eyes. "I do not *bash* into furniture."

He arches one brow.

"Hardly ever," I say. "And only when the furniture is in a ridiculous spot. There is always far too much of it. A random chair here. A stray ottoman there. Vases and statues and useless little tables. Every room is an obstacle course."

Mrs. Rendall laughs softly, which reminds me she's there, holding the lamp just out of our view. I settle for glaring at Gray, and the corners of his mouth twitch, and I have to admit I'm mostly grumbling because he's right. Even with layers of Victorian clothing, I get enough bruises that he really could start his study there.

"As for this," he says, tapping the bruise on Sinclair's back. "It's more of an impression than a bruise. Do you note the shape of it?"

I need to move to check it from a couple of angles. Then I say, "Foot-shaped. Or boot-shaped. Not a kick—that would only be the toe. More like someone stepped on him."

"Or . . . ?"

"Put their foot on his back to hold him down." I move for a closer look and Mrs. Rendall adjusts the lamp without prompting. "It's a light bruise. Would death affect that?" I look up at Gray and clarify, "Would the fact that Mr. Sinclair was either dead or close to death affect lividity? Making what might become a deep bruise normally seem light?"

"Excellent question," Gray says. "And one to which I do not have a definitive answer. I will add it to my proposed study. You will recall that we saw bruising in the murder of Sir Alastair, where the killer appeared to use his foot against the victim's back."

"For leverage."

"In that case, the purpose seemed clear and the strength appropriate. The bruising was not significantly less than I would expect. However, we do not know what amount of force that killer used."

"How did it compare to the bruises on my back?"

Gray hasn't been standing there, talking. He's been poking and prodding at the bruise. Now he stops. "Bruises on your back?"

"From when the same was done to me. I survived, which provides a comparison."

Mrs. Rendall gives a quick intake of breath, and I realize that may have sounded cavalier.

Hey, remember when I was strangled, a would-be killer's foot on my back for leverage? How did those bruises compare?

It's not just Mrs. Rendall who reacts, though. Gray goes ashen and the fingers on his extended hand curl under.

"That was thoughtless of me," he says, his voice low. "I did not intend a reminder of your ordeal."

I smile up at him. "I didn't take it as a reminder. Not an unwelcome one, at least. It only made me think that the two incidents provide a comparison that could be helpful here."

"Yes, well, still, I . . ." He trails off and then clears his throat. "It was still a reminder, and for that, I apologize."

I peer at him, his gaze on Sinclair but unfocused, his hand fisted, and I realize that the recollection bothers him more than it does me. Yes, I was strangled, but it sent me back to my own time, where I resolved the issues that had kept me from settling into this world.

It'd been less a death than a rebirth, if you want to be poetic about it. But to Gray, I'd nearly died. Or, at the very least, I'd nearly disappeared forever, back to my own world, and when I look at him now, his gaze distant, that hand fisted and shaking slightly, I want to send Mrs. Rendall on some errand. I want to stop and take a moment and pursue this.

Apologize for bringing it up? Reassure Gray that I'm fine? Or just take a moment, free of distractions and witnesses, to absorb that look on his face, to wonder exactly what he felt when he thought I was gone, why the reminder would still affect him so much?

But I'm not getting that moment, am I? Oh, I *could* send Mrs. Rendall off on some pointless errand. Yet the moment I think that, guilt jabs through me with an ice-water reminder that this is an autopsy, damn it. A good man—a friend of Gray's—is dead, and that is all that matters.

I shake my head. "It would hardly signify anyway, I suppose. While the intent was the same, it wasn't the same circumstances or even the same actor, so it would be a horribly flawed scientific comparison."

"I fear so," Gray says, his voice scratchy. "It was a good idea, though."

"The point being simply that my question has no definitive answer. The bruising here is light, which may or may not indicate the amount of force used."

Gray's hand relaxes. "Yes."

"The fact that it's light only means we don't have a full print. There seems to be a toe and heel, but it's hardly a discernible footprint we can match to a boot. I couldn't even guess whether it's a man's boot or a woman's."

"I would concur. It appears to be a foot, applied fully, rather than through a kick. As for the purpose, I would speculate restraint."

I nod. "Mr. Sinclair is hit from behind and falls face-first. It's a hard drop, considering the broken nose. It's rare for a head injury to be instantly fatal, so the killer puts their foot on Mr. Sinclair's back to hold him down. Yet the position we found the body—and the open eyes—suggest Mr. Sinclair *did* die immediately. There was no need to apply greater pressure to hold him down, hence the light bruise."

"Again, I concur."

"Can you determine whether the head injury *was* instantly fatal?"

Gray purses his lips. "Possibly, but either way, I am not certain it matters."

My brows rise as my lips twitch in a smile. "No?"

Mrs. Rendall shifts the light, again reminding me she's there, which also reminds me that my question is less than appropriate for an assistant.

"Apologies, Dr. Gray," I say. "I do not mean to question your expertise."

"Apology accepted," he says, and his tone is serious, but his eyes dance, letting me know he's playing along for our audience. "But please continue. I welcome your insights, Miss Mitchell."

"They are the insights as a reader of detective fiction rather than a detective, which I am not. Proceed, please."

His eyes twinkle more. "Noted. I welcome the observations of an *amateur* detective."

"Imagine the blow was never intended to kill him. Perhaps it was a warning. Or meant only to prevent him from seeing something. He is knocked unconscious and his attacker leaves . . . and then someone else kills him. In that case, knowing whether death was instantaneous would matter."

"I stand corrected. However, I have noted something that suggests death *was* instantaneous, though not from the blow to the head."

I frown and sweep my gaze over Sinclair's body. "Should I be able to see it?"

"Perhaps. It is visible from this perspective."

I walk along Sinclair's body, searching his back for bruises or pinpricks or anything that could indicate a cause of death. When I pause to probe his head wound, Gray says, "*Visible.*"

I survey the body again, slower. At the feet, still seeing nothing, I ask Mrs. Rendall for the light. As she hands it to me, her gaze darts left, as if giving me a hint.

Great. So I'm the only one who doesn't see it?

I remind myself that Mrs. Rendall is a doctor's wife, one who has probably also been his nurse for decades. She's being very circumspect here, listening to us without speaking up, but that doesn't mean she's an amateur when it comes to medicine.

Her gaze flicks again, and this time I can follow it. She's indicating Sinclair's neck. It takes me a moment. Then I see it.

Without speaking, I move up to Sinclair's neck and lower the light next to it. There's no damage to the skin, but something is . . . not right.

"His neck is broken," I say finally. "I know that is not the medical term for it."

Gray nods. "There appears to be a traumatic injury to the cervical portion of the spine. Specifically the first vertebrae. I did not see it at the scene, but now that the body is unclothed, the damage is evident. As I do not see any other obvious signs of injury in that area, my initial theory would be that it was caused by the blow to the head."

"The blow was hard enough to snap his neck forward and back, with enough force to fracture the C1 vert . . ." I trail off, not sure whether that's common usage yet. "The top vertebra. The higher the vertebra the more serious the injury. At the top . . ." Again I trail off, sneaking a look at Gray this time, uncertain of that part, too—how much is known about spinal injuries.

"The higher the injury, the more severe the damage," Gray says. "That has been established through vivisection."

I swallow and hope my expression stays neutral. I've learned more about vivisection than I ever wanted to. In fact, I think I'd have been happier never knowing about it at all.

I also acknowledge that my revulsion comes from living in a world where anyone who would do such a thing is a sadistic bastard. But that's a viewpoint of privilege, specifically the privilege that comes from the fact that we no longer need to do such things because of the medical advances that . . . came from doing such things.

What is vivisection? Well, if dissection refers to cutting into a dead animal and "*vivus*" is Latin for living . . .

When it comes to spinal injuries, I can presume doctors realized that injuring different areas of the spine had different effects, and the higher the injury, the worse those effects. To properly study what parts produce what injuries . . .

I'm not going to think about what they would have needed to do with animals, but I understand the need for it. Those experiments having been conducted, doctors like Gray now understand how those injuries will manifest, and that is critical knowledge, however it came about.

Gray continues, "A fracture at this level can separate the brain from the rest of the body. Without the brain to regulate the body . . ."

"The organs aren't getting any signals and stop working. The lungs don't take in oxygen. The heart doesn't beat."

"Yes. Ezra mercifully appears to have lost consciousness from the blow, the impact sudden enough that it might explain his eyes remaining open."

Mercifully, because otherwise, he'd have been alive and fully paralyzed as his body shut down.

"That is my initial theory," Gray says. "Now we need to confirm it, as best we are able."

Confirming that means cutting into Sinclair's neck to examine the spine. Gray conducts the internal examination, which confirms separation at the C1 vertebra.

In the end, I don't get to watch Gray perform a full autopsy, because it isn't necessary. We know what killed Ezra Sinclair, and anything more would be an unnecessary intrusion.

SEVENTEEN

Once the postmortem is complete, we need to wrap Sinclair's body and take it back to the estate. There's nothing else we can do with it. A city like Edinburgh has a morgue, but towns and villages do not.

In my time, the body would be transported to an undertaker, but when I first told Gray that, he'd been baffled. What would an undertaker do with the body? In that capacity, Gray has nothing to do with the dead themselves. He just makes the arrangements for the funeral and burial.

Bodies are often kept in the house of the deceased, where the women in the family will tend to it before burial. That burial will come as soon as possible because . . . Well, as comfortable as Victorians may be with their dead relatives, they don't want them in the house after they get too far down the path to decomposition.

With Sinclair being a murder victim, Gray won't want him buried any sooner than necessary. Lacking the proper storage facilities, though, all he can do is wrap the corpse tightly and keep him at the estate.

Simon and Gray brought Sinclair in fully wrapped, and that's how they'll take him out.

We thank Dr. and Mrs. Rendall for their hospitality, and then go to fetch Simon. While Gray talks to him, I open the coach door. The June sun is blazing, and the coach is going to be an oven, which is never good for dead bodies.

I prop open the door, and I'm inside wrestling with a sticky window when I fall on my ass, thankfully landing on the seat. As I go to rise, though, something crinkles. I turn and find a piece of paper half wedged in the seat. One glance tells me it's not something that just fell out of a pocket. It's old paper, tattered and creased from folds, with smudge marks from ink.

One side of the paper has multiple bits of writing on it. Like a piece of scrap left on a desk for jotting notes. The paper is coarse, the writing on it from different hands.

We aren't in a time period when you can grab a hundred-sheet notebook at the dollar store. Paper is plentiful for someone like Gray, but like most things in this world—from clothing to household wares—if you're poor, you reuse it until it's falling apart.

That's what this is. A piece of paper that has been used and reused. Different handwriting suggests multiple writers, all of them semiliterate, using mostly pencils. I see a few dates, as if someone wrote them down to remember them. There are a few rough calculations, too. Other writing seems to have been deliberately smeared with fresh ink. To hide what was beneath? When I hold it up, I realize that one edge has been carefully torn away. A larger sheet, then, ripped down to a smaller size, maybe four inches by two.

How did this get into the coach?

It's not Simon's or Alice's. They both have good penmanship and access to quality writing utensils and paper.

Did someone sneak into our coach while we were inside the Rendall house? Looking for valuables and accidentally dropping this? Maybe, but I'll give the locals the benefit of the doubt and consider it more likely that if someone entered our coach, it was purely out of curiosity.

I can imagine a child or teenager sneaking into this "fancy" coach for a look. I can also imagine a piece of paper dropping out of their pocket. But the page really looks as if someone blotted out some of the writing before leaving it, and that clean torn edge—while the others are dog-eared and tattered—suggests it was ripped recently. Someone took an old piece of paper and studiously removed any identifying bits . . . before accidentally dropping it in our coach?

That's when the answer hits me, making me groan with the obviousness of it.

I turn the paper over.

"Excellent detective work, Mallory," I mutter to myself as I see the writing on the other side.

Someone has indeed written on the back, which is otherwise blank.

Whoever wrote the note doesn't appear to have much experience with a pen and ink, because it's badly smeared, with letters running together. It takes me a couple of minutes before I figure out what it says. And when I do, I'm out the coach door in a flash, hurrying along the Rendalls' front path, where Gray and Simon are circling the cottage to get the body from the back.

Simon hears me first and glances back. I wave the note and hurry to catch up.

"I found this in the coach," I say.

Gray takes it and frowns down as he works on deciphering the hand.

I put my finger on the words and read, "'He deserved it for what he did to Nora.'" I look up at Gray. "That's what it says, right?"

"It certainly does appear to be. *He deserved it . . .*" Gray's head snaps up, and he meets my gaze.

"I'm guessing they mean the murder," I say. "Someone saw us carrying the body into the doctor's and figured out why. We already know the rumor was circulating."

"The rumor being that *Archie* was dead," Gray murmurs. "Murdered. But the body we carried out was obviously not Archie's." He stops and then shakes his head. "No, the body was wrapped in a sheet."

I nod. "That boy who ran into the Rendalls' said His Lordship had been murdered. Archie isn't a lord, but the Hall siblings called him that."

"But how did this get in the coach?" Gray's gaze rises to Simon, who has been quietly listening. "Did you step away from it?"

Color rises in Simon's cheeks. "Er, yes, sir. An older fellow needed help and, er, I did not think anything of leaving the coach. I checked to be sure you had not left anything valuable inside. If you would have wished me to stay with it, I apologize—"

"You were not required to stay with it. I am only trying to understand how this was left."

Simon still shifts in obvious discomfort at Gray's abrupt tone and lack of body-language cues. I've known Gray long enough to recognize this tone as efficiency rather than curtness or annoyance, but Simon isn't so sure.

"May I speak to Simon about this?" I say to Gray. I flash a smile. "Practice my interview skills?"

Gray doesn't miss a beat. "That is an excellent idea. I will tell the Rendalls that we are briefly delayed in our departure."

"Can you also ask whether Dr. Rendall saw anyone near the coach? Maybe get the name of the boy who came running to tell them of the murder?"

"Certainly."

As Gray heads into the Rendall house, I lead Simon out toward the road. There's a huge old oak tree nearby, the canopy providing welcome shade and a bit of shadowed privacy. I wave Simon there.

"I was set up, wasn't I?" Simon says.

"Hmm?"

"Being led away to help that fellow. Someone wanted me to leave the coach unattended. In the city, I would never have fallen for it."

"I hadn't thought of that. Maybe? It's just as likely that whoever left the note was watching for a chance. Can you tell me what happened?"

Simon leans against the thick trunk as he relaxes. "I moved the coach, getting Folly out of the sun. Then I heard a shout. There was a cart full of logs that seemed to have struck a rut in the road and the logs tumbled out. Seeing me, the cart driver waved for help, and I went to provide it."

"Where was that?"

He points. "In front of the third house there. You can see the rut in the road."

"Would you know the man if you saw him again?"

"I would. He was elderly, which is why I was quick to help. He said he lived a few cottages down . . ." Simon walks onto the street and shades his eyes. "There. The cart is in front of the house, and he is unloading it."

I walk out onto the road for a better look. While the man is a few hundred feet away, he's clearly gray-haired and stout, and very obviously unloading a cart of logs.

Simon continues, "He'd received permission to chop up a dead tree in the kirkyard and he was taking the pieces home to dry for next year." He pauses, still watching the man. "While I ought to have been more careful, there was nothing suspicious in it."

"I agree," I say. "I'll note the house, but I'd be shocked if it were a setup. Someone took advantage of you stepping away from the coach to leave a note."

Simon's voice drops, though there's no one else around. "Is Dr. Gray annoyed with me? If he is, I would rather he said as much."

"He's not," I say. "That's just his face."

Simon laughs under his breath. "Good. I trust you would tell me if he was."

"I would. Now, before you were called away, did you see anyone lingering about?"

"There have been many people lingering about. I believe most of the village has found some reason for walking past the coach. I have been asked at least a half-dozen times what happened up at the castle." He lifts his hands. "I said that I am merely the coach driver for one of the wedding guests. For those who know that we transported a body, I said I only do as I am asked, and I was given no further details."

"Am I right that people seem to think the victim was Mr. Cranston?"

He nods. "Several of them believed the deceased was the lord of the estate and that he was murdered."

"Did you notice anyone lingering for longer than is polite?"

"A few lads. I ran them off. They seemed mostly curious. One tried to offer me a ha'penny for a look inside the coach." He rolls his eyes. "As if I would endanger my position for that."

"It'd take a half crown?"

He laughs softly. "I do not think there is any bribe worth that, although I did feel bad for not letting him have a peek. I understand the curiosity. They do not see many such coaches here." He pauses and then curses under his breath. "And if I was concerned about village lads poking about the coach, I ought not to have walked away from it to help that fellow. In my defense, the boys were long gone."

"And you knew there was nothing of value in the coach. Dr. Gray would have told you to go and help. I will take a description of the boys, though."

"Because the one who wanted to pay for a peek might have really wanted to plant the note."

He tells me what he can remember of the boys, especially the one who offered the ha'penny. Then he glances at the Rendall cottage before lowering his voice. "There is something else I need to speak to you on, Mallory. A . . . situation. At the estate."

I stiffen. "Has someone been giving you trouble? Or is bothering Alice? I've been trying to pay attention, but things have . . ." I flutter my hand. "It's been a lot."

"With the murder and all?" He smiles. "No one has been giving us trouble, and if they did, we can take care of ourselves. You are not responsible for us, but it is sweet that you try to be. You are . . ."

"Not Catriona," I murmur. For everyone else, this is a good thing. Simon is the one exception. Catriona's only friend, and the one person who misses her, however much he tries to hide it.

"No longer the Catriona I remember," he says carefully, "but there are times . . ." He sighs and shifts his weight. "Am I a terrible friend if I admit that there are times I remember you are not her and I am relieved? There was more to her than others saw, but I was not blind to the rest, and I was always waiting for her to betray Mrs. Ballantyne and Dr. Gray's trust. I had even begun to suspect she was . . . unkind to Alice."

I school my features, emulating Gray's blank mask. "Alice has not said anything of the sort to me."

He exhales in obvious relief. I'm not lying. Alice hasn't admitted anything.

"Catriona was not an easy person to like," Simon says. "But I did care for her." He glances over. "It seems odd sometimes, speaking to you this way, as if you and Catriona are different people. That is what it feels like, though. As if she left, and her sister came. I miss Catriona, but you are . . ." He clears his throat. "Better for all."

A moment of silence passes before he glances at the cottage again and says, "At this rate, I will not say what I need to say. It is about last night. When the murder occurred. I know everyone must tell where they were, and I ought to say I was in my bed. But I was not."

"Ah."

"Nor was I alone, which is the greater problem. I was with Mr. Cranston's valet." He glances over. "If you would like me to say we were discussing horse care, I can say that."

I sputter a laugh. "No need. So you hooked up—got together with—Mr. Cranston's valet." I waggle my brows. "He's very handsome."

I expect Simon to blush, but he only rolls his eyes. "He is, but I am hardly smitten. Grooms and valets and lady's maids often accompany their employers on such trips, and it is not uncommon for servants to mingle." He gives me a sidelong look again. "Is that more than you wish to know?"

"I know Catriona was very straitlaced"—"prudish" would be the word—"but that's not me. You're saying that staff who accompany their employers on holiday have some fun among themselves, which makes sense. Easier than hooking—getting together with people you run into regularly. That's what you were doing with the valet."

"Yes. Holidays such as this are particularly useful for finding . . . others who share my inclinations."

I nod. That also makes sense, especially in Simon's case, where being gay got him into trouble. He's extremely circumspect these days. Hooking up while on holiday would seem like the safest choice. Unless you do so on the night a guest is murdered.

"You and Mr. Cranston's valet were together last night," I say. "And you're not sure how to answer if Constable Ross asks where you were."

"Yes."

"Well, I wouldn't be surprised if he doesn't bother. He's never investigated a murder before. But you two need to make sure you tell the same story, and I'm going to strongly suggest you stick to a variation on the truth. You joked about discussing horses. You can go with that if you like. For the investigation, *why* you were together isn't as important as the fact you were not in your respective beds."

He gazes out at the road, and I know that wasn't what he wanted to hear.

"You can't lie, Simon," I murmur. "I'm sorry. You cannot risk getting caught up in a murder investigation." I lower my voice. "I think you know that."

That's how he ended up in Isla's employ. He'd been framed for murder. Very clumsily framed, according to McCreadie, but when it involved the murder of a powerful man and his gay lover, it was damned easy to lay the blame at the foot of that lover's best friend . . . who was also gay.

"Dr. Gray will know the truth," Simon blurts after a moment. "Dr. Gray and Detective McCreadie and Mrs. Ballantyne. They will all know why I was with Mr. Cranston's valet, and they will think I do not appreciate the second chance I have been given."

"That's not . . ." I pause a moment, thinking of how to frame this in the most period-appropriate way before realizing I have no idea how to do that. "The only second chance they were giving you was an opportunity to start over in a new job, in a safe place. No one expects you to change who you are. That'd be like expecting Dr. Gray to change his skin color."

Simon slants me a look. "It is not exactly like that, Mallory. People like me *do* change who they are, if they wish to fit into the world."

"Change who they are? Or hide who they are?"

He shrugs. "People expect the first and get the second. I cannot change my nature, but I can suppress it, so as not to embarrass my employers. I have been very discreet. Even last night, I would have refrained, had we not been sampling a bottle Mr. Cranston gave us."

I meet his gaze. "I am one hundred percent certain that neither of our employers—or Detective McCreadie—would be shocked or disappointed to learn you'd slipped off with Mr. Cranston's valet. I understand the matter must be handled delicately, and I think handling it delicately means I need to warn them. May I do that?"

He leans back against the tree. "Is that necessary?"

"If you prefer, I would only tell Dr. Gray."

"Of the three, he's the last I'd choose."

"Then you've misjudged his character gravely. But if you are set against it, I'll tell none of them, and we can hope that Constable Ross doesn't ask where you were. And that no one else saw you and reports it and then Ross decides it's very suspicious that you and Mr. Cranston's valet didn't see fit to tell anyone you were together last night."

Simon sighs.

"*Did* you see anything?" I say. "That's more important, as far as I'm concerned. If you saw something but you don't want to tell Ross, tell me and I'll see if there's another way to handle it."

"I saw you," he says. "That is the other part of my dilemma. Both

Theodore—the valet—and I saw you and Dr. Gray heading up onto the hill. Together. At night."

"Ah. Well, we both had bad timing, didn't we? Don't worry about that. If it comes to it, go ahead and admit you saw us. We've already discussed it with Detective McCreadie. He knows we were out, and that we'll need to tell Constable Ross."

"And *what* will you tell him?"

I shrug. "The truth. I'd had trouble sleeping, so Dr. Gray took me for a moonlit walk."

Simon stares at me. "That is even worse than my horse excuse."

I cross my arms. "In my case, it's true. I even have the note to prove it. Dr. Gray invited me on a walk, and he brought a basket, and we had a picnic."

Simon studies my expression until I say, "We *did*. We are friends. I know that's hard for everyone to understand."

"Because it is obvious to everyone with eyes that your feelings for him go beyond friendship, Mallory."

My cheeks blaze. "We are friends," I say firmly.

He watches me for a moment and then rubs his mouth. "I have not known how to discuss this with you, but as someone who is also your friend, I feel it must be said." He meets my gaze. "Take care, Mallory. You tread a path nearly as dangerous as my own."

"I'm not treading any—"

"What if Dr. Gray intended more than a picnic?" He raises his hands against my protest. "I am not saying he did. I am saying what *if* he had. If he made advances, would you have received them?"

"He did not, and he will not, so the point is moot."

"No, the point is not moot because if you think he will never make those advances, then you are as blind—" He rubs his mouth again. "Dr. Gray is an honorable man, and if he has any intentions, they are honorable, but what he intends and what will *happen* are two very different things. You were a housemaid. He has elevated you to the position of assistant, but that does not change the fact you *were* a housemaid, one with a very dubious background. He would say that does not matter. So would Mrs. Ballantyne. They are correct that it *should* not matter, but just because a thing should be acceptable does not mean it is."

I say nothing.

He continues, "I made that mistake. I told myself that as long as I was not hurting anyone, then what I did was my own business, and I shouldn't need to hide it. I was young and naive, and I nearly paid the price with my life. I'm not saying it's the same for you. But I *am* concerned. For your sake. There's the world within our town house, and there's the real world, and we can do as we like inside those walls, but we cannot *stay* inside them."

I still say nothing. I can't, because I know he has a point, and my only argument is that it's a moot one. And if a little voice in my head whispers *What if it wasn't?* I shove it back into silence.

My feelings for Gray don't matter because they aren't reciprocated, and I'm okay with that.

Okay with that? Or relieved, because if they were reciprocated, I don't even know how I'd deal with that. I'm his employee, and if we ever tried moving beyond friendship and it didn't work out, I could lose everything. My home, my job, my friends.

My heart picks up speed, something almost like panic rising.

Almost like panic? No, that's actual panic.

Simon continues, "I don't want to see you get hurt, Mallory, and I don't want Dr. Gray to be the one to hurt you. Because he would not mean to. It's easy to jump in with both feet and tell yourselves you'll figure it out later but . . ."

"I know," I say. "Nothing is happening. Nothing will happen. I appreciate the concern." I look up at him. "I truly do. But it is misplaced."

"I hope so," he murmurs. Then his head jerks up and he straightens, calling, "Dr. Gray."

Gray is approaching slowly, watching for any signal that we aren't finished with our conversation. Then he says, "I think you need to come inside, Mallory. I have asked the Rendalls about the note, and they have said something you need to hear."

EIGHTEEN

We find the Rendalls in their living room, both looking pale and worried. Seeing that, I slow and glance at Gray. He strides in as if not detecting their unease. Probably because he actually doesn't detect it. Gray always says I'm better at reading people. It's not that he lacks empathy; he just doesn't pick up on body language and emotional cues as well as I do. His gift is for reading and interpreting evidence.

I take a seat. "Dr. Gray has shown you the note."

Dr. Rendall nods. His wife only grips her hands tighter in her lap.

"I am sorry if it has caused you distress," I say.

Out of the corner of my eye, I see Gray blink. Then distress flickers over his own features. Yes, he didn't notice it, and that bothers him.

"My apologies," Gray says in a low voice. "I did not intend to upset you."

Mrs. Rendall manages a weak smile. "We are not upset. Just . . ." Her gaze goes to me. "As Miss Mitchell said, we are somewhat distressed by that note. Of course you had to bring it to us, and of course we had to tell you what it means. We do not believe that is connected to poor Mr. Sinclair's death, but now that the note has been given to you, you must give it to Petey—Constable Ross—and we . . ."

Her husband completes the unfinished thought. "We fear he lacks the expertise to properly handle such a thing."

"That he might take the note as evidence," I say, "when it does not accuse anyone of killing Mr. Sinclair. It only says that the victim—presumably Mr. Cranston—deserved his fate."

"Exactly so," Mrs. Rendall says. "Constable Ross is out of his depth, and we have known him from the hour he first drew breath—I was there as midwife. There are children who are quick to admit they do not know a thing, in hopes of learning it. And there are children who see that as an admission of failure."

"It is admirable to want to solve problems yourself, rather than relying on others, but there are times for self-led education and times when . . . it is not the best course of action."

Mrs. Rendall laughs softly. "That is a very diplomatic way of putting it."

"In this situation, while Constable Ross may not wish the assistance of others, I can assure you that those others are present to oversee his work. We mentioned that we are here with a criminal officer who has conducted several homicide investigations. He will respect Constable Ross's jurisdiction in this case, but he will not allow a miscarriage of justice."

There's a moment of silence, and I replay what I said, wondering if I messed up with some anachronistic phrase or concept. Nope, I just started talking like a cop again.

"Very well said," Mrs. Rendall murmurs after a moment. "Thank you. We are fond of Pet—Constable Ross—and we believe he will one day make an excellent first constable, but we do appreciate that there will be more experienced eyes on his work."

"As for the note," Dr. Rendall says. "We can give no insight into the writer, as we have already told Dr. Gray. The penmanship is unremarkable, and the poor penmanship is, sadly, common. As for the sentiment, there are those who might have shared it if the victim really were Mr. Cranston. We would not. What happened to Nora . . ."

He trails off and when silence falls, I say, softly, "Mr. Cranston is believed to have taken advantage of her?"

They both blink. Then Mrs. Rendall says, "Oh dear, no. Yes, I suppose that is what it would sound like, isn't it? A wealthy gentleman from the city being blamed for doing something to a woman. No, that is not it at all."

"Good. So Nora . . ."

"Nora Glass," Mrs. Rendall says somberly. "The second-eldest daughter of our blacksmith. Some children love to ramble off on their own, and she was one of those. A dreamy girl who would be gone from sunup to sundown if she had her way of things."

I don't miss the past tense, and my gut seizes as I begin to suspect where this is going. A girl who likes to wander. A nearby estate with deadly traps.

Mrs. Rendall continues, "Nora knew she was not supposed to go onto the grounds, but she was twelve, at the age where children begin to think for themselves and decide that their parents are still treating them like children."

I swallow. "There are traps on the property."

Mrs. Rendall looks up sharply. "No. I mean, yes, we know about those, but so did Nora. She is cousin to the Hall children, who grew up there, and they made sure she knew about the traps. But she was accustomed to her uncle being the gamekeeper. It was the new fellow who caught her wandering about."

Again, my gut clenches, so sure once again that I know where this is going.

"What did he do?" I ask.

"Frightened her off. Shouted at her in his native tongue, and she had no idea what he was saying, but she understood his tone and ran like the devil himself was on her tail."

Ran and fell? Stumbled over a cliff edge? Or tripped and incurred an injury that turned septic? There are so many ways to die in this world.

"What happened?" I ask.

"She made it safely back with a grand story." Mrs. Rendall's lips curve in fond recollection. "That is the sort of child she was. She might have been sent home in a terror, but she soon turned it into a story. Few people had met the new gamekeeper and now she had a fine tale to tell. How he leaped out of nowhere, this wild-haired man who cursed her in his native tongue. Each time she told the tale, it grew grander. And then . . ." Any trace of a smile evaporates. "Then, a week later, she took ill."

"Measles," Dr. Rendall says. "There was a fellow traveling through whose horse threw a shoe, and he told Nora's father how he'd come through a village where a child had died of it. He showed no symptoms himself, and the Glasses thought little of it. Nora had been in the blacksmith shop with the man. She loved to speak to travelers and hear their stories."

"He was infected, simply not showing symptoms," I guess. "She caught the measles from him."

Dr. Rendall nods. "One of her younger brothers also came down with it soon after. He survived. Nora did not."

I glance at Gray. I'm missing something in this story if the villagers blame Cranston for Nora's death.

"Do people think she caught it from the gamekeeper?" I ask.

"In . . . a manner of speaking," Dr. Rendall says.

Mrs. Rendall shifts in her seat, obviously uncomfortable. "Some believe he cursed her."

"Cursed? Oh."

She'd said Nora told stories of Müller cursing her in his native tongue. I'd interpreted that to mean swearing at her.

When the Rendalls don't elaborate, Gray says, "A village like this would not see many people who speak another language. There is always . . . suspicion."

Mrs. Rendall sighs. "Dr. Gray is being polite. I suspect he has been the victim of such suspicion himself. People here often never travel more than a few miles from their home. They only see others like them, and they respond poorly to all outsiders, but particularly those who do not look or sound like their neighbors. Nora did not mean any harm. I do not even think she believed he was uttering curses."

"She embellished her story for the audience," I say. "He shouted at her in another language, and since she didn't know what he was saying, it would be easy to claim he cursed her. Dramatic license."

"Dramatic . . . ? Oh, yes. I see. That is it precisely. She meant no harm, and it would have fallen on the adults to gently tell her that she ought not to interpret a foreign tongue in such a way. But even those with a greater knowledge of the world might not have seen the harm in it. She was a child having a child's fun."

"Which took a sinister turn after her death."

Mrs. Rendall squeezes her hands in her lap again. "I know how this must look to you and Dr. Gray. The simple countryfolk and their wild superstitions."

"Not at all," Gray says smoothly. "There are as many superstitions in the city. A young girl died, and people want answers. I have seen that both as a doctor and an undertaker. Those in medicine understand"—he glances at me—"to some degree how diseases are transmitted, though we still have much to learn. Yet we have a history filled with people trying most desperately to explain what often seems supernatural in origin."

Dr. Rendall nods. "The answers we have are too new for most people. They grew up believing miasmas caused illness, and that is what they continue to believe. While most no longer believe in curses, it only takes the tragic death of a child to resurrect old fears and beliefs."

"Progress comes slowly," Gray says. "Set back, as you say, in the face of tragedy."

"So people thought," I say, "that the gamekeeper—Mr. Müller—cursed Nora."

"*Some* people," Mrs. Rendall says firmly. "Most knew better."

"But the note seems to blame Mr. Cranston for her death."

"Mr. Cranston is . . . not a popular figure in town," Dr. Rendall says carefully.

"We have heard that. In this case, he is responsible for bringing Mr. Müller—and letting Mr. Hall go—and so if Mr. Müller cursed Nora, her death would be Mr. Cranston's fault."

"I presume that is the thinking."

I glance at Gray. While part of me wants to pursue this lead, Sinclair's murder is not our investigation. Also, the Rendalls are already uncomfortable with the note. They're worried that Ross will jump on it and blame one of the locals for murdering Sinclair. Which means I can't ask whether they think it's possible.

Is it possible? Suspicion and resentment have had time to fester. Someone might have decided to avenge Nora. Her father is the blacksmith. That means he's going to be a guy with some muscles, one who could easily have cracked open Sinclair's skull.

"Do you have anything more to add, Miss Mitchell?" Gray prompts.

I shake my head.

It should be a lively coach ride back to the estate. With the postmortem, the note, and the story behind the note, our brains should be percolating and boiling over in a rush of words, Gray and me bouncing ideas off each other and zooming through all the implications.

Except this isn't our case.

Oh, it's never "our" case. It's always McCreadie's. Yet we happily gather information for him, knowing he'll use it. With Ross, we can't be sure of that. Hell, we can't be sure he won't discard evidence just because *we* uncovered it.

Finally, as we reach the long road into the estate grounds, I say, "I think it's best if you speak to Ross directly, instead of giving him your findings through Hugh."

"Yes."

When I lapse into silence, he gives me a sidelong look. "You want to say more."

"No, that's it."

"Mallory . . ." He tilts his head down to catch my eye. "You fear insulting me by advising me on how to best deal with Constable Ross. My manner can seem haughty, even imperious, to those inclined to see that in me. The perils of being partially raised by Annis."

I have to laugh at that. "True. But in her case, she actually *is* haughty and imperious."

"Perhaps *you* should speak to the constable?"

I shake my head. "He's sensitive about anything he perceives as big-city folks looking down on villagers. He'd interpret it as you sending your assistant because he's not worth your time."

"You are suggesting I speak to him the way you speak to Addington. Behave as if I think he has the situation under control when I know he does not."

"Addington buys it. I think Ross will, too." I gaze out the window at the passing valleys. "I'd like to take a look at Archie's collection of shillelaghs. Do you see any issues with that? I'd rather not set Ross on that trail until I've taken a look."

"Because he might see a bit of blood on one and helpfully clean it with his handkerchief?"

I shudder. Then I lean toward the window. "Is that Hugh and Isla?"

Gray moves to look out. Two figures sit on a bench by the smallest lake.

"It does appear to be," he says. "Shall we stop and speak to them?"

I give him a hard look. "Your sister is alone with Hugh, in a pretty and romantic setting, the two of them engrossed in private conversation. Are you seriously asking whether we should interrupt?"

"Er. Yes. I see. I will leave them to it."

"You'd better," I say with a glare.

His lips twitch. "I would say that you are wonderfully protective of your friends, but I cannot help but wonder, in this case, how much is protecting them and how much is indulging your hidden hope to see romance blossom."

He's teasing me—and he clearly means my hope with Hugh and Isla—but it recalls too much of that conversation I just had with Simon, and I shift in my seat. Then I cover it with a roll of my eyes. "Hidden hope? My hopes for those two are not at all hidden. At least not from the guy who shares them. You would like to see some movement there, yes?"

He sighs dramatically. "I have been waiting for *years* to see some movement there. I know they cannot be rushed, particularly with Isla's widowhood, but they are taking a damnable long time to get to it."

He glances out to watch them as they disappear from view. "In full confession, I had even entertained hopes that this shared getaway—to a wedding no less—might spur them along. Which only proves I am terribly obtuse when it comes to evaluating emotional situations."

I smile. "Hoping your sister hooks up with Hugh at his sister's wedding . . . with his ex-fiancée in attendance?"

"Define 'hook up'? I am beginning to think I understand what it means, but when you put it in that context, I wonder whether I'm wrong."

"Nah, you just hope you're wrong because you're a very proper Victorian who wishes for his sister to have a very proper romance, which will end in a very proper marriage."

His eyes narrow. "Now you are mocking me."

"Perish the thought." I lean back. "I would only mock you if you were startled by the thought of your widowed sister having an affair. It is not as if you've done any such thing yourself with widowed women."

Color touches his cheeks as his eyes narrow more.

I continue, "Your sister will do what she wants, and if you hope to see her happily married, I might remind you that she has been married, and it was not happy. That can have a . . . chilling effect."

He thumps back in his seat. "I had not considered that. You are right, of course." He gazes out the window. "You are also correct that I am being hypocritical. In my defense, I would not begrudge Isla any joy, including an affair. But yes, my ultimate hope would be to see her in a happy marriage. Not because I think women should be married, but as compensation of a sort. Making up for the hell Lawrence put her through." He looks at me. "Is that patronizing?"

I reach to touch his knee, my fingers barely grazing it. "No, it's kindness and caring. In the end, it might be what Isla wants, but don't be surprised if it's not. My bigger concern is that, if it's what Hugh wants and she refuses . . ." I pull back and shake my head. "That's putting the cart well before the horse, and also none of my business."

"As we both want the best for them, I believe we can consider their happiness our business. Thank you for pointing out that she may be hesitant."

I nod. "She's gun-shy. I'm not sure that's a saying here but—"

"Dr. Gray! Mallory!" A voice comes from outside the partially open window. We're drawing up on the house, and Fiona is running toward us, skirts hiked, Violet following at a brisk walk.

Gray raps the roof for Simon to stop, and he barely has the door open before Fiona is there.

"Have you seen Hugh?" she says. "I cannot find him anywhere, and we need him immediately."

Gray and I glance at each other, neither quick to say McCreadie is with Isla.

Fiona doesn't wait for an answer. "His boots are gone, and he did not tell anyone he was leaving, and we need him now."

"What has happened?" Gray asks.

"That man—that constable." Fiona spits the words, her hazel eyes flashing. "That insufferable fool has . . . has . . ."

She seems unable to get the words out in her anger, sputtering until Violet moves up beside her.

"Constable Ross has taken Archie," Violet says. "He has arrested him for Ezra's murder."

NINETEEN

We are heading out with only Violet. She managed to steer Fiona back into the house, telling her she needed to be there in case McCreadie returned. I breathe a sigh of relief at that. Fiona is adorable, even in her fury . . . though I'm sure she'd hate me saying that. Her fury, though, also means she's not the best person to calmly tell us what happened, and she's not likely to stay silent while Violet explains.

Once Fiona is gone, Gray seems to realize where we are going and looks over at me in alarm. I shake my head, hoping he'll correctly interpret that to mean I'm aware and will handle it. I'm not leading Violet to where Isla and McCreadie are sharing a private moment. I wouldn't do that to any of them.

"Archie went without complaint?" Gray asks as we walk down the road toward the ponds.

"I do not believe my brother is capable of doing anything without complaint," she says tartly. Then her voice drops. "Except agreeing to marry Fiona. That surprised me. I thought he would bluster and rage and refuse. He did not. He knew . . ."

Her fingers press into her skirt in a smoothing gesture. "It was necessary, and he did it, and it was the same here. In this case, he initially objected. As did I. Fiona objected most strenuously. Even Mrs. Hall came out to see what was the matter and told Constable Ross he was making a mistake. But Archie's protests were the least strident. He calmed us and told us Hugh would set this straight and he would be fine."

I certainly hope so, though I bite my tongue and let Gray continue the questions.

"Do we know why Constable Ross arrested him?" Gray asks.

"That is the worst of it," Violet says. "At least if the constable had found some evidence that seemed to indicate Archie was responsible, I would understand why he felt the need to arrest him. The constable is young and new at his job, and in his enthusiasm, he could be forgiven for making a mistake." She glances over at us. "It was the coat."

"The . . . ?" Gray says.

"The coat Ezra was wearing when he died."

"Archie's coat?"

"Exactly. That is the proof that Archie killed him."

"I . . . do not understand."

Violet gives a humorless laugh. "No one does. Except, apparently, Constable Ross. Oh, and Edith. Edith Frye is convinced he is correct. That woman does not have the sense God gave a gnat. No, that is wrong. She has a gnat's full measure of sense, along with the cruelty of a jackal, always sniffing about, looking for trouble, delighted when she finds it." Violet pauses, her cheeks flushing as she glances at me. "My apologies, Miss Mitchell. That was rude and petty. I am overly distraught."

"You are understandably distraught," I say. "As for Mrs. Frye, I suspect that comparison does a disservice to jackals."

She covers her mouth against a snorting laugh. "Yes, I ought not to disparage jackals. Or gnats. As for the coat, Constable Ross says that is the cause of the murder. It is a very fine coat, you see."

"It is," I say.

"And being a fine coat, Archie would be furious at Ezra borrowing it. Driven to a blind rage, seeing his oldest and dearest friend out for a walk, dressed in *his* coat."

"So his theory is that Mr. Cranston killed Mr. Sinclair for wearing his coat?"

"But of course."

It takes me a moment to find words. Then I say, "I can understand that

Constable Ross does not know Mr. Cranston, but even if *anyone* would murder a friend for borrowing a piece of clothing, what about the fact it was the middle of the night? Did Mr. Cranston wake with the dread feeling that his coat was not where it should be, thunder downstairs, find it missing, and storm out at night determined to apprehend the thief? And then happen to find him, on an estate of hundreds of acres? Realize it's his best friend . . . and still kill him?"

Violet's lips twitch. "Fiona is right, Miss Mitchell. You are a very fine detective in your own right." She slows. "Did that sound superior of me?"

"It did not. As for being a fine detective, I'd like to think I'm growing into a decent one, but this is common sense." I rein in my outrage and take a moment to consider it all. "Not to give Constable Ross too much credit, but I suppose, given that Mr. Sinclair was struck from the rear, he could argue that Mr. Cranston didn't know who he was hitting."

"Yes, I suppose we must allow that would not be as outrageous as killing his best friend over a borrowed coat. Constable Ross believes Archie wanted to go for a walk, found it missing, went out and saw a shadowy figure wearing his coat. Given Archie's problems with the locals, he presumed it was one of them and, outraged, hit the man, intending only to injure him. To his horror, he discovered he had killed his best friend."

She takes two more steps and then adds, "I will even credit Constable Ross's imagination here. If the accused were not my brother, I would think it an excellent tragic tale."

Gray says to me, "I understand that Archie may seem exactly the sort of man who would lose his temper and strike someone. But he is not."

"Full of sound and fury," I say.

"Signifying nothing?" Violet smiles over at me. "You know your Shakespeare."

"I am disturbingly fond of *Macbeth*, as my father always said."

That makes her laugh. "I have heard others say it is a warning about overly ambitious women, but I have always seen it as a warning about what happens to women who have no way to exercise their ambitions, except through their husbands. As for Archie, you are both correct. In the more colloquial sense, I would say he is all bark and no bite. He has no taste for physical violence, either in a fit of temper or as a bit of masculine fun." She glances at Gray and smiles warmly. "Hugh once said you enjoy fisticuffs, and I thought that did not suit you at all. Likewise, I believe, an aversion to it does not suit my brother."

"Yet he is averse to it," Gray says. "He never engaged in schoolyard rough-and-tumble."

I step over a fallen branch. "And while the theory seems plausible on the surface, I cannot imagine anyone finding their coat gone and presuming someone broke in and stole it. Any normal person would assume they'd either misplaced it or someone borrowed it. Also, this morning, Mr. Cranston said Mr. Sinclair was in the habit of borrowing his coat. That would be his first thought if he found it missing. I'll need to tell Constable Ross about that." I gaze out along the road and think. "Or, no, I actually shouldn't or he might decide Mr. Cranston was establishing an alibi."

"Yes, I would not give his imagination any more fodder," Violet says. "However, Fiona and I have both heard Archie grumbling at Ezra for borrowing his coat. We can tell Constable Ross that . . . without the grumbling part. We can establish the borrowing as normal behavior, one that did not truly bother Archie."

"There is also the matter of the coat itself," Gray says. "It is very distinctive. I fear it was not a coincidence that Ezra was attacked while wearing it."

Violet shivers. "You believe my brother was the target."

"Which means the killer would not be Archie," Gray says. "Archie realizes he was the likely target, which may explain why he did not protest too much about being taken into custody."

"Because he'll be safer there," I say.

"Yes."

I slow my steps. "Do you remember which lake we saw Hugh sitting at? I thought it was the largest one, but now I am second-guessing. There are several that look similar."

I swear I hear Gray's exhale of relief, as he realizes my plan for keeping Violet from stumbling on McCreadie and Isla.

"I thought it was the largest one, as well," he says. "That is just to our left up here. Why don't you and Violet take a look at that one, while I check the next?"

"Excellent idea."

I lead Violet to the largest lake, which is definitely not the one where we saw McCreadie and Isla. Gray continues along at a brisk walk toward the correct one, about a quarter mile down.

Violet and I round the lake, being careful to stay on the path. We've come full circle when Gray and McCreadie appear by the road, Isla nowhere in sight. We join them, and as soon as we draw close, McCreadie's grim expression says Gray has already filled him in.

McCreadie's attention goes straight to Violet. "We will get this sorted."

Her lower lip wobbles, but she pulls it in and straightens with a stiff nod.

"I am sorry, Violet," he says softly. "I am truly sorry."

Her gaze lifts to his and her knees wobble. He reaches out, and she falls against his shoulder and begins to cry.

We're at the house now. Violet's breakdown had been so brief that I wouldn't even call it a breakdown. She allowed her composure to crack just long enough to show how she really felt about all this. Then she gathered it up again with red cheeks and murmured apologies, and insisted we return to the house before Fiona came looking for us.

When we get there, Isla is coming down the stairs, as if she'd been up there the whole time. She even has a book in her hand.

McCreadie ushers everyone into the largest of the sitting rooms. We all take seats and, for a moment, there's an odd silence, as if we're all waiting for something.

Waiting for Cranston, I realize. He might be loud and even obnoxious, but he's the sort of person that others acknowledge as leader without realizing it.

Now we've settled, and everyone waits for their host to come rolling in and take over. McCreadie seems to realize that at the same time I do, and he rises, clearing his throat.

"We are all aware of what has happened," he says. "First, let me assure you that the charges should not stand. There is a long way to go between arresting a fellow and convicting him of a crime, and whatever First Constable Ross's position in the village, he should still concede to the higher authority of the law."

There are two "should"s in that speech. I don't know whether McCreadie has intentionally chosen that word, but I feel the full weight of it. He isn't saying the charge *will* not stand or that Ross *will* bow to the authority of law.

Only Isla catches the nuance. Her lips tighten in worry. The others hear what they want to hear. Reassurances that all will be well.

"So how do we go about correcting this?" Fiona asks her brother. "Do you send a letter to the courts in Edinburgh, asking them to take over the case? Or to the police office, asking that you be allowed to replace Mr. Ross?"

"I have no jurisdiction here, and a higher court cannot intervene at this early stage. But we must remember that it *is* an early stage. While I could speak to First Constable Ross and try to convince him that his reasoning is unsound, I fear that might misfire."

"Misfire?" Fiona says. "How?"

When McCreadie is slow to answer, I say, "Detective McCreadie already offered his assistance in the gentlest way possible, and Constable Ross took offense."

"He is young and ambitious," Gray says. "He wants to do this on his own, and I agree with both Hugh and Miss Mitchell. He could do more than refuse to listen."

"He could dig in his heels," Violet says. "Determined to prove he is correct."

"So we give him another suspect," Fiona says. "The actual killer." She looks at her brother. "If Mr. Ross thinks he has his culprit, then you are free to discover who really murdered Ezra. I do not like the idea of Archie being kept in custody, though. Is that what they will do? Put him in the local prison?"

"I doubt there is a local prison," McCreadie says. "I will need to find out where they are holding him."

"I will handle that," Fiona says firmly. "You need to solve the case. You and Duncan and Mallory and Isla." She tries for a smile, but it's strained. "That is what you do, is it not?"

McCreadie falls silent for a moment. Then he says, carefully, "Of course I will investigate, and that will be easier without First Constable Ross about. We will need to tread with caution, though. If he learns of it, that may be the thing that sets him more firmly on his course."

"Then he shall not learn of it," Fiona says. "He believes he has his man, and he gave no indication that he intended to return even to gather evidence. Violet and I will see to Archie. We will discover where he is being kept and protest against his incarceration, which will throw Mr. Ross off the trail."

"Clever," Violet murmurs. "With his suspect's sister and fiancée wailing, he will believe we have all accepted Archie's arrest as fait accompli."

"And if he grows suspicious," Fiona says, "I will wail and rail louder to distract him."

McCreadie raises a hand. "As long as you do not distract him from continuing the investigation himself. It would be better for all if he did so and discovered the true culprit—or at least discovers that he is mistaken about Archie."

"Unless he is not."

Everyone follows that voice to the woman in the corner. Edith Frye. Beside her, James shifts in his seat and takes great interest in a mounted deer head.

"Well?" Edith says. "Are we all going to ignore the elephant in this room? The possibility—nay, the *probability*—that the young constable is correct?"

"And Archie murdered his best friend for borrowing his coat?" Fiona says. "Does that make sense to anyone?"

McCreadie clears his throat. "The theory, as I understand it, is that Archie did not know it was Ezra and did not intend to kill the thief. As Archie's friend, I do not think that is what happened. As a criminal officer investigating a murder, I must consider all possibilities."

"Fine," Edith says. "You can consider it. We wish you all the best with this little mystery game, but we came for a wedding and the groom is in jail. So we will be going." She rises. "Come, James. I will have our girl pack while you tell the groom to ready the horse."

"That will not be possible," McCreadie says.

Edith turns to him, her eyes narrowing. "What will not be possible?"

"Leaving. Or, perhaps I should say, I do not recommend it."

She snorts. "I don't give a fig what you recommend."

"But you should because if I prove Archie did not do it, then Constable Ross needs to reopen the investigation, and he will discover that two people left the house in a terrible hurry."

Edith stares at him. "Are you accusing me of killing Ezra?"

McCreadie gives the most casually elegant of shrugs. "I accuse no one without proof. However, I certainly will investigate you. As for First Constable Ross, I doubt he will consider you a viable suspect. James, though?" He turns to the other man. "There has always been friction between you and Ezra."

"Wh-what?" Frye says.

"Friction. Jealousy. You look up to Archie. Always have. You took up with Edith after—" McCreadie clears his throat. "Yet despite your admiration, you could never wedge Ezra from his side. You invested heavily in Archie's whisky company, proving your support and loyalty, and still he chose Ezra to be his best man."

Frye's mouth works. "That's not—I—"

"Also, you argued with him last night. We all heard it."

"That was *business*."

"I am not saying your actions are suspicious. Only that they may be seen as such to an outsider, such as Constable Ross. I would suggest you stay to show you have nothing to fear, but that is up to you."

McCreadie turns to Violet. "On that note, I fear I must also ask you to keep your parents from joining us, if that is possible. I understand they may wish to support Archie, but more people in the house will only hamper the investigation. They will also have questions, understandably."

Violet nods. "They will question the investigation, you mean. *Your* investigation specifically, given . . ." She swallows and straightens. "There will be friction that we can ill afford. I will not tell them that Archie has been arrested. That would bring them running. But after Ezra's death, Archie postponed sending a coach for them. I will now send a letter telling them of that and saying they must stay a while longer."

"Thank you. Fiona? Will you add a letter to our parents, please?" A twist of a smile. "Probably best coming from you."

"Of course."

"We shall begin with that, after which I will interview each of you, to properly construct the timeline. I apologize if you have already given that information to First Constable Ross."

Fiona snorts. "We gave nothing to him, as he requested nothing from us. Yes, Violet and I will pen our letters, and then come speak to you when we are done."

TWENTY

I don't sit in on the interviews, partly because McCreadie and Gray don't need my help and partly because it seems a very boring way to spend the next couple of hours. Or maybe that's the same reason.

I have other avenues to pursue. I start with Cranston's collection of shillelaghs. They're kept in the cloakroom, which is actually more like a sitting room. It's about ten feet square and includes wardrobes for hanging cloaks and coats and other outerwear. It also has a few low settees, which are useful for taking boots on and off, but also seem to be designed for sitting. This isn't unique to Cranston's estate. I've seen these in other big houses, where they seem to be a spot where you can comfortably transition from outerwear to innerwear and freshen up a bit. Most have mirrors. Some even have a washbasin.

The shillelaghs are arranged in stands, both for decoration and utility. The utility being as walking sticks rather than weapons, but the room *is* conveniently close to the door, in case of invasion.

I'd noticed the shillelaghs yesterday, and while Isla had taken her time changing out of her boots, I'd examined and admired the walking-stick clubs. I know a bit about shillelaghs, mostly from a case back home where one had been used in an assault, prompting me to do some research. As with anything that catches my interest, I delved in deeper than I needed to. I even have a shillelagh back in my Vancouver condo, a gift from colleagues, that assault being the first case I cleared as a detective.

Shillelaghs are sometimes made from oak, but that's rare enough in Ireland that blackthorn is more commonly used. I will admit that I thought blackthorn was a tree until I came to Scotland and discovered it's a shrub. It's also known as sloe, and if I'd known that, I'd have realized it was a shrub, sloe berries being used for sloe gin.

The fact that it's a bush explains the signature knotty look of a shillelagh. It's a long and relatively slender stick with a thick knob at the end. Traditionally, the stick is cured in a chimney, for up to a year, turning the blackthorn literally black. The club is then polished and oiled, and sometimes, to add a little extra heft, that knobby end is filled with molten lead.

Yesterday, I didn't count how many shillelaghs Cranston had in the cloakroom, but now that I'm examining them, I don't think any are missing. Each of the three stands holds four, and I recall seeing two empty slots. So space for twelve shillelaghs but only ten in the collection.

I make my way around each stand. With gloved hands, I carefully lift each shillelagh to examine it. Of the ten, six have smooth rounded or cylindrical ends that wouldn't have made the mark left in Sinclair's skull. The knots on two are too shallow for the wound. The final two have the sort of knotty ends that would work.

I'm turning one over in my hands when someone clears their throat behind me. The housekeeper, Mrs. Hall, stands there, her hands on her hips.

"What might you be doing, lassie?" she says. "If you're thinking of taking one of those for a stroll, think again. They belong to Mr. Cranston, and I'll not be having anyone take them out while he is not at home."

"I'm not looking for a walking stick," I say. "I am helping Dr. Gray and Detective McCreadie, who are trying to free Mr. Cranston."

Her gaze goes from me to the shillelagh, with a look that clearly asks how the walking sticks are connected to that.

"I'm looking for anything of value that might be missing from the estate," I say. "Are these all accounted for?"

"Yes," she says. "Mr. Cranston is still adding to the collection. That is why there are two empty spaces."

"Do they get used as walking sticks?"

"Sometimes. By Mr. Cranston and Mr. Sinclair, mostly." She lowers her hands from her hips and sighs. "Petey Ross is a fool. Always has been.

Always will be. His grandfather was a fine constable, but sometimes, when folks reach an age, they declare they are done with work. They want to be done so quickly they cannot bother passing on what they know."

"The senior Constable Ross didn't properly train his grandson."

"The boy could get help from constables in other towns. But no, he must do it all himself." She moves to straighten a shillelagh. "Embarrassing, it is. Makes us all look like simpletons. Typical village folk who do not know their arse from their elbow. And now look at what he's done. There's a fine detective in the house, and Petey ignores him and arrests the master. The *master*."

"And that is . . . embarrassing?" I venture.

"No," she snaps. "It is ridiculous. Mr. Cranston killing Mr. Sinclair over a borrowed coat? Mr. Sinclair took it all the time." Her lips tighten. "I had half a mind to hide it from him. It's a fine coat, and he had his own, but all Mr. Cranston would do is grumble because he is not the sort to actually complain about such a thing. Kill him for it? Kill *anyone* for it?" She snorts. "Preposterous."

"People have killed for less."

"Oh, I don't doubt it. But not Mr. Cranston, and clearly not for a borrowed coat."

"That is what everyone says, which is why Detective McCreadie is investigating."

She stops fussing with the clubs and nods. "The detective seems a fine man. He will set this right."

"Has he spoken to you yet?" I say. "He needs to talk to everyone in the house, to establish a timeline."

"He has not, but I will be ready when he does."

"About that . . ." I lower my voice. "He's going to need to speak to your children, too."

She tenses so hard the keys on her chatelaine jangle. "My children? They do not live here."

"Dr. Gray believes they were on the property last night." *Apologies, Duncan.* "A deer was killed and partly butchered."

"And you blame my children?" Her voice rises, but there's a shrill ring of insincerity in her outrage. "They were inside all night—"

"The deer was killed with a bow, which we know they use. The footprints indicate it was your daughter—the pattern of her gait is distinctive. It took place close to where we found Mr. Sinclair."

Genuine fear touches her eyes even as they narrow. "My children were in bed—"

"We think they might have seen the killer. Or heard something. They left the stag half butchered, as if something made them beat a hasty retreat before finishing."

She gives a soft exhale, as if of relief, though her face stays stony. I'm not accusing her children of killing Sinclair. I'm enlisting them as witnesses.

I meet her gaze. "Mr. Cranston will not care about them hunting a deer if their testimony sets him free. Neither will Dr. Gray nor Detective Mc-Creadie care about the stag. It seems silly to keep all the game for one man who does not even live here."

"I will speak to them," she says. "I know nothing about any deer, and I am sure there is some mistake."

"Perhaps they were only walking and came upon the stag already dead," I say. "That seems reasonable."

"It does," she says firmly. "Whatever the situation, they will not with-hold any information that would see Mr. Cranston set free."

I hesitate, then I meet her gaze. "Not even when he is responsible for taking their father's job and turning them out of their home?"

"That was not Mr. Cranston," she says sharply. "He was misled, and the situation would have been rectified."

"Misled?"

She sweeps her skirts past me as she heads for the door. "I will speak to Detective McCreadie when he is ready for me."

After Mrs. Hall is gone, I consider everything she's said. Then I return to the shillelaghs. An examination of the two knobby ones doesn't reveal any obvious damage or trace evidence, but we'll conduct a proper exam-ination.

McCreadie and Gray are still in the large sitting room conducting their interviews. I pause outside the door long enough to hear them asking Fiona where she'd been last night. In bed, she says, which I'm going to guess will be everyone's answer.

One of the women was out there. I think back to last night, the figure I'd spotted, and I curse myself for not taking a closer look.

Could that figure have been carrying a shillelagh? Could a woman have clocked Sinclair hard enough to snap his neck and dent his skull? It depends, I think, on how angry she'd been.

If any of the women had a motive to kill Ezra Sinclair, I haven't seen it. They all treated him as a good-natured and kindhearted fellow, innocuous in every way. Especially innocuous compared to Cranston, the guy who had almost certainly been the real target.

Fiona was bristling with outrage and indignation at Cranston's arrest. Could that be a cover to disguise the fact that she was secretly relieved? That she'd failed to rid herself of a brutish bridegroom last night, but had ironically managed it despite killing the wrong person.

Mrs. Hall said she didn't blame Cranston for her family's situation, but I find that hard to believe. What would happen if he died?

What about Edith? She'd been upset with Cranston over the investment, and they did have a romantic past.

The only one I can't find a motive for is Violet, but that doesn't mean she didn't have one.

But just because a woman was out last night doesn't make her a killer. I'd been out, too.

Could Sinclair have been having an affair with one of the women? Maybe Fiona? Sinclair had gone out of his way to be kind to her, as one might to the young bride of his best friend. He'd been solicitous and quick to include her in conversations, which is too risky if they were hiding an affair.

For Fiona's part, there were no shy or flirty glances. She was friendly and relaxed around Sinclair, just as she was around Gray. Friends of her older brother and her fiancé, nothing more.

If someone had been meeting Sinclair for romance, I'd say it was Violet. They're both single, attractive, quietly decent and intelligent people, who've known each other for decades. On paper, they'd make a good match, but that can be awkward if the guy is your brother's best friend. Just look at Isla and McCreadie's excruciatingly slow dance.

I think back to how Violet and Sinclair have behaved around each other. Sinclair has been friendly, but Violet never initiated conversation with him.

In fact, when I think about it, she'd seemed to distance herself from him, walking with others, sitting near others. Far from being proof of disinterest, a careful distance between the two could mean they were having a secret affair.

These thoughts preoccupy me as I head outside for the stable. I need time alone with my detective brain, and I'll use that opportunity to visit guests who won't interrupt my thoughts—the wildcat kittens.

They're being tended in the barn. When Fiona asked to keep them there, Cranston had only hesitated, as if thinking it through. Fiona hadn't seemed the least concerned that he'd say no, but Sinclair had leapt in to her "defense." I got the feeling that had irritated Cranston, as if he'd expected his best friend to know—as Fiona seemed to—that he was thinking it through, rather than preparing to refuse. In the end, Cranston had not only allowed it but given her a prime spot: a tiny storage room in the half-empty hayloft.

I climb the ladder to the loft and discover Alice coaxing the injured kitten to eat.

Seeing me, she rises, smoothing her skirt. "Does Mrs. Ballantyne need me?"

"No, I just came to see the kittens. How's our little patient doing?"

She lowers herself to the floor again. "She is not eating, and Miss Mc-Creadie said I could help with the feeding."

"Her leg is probably hurting, and she's likely confused by that."

"That is what Miss McCreadie said."

"Dr. Gray has pain medication. A wee bit could help her find her appetite." I stroke the kitten's back and she manages a purr. "Would you like me to ask him?"

"Yes, please. Also . . ." She lowers her gaze as she holds the mash to the kitten's mouth. "It would be easier to care for her in the house."

"Ah."

"I know wildcats are not pets, but she is a patient, and Miss McCreadie says she will likely never be able to be released anyway."

"There are three-legged cats in the wild, but usually they are grown cats who lost a leg to injury and adjusted, having already learned to hunt."

"We could keep her in our room. Then I could nurse her properly and be there during the night. I cannot come out here after dark."

"I will speak to . . ." I trail off, not sure who I'd speak to. The owner of the house in police custody? Fiona, the not yet lady of the house? I could also ask Violet, as the owner's sister, but that might put her in a bad spot between her brother and his fiancée.

"I will speak to Fiona," I say. "She might, however, need to check with Mrs. Hall."

Alice's face fell. "Mrs. Hall will not allow it."

I smile. "I get the sense Mrs. Hall likes Fiona, and that it will be like Isla asking Mrs. Wallace."

A faint smile touches Alice's face. "Mrs. Wallace would say yes, even if she grumbled about it."

I promise to speak to Fiona. Then I take a few moments to linger and play with the two males. Alice is too intent on feeding their injured sister to pay me any mind, which allows me to fall into my thoughts.

Those thoughts turn to the kittens. Who murdered their mother? Müller. I'm reasonably sure of that, but it also makes me wonder whether there could be any connections between that murder and Sinclair's.

It feels as if these two deaths should *be* linked. One morning, we find a dead wildcat placed in a trap after being poisoned. The next morning, we find a dead man murdered, likely after being mistaken for the estate owner.

There's no obvious connection. It's not as if the wildcat was a trial run. Sinclair certainly didn't die because he realized the cat had been poisoned—no one's committing homicide to cover up felicide.

Maybe a connection isn't so ridiculous, though. Perhaps the wildcat's death led to a cascade of events that ended in Sinclair's murder.

Cranston realizes Müller poisoned the cat, and he's livid . . . especially knowing how Fiona would react if she found out. Cranston confronts Müller. Tells him he's sacked. Müller sees what he thinks is Cranston walking around that night and takes matters into his own hands. If Cranston is dead, no one will know he fired Müller.

Or Sinclair figures out that Müller killed the cat, and he's equally livid, since Sinclair recommended Müller for the job. He goes out at night and confronts Müller. Sinclair threatens to tell Cranston, and when he turns around, Müller clocks him.

Yep, I have a lot of theories, but I feel as if I've jumped ahead to take the midterm after only attending half the lectures. I need to slow down and accumulate more data, starting with talking to my partners in crime-solving.

TWENTY-ONE

I'm nearly at the house when I hear Gray's low voice. Now, some people tease that I am particularly attuned to the sound of his voice. Maybe. Probably.

I follow that voice into the garden, where I find McCreadie and Gray in quiet conversation.

"A post-interview analysis, and you didn't invite me?" I say.

Gray fixes me with a mock glare. "Perhaps because you abandoned us and went haring off in search of more interesting leads."

"Mmm. Guilty. So did you find anything?"

McCreadie shakes his head. "We are taking a break from the tedium. The stories are all the same. They were in their beds last night from dusk until dawn. They did not hear Ezra or anyone else leave. They saw nothing. They know nothing. They certainly do not know why anyone would want Ezra Sinclair dead. Now Archie on the other hand . . ." He sighs. "I am glad Archie is not around to overhear his friends and family list all the people who might wish him harm."

"But it's good that he's not here," I say, "so they feel free to speak plainly."

"True. But even then, the prevailing theory is that the killer only took a swing at the person they presumed to be Archie, reacting in anger, with no wish to kill him."

"Except they took a swing at him with more than their fist, which implies real rage, whether the intent was to kill or not." I move closer and lower my voice. "To that end, I have examined the shillelaghs. According to Mrs. Hall, none are missing. Unless she's the killer and is just saying that."

"But the number of them could be easily verified with Archie," Gray says.

McCreadie raises a finger. "Unless Mrs. Hall knows one is missing and is covering for Archie, who will agree that yes, they are all accounted for."

"Anyway . . ." I say. "They all seem to be there, and two fit as possible murder weapons. We'll want to examine them for forensic evidence. I'll let someone else ask Mrs. Hall."

"Hugh can do that," Gray says. "But he will *inform* her, not ask her."

McCreadie shakes his head. "And here is why I should indeed be the one to speak to her. Because I know to phrase it as a question, even if it is not."

"Also, you're the nice one," I say.

McCreadie sighs. "That will go on my grave, I fear. 'Here lies Hugh McCreadie. The nice one.'"

"Not to aim that joke at poor Ezra but was he *really* the nice one?" I ask. "Is it possible he had a dark side?"

McCreadie bursts out laughing. "I fear not. Though it may have made him more interesting." His face twists in a grimace. "That was unspeakably rude. And perhaps self-insulting, as I just admitted to being the nice one myself. But Ezra was best known as Archie Cranston's friend."

"As you have seen," Gray says, "Archie casts a long shadow."

"Which blotted out his friend," I say. "Archie is loud, abrasive, and larger than life. He takes charge. Everyone notices him."

"It happens," McCreadie says.

Gray's brows shoot up. "Why are you both looking at me?"

McCreadie pats his arm. "You are never loud."

"I realize I can be difficult at times, but I do not think I am abrasive."

"Fine-grit sandpaper," I say. "Archie is coarse-grit." I raise a hand against Gray's protest. "Fine-grit smooths and polishes. Take it as a compliment. You are only as abrasive as you need to be."

Gray grumbles under his breath.

"Back to the shillelaghs, I'm guessing you do want to examine them, Duncan?"

He turns a hard look on me. "You're distracting me with science treats."

"Now, now, no need to get abrasive."

McCreadie lifts his hands. "I am removing myself from the line of fire and speaking to Mrs. Hall about the shillelaghs. I will meet you in the parlor, as we seem to have commandeered it for our police office."

When he's gone, I look at Gray. "Do you know where I could find Fiona?"

"I am not certain I can answer that without being abrasive."

I smile up at him. "I like your abrasive bits. They are one of the many things that make you interesting."

Spots of color touch his cheeks as he shakes his head. "You do that to disarm me."

"Do what?"

"Compliment me."

"Would you rather I needle you some more?"

"I am not certain," he says as he turns back to the house. As he walks away, he murmurs, under his breath, as if I'm not supposed to hear it, "I rather like that too much as well."

First, we track down Fiona, who is in the yard playing croquet with the other women. I take her aside before asking about moving the injured kitten—otherwise, I envision Edith flying into a tizzy at the thought of an animal in the house. Fiona says the move sounds like an excellent idea, and she excuses herself from the game to speak to Mrs. Hall.

A few minutes later, Gray and I have the suspect shillelaghs in the parlor. What we don't have? Gray or Isla's laboratory equipment. We don't even have a magnifying glass.

McCreadie brought us the shillelaghs and then had to go interview the staff. I've told him about Simon and Cranston's valet. Better that he's prepared for that revelation.

Now Gray and I are standing at a table we pulled into the middle of the room. The shillelaghs rest atop a white linen cloth. Testing for DNA is out of the question, obviously. We shook the clubs over the cloth first, in case any dirt or hairs fell off. Nothing did, and I'm not sure how useful that would be. Useful in the sense it would suggest the shillelagh might have been used to kill Sinclair, but any detritus could also be from its use as a walking stick, and without a microscope, we lack a way to compare dirt or hairs.

In this era, checking for blood requires a microscope. There's no luminol or other tests. I'm still trying to figure out how to rig up a black light, if that's even possible. The hack I know—wrap colored cellophane around a flashlight—doesn't work without cellophane or flashlights.

"We could rub it with a cloth and see whether any blood comes off," I say. That's not exactly hard science, but even if we did find blood, we're decades from being able to analyze it. We can only say that the object seems to have blood on it.

"We will likely need to do that," he says. "First, though, we will want to examine it for signs of damage. I do not see any with the naked eye, but let us take a closer look with a lamp."

"Is it possible to make a magnifying glass? I did that as a kid, using the base of a plastic bottle and a drop of water, but you guys haven't invented plastic, and we can't easily cut glass."

He considers. "True, but the principle should work. It's the convex surface of the magnifying glass or the droplet that we require. Let us hunt down a glass bottle and some water."

With the bottle and the water, we're able to test several ways of magnifying the surface of the shillelaghs. While a drop of water works for a very limited area, it does mean we're wetting a surface that may contain evidence. Putting water in the glass bottle gives us a less magnified view, but a much larger surface, without the risk of washing away trace.

When I heartily wish for the concentrated beam of a flashlight, Gray fashions a cone for the lamp, which allows for a much brighter light source. As much as I long for my old equipment, I have to admit there is magic in this, hearkening back to childhood, figuring out the world and the science behind it.

So we have our makeshift magnifier and our makeshift flashlight and . . .

"Nothing," I say, sighing dramatically. "All that, and we still didn't find anything to suggest that either of these clubs were the murder weapon. Even rubbing the ends with a cloth didn't reveal traces of blood."

"I am sorry," Gray says. "I know it was disappointing."

"Kinda fun though." I sneak him a smile. "Even if it is a waste of valuable time."

"But is our time so valuable?" He sets the lamp down on a side table. "Unless you would rather have been playing croquet . . ."

I shudder. "Now, if I were playing croquet with you and Hugh and Isla, it'd be fun, but not with Edith." I place the water jar by the lantern.

"Also, one could say it was a valuable use of our time in the sense that we now know how to make do in the field, if we lack the proper equipment. We spent time learning while we could afford to spend it."

"Or we learned to start carrying around a magnifying glass." I glance up at him. "I don't suppose they have portable microscopes yet?"

"Hardly."

"Yeah, not even sure that's a thing in my time." I look back at the shillelaghs. "Okay, so there's no sign of blood on these and no sign of damage that could have been caused by striking Ezra in the head. I don't know that there *would* have been damage to the clubs, though. I also don't know that there *would* have been blood from a single blow. We could have hoped for hair, but that isn't likely without damage to the wood."

"You did lift finger marks. That was cleverly done."

"Now you're just throwing me a bone." I sigh and drop onto the settee. "You know whose fingerprints I'm going to find? The guy who's been arrested, because they're his damn walking sticks, and if I find that, I need to be sure Ross doesn't find out or I'll have put the noose around Archie's neck myself."

"But what if there are other prints? Prints that have no explanation for being there?"

"That'd be a whole lot more helpful if we had any proof that one of those clubs was the actual murder weapon. I thought I was being so clever. Oh, look at that wound pattern. It could be one of those shillelaghs from the house." I sigh again.

"There might be another way to test that theory," Gray says.

"Like what?"

"Compare the pattern of bumps to the actual wound."

I straighten. "Right. We'll need to unwrap Ezra and examine . . ." I trail off as Gray pulls a piece of paper from his pocket.

As he unfolds it, my eyes narrow. "What is that?"

"A saved step," he says as he opens the paper to show a wound pattern. "Do not give me that look. Am I to be penalized for thinking ahead?"

"No, you're to be penalized for not giving me that before I started rounding up bottles and lanterns."

"But you were having so much fun. It didn't seem right to interrupt."

I make a rude gesture, and he only laughs and hands me the paper.

"Even if this matches," he says, "we would have wanted to test for the rest. And if it did not match, we would still have tested to be sure."

I snatch the paper with a sniff, and the damn man has the audacity to laugh again.

I smooth out the paper and bring the lamp back over to improve the lighting at the table. Gray waits patiently as I study the page. There are two things on it: a sketch of the wound pattern and an actual print he must have taken before the body was moved and the head wound cleaned.

It's a distinctive pattern, at least in the sense that it's not just a divot in Sinclair's scalp. There's the main indent, but also a spot on it where the weapon struck deeper and another partial deep crater on the edge of the main one.

Both shillelagh heads are roughly the same size. I'll measure them, of course, but weapon-matching is not the exact science I used to see on TV. Even Gray knows that.

Okay, I should say Gray *especially* knows that, since it's one of his main areas of research. He realized years ago that it might be possible to match wounds to weapons, and he's published several papers on it. What he's learned, though, is that there's wiggle room, mostly because, well, flesh wiggles. He can tell whether a stab was made by a kitchen knife or a switchblade. But if he has potential weapons with similar blades of slightly different sizes, he can rarely choose one with enough certainty to risk a suspect's life on it.

Likewise with blunt force trauma, it's not as if the scalp and skull took a perfect impression of the weapon. The amount of force used plays a role, as does speed, tissue elasticity, length of contact . . . These are all things I vaguely knew as a detective, but I've now actually helped Gray prove them.

Science isn't magic, and I appreciate that Gray recognizes the fallibility of his work. Putting too much faith in forensics—especially early forensics—sent many people to the gallows. Hell, it continues to send people to death row, when juries raised on *CSI* get overly excited about scientific "proof."

Even after measuring, we can only say that both shillelaghs are possible murder weapons, based on the width of their club-like ends. Then we try matching up the knobs, but that's trickier than you'd think. We end up with two possible points of impact on each shillelagh.

"I believe we require a demonstration," Gray says.

"Uh . . ."

"Stand right there, face the window, and let me club you in the back of the head. Then we can see which knobs line up correctly." He catches my look and raises his brows, eyes twinkling. "For science?"

"You believe that's a valid science experiment?"

His lips twitch. "I do. The question is whether you are committed enough to try it."

"No, it's whether *you're* committed enough. Because I'm nowhere near Ezra's height." I lift a shillelagh with my bare hand. "Turn around, Doctor."

He smiles and shakes his head. "I was joking, of course."

"He says now," I mutter. "You do realize the implications of a man threatening to hit a woman in his employ."

That smile evaporates. "I did not intend—"

"I'm kidding, but you deserved that. Okay, I get what you're saying, though. We need to test out the clubs to see which knobs would match up with a blow and whether they fit the impression. You'll need to stand in the line of fire, since you're tall enough to see the knobs when I swing the club."

He stands with his back to me. I arrange my gloved hands on the club until I find a position that would work. I swing and stop a little lower than his head, Sinclair being a couple of inches shorter.

"Okay, turn," I say.

He does and compares the knobs to the marks on the paper. He shakes his head, and we do it again with another position. Again, it's not a match.

"Those are the only two ways to swing it with the right weight," I say. "The bulb is slightly off to the side, so you need to hold it just right. Let's try the other one."

The other shillelagh has a more centered knob, but the stick is slightly bent, meaning there are only a few ways to comfortably swing it. I get a good and natural grip and feign clubbing my boss.

Gray turns, lifts the paper, and, before he can say anything, I say, "That works, right?"

"Your mind-reading is improving."

"Nope, just my Duncan-reading." I jiggle the club. "Can you come hold it and I'll take a look."

He does. I walk over, rise onto my tiptoes, and see that the knobs do indeed line up.

"One more thing." I grab a pillow and lift it. "Swing as if this is Ezra's head. I doubt height will change anything, but you might swing differently than I do."

The knobs still line up. To be absolutely certain, we dust them with some of the lead powder I'd used for fingerprinting. Yep, lead powder. I really try not to inhale.

Once that's applied, I get an impression of the club end, and it does indeed match. We set that aside for McCreadie to see and evaluate.

"Care for another experiment with the shillelagh?" Gray asks.

"Does it involve clubbing me like a baby seal?"

His brows shoot up. "Do I want to know what that means?"

"Nope. Okay, what do you want to test?"

"Height differential. We know how tall Ezra is. Now that we have what is almost certainly the murder weapon, we can test whether the killer is more likely to be my height or yours."

We rearrange furniture to get that pillow at Sinclair's head level. Then we both swing the shillelagh.

Our question isn't answered as neatly as we might have hoped. The blow came from directly behind, which is not the proper way to swing a shillelagh. The stick is intended for fighting, not sneaking up and clubbing someone. Gray's natural blow would crack down a little higher on Sinclair's head. Mine would be lower. That doesn't rule out anyone except Alice and *maybe* Violet.

We finally stop, both slightly winded.

"Okay, so we have a potential weapon and a possible height range *if* the killer used that weapon. I lifted four sets of fingerprints from it. One matched the prints we took from Ezra. Even if we identify the others, they won't point to the killer. Also, there are a whole bunch from one person, and I'm going to guess that's Archie, which doesn't help his case."

"Having a potential weapon is progress," Gray says as he dabs sweat with a handkerchief. "And while it's disappointing that we could not definitively narrow down the height of the killer, it does mean we continue to have the full range of suspects to consider."

"Not sure that's a plus," I say. "But okay. Fingerprinting can wait. It'll be useless until I have Archie's to exclude. Time to catch up with Hugh?"

"Also tea, as we seem to have missed lunch."

"Do you want me to see what's left over from lunch? Skip tea instead?"

He gives me a hard look, and I laugh and then follow him out the door.

TWENTY-TWO

We find McCreadie and tea in the same place—the largest of the sitting rooms, where everyone has gathered.

"I was about to get you," McCreadie says. "Right after I picked the best cream pastries from this tray. Oh, I do believe Mrs. Hall wanted to speak to you. I could be mistaken, but you ought to go see."

When Gray only shakes his head and sits down, Edith makes a little noise of affront, as if Gray is being incredibly rude.

"Mrs. Hall does not need to speak to him," Isla explains. "Hugh is teasing him about missing out on the pastries."

Edith makes another noise, this one clearly conveying that we all have a very odd sense of humor.

"You do not mind having tea before we talk, do you?" McCreadie says to me as he raises his cup. "Of course not. You will be in no rush to hear anything I might have to say."

I peer at him. That mood suggests he found something.

"We have something, too," I murmur as I lean toward him to take a pastry. "But I am certain you can also wait."

A pause. Then McCreadie lifts his cup and pushes back his chair. "I do hate to be rude, but Duncan, Mallory, and I must take our leave. We have business to discuss."

* * *

We take our tea and plates outside to a small wrought-iron patio table. It's breezy, but private, and we tell McCreadie what we found with the shille-laghs. He's relieved that we seem to have a murder weapon, but also points out the complications of it.

"How does this affect the possibility that the killer is not a guest or staff?" he asks.

I nibble at a petit four. "It depends. How easy would it be for someone else to get inside the house? Are the doors locked at night?"

"I do not—" McCreadie stops short. "No, that is a lie. I know the answer, from our interviews."

"Ah, yes." Gray looks at me. "Violet wants us to speak to Constable Ross and tell him to think it through. There is no logical reason for Archie to ever think someone walked in and stole his jacket."

"Because the door is locked?" I venture.

McCreadie shakes his head. "Because the house is too remote for such a thing. No one is coming all the way from the village—risking being shot by Mr. Müller—to steal a coat. However, that did make Duncan ask about the doors. She says they are not locked, for the same reason."

"Because the house is too remote, even if Archie is concerned about the villagers."

"But he is *not* concerned about them," McCreadie says. "Not truly. He is frustrated, and so he bellows and blusters."

"He could try talking to them. The issues seem to have started with the previous owner, so Archie has the chance to resolve them."

McCreadie shakes his head with a faint smile. "But bellowing and blustering is so much more fun."

"Fun?" I say. "Or more befitting his persona? A man of action. A man of privilege. A man who does not negotiate with mere peasants."

"Mmm." McCreadie leans back, his face scrunching. "That is his persona, yes, but it is not truly him."

Gray makes a small noise in his throat.

"Yes, Duncan, you and I disagree on that, but I know Archie better, and he has let me see that better side of him. You and Archie are like two alpha dogs, unwilling to cede territory, circling one another, growling and unable to see past those snarls and flashing fangs."

"I do not snarl or flash my fangs at Archie, whatever the provocation."

"*Whatever* the provocation?" McCreadie says. "I remember you taking a swing at him."

Gray sniffs. "Ancient history."

"Only because you have barely exchanged a dozen words since we left school."

I say, "I overheard Ezra saying something to Archie about learning a lesson about provoking you. What happened?"

"I threw a punch," Gray says. "Not to strike him down but to challenge him to a fight."

"And?"

"He walked away. As I said, he does not fight. Even if it meant suffering the shame of refusing."

I have to choke back a laugh. That would be mean, laughing at the obvious frustration in Gray's voice. But I'm beginning to get a deeper view of the dynamic between the two. Cranston insulting and needling while Gray takes the high road, because that's not Gray's style. Then Gray invoking his style with a challenge . . . and Cranston taking the high road and refusing.

Two alpha dogs indeed. Or more like a cat and a dog sharing the same turf, the cat endlessly provoking and toying with the dog, only to run away when the dog retaliated.

McCreadie looks at me. "Duncan will disagree, but I believe Archie will negotiate with the villagers. He will not want conflict once Fiona is mistress here, and he has realized that bringing in Müller made things significantly worse. Now he needs to find a way to step back without losing face."

"Fire Müller. Rehire Mr. Hall. Come to some agreement for villagers using the land. I understand why he'd be stalling—he's the new owner and can't look weak. He also hired Müller on a six-month contract. But he's also amassing enemies on both sides. The villagers don't realize he'll eventually back down, and Müller almost certainly realizes he's on the way out. Which makes them all suspects."

McCreadie tilts his head. "I agree that anyone *could* obtain the shillelagh. However, I consider it unlikely that a random villager would know where to find it. Also why choose that when so many weapons are at hand? No, if it was someone from the outside, it would be Müller. He would know about the shillelaghs and, if the police realized that was the weapon, he would seem an unlikely suspect. He is the gamekeeper. Would he not use a gun? A trap? Even a shovel?"

"I'd add Mr. Hall and his kids to that group. Same reason. They know the house and they have more obvious weapons. Also, we know the kids come and go. Seeing them here wouldn't seem odd."

"So the weapon being from the house only slightly reduces the list of likely suspects," Gray says. "That is our news then. And you also found something, Hugh?"

McCreadie's eyes widen. "What makes you think that?"

I glare at him. "You teased about it inside."

"And it worked. You rose to the bait and told me the results of your examination of the shillelaghs." When both Gray and I turn on him, he lifts his hands. "Now I am truly teasing. Yes, I have something. Like your clue, it does not solve the mystery—or exonerate Archie—but it does answer questions. We know Ezra was almost certainly killed by that shillelagh from Archie's collection, and we also know, with equal near certainty, that the woman you saw out last night was slipping out to meet someone, that someone almost certainly being Ezra."

I sit back in my chair. "You beat me to it. That is my theory as well—that the woman went to meet Ezra."

Gray looks over. "Which you did not share with me?"

"Or Hugh, because it was just my brain thumbing through possibilities. Still, the main two reasons for a woman to be out would be kissing and killing."

Gray's brows shoot up. "I am not certain what that says about women. Or, more correctly, about your opinion of them."

McCreadie makes a noise suspiciously close to a snicker. "Given that you were out with Duncan, Mallory, I must ask which of those two you had in mind."

I shake my head. "I mean those are the most likely reasons for a woman to be out *here* last night. On an estate where we know there are traps. Either she was the killer or she was going to meet a lover. The most likely suspect for the role of lover would be Ezra, since it would explain why *he* was out as well."

I turn to McCreadie. "So your clue? Who was it? Was she definitely going to meet Ezra?"

"And this is where my clue becomes, like yours, less than as helpful as one might hope." He pushes back his chair and stretches his legs. "What I have is a maid who found a note in Ezra's wastebasket. A partial note, discarded because of an inkblot. It was unaddressed, which is not surprising. When sending such notes, one cannot risk them falling into the wrong hands."

"Have some experience, do you?"

Color touches his cheeks, but he goes on. "It was only the opening lines, in which Ezra asked the recipient to meet him at the bench by the smallest lake. He said he knew he should not send the letter, but he could not stop thinking about her. The maid found it in his room. She claims it was dropped near the wastebasket and so she dared not presume it was rubbish."

"Giving her an excuse to read it."

"Yes. When she realized it was of a personal nature, she burned it to protect Ezra, whom she seemed to have thought very highly of. A bit of an infatuation. Nothing new there, hmm, Duncan?"

When Gray doesn't answer, McCreadie says, "Ezra was always very popular with the maids. It is his kindness they respond to."

"So this one had an infatuation," I say, "which wasn't affected by the fact he was writing love notes to another?"

McCreadie smiles. "Heavens no. That only proved he had a tender and romantic heart, which is what all young ladies wish to see in the object of their infatuation."

"Could she identify the handwriting?" I ask.

Gray frowns. He's been quiet, but this catches his attention. Then he nods. "Ah. Yes. Because it could have been placed there by another."

"I considered that," McCreadie says. "And so I found samples of his writing, Archie's, my own, and Duncan's. We had all made notes on a plan of the wedding arrangements. Fiona and Violet's writing was there as well. I asked the maid to choose the writing she saw. She chose Ezra's."

"Then the question is who he was seeing. There's Edith, Violet, and, er . . ."

A smile touches McCreadie's lips. "My sister, whom you do not wish to mention. My sister must be a suspect, however little I can imagine her doing this." He tilts his head. "No, I can imagine her striking Ezra in the head if he attacked her, but since I cannot imagine *him attacking anyone* I would struggle to see my sister as the culprit. I would also struggle to see her slipping out for an assignation two days before her wedding. Some young women—and men—would consider that romantic. Fiona would not, however popular Ezra might have been with the ladies."

"Not just the maids then?" I say.

"Not just the maids. I have never quite understood it myself." Mc-Creadie flushes slightly. "And that was rude. I only mean that he attracted what always seemed an inordinate amount of interest from young ladies. I suppose it is his kindness. Otherwise . . ."

"He's otherwise middling," I say.

McCreadie looks uncomfortable.

"That's not an insult," I say. "We're trying to cast him in the role of secret lover, and so we need to dig deeper there. In your friend group, he was not the loudest, the handsomest, or the cleverest." That would have been Cranston, McCreadie, and Gray, respectively. "But he was kind and considerate, and often times, women appreciate 'middling.' It's less daunting."

McCreadie considers. "Yes, I suppose I can see that, and I did not intend any insult to Ezra. I remember always wondering at the attention he garnered, and perhaps, when I was young, I envied it. When we envy a thing, we seek to declare the object of our envy unworthy. But yes, to circle back to the question, women find Ezra attractive, and he was always exceedingly discreet, even as a young man, so we can cast him in the potential role of secret lover here. While I cannot see Fiona as his partner, I know we must consider her."

"Should we add the maids to that list?" Gray asks.

"Technically yes," I say. "Though my sense on seeing the woman was that she was a guest. A maid would carry herself differently. What about Edith?"

McCreadie stares at me as Gray smothers a laugh.

"I . . . do not mean to be rude," McCreadie says, "but I cannot imagine Edith inspiring that kind of romantic longing in anyone, even her husband." At my sputtered laughter, he says, "All right. That *was* rude. But you know what I mean."

"Poor Edith," I say.

"Poor James," Gray says, and McCreadie coughs on a laugh.

"All right," McCreadie says. "If we are done being cruel to the Fryes, might I suggest we set this lead aside for now. We could re-question the ladies, but with such a delicate matter, I do not expect to get an answer. I would rather discover who was out last night and then confront her. For now, there is one more person I really must interview."

"The prime suspect?" I say.

He glances at me.

I shrug. "Müller is a very good suspect. In trouble with Archie over the traps and almost certainly about to lose his job. Also, the village blames Archie for that little girl's death because of something Müller did. Another reason to get rid of the gamekeeper, which means another reason for Müller to get rid of *him*."

"Also, he seems a terrible person, which is your favorite sort of suspect?"

I smile. "It is."

TWENTY-THREE

I don't get to join the interview outing. I've already gotten the very strong impression that Müller considers few people worth talking to, and women are refused that questionable distinction altogether. Müller seems to like McCreadie well enough and tolerates Gray, so it makes sense for those two to perform the interview. Does that rankle? Yes, but mostly just because Müller is a key suspect, and I want to be there.

With that avenue cut off, I'd like to get Cranston's fingerprints to exclude them. McCreadie agrees I should be the one to do that and the one to speak to Cranston, because in this case, my sex and lack of status help. There's no way Ross is letting either McCreadie or Gray near his suspect. Me, though? Accompanying the accused man's fiancée, who is bringing him food and a change of clothing? We couldn't possibly be up to anything.

That'll need to be done this evening, when it makes sense for Fiona to take dinner and clothing. In the meantime, then, I'm doing a bit of busywork with Isla. From the note the maid found, it seems that Sinclair planned to meet his beloved at the same bench where we'd seen Isla and McCreadie earlier. Hey, it's a very romantic bench.

Isla and I are heading there to look for clues. The theory is that Sinclair went to meet the recipient of that letter, but was cut down on his way. His body had been found on the other side of the road, but he *had* been heading in the bench's direction, as if circling wide to keep anyone from spotting him walking with whomever he sent that note to. If that's what happened, then there might be signs of the woman at that bench, where she would have waited before giving up.

Is it also possible that she went to meet him with that shillelagh in hand, intending to kill him? Yes. I struggle to envision Sinclair as the kind of lover who'd incite a woman to murder, but I can't discount anything based on a two-day impression.

"Perhaps there were two women," Isla says as we walk. "One received the letter, and the other learned of it and killed him for being unfaithful."

"Ezra Sinclair as a two-timing cad?" I say.

"I do not know if I see him in that role," she says, "but I could imagine him leaving an unhappy lover in his wake. He has moved on, most politely, but she cannot let him go." At my look, she says, "He did have a certain way about him that I could see women finding attractive."

"Huh. You know when Hugh, Duncan, and I were discussing the women Ezra might have been meeting, we forgot about you."

Her cheeks heat as she shoots me a murderous glare. "It was not me, in case there is any question on the matter. I would not be running over the moors chasing romance with a near stranger. I said that I could see other women finding him attractive. He was . . ." She hesitates. "Not to my taste."

"Your taste being . . . anyone in particular?" I tease, but she only rolls her eyes.

"Of the other women in the house, can you see him being to *their* tastes?"

"I do not know them well enough. Ezra Sinclair was a type, one women can find attractive, but I did not."

"A middling sort."

She glances over.

I shrug. "We discussed this. Hugh says women had always found Ezra attractive, and I think it's because he was very average. Nonthreatening. Attainable. Also, kind, which goes farther than most people give it credit for."

"Kindness goes very far. Ezra . . . Yes, middling, as you say, but also comfortable and very attentive."

"Attentive? To anyone in particular?"

She waves a hand. "In general."

"So no one in particular that you noticed?"

As she walks in silence, her hand slips into her pocket. Looking for her mints. When I met Isla, she had a nervous habit of popping them, arising from her asshole of a husband insisting she had bad breath. A habit rooted in shame and humiliation became an anxious compulsion, one she's been breaking. Seeing her reach for the tin, though, tells me that my question makes her uncomfortable.

"Isla?" I say. "Do you know who that note was for?"

She shakes her head.

"But you have a suspicion?"

"Violet," she blurts. Then she clenches her fists. "And I fear that says more about me than her, so you ought not put much faith in it. I thought I sensed a tension between her and Ezra, one that might speak of a hidden attachment. But I did not see anything overt, and I fear I . . ." She swallows. "I hoped to see an attachment. Ezra seemed a decent fellow, and she seems so sad."

Isla wanted to see a sign that Violet had a new love, proof she was over McCreadie, and she's uncomfortable because that hope would only partly be rooted in concern for Violet.

"I knew of the broken engagement, of course," she says as we walk. "It was the cause of Hugh's estrangement from his family. He made a hard choice, and it cost him. But I did not ever consider how it affected Violet. I had very little contact with her, only passing in social circumstances. Now I understand what she went through, and the man who put her through that is . . ." She swallows.

"A very dear friend of yours."

She nods. I haven't pressed her to admit how she feels about McCreadie. Part of me wants to push, but a bigger part realizes she'll push back, possibly by shoving her feelings even deeper into hiding.

She slows to touch an overhanging branch, shielding her expression. "Is it wrong that I am not furious with Hugh? Am I being deliberately obtuse? Or, worse, one of those women who absolves a man simply because she knows him. *Oh, he did not mean it. You do not understand him.*"

"Except"—I lower my voice—"you do understand him, and you know he did not mean to cause her pain."

"He was thoughtless," she says, abruptly resuming her walk. "Young and careless and inconsiderate, and I *am* angry with him for that. But I also understand that he did not foresee the consequences for her. Young men never do."

"I get the sense he sees them now."

She nods. "He does, and that is why we were together earlier. Because he is feeling melancholy and wished to talk. He wanted to believe Violet had moved on with her life and understood they would have been a poor match. But I am not sure they would have been. Perhaps not the most joyful of unions, but better than—" She clears her throat. "Better than most."

"Hugh wants more from a marriage," I say softly. "And I'm sure he told himself he also wanted more for Violet, but as you say, men don't think about such things. It was an arranged marriage, and that brings in all new levels of blame and guilt."

"All that blame goes to the woman," Isla says. "It is as if Hugh changed his mind about buying a horse. No one else will want that horse because clearly it is deficient. At best, you can hope to sell it cheap." Her voice goes harsh. "We are not *horses*."

I take her arm and hold it as we walk.

"I fear . . ." She trails off before trying again, her voice a little firmer. "I fear . . . Oh, I do not even know how to say this."

"It's just us, Isla. Nothing you tell me goes back to Duncan." I lean around her to meet her gaze. "You know that, right?"

She nods, her eyes glistening. "I do, and thank you. I know how close you and my brother are, and I appreciate that I do not need to worry about that."

"He tells me nothing that you say to him in confidence either. Just as I'm not worried about you sharing something I said in confidence. We've worked all that out, thankfully."

We worked it out with a stumble. A serious one. I confessed my truth—about time traveling—to Isla first, and that hurt Gray, more than I would have expected.

Isla walks in silence until we can see the lake, and then she blurts, "I fear the broken engagement was my fault." Her head jerks, as if she is trying to pull back the words. "Not entirely. But partly. Then I think that, and I am . . ." She struggles for a word. "Uncomfortable. It feels like hubris."

"Okay," I say slowly.

"I kissed Hugh. It was awful." Her eyes widen. "Not the kiss." A choked sound that isn't quite a laugh before she flushes. "That was not awful at all."

"You kissed Hugh this morning?"

"What?" She stops and turns to look at me. "No, not this morning. Before my marriage."

"You kissed Hugh when you were young."

"No." Another flush, this one paired with a guilt-ridden glance away. "Right before my marriage. The *day* before."

"Oh."

"That was the awful part," she says. "It was the day before Lawrence and I planned to elope. Hugh was about to leave for London, and he came by to see Duncan, only Duncan had forgotten he was coming by, forgotten Hugh was leaving at all. You know how he can be." Her lips twitch in a half smile. "I was there alone, and I invited Hugh to tea and he kissed me."

"During tea?"

Her cheeks flame. "I stood to ring for the maid, and Hugh rose as well, and I was so close I nearly crashed into him. He told me Lawrence was not the man for me. He did not know of the elopement, of course, only that there was tension over our courtship, my parents refusing to let us marry. I had pretended the relationship was over, but Hugh knew better. He begged me to listen to my mother and Duncan. Then he kissed me. And I . . . I kissed him back."

"Ah."

"I fled after that. Said I did not mean it and ran upstairs, and Hugh did not follow. He left for London, and I spent the rest of the day in a state of nervous confusion. That kiss was . . . Confusing. I ought to have refused it. I ought to have been horrified by it. But I was not, and yet I loved Lawrence. I was *marrying* Lawrence."

Her gaze turns my way. "I felt like a harlot. You will understand how ridiculous that is, as I do now. At the time, though? To be in love with one man and let another kiss me? To *enjoy* that kiss? To want to run after Hugh and ask what he meant by it?"

She crosses her arms, as if suddenly chilled. "I panicked. I should have analyzed the data and determined the cause. The cause being that I had convinced myself I was in love with Lawrence because he made me feel loved. He showered me with praise and affection, and I had never experienced that from a suitor."

"In my time, we call that love bombing," I say.

A brittle laugh. "That is exactly it. He bombarded me with what seemed like love when it was only artillery intended to break down my defenses and win himself a wealthy bride. He was so handsome and well regarded that I could not help but bask in his attention. If his kiss did not ignite me the way Hugh's had—" She clears her throat. "The point is that, in my guilt and shame and confusion, I only became more determined to marry Lawrence. Which I did."

"And then . . ."

"And then Hugh cut his trip short, came home, and ended his engagement to Violet."

"Oh."

She slants a look my way as we resume walking. "Once, after a glass of whisky, I said that I hoped it had nothing to do with our kiss, any guilt over it. He said no, that he had already been in the throes of uncertainty about the engagement when he kissed me, and he apologized for that. He blamed his confusion."

"Over his engagement."

"Yes, he said he was not himself. He was confused and worried that I was still seeing Lawrence, and in the turmoil of those emotions, he kissed me, and he was sorry if that had been upsetting. I said no, that it had been a time of confusion for me as well. We left it at that."

"Okay."

"But I have since wondered whether it could have been more. Whether he might have had deeper feelings for me."

I'm about to answer that question when her next words stop me.

"I feared he might have had deeper feelings," she says. "And then I feared he did not." She flutters her hands. "Worse, it is what I still fear."

"That he has deeper feelings for you? Or that he does not?"

"Both," she says with obvious exasperation. She stops on the edge of the lake and looks out over it. "When we were children, Annis always counseled me not to be a foolish girl. To her, that was the worst thing a young woman could be, and so it became the same standard for me. Whatever else I might be—odd, awkward, wild in my thinking and my habits—at least I was not foolish. Then I grew up and became exactly that. The foolish girl who fell for Lawrence Ballantyne. After that, one would think I had learned my lesson. But clearly I did not, because I have grown into a foolish woman who, at the same time, both wants and fears a man's romantic regard."

Her words are like the swing of an anvil, and I'm half inclined to duck my head to avoid the blow. Wanting a man's attention while being terrified of what it would mean? Why no, I've never felt that at all.

I say, very carefully, "That doesn't seem all that foolish to me." I clear my throat and shove thoughts of Gray aside to focus on Isla. "You have deeper feelings for Hugh?"

"Yes." She blurts the admission like she's confessing to wanting him dead. "I am a fool."

"I can't imagine thinking any woman foolish for liking Hugh. He is very easy to like." I quickly add, "Not that I have any such feeling for him."

She turns a small smile on me. "You do not need to explain. I understand very well where your affections lie, and what your feelings are for Hugh. Friendship. As mine should be."

"Why?" I move up beside her to look out at the lake. "If I said I'm certain that he feels the same—"

"Do not. Please."

"Okay." I stand there, thinking.

She said she fears he doesn't feel the same. That makes sense; who wants to like a guy who doesn't like them back? In my case, I'm just hoping my feelings for Gray subside, like an inconvenient crush.

Yet she also said she fears Hugh feeling the same, and she just stopped me from saying I believe he does. Why would she not want Hugh to return her feelings?

The thought of Gray having feelings for me makes my heart jump . . . but it also makes my stomach drop, a little voice in me screaming *No, no, no!* That way lies heartache, because as much as I want to insist Simon is wrong, deep down, I fear he isn't, that Gray and I would both be hurt.

I continue, slowly, "You're afraid of Hugh having deeper feelings for you because it's safer to stay friends. You have that much, and you don't want to lose it."

"Yes."

"And you're afraid you would lose it because your only experience with love is heartbreak."

Her shoulders roll in discomfort. "Humiliation and shame. Not heartbreak. I never loved Lawrence. I only told myself I did."

You don't elope with someone you don't care about. Even if it hadn't been a great love, there'd still been heartbreak, on top of the humiliation and shame. Also, disappointment. Crushing disappointment.

She pivots to me. "What if Hugh *does* care for me? What if he kissed me because he cared for me back then? What if everything could have been different? If I could have ended things with Lawrence and been with Hugh instead." Her eyes glisten. "What if I could have been happy?"

I take a moment before answering slowly, "How did you feel about Hugh when he kissed you? Did you love him?"

"What?" Her brows knit and she gives a short laugh. "Of course not. He was my younger brother's friend. I was very fond of him, naturally, but he was . . ." Her hands flutter again. "Hugh."

"And after that kiss? Did that make you think of him as more than Duncan's best friend?"

Her face reddens. "Yes, but not as a possible husband. If I am to be forthright, as I know I can be with you"—her face goes even redder—"what it awakened were thoughts of desire, of physical want."

"The thought that you might like to take Hugh as a lover. Not the thought that you might like to run away and marry him."

If her face goes any redder, it'll burst into flames. "Yes. That. If I saw him as more than Duncan's friend, it was that I saw him as a desirable man. But not as a husband."

"Well, then, I don't think you can look back and wish you'd made another choice. I don't think there was a choice to make. Not between Hugh or Lawrence, at least. You thought you loved Lawrence, and I suspect, at that age and point in your life, you were more interested in love than lust."

She nods, her gaze lowered.

"Those deeper feelings for Hugh, did they come more recently? Since Lawrence died and your friendship deepened?"

"Our friendship deepened before Lawrence's death, but yes, those feelings came only after my marriage had ended—in theory if not in fact. After Lawrence and I decided to live separate lives."

"If Hugh had deeper feelings for you when he kissed you, that could have something to do with why he ended his engagement. He realized he wanted more from a lifelong partnership. If you're worried that he ended his engagement *before* discovering you'd eloped?" I shrug. "He could have returned to Violet. She'd have taken him back."

She nods, her gaze down.

"But whatever Hugh felt, you didn't feel the same at the time. You didn't choose between two men and pick the wrong one. You believed you were in love with one guy and chose to marry him." I look her in the eye. "If you think you'll make the same mistake with Hugh, he's not Lawrence."

"I know. But even if Hugh does feel that way about me, he's impetuous. He could think he wants to be with me and then change his mind."

"He *was* impetuous. That's the young man who offered to marry you so you could study in England. The one who kissed you and begged you not to marry. The one who broke off his engagement. But that isn't the man who had to deal with the consequences of that breakup—hurting Violet and being disowned by his parents—and still never went back on his decision. The one who is, if I'm right, courting you at the speed of molasses because he knows that's what you need."

Her lips twitch. "I am not overly familiar with molasses, but I presume it moves slowly."

"So slowly. But it's worth the wait. As Hugh thinks you are."

Fresh spots of color darken her cheeks.

"Think about it," I say. "There's no rush, obviously. But if you have any doubts how Hugh feels? I've been here over a year now, and I've never seen him look at another woman. How long has it been since he date—courted someone?"

"I—I would not know. He hardly shares that information."

"True, but I'm going to bet that you've known there were women, in the past, and now there aren't. Maybe he just can't find any. It's too bad he's so unattractive and ill-tempered."

She smiles and shakes her head. Then she gestures at the bench. "We have long since arrived at our destination, and I know you need to investigate."

"Sure, but there's no rush. We can keep talking. Give me time to mention the way Hugh looks at you, the way he finds excuses to touch your hand, the way he jumps when you want something—"

"Investigate," she says, jabbing a finger at the bench. "Or I will turn the discussion to how you feel about my brother."

"Why, would you look at that? It's the bench I need to examine for potential evidence."

She shakes her head and leaves me to it.

TWENTY-FOUR

So the bench trip is a bust. Or it would be, if not for that conversation with Isla. Is it wrong to say that I'd take her admitting her feelings for Hugh over a piece of murder evidence any day? Bad Detective Mallory. Okay, if it was a piece of evidence that would catch the killer before they struck again, I'd need to go with the clue instead. But if it was something like a footprint in the damp earth that I could trace to the woman Sinclair had been meeting—who likely wasn't his killer—I'll stick with Isla's long-overdue confession.

I actually do find a print in the damp earth. It's a man's boot and almost certainly McCreadie's, which I know because I've had to exclude his prints before. I still measure and sketch it.

I find nothing else. No evidence to tell me who the mystery woman was. No evidence to suggest she even made it to this bench. But being here, I can better map out the route she'd have taken and confirm that the woman we'd seen last night definitely *could* have been heading here. I can also confirm that Sinclair was probably heading here, having circled through the field on the other side of the road to avoid them being seen together.

McCreadie and Isla had chosen this spot because it's not only pretty but isolated. Or so it seems when you're sitting here. Gray and I had spotted them from the road, but looking up from here, I wouldn't see passing coaches or pedestrians . . . and would reasonably assume they couldn't see me either.

It's the perfect spot for a rendezvous.

Now, how is it for witnessing a homicide?

"Alarming how quickly your mind moves from romance to murder," Isla murmurs when I tell her that. "I know only one other person who could veer so naturally and adroitly. Perhaps I should introduce you to him. No, wait, you are working for him."

I ignore that. "It's a perfectly natural change of subject, considering that the romantic rendezvous is connected to the murder, at least in the sense that it explains why Ezra was out last night."

That gleam in her eye disappears as her face drops. "He came to meet a woman, who might have been Violet Cranston. Her chance at finally finding happiness."

"We don't know it was Violet," I say firmly. "But if the woman I saw last night sat here, I'm wondering whether she could have heard anything. Can you sit while I go up the hill? I want to try shouting from the murder scene."

"To see whether I can hear you."

"Right."

"Do not forget the traps."

"Oh, I won't. Duncan and Hugh are going to ask Müller to remove them, in light of what happened and the number of people who need to be tramping through these fields. For now, I'll just walk carefully."

"*Very* carefully. Please."

I head directly up the hill to the road. From there, I realize I can't see Isla. It was the extra height of the coach that gave us the proper vantage. Once on the road, I look around to get my bearings. Then I head almost directly across and into the brush. Within twenty feet I reach the spot where we'd found the abandoned deer kill. I make a quick note of that. Then I veer left and count off the distance in paces.

Seventy-two paces.

That makes it very likely that whoever had been field-dressing the deer had heard something—or someone—related to the murder. They'd definitely have heard a cry. Maybe even the thwack of the club hitting Sinclair's head.

They're butchering the deer when they hear someone. Would movement make them bolt, half their catch abandoned? Probably not. They'd have braced and waited. But a cry? The sound of violence? That would make them grab what they could and go.

I look around the spot. I'd like to come back with Gray and McCreadie for another look, now that Ross won't be running us off his crime scene. For now, I yelp. It's a normal-volume yelp, as if I'd been caught unawares. Then I say "Hey!" with my voice raised. Finally, I take a deep breath and yell, a soundless cry of pain and surprise. There, three vocalizations to determine which—if any—Isla could hear from her spot at the lake.

I'm making my way back when someone shouts, "You there!," and I turn to see Müller stomping toward me, hunting rifle under his arm, the barrel pointed at me. My hand slides into my pocket, where I am indeed now carrying my little derringer.

"Lower the rifle," I call back.

His steps slow, and even from twenty paces, I see his face screw up in confusion.

"You are pointing a rifle at me," I say, my fingers finding their grip on the derringer, still in my voluminous pocket. "Move it away from me *now*."

His eyes narrow, and that gun barrel doesn't budge.

I pull out the derringer and point it at him. Seeing it, he blinks. There are many emotions he could show at that moment. Surprise. Confusion. Grudging respect. Even amusement. Instead what fills his eyes is a hate sharp enough to make my breath catch.

Wrong move, Mallory.

Yes, I've pissed off a guy with a gun, but taking out mine wasn't necessarily the wrong move, if the alternative was letting him think he can aim his rifle at me without consequence.

"What do you think you will do with that little thing?" he says.

At this point, it would be lovely—and badass—to turn the gun and fire it at a nearby tree, in a satisfying display of marksmanship. But that's a whole lot less risky with a modern gun that takes more than two rounds.

Instead I say, "I am alone out here, where a man has been murdered, and someone is pointing a gun at me. I would be a fool not to at least try defending myself."

"I am pointing the gun because you should not be here, little girl."

I bristle at that. Even in Catriona's body, I'm hardly a little girl.

"I am looking for my employer," I lie. "Dr. Gray came to speak to you with Detective McCreadie. Have they found you?"

He grunts. "I saw them heading for my cottage, so I turned and walked the other way. I have no time for their nonsense. Not for yours either. Walking around out here and screaming."

"I was testing how far away Mr. Sinclair's cries could have been heard."

Müller eyes me. "I thought you were looking for your master."

My jaw clenches at the word "master" and I tell myself it's commonly used in this period. Except the way Müller says it puts my teeth on edge.

"I am," I say. "But I paused to conduct an experiment. I am a scientist's assistant, after all."

"Mallory?" a voice calls, and I look to see Isla hurrying over the field. "I heard you shout." Spotting Müller and the two guns, she stops short.

"It is fine," I say. "We startled one another, and we were just about to lower our weapons."

I force myself to withdraw the derringer. Only once I do that does Müller follow suit, with a little sniff of satisfaction that I backed down first.

"It seems Mr. Müller missed your brother and Detective McCreadie," I say sweetly. "He has not yet been interviewed. We ought to escort him to them."

"You will do no such thing, girl," Müller says. "I am busy—"

"Doing something that is more important than helping find a killer? You knew Ezra Sinclair. Surely you want his murderer caught. You must also want Mr. Cranston released."

"Released?"

"First Constable Ross arrested him for the murder."

Müller lowers the rifle further and snorts. "Fool," he mutters, though I'm not sure whether he means Ross or Cranston.

"Right now, nothing is more important than helping your employer," I say.

His expression suggests he's not so sure of that.

"You *do* want to keep your job, I presume?" Isla says.

He doesn't even look her way. "Do I still have a job? Mr. Cranston seems to be reconsidering after the nonsense with that wildcat." He rolls his eyes. "Letting me go because I caught the cat he wished gone? Oh, but the girl was upset. We cannot have that."

"The *girl* is about to be your employer," Isla says.

His expression grows crafty. "Is she now? Does she plan to marry a man accused of murder? I hear that is a hanging offense in this country."

"But if Mr. Cranston is hanged, the property goes to her, as his fiancée," Isla says. "That is Scottish law."

Müller hesitates. He doesn't know enough about his adopted country yet to call bullshit on Isla's lie.

"What time did you retire to bed last night?" I ask.

"By ten. I must be up early, and so I am in bed at dusk, which is later than I like in this cursed cold land."

"Did anything disturb you in the night?"

Müller eases back. "No. I sleep soundly."

"What time did you rise?"

"Dawn, also earlier than I like. It is not natural for the sun to be up so long."

His distracted answers suggest his mind is elsewhere—probably mulling over what I said about Fiona. He's responding on autopilot.

While it's tempting to take advantage of his distraction, I have a feeling any hard question will snap it. I'd love to ask whether Cranston confronted him later over the wildcat, but if Müller realizes he's a suspect, he'll also realize he shouldn't let that slip. I'll leave those questions for McCreadie. Keep this simple, treating him as a witness, not a suspect.

"Dr. Gray and I found that partially butchered stag," I say, angling in a new direction.

"Poachers," he spits. "That lame girl and her brother. They do not even bother to hide that it is them. They are insolent and disrespectful, and at home, they would have been hauled before the magistrate, their hands chopped off."

"Both hands?" I say. "They're being punished for stealing, but afterwards, they would need to rely on charity. Seems counterproductive."

His eyes narrow, as if he can't tell whether I'm being sarcastic or just prattling. "They take one hand only. From each of them."

Is that really still the law in nineteenth-century Austria? Somehow,

I doubt it. Of course, it could have been the "law" where he worked—punishment inflicted by the local lord.

Müller continues, "Cranston is too soft on them. He feels *bad* for what he did to their father." His lip curls, in obvious disdain. "He is weak. My former employer was not weak."

"It does not sound as if you much like this position," Isla says. "I am surprised you took it."

"My former employer died, and the son was but a shadow of the father. When Mr. Sinclair told me of this position, he said his friend was a strong man, a man of action. I believed him." Müller spits to the side.

"Are you hoping to return to Austria then?" Isla asks.

Müller only gazes off into the distance, as if that's answer enough—he's not sharing his thoughts with a mere woman. Unless, of course, it's thoughts on the "weakness" of his current employer.

I think through my next question. I won't get many more. Should I pursue the dead-deer lead? No. If Müller killed Sinclair, then I can't suggest that the Hall kids may have witnessed his crime.

"About the traps—" I begin.

His jaw sets. "I am not removing them."

"Did someone ask you to?"

He gives that distant look again. Not answering.

"If you need Mr. Cranston's order, we can still get that," I say. "I will be visiting him tonight."

"I have already given him my answer."

Well, that also answers my question about who ordered the traps removed. How the hell can Müller refuse a direct order from his boss?

"I was not going to ask about removing them," I say. "I wanted to ask whether there are any in this area."

That crafty look again, as if he doesn't want to answer because he likes seeing Cranston's guests gingerly picking their way through the fields.

"It will be important for the investigation," I say. "Mr. Sinclair was out here at night. He knew where the traps were. If there are some here—and he came into this field—it might suggest he was being pursued."

Do I really think Sinclair was being chased? No. Everything indicates ambush. So why ask about this?

"There are no traps in this field."

I frown. "Are you certain? I saw something gleaming over here."

I start to walk, and he follows to prove me wrong. He walks right into a bit of marshy lowland and looks around. When his attention is diverted, I slip a few coins from my pocket and toss two.

"I see nothing," he says with satisfaction.

"No? Then what is that?" I point at the coins.

He strides over, bends and scoops up the coins. Then he shakes his head and holds out a shilling between his thumb and forefinger. I let him drop it into my palm.

"Oh," I say. "How peculiar. Is the other one also a coin?"

He lifts a guinea . . . and then smirks as he drops it into his pocket.

"You have wasted enough of my time with your foolishness," he says, turning on his heel.

He strides off. Isla and I stay where we are until he's out of earshot. Then she indicates the coin in my palm.

"Finger marks?" she says.

I smile and point down at very clear boot treads in the soft earth. "And footprints. Thank you, Mr. Müller. You were very helpful."

She laughs softly as I wrap the coin in my handkerchief and then bend to measure the footprints.

TWENTY-FIVE

"Tallyho!" a voice calls when we reach the road.

We look to see McCreadie waving.

"Is that supposed to mean they've spotted foxes?" I say.

"I do not know whether I like being compared to a vixen," Isla murmurs.

"Handsome, crafty, and clever," I say. "I'll take it. In my world, 'fox' is old-fashioned slang for an attractive woman."

"I will never fail to marvel at how you can refer to something as 'old-fashioned' when we do not even have it yet."

"A hundred and fifty years is a whole lotta generations with a whole lotta slang. I'm not even sure that one was used over here. Probably not. 'Tallyho' still is, mostly as a greeting between toffs."

"Mallory just called you a toff," Isla calls as they draw near.

"She had best not be referring to me," Gray says.

"No, to Hugh," Isla answers.

McCreadie's mouth opens and then closes. "I . . . feel as if I should take offense, but it depends on how she means it. If she is saying I dress as an aristocratic gentleman, then I am not certain I should argue."

"Sure, take it as a compliment. That's definitely what I meant."

"Did you have a lovely walk?" Isla asks as they catch up to us. "I hope so. It is a beautiful day for a stroll, and you need not worry about Mr. Müller. Mallory has already interviewed him and obtained his prints, both finger and foot."

I lift my hands. "I didn't fully interview him. I got in a few questions before he declared me too female to acknowledge. Mostly, I wanted to get the prints."

"Which was very cleverly done," Isla says. "She lured him into a soggy patch for the footprints and dropped a coin for the fingermarks, all the while pretending she had seen a trap, so he could feel most superior about proving her wrong."

McCreadie tips his hat to me. "Once again, I bow to your skill, milady."

"Thank Müller, for having such a low opinion of my intelligence that he didn't question my awkward tricks. As for the interview, he dodged you two. He saw you heading for his cottage."

McCreadie smiles. "I know, and having spotted him making haste in the other direction, I used the opportunity to search his cottage."

"Nice. Find anything?"

He glances at Gray, who takes out his handkerchief and opens it to reveal a hair ribbon, a tin ring, and a scrap of fabric. I frown at the objects. The ribbon is embroidered and distinctive. Taken together, that and the small ring seem like mementos, probably from a young girl.

"Does Müller have a daughter?" I ask.

McCreadie lifts a finger. "A plausible explanation. A daughter who perished—or whose mother took her away—and he keeps these reminders of her, which we have cruelly stolen."

I take a closer look at the fabric. It's dingy white, with ragged lace and torn edges. I lift it gingerly in one gloved hand.

"Oh my," Isla says, recognizing the fabric a moment before I do.

It's a piece of fabric ripped from bloomers. Women's—or girls'—underwear.

"It was under a floorboard," McCreadie says. "I have taken to checking for them, as well as under the mattresses, thanks to Mallory. She is correct—in thinking they are being clever, people can be very predictable."

"You found all these under a floorboard?"

McCreadie nods. "The fabric was wrapped around the ribbon and ring."

A girl's ring and hair ribbon, hidden inside a piece of girls' underwear, the bundle hidden in the gamekeeper's cottage.

"It has not been his cottage for long," Isla says. "I feel obligated to point that out."

"True," McCreadie says. "But there were marks on the wood where it was pried up. Fresh marks that indicate the spot had only been opened recently."

A ring. A ribbon. Underwear. All belonging to a girl. Recently hidden from sight.

After a twelve-year-old girl fled from the gamekeeper here.

Yes, Nora might have died of measles, but that doesn't mean Müller didn't do something to her. Something terrible.

We need to dig deeper into Nora's case. That will mean speaking to her family and, perhaps more importantly, her friends. I think back to the children Simon had seen lingering around the coach and the note I found in there. That note linked Nora's death to Cranston. Childish superstition from the stories she told of having been "cursed" by Müller? Or was there more to it?

As a female constable, I'd worked my share of sexual-assault cases, not so much investigating as interviewing the survivors. Some of those had been children. I imagine twelve-year-old Nora roaming around the estate grounds. Müller catches her. Really catches her, not just shouting in Austrian as she flees.

I won't speculate on what happens after that, on an empty estate with the owner in Edinburgh. Afterward, how does Nora deal with the trauma? She's twelve, still a child, but in this world, she's a young woman whose marriage prospects have been irreparably damaged, and she's old enough to know that. Instead she weaves a story where she escaped ahead of the irate gamekeeper, her attacker reduced to an impotent buffoon, running after her and shouting in his own language.

She said he cursed her. And, if he did what we fear, that's not completely untrue. He cursed her to a life of shame and humiliation if anyone found out what happened.

What if she did tell someone what happened? It'd be a friend, rather than an adult. A friend who couldn't do anything about it, because Nora couldn't afford for anything to be done.

What if it's a half-told tale, full of holes to cover Nora's shame, and the friend misinterprets her to mean Archie Cranston is the culprit? Or blames

Cranston because it happened on his land, and Müller is his employee? That friend leaves a message in Gray's coach.

He deserved it for what he did to Nora.

We can't interview Nora's family or friends just yet. We need more information to narrow down our questions. I'd also like an excuse to speak to Nora's family without arousing Ross's suspicions.

I have an idea about that, and I add it to the list of things I hope to accomplish at my next stage of the investigation: accompanying Fiona to see Cranston in jail.

TWENTY-SIX

I know a little about jails in this period and region. Jail as in "a temporary holding place" rather than prison as in "a place where sentences are carried out." Most of my knowledge comes from my childhood interest in the macabre that has persisted well past childhood. One might think jails and prisons wouldn't qualify as macabre, but having spent a night in an Edinburgh lockup, I can say hell, yeah, that qualifies.

I've visited old village lockups in England. They're basically a closet-sized stone cell in the middle of town. I can just imagine what it'd have been like to be confined there at night. I'm not claustrophobic or afraid of the dark, but something tells me I would be when I came out.

Did Scotland have those? I'm not sure. I know they did have the uniquely Scottish tolbooths—buildings that were originally intended for the collection of tolls and customs, and eventually included jails and law-enforcement bureaucracy. I suspect this village is much too small for such a thing. Maybe Cranston will go to one when he's transferred to a larger locale. For now, I have no idea where they'll keep him.

I soon find out.

This village isn't big enough for a proper jail. But, like some tolbooths, the sole administrative building serves as a combination of everything from police office to town hall. That's where the cell is—an outdoor makeshift lean-to shored up with iron bars.

Ross allows us entry. Not only does it save him from feeding the prisoner, but Fiona has brought a spread big enough for three, and he takes more than half for his own meal. He also happily accepts the coins she brought "for anything Archie might need."

I had been concerned that Ross might not let me accompany Fiona. What if McCreadie was trying to sneak Gray's assistant in to question Cranston for him? Silly question. I am the pretty young woman Dr. Gray *pretends* is his assistant. Even if they'd given me a list of questions, I probably couldn't read them.

Oh, Ross remembers me. His stares and flushes make that much clear. But he doesn't for one second doubt that I've only come to accompany Cranston's fiancée. Nor does he seem to recall that Fiona is also Detective McCreadie's sister.

Ross takes us out back to the lean-to. "Cranston?" he calls. "You have a visitor."

"*Mr.* Cranston," Fiona says smartly. She looks at him. "When my bridegroom is released, this will go much easier for you if you have treated him with respect."

Ross blinks, and I have to bite the inside of my cheek. Until now, she has been the perfect model of maidenly decorum, with downcast eyes and a quavering voice. Now that she got what she wanted, she returns to form.

Ross doesn't seem to know how to respond and opens the door. "You will have to go inside. I cannot leave it open."

Fiona swans in as if he's holding the door to a ball. I follow and squint against the interior gloom. The only light is sunshine sneaking through cracks in the rough construction. It's half the size of a county jail cell. There isn't even a cot—just a few bales of hay. That's where Cranston sits, rising quickly as he realizes he has visitors. Even in the dim light, he's a mess, his shirt dirty and wrinkled, hair standing on end as if he's been running his hands through it.

"Violet," he says. Then he stops. "Fiona?" He quickly pats down his hair and pulls his shirt straight, and his voice lowers a little. "What are you doing here?"

"Come to bring you dinner." She lifts the hamper. "Also clean clothing and a few other amenities. I am sorry if you were expecting Violet. Of course she wanted to come, but I asked whether I might instead."

"Oh?" He sounds confused, as if unable to comprehend why his fiancée would want to see him.

"I apologize for the disappointment."

"What? No." More shirt straightening. "I simply did not expect . . . . This is not the place for you, and I am the one who should apologize. I expected you to be on your way to Edinburgh by now."

Her brows shoot up. "Fleeing my falsely imprisoned bridegroom? Do you really think me that sort of woman, Archie?"

"I . . ." He swallows, seeming thrown and almost shy. Then he looks at me and seems to pounce at the distraction. "Miss Mitchell. Dare I hope Hugh sent you and that he is working on freeing me?"

"Indeed," I say. "That is the real reason Violet could not come. She knew Fiona wanted to and I needed to. Detective McCreadie has questions, and Constable Ross was never going to let him ask them himself. He cannot know we are investigating at all."

Cranston's shoulders roll back. "Hugh *is* investigating then."

"Did you think my brother would forsake you?" Fiona's lips curve. "His soon-to-be brother-in-law?"

A look passes over Cranston's face, and I try to read it. Shame? Discomfort? He says, softly, "I understand that you may not wish to wed, Fiona. Even if I am freed of the charge, it will stain me."

"If you are trying to get out of the marriage, say so," she says tartly.

He blinks, taken aback. "Not at all. But I would understand—"

"We will discuss that later, and if you wish this to serve as an excuse to end the engagement, I trust you will be honest. For now, answer Mallory's questions."

His lips twitch, and he looks more like himself. "Yes, my lady." He turns to me. "Ask away."

I start by telling him what we know of the reason Ross has arrested him. Then I say, "Has he indicated he has evidence?"

A derisive snort. "No. He is certain that his theory is enough."

"At the site of Mr. Sinclair's murder, you presumed you were the target."

Beside me, Fiona stiffens.

Cranston meets my gaze. "Is that not obvious? Ezra was walking my estate grounds in the darkness of night, wearing my coat. Someone approached from behind and struck him."

"Thinking it was you."

"No one would have cause to kill Ezra. Me on the other hand?" A humorless smile. "The list is long and varied."

"Is it?" Fiona says. "You upset and anger people, but have you done anything to truly make someone wish you dead?" She looks at me. "Apologies. I did not mean to interrupt."

"It is a valid question," I say. "The problem is that people's reasons for murder rarely make sense to anyone else. Also, it is not clear that murder was the intention. A single blow to the head is not usually fatal. However, I definitely need a list of everyone at the house or in the area who might have reason to harm you, Mr. Cranston. If we can even prove that you were the likely victim, it helps your case."

"Because I would not murder myself? That was, sadly, my primary defense. That I was almost certainly the intended victim, having angered so many people. I have been composing a list." He looks at me. "Are you ready?"

I take out my notepad and pencil. "Proceed."

His list is very close to our own. Ross has already told Cranston that he suspects he only meant to hurt Sinclair, and so Cranston gives me everyone in the area with a grievance.

Edith Frye, for suspecting he's cheating them on the investment, which he swears he is not. James Frye would seem a possibility, but Cranston doesn't think he has it in him. That could seem like an insult, but he doesn't seem to consider it one, which tracks with what everyone has said about Cranston himself eschewing violence.

Mr. Hall, the former gamekeeper, and his children make the list. They have a serious grievance, which Cranston surprisingly recognizes as valid. He doesn't apologize for it—just says they have reason to want to frighten him or get revenge.

Müller is next on the list. As we suspected, Cranston planned to fire him, and he's not surprised that Müller understood his predicament.

"We spoke," Cranston says. "Or I spoke and he listened, which he did not much like. I was furious about the traps. He made it seem as if I were lying about expressing concern over them. He acted as if I ordered the killing of the wildcat. Both were false, and to question me on that, in front of others, was the height of duplicity and insolence."

I'm still not completely convinced Müller *was* lying about those two things, but I won't get clarity on that with Fiona here. If Cranston is exaggerating, it's for her sake. I'm not even sure he'd admit to anything without her around. He's adamant in that way of people who are either telling the truth or have convinced themselves they are.

"Anyone else?" I say.

"Locally, no."

"Mrs. Hall?"

He shakes his head. "I realize some would question the wisdom of keeping on the housekeeper whose husband I let go. But it would have been cruel to also release her when I had no cause."

"She does have access to your food."

"And would poison me?" He shakes his head. "She is a sensible woman who understands I made an estate-management decision. Most people who purchase a property do the same."

"They bring in their own staff. You believe she understood that but her husband did not?"

"I do not know her husband well enough to say. That is why he is on my list."

"And their children?"

"They are angry. To them, I stole their family home and disrespected their father. It did not even help that I tried to hire them on."

I frown. "You tried to hire Lenore and Gavin Hall?"

"Yes. The girl to work in the house and the lad to do some labor about the estate. The boy refused, but Lenore worked with her mother for months. It seemed to go well enough, and then she quit. Ezra thinks she had hoped if she proved a good worker, I would hire their father back and return them to the cottage. I did not—could not, as I had a six-month arrangement with Müller—but the girl apparently does not see it that way, and she has avoided me ever since."

"You offered Gavin a job on the estate but not his father?"

Cranston sighs. "Ezra convinced me that it would be insulting to Hall and offensive to Müller."

Sinclair had a point. Firing Hall as gamekeeper and hiring him back to work a lesser position *would* be insulting, and Müller wouldn't want his predecessor on the estate, judging how he managed it, maybe even sabotaging him to get his job back.

"How about the locals?" I say. "Is anyone angry enough to wish you harm?"

Cranston throws up his hands. "Probably? They act as if I am some ogre who bought the estate and erected a moat filled with crocodiles. I purchased the property and continued on in the same manner as the previous owner. Yet it is *me* they are furious with."

Fiona says, carefully, "My sense, Archie, is that they were equally angry with the previous owner. He built the house and kept them off an estate they long considered community land. They hoped that would change when you bought the property, and it did not."

"Then tell me so," he says with exasperation. "Form a delegation. Have the village head or whatnot come to me and discuss it. People barely say a word to me. They only look daggers and act as if I refused to hear them out when they have not said a word."

He looks at me. "That is an issue to be solved another day. You ask whether any of them would wish to harm me. Club me over the head to show I am not safe in my fiefdom? Yes, I can see that. But do not ask me who."

"Because you do not know any of them," Fiona murmurs. "You have not tried to meet them. Have not frequented their shops. Have made no effort to learn anything about the village at your gates."

He sighs, deeply and dramatically. "I only wished for a country estate. I had no idea there would be so many complications. I am not a lord."

"Maybe not," I say. "But that social construct is built into the land. The construct and the compact. They expect certain things from you, and if you do not provide them, they will see it as churlish arrogance."

Cranston peers at me. There I go again, not talking like a young woman lifted up from the working class.

"Well put," Fiona says. "But as you say, Archie, all that can be resolved later, and I will be there to smooth the waters. We will begin with a summer picnic on the estate."

Cranston groans. "I bought the place to escape all that."

"Too bad. You will endure the occasional social event."

"Are the gallows really so terrible?" he murmurs. "I hear it is quick."

"You are joking," Fiona says. "But do not talk like that. This is a mistake that will be rectified."

"On that note," I say, "are there specific villagers with more reason to dislike you than others?"

He throws up his hands again.

Fiona leans in and stage-whispers, "That would require him knowing their names. *Any* of their names."

This is the first time I've seen Fiona and Cranston together in anything other than a large group. Their energy is . . . interesting. Fiona is relaxed, teasing him and making plans for the future, and he is acting as if he's not sure what to make of that. As if he really did think she'd be long gone.

It's an arranged marriage, and to me, with my twenty-first-century Western sensibilities, I'd expect Fiona to jump at the chance to escape it. Even Cranston might, if he had hopes of more than a domestic partner to manage his household and bear his children.

It's obvious that they know one another, in the way children of long-connected families do, but it's also obvious that those families didn't bother with even a sham courtship. It's like being told you'll marry the son of your dad's work partner, a guy you've seen at social events for years but barely exchanged five words with. I'm horrified at the thought, but the only thing that seems to horrify Cranston is his bride's youth, which may come from having known her *since* she really was a girl.

As for Fiona, I don't even know what to think. I do get the sense that this wouldn't be the worst marriage ever, as arranged marriages go. Not a love match, but a decent working partnership, the sort Isla had fore-seen between McCreadie and Violet. The romantic in me always hopes for more, but the realist looks at all the spectacularly shitty "love matches" she's seen and has to admit this might not be as horrifying as it appears.

"I do know some of their names," Cranston says with a mock glare at Fiona. "Constable Ross for one."

She snorts.

"And Doctor . . ." He trails off and then comes back with, "There is a fine doctor and his wife, both elderly. The name escapes me."

"What about Nora?" I ask.

He frowns. "Lenore Hall?"

I shake my head. "Nora Glass."

His eyes roll up in thought. Then irritation sets in as he shakes his head. "If you are testing me, Miss Mitchell, I have already admitted I know few of the villagers. Several of the young women have worked at the estate, but I do not know any by that name."

"Nora Glass is—was—twelve. As far as I know, she never worked at the estate. She died earlier this spring after contracting measles."

He blanches. "Of course. Yes, when I returned last month, I heard that a village child had died." He sneaks a look at Fiona. "I ought to have offered condolences, I suppose."

"Yes," she murmurs. "But again, I will handle these things, and no one would truly have expected it of a bachelor." She frowns at me. "Did someone take umbrage at the lack of condolences? Enough to attack Archie over it? I cannot see that, but I do not know the local customs."

I shake my head. "I didn't hear anything like that. I did hear, though, that Nora was on the estate grounds shortly before she took ill."

"What?" Cranston says, his surprise seeming genuine.

"She liked to walk on the grounds. Mr. Müller caught her and ran her off."

He stares at me. "And then continued insisting we leave out those traps? Knowing *children* played there?"

I note his use of "children." Nora was twelve, on the cusp of puberty. In my experience, men who prey on children of that age are quick to mentally push them into the realm of adulthood. Young woman. Teenage girl. Not a child.

"Müller did not tell you about her?" I press.

"Certainly not. Likely because it meant I'd never have allowed the traps. I was already concerned that they might hurt someone."

"Isn't the point of traps to hurt someone?"

He gives me a hard look, as if I'm baiting him. "No, the point is to keep people out of the fields. To discourage poaching."

"Poaching was a serious problem?"

"The former owner said it was. I have not been here long enough to judge for myself, but with all that is being said, I begin to wonder if his account was not exaggerated."

"You heard about Nora's death when you came back last month. When exactly was that?"

He provides the dates in May, which are a couple of weeks after Nora died. Before that, he'd been up briefly in March, but the mud made him decide to wait until spring. He'd been up frequently last fall, hunting, and again in December, hosting friends, but since the new year, it'd been only the early March and late May trips. If that's true, he wasn't here anytime close to when Müller ran Nora off.

"There are villagers who may blame you for Nora Glass's death," I say.

He frowns. "They think she caught the measles on my estate? Duncan could set them straight on that." He pauses. "Or do they think she caught it from Müller? I know there has been grave suspicion about him, as a foreigner."

I tell him about the so-called curse and add, "The blame seems to come because you hired him."

"Hired a foreign devil to chase off children and kill them with foreign curses?" He looks at Fiona. "You really believe we can socialize with these people?"

"Obviously not everyone thinks Müller cursed Nora," I say. "It might only be a tale told among the children."

"I am now a monster in the tales of the local children? Lovely."

When I tell Cranston about the note, his shoulders slump and he shakes his head, muttering about the mess he's gotten into.

"Detective McCreadie needs to look into it," I say, "on the chance—however slim—that the killer targeted you for that. The problem is that he does not dare start asking questions in town, or Constable Ross will know he is investigating. We need an unrelated reason for speaking to Nora's family. Fiona mentioned that you ought to have sent condolences. Might we do that, on your behalf? Claim that you only just heard of Nora's death and, although you are obviously unable to visit yourself, you wanted to send something?"

His eyes narrow. "Will that not look like blood money, if they believe me responsible?"

"It would be a gift, not money. If they take offense, they will say so. If they feel, in any way, that you owe them, while I know that would be uncomfortable for you, it helps with the case. It would get them talking."

"Fine. Whatever Hugh deems fit. I trust him to handle this correctly. Now, if you have more questions, is there any chance I can answer them while eating? I have not had a bite since last night."

I pick up the basket. "Of course."

TWENTY-SEVEN

Before Cranston eats, I get his fingerprints, explaining that we believe the murder weapon may belong to him and we want to exclude his prints. He's a little concerned, obviously, that his prints on the weapon could be used to convict him, but I promise that information will not be shared with Ross.

Then I continue questioning Cranston as he eats, stopping only when Ross decides visiting hours are over. I've learned enough, and if we have more questions, Fiona sweetly requested permission to bring more food for both of them. A bachelor can never turn down free food, especially when it is excellent.

We return to the estate after that. Visiting Nora's family will need to wait until we've had time to prepare. I also have to discuss that with McCreadie. If there's any way he can be present for the interview, that's best, but I'm not sure it's feasible.

By the time we return to the house, it's mid-evening. I start by comparing the fingerprints to the ones I've lifted from the shillelagh. As expected, Cranston's prints match the one I found the most of. Because it's his shillelagh. That doesn't help. I have two other prints, but we've decided not to get exemplars from anyone else until we have a suspect. Everyone in this house could have handled it—from Mrs. Hall to the maids to the guests. Handling it for cleaning or just taking a closer look.

When we have a suspect, then we'll want to know whether their prints match the two unidentified ones.

I walk the gardens with Gray and McCreadie to explain what I got from Cranston. Then I tell them what he said about Nora.

"As leads go," McCreadie says, "I am not certain how useful this one is."

"In regards to Ezra's death, you mean."

He nods as we turn a corner. "Naturally, if Müller molested the child, Archie must know so he can sack him. However, the stronger lead would be that Archie molested the girl and someone tried to kill him for it. That is not impossible. It is, however, unlikely."

"Given the timing of Archie's visits and the fact he had no contact with the villagers. Nora wouldn't have been wandering around the grounds in March, when Archie says it was a bog. Also, he spoke of her as a child, and I didn't pick up any sense that he was dissembling."

"Archie is terrible at dissembling," McCreadie says. "He does not have the temperament for it." He looks at Gray for confirmation and Gray, walking silently behind us, nods.

I say, "If Müller assaulted Nora, it seems a stretch to attack Archie because he's Müller's employer."

"Could the killer have mistaken Ezra for Müller?" Gray says.

I look back at him. "Good question."

McCreadie nods slowly. "We keep presuming the killer thought Ezra was Archie, but that is purely based on the coat. Müller is also of a similar size and more likely to be wandering the grounds at night."

"Only those who know Archie would recognize the coat," I say. "And it's very clear he wasn't socializing with the locals."

"Yet the shillelagh indicates the killer had knowledge of and access to the house."

I tell them what Cranston said about briefly employing Lenore Hall.

"I did not know that," McCreadie says. "So she spent time in the house after Archie bought it."

"When the shillelaghs were on display," I say. "We definitely need to speak to Lenore and Gavin."

"That will not be easy," McCreadie says darkly. "It appears they have gone to visit their grandmother in Dundee."

"What?" I say, stopping and turning to face him.

"We learned of it this evening," McCreadie says.

I wince. "That's my fault, isn't it? For telling Mrs. Hall that you'd like to speak to them as potential witnesses."

"No. They left early today, without their mother's knowledge."

I curse under my breath. "I should have moved faster. They were the obvious suspects for the dead deer, which made them witnesses."

"To a murder that was not ours to investigate," Gray says. "This has been a tangled mess, and it is no one's fault but that constable's."

When we don't answer, Gray presses on, "Hugh, you had no authority to investigate until Archie was arrested, and even then, you have only a moral authority. You cannot even openly investigate, for fear the local constable will retaliate. It is ridiculous and unconscionable, but it is the restriction you must work under, which means you and Mallory cannot blame yourselves for not interviewing witnesses who seem to have left before Ezra's body was discovered."

"How far is Dundee?" I ask. "I know it's an hour or two by car, but I'm afraid to ask what that means here."

"It is nearly as far as returning to Edinburgh," McCreadie says. "If we decide that we absolutely must speak to them to solve the case, we shall do it, but not until then."

Because it would take at least two days from the investigation. One day to travel there and question the Halls and another to return after Folly rested overnight.

"The alternative," McCreadie continues, "is that one of us goes to speak to them while the others remain here investigating. But if I were to go—which would be most feasible, as Mallory cannot go alone—I would not know what you had uncovered in the meantime."

"We could have vital information you need for your interview," I say. "And you wouldn't get it until you were back. I really miss cell phones. Hell, I miss *telephones*."

"Poor Mallory," McCreadie says, "stuck with our primitive methods of communication."

"The problem," Gray says, "is that if Lenore and Gavin Hall suddenly departed, it makes them excellent suspects."

"Or just excellent witnesses," I say. "Imagine you saw a murder and believed the killer may have also spotted you. You might decide to go visit a distant relative for a while. Especially if you were committing a crime when you witnessed the murder. Either way, it means we really should talk to them. But Hugh's right—it's so early in the investigation that he'd be rushing off without all the facts."

I look at McCreadie. "Is there any way to compel them to return?"

"As potential witnesses to a murder?" He shakes his head. "Even if I were the officer in charge of the case, I could not do that. I would need to chase after them."

"There is Mrs. Hall," Gray muses. "We wish to speak to her children, and she is here, in Archie's employ."

McCreadie's brows shoot up. "Are you suggesting we use her position as leverage to compel her children's return?"

"In the pursuit of a killer, I do not think strong persuasion is out of line."

"Oh, I am not complaining. I am only surprised. Terribly Machiavellian of you, old chap."

Gray rolls his eyes, and then slides them my way. "Mallory?"

"From what I've seen of her, she won't respond well to blatant threats. Considering Lenore and Gavin are young adults and still come to visit her at work, I'm guessing it's a good relationship. I would suggest obvious manipulation."

"*Obvious* manipulation?" Gray says.

I shrug. "Don't try to trick her. Let her see that she's being bribed, but also let her see that it's in her family's best interests. Archie is definitely firing Müller, and he seemed inclined to rehire Mr. Hall. If Archie agrees, let Mrs. Hall know that's the plan . . . and that it's important for her children to return to give their testimony. Tell her they'll be protected—we'll send a coach if that helps—and that we consider them witnesses only and understand why they'd be spooked if they saw the murder."

McCreadie nods slowly. "That could work. Mrs. Hall will see the bribe, but we are not insulting her intelligence by pretending the two things— her children returning and her husband being rehired—are unconnected. We need only to get Archie's agreement."

"Which can be done tomorrow when Fiona takes him food."

TWENTY-EIGHT

Once again, I can't sleep. This time, even having a tiny furry roommate doesn't distract me. I cuddle the wildcat kitten, who has decided she will tolerate such things, and I play "catch the finger" with her for a few minutes, until her excited squeaks have Alice tossing and turning. With one last apologetic pat, I set the kitten back in her box, put on my wrapper and slippers, and then head into the hall.

Of course, once out of the room, I have no idea what to do. I wouldn't bother Isla. While I'd love to poke my head into Gray's room, hoping the sound will wake him, that's wrong. Plus it runs the risk of me being caught coming or going from his bedchamber.

I wander downstairs. The house is silent and still. As I scan the hall, I remind myself that I'm not nearly the "guest" I was on my first night here. Everything is so topsy-turvy that no one would blink twice at Gray's assistant availing herself of the library at night.

I slip in there, and once I do, I need to kick myself for being a lousy detective. Apparently, I haven't paid nearly enough attention to this room or I'd have noticed that the library has a distinct lack of books.

There's a desk and bookshelves, but those shelves are mostly bare, the few items gracing them being knickknacks that seem to have been left by the previous owner. Just random Victorian bric-a-brac, mostly imitation antiquities, like a statue of a Greek nymph and a Chinese vase. The half-dozen books also seem to have been left behind, all nonfiction of the sort guaranteed to cure my insomnia.

I should have brought a book. Gray's house is certainly full of them, fiction and reference, and no one would have objected to me taking one on the trip. I'm just still too accustomed to my world, where I always have a device, and that device will hold my latest novel plus a virtual to-be-read shelf.

I should ask whether Isla brought books. I remember her coming downstairs today holding one, and I'm sure she brought a backup. For now, I'm stuck leafing through *The Wealth of Nations*. Yes, I know it's a classic, written by a Scottish economist and philosopher, but holy shit is it boring. The guy will make an interesting point and then go on for dozens of pages explaining it with examples that probably made sense to an eighteenth-century reader—or a historian—but I'm *dying*. So when footsteps sound in the hall, I shut the book in relief.

I resist the urge to hide, but I don't call out a greeting either. Those footsteps are moving so slowly and lightly that it's clear the person doesn't want to be heard. After they've gone past the library door, I slide the book aside and rise.

The footsteps continue deeper into the house. I tilt my head, frowning as I try to figure out where they're going. The kitchen for a snack? No, the steps are coming back my way.

I hold my breath and wait. The footfalls pass and return to the stairs. Going back up? That's odd. Is someone sleepwalking?

I creep to the door as a stair creaks, as they return upstairs. Were they down here checking whether anyone else was awake? Like me, unable to sleep, hoping for company?

Gray wouldn't creep about. Isla and McCreadie might, not wanting to wake anyone. Or could it have been Alice, waking to find me gone? That's the most likely answer.

I head back to the stairs. As I near them, though, the door that clicks shut is on the next level. Not Alice then. If it was Isla or McCreadie, I'm sorry I missed them.

I creep up the steps in hopes of hearing a noise in one of their rooms. If I do, I can softly knock and let them know I'm awake at this ungodly hour, too. Insomnia loves company.

I pause at the top and listen. The faintest swish of fabric comes. I follow it to my right, across the hall from Gray's room. Who was sleeping in there? One of the men, I think. Sinclair or Cranston. The women's rooms are all down farther, with Isla's.

No, that wouldn't be Cranston's chambers. He has the main bedroom, and if I recall correctly, it's up another set of stairs. These are all guest rooms.

Then I realize whose room that is. I'd stood atop these stairs earlier today as Simon and another groom came up . . . carrying Sinclair's body.

Someone is in Ezra Sinclair's room. Where his dead body is laid out.

I hold my breath as I creep toward the door. I'm careful not to step in front of it, in case my slippered feet shadow any light underneath.

The interior has gone silent. Even when I strain to listen, I pick up nothing.

The obvious reason for someone to be in Sinclair's room is to retrieve something. Evidence that might indicate Sinclair was the actual intended victim? Planting a clue to divert attention? Or planting a clue to exonerate or convict Cranston?

I wait another minute as I listen, but when no sound comes, I take hold of the doorknob, turn it slowly, and ease the door open a crack.

At first I see nothing. There's no sound either—no one gasps or scuttles for a hiding spot. Cold air blasts out, from the windows all being opened to delay decomposition. Then I catch a figure seated in a bedside chair.

Is someone paying their respects? If so, I should retreat. That would be the polite thing to do. But I'm no longer just a guest in this house. I'm a detective solving the murder of the man lying on the bed.

I ease the door another inch, until I can see the form better. It's a woman. A dark-haired, petite woman.

Violet Cranston.

I consider my options, but really, there are no options. Sure, I could back out and leave her to her silent vigil, but if I did, I'd be a decent person and a shitty detective.

"Oh!" I say as I push the door a little further open. "I am so sorry."

She whirls, sees me, and scrambles to her feet.

I step in and close the door, and then move close enough to speak softly. "My deepest apologies. I was coming downstairs when I thought I heard someone in here and I feared it might be . . ." I trail off as my gaze shifts in discomfort. "I do hate to suggest this, but I feared one of the servants might be taking advantage of Mr. Sinclair's death to pocket a valuable or two."

She doesn't answer. I wonder whether my explanation landed wrong. Then I see her, face drawn, breath held, and I realize she's barely heard my excuse. She's waiting for me to ask hers.

Uh, so, what exactly are you doing in here with a dead body, Miss Cranston?

"I am sorry to interrupt your grief," I say. "Might I bring you tea from the kitchen?"

She visibly relaxes as she realizes I don't see anything odd about her sitting beside a dead man. Certainly, in my time, finding someone sitting with a sheet-wrapped corpse in the middle of the night would be concerning. But Victorians are much more accustomed to death and more comfortable with the dead. Also, would I really think it odd if someone wanted to sit, alone, with the body of a loved one in a funeral home? No.

But would I have considered Violet close enough to Sinclair to visit his body? While he was her brother's best friend, I don't get the sense they were like Isla and McCreadie, growing up together and staying close. Cranston hasn't lived with his family for years.

Would Violet sneak in here, in the middle of the night, to sit vigil with her brother's friend?

I remember my thoughts and suspicions from earlier.

According to that maid, Sinclair wrote a note to a woman in the house, asking her to meet him at the lake. The most likely person he'd been meeting, I had decided, was the one now sitting beside his body.

Violet hasn't answered my question about the tea, so I decide to skip it or she might not be here when I return.

"I am sorry to intrude," I say again. "However, since I am here, I feel there is something I must warn you about."

Her brow furrows, as if she's wondering whether she heard me right. "Warn me?"

"It is about last night," I say. "I saw something, and it concerns you. I do not believe it signifies, but as Detective McCreadie and Dr. Gray are now on the case, if I were to keep this from them, I could lose my position."

I lean in and whisper, "I saw you going out. I do not sleep well in strange places, and I have been up every night, wandering as I try to sleep. I was gazing out the window when I saw you hurry past. I became alarmed, knowing of the traps and what they did to that poor wildcat. I pulled on my boots and went out after you. I saw you heading up the hill to the south, on the road, but once I crested the hill, you were gone. I realized then that I might be interrupting a romantic rendezvous and quickly retreated."

She says nothing. Just watches. After all, I haven't asked a question, have I?

I continue, "I wouldn't have mentioned it to Dr. Gray or Detective Mc-Creadie. Obviously you are not the killer. But then Detective McCreadie learned of a note sent to one of the women, from Mr. Sinclair, inviting them to join him at the small lake, which is exactly where you seemed to be going."

Still she says nothing. Smart, really. If there's one piece of legal advice that clients often ignore, it's this: Don't volunteer information. Especially don't volunteer it when the cops haven't asked an actual question. That goes for the innocent as well as the guilty.

"I will need to speak to Dr. Gray," I say. "That is one of the things that has kept me up tonight—the fear that I have already held back too much. It will help, though, if I can say I spoke to you about it already. Dr. Gray will see that you had nothing to do with Mr. Sinclair's death and there might be no need to bother Detective McCreadie with it."

Oh, that's low. Very low. I should be ashamed of myself. But I need to take the shot. I am here to solve a case, not to be nice, even to a woman who probably deserves a little more niceness in her life.

Sure enough, Violet flinches at McCreadie's name, and a look like horror crosses behind her eyes. I said I'd seen her, but she hadn't taken that to the obvious end point—that I needed to tell her former fiancé she'd been meeting a man last night.

"I know it was you," I say, my voice lowered. "If I could say I was not sure, I might be able to ignore it, but I cannot."

"It was not what it seems," she says quickly. "I realize how it might appear, but Ezra is"—her gaze shoots to the bed—"*was* my brother's best friend. I have known him for most of my life. Yes, he sent me a message. Yes, he asked me to meet him at the lake. I expected he wished to offer quiet sympathy, away from prying eyes. He knew I have been upset. It was not easy, being here." She looks up at me. "I do not expect you to know this, but I once had an attachment to Hugh McCreadie."

"You were engaged," I say softly.

The look that crosses her face now is pure humiliation, and I hate that look so much. I hate that—years after a man decided not to marry her—she still bears that brand, feels that shame. That the world *expects* her to be ashamed.

"I heard it ended," I say. "It was arranged by your parents, and you and Detective McCreadie decided you did not suit."

Those simple words—making the decision seem mutual—have her relaxing.

"Yes," she says. "We did not suit, sadly. It can still be difficult, though, seeing him."

"I can imagine."

"I believe Ezra wished to lend me the proverbial sympathetic ear. Even a shoulder to cry on, if that was what I required. He was always kind to me. He treated me as if I were *his* sister."

She quickly adds, "Not that I was in need of a better older brother. Archie is the best a woman could want. He has always watched out for me. But he can be . . . less than observant. If I admitted it bothered me to have Hugh here, he would have made arrangements for me or Hugh to stay elsewhere. But if I act as if it does not bother me, he does not see that it does. Some people need to be told a thing directly. They are not good at interpreting signs. That is my brother."

"But Ezra was different."

She manages a wan smile. "I have always thought the best friends are those who complement one another. Like Hugh and Duncan. That was Archie and Ezra. My brother cannot see anything that is not held in front of his face, while Ezra saw everything. He always knew what I needed. Last night, I needed a friend, and so I believe that is what he wanted to give me. Trusting him implicitly, I went out."

I let the silence stretch. I can tell there's more she wants to say, and after a moment she does.

"In light of what happened, though," she says, "I have wondered whether he might have wanted to tell me something else."

"Something that got him killed?"

She shakes her head. "I cannot imagine that. I know people believe Archie was the intended victim, and I would agree." A weak smile. "My brother has that effect on people."

"But Mr. Sinclair did not."

She hesitates before shaking her head.

"You were thinking of something," I press.

"Only that . . ." She trails off and plucks at her skirt. "I am overtired, and my mind is wandering."

"When it comes to murder, Dr. Gray always says to tell him everything and he will determine what is important." He says nothing of the sort to me, since that would be really condescending when speaking to a professional police detective, but it makes Violet nod in understanding.

"Yesterday, after that terrible business with the wildcat," she says, "I saw Ezra speaking to Mr. Müller, who was most agitated. Later, I overheard Ezra with Archie, and Ezra seemed to be trying to dissuade him from letting the man go. That struck me as odd."

"It was Mr. Sinclair who recommended Mr. Müller," I say.

"Yes, but Ezra has apologized for that. He seemed most embarrassed to have made a poor recommendation. So why would he then argue to keep the man on?" Violet shakes her head. "I do not understand."

Sinclair argued to finish Müller's contract . . . after speaking to the man. What did Müller say?

I'll need to confirm this story with Cranston. For now, I consider whether to push Violet. She's admitted to being the woman at the lake. That's one mystery solved. But according to the maid, the note said that Sinclair knew he should not send it, but he could not stop thinking about her. That sounds romantic in nature, so my gut tells me Violet is lying about that.

Or is "lying" too strong a word? It implies deliberately misleading me on an investigation when I suspect the truth is much more forgivable.

Violet says she suspected Sinclair wanted to provide a sympathetic shoulder to cry on. But the other day, I overheard Sinclair asking *Fiona* to be that shoulder for Violet.

Speaking to Fiona, Sinclair had acted as if he wasn't close enough to Violet to help her. Which doesn't seem to have been the case.

Whether Violet and Sinclair were romantically linked or not doesn't affect the investigation, as far as I can see. But it would have a huge effect on Violet, emotionally and socially. One fiancé dumps her and the next candidate is murdered? Tongues would wag, and her marital prospects could plummet to zero.

Except . . .

That would presume anyone knew Sinclair was courting her, which obviously they did not, with Sinclair going so far as to enlist Fiona's help in comforting Violet.

I need to work this through more.

"I must ask if you saw or heard anything last night," I say.

Her shoulders droop as she blinks back tears. "I only wish that I had. I presume Ezra was attacked while I sat waiting. If I knew anything that could free my brother, I would have already put aside all propriety to admit to being out there. But I did not. I was sitting on the bench, lost in my thoughts."

Facing the lake, turned away from where Sinclair was. Also away from where the Hall kids were field-dressing that stag, which they'd do as quietly as they could. From that distance, she wouldn't have heard soft voices. A shout, yes, but there's no reason to think Sinclair's death was anything but silent, save for the thud of the blow, which she'd have been much too far away to hear.

"Did you see or hear *anything*?" I press. "Even unrelated to what happened to Mr. Sinclair?"

She shakes her head. "If I had, I would have retreated to the house. The night seemed empty."

Empty . . . except for Sinclair coming to meet her, a killer sneaking up on him, the Hall kids field-dressing a deer, plus Gray and me having a picnic on the hill.

Yet everyone out there had a reason to be quiet. No one would have had a lantern. And the estate is large enough that it really would have seemed empty.

I'd spotted Violet, and I believe the two teens saw or heard something. But otherwise, we all kept to our bubbles of illicit nighttime activity.

I ask Violet more questions, mostly nailing down the timeline. When did she leave the house? When did she return? Did she go straight to bed? What time did she get up in the morning? She answers them all readily . . . until I hit the last question.

"The note from Mr. Sinclair," I say. "Might I see that?"

She pauses long enough that I know there's not a hope in hell of seeing that note.

"I would keep it to myself," I say. "I can tell Dr. Gray that I read it but returned it."

"I will look for it," she says. "I believe I threw it into the fire, but I will look."

Yep, I'm definitely not getting that note. Which suggests it was indeed a final copy of the romantic missive the maid read.

"That is fine," I say. "Thank you. And now I will leave you to your grief."

TWENTY-NINE

Despite being up half the night, I wake at the crack of dawn and feed the wildcat kitten while Alice gets a rare lie-in. When I hear people below, I head out. On my way down, I pause outside Isla's door, but it's shut and no sound comes from within, which means Alice isn't the only one enjoying a late rising.

"Mallory?" Gray's murmured voice reaches me from the stairs, and he comes back up to frown at me. "Is everything all right?"

"I have a question," I say.

His face relaxes into a faint smile. "Ah, nothing new then. I presume it is something only my sister can answer?"

"No, you'll do."

His brows shoot up. "I am honored."

"May we speak after breakfast?"

He moves into the hall, closing the gap between us as he lowers his voice. "Privacy is required, I take it?"

I nod.

"Then, if you are not famished, you ought to accompany me to speak to Simon at the stables."

"Is something wrong?"

He lowers his head toward mine. "It is an excuse."

"Ah, all right then. Let us go and speak to Simon."

* * *

As we leave the house—and I'm sure no one is outside to overhear—I tell Gray about Violet.

"Well, that answers the question of whom we spotted that night," he says, "as well as confirming that the maid *did* read a partial discarded note."

I nod. "As for the final version, when I asked for it, Violet went very quiet. She agreed to look for it but warned she might have thrown it in the fire."

"If she did not, then she has now."

I shake my head. "It was the last note sent by a friend. If she burned it, she did so as soon as she read it. She could have hesitated because she realized she no longer had it and worried that looked suspicious. But I think she didn't want me reading it because it would confirm Ezra was more than a friend."

Gravel crunches under his boots. "Then that is a tragedy."

"Violet deserves a happily ever after."

"She does. Hugh truly did not mean to put her through that, and I think, if I might be so cruel, that it was best if he did not foresee the consequences, or he would have changed his mind. That would have been good for Violet, but *she* is not my dear friend."

"Hugh's happiness is far more important to you. I agree. It was an awful thing for Violet, but they're both better off for it."

Even as I say the words, I wonder how true that is. Would Violet rather be where she is—single, rejected, and shamed—than married to a decent man who didn't love her?

I think most women in this time would choose the decent man who would treat them well even if he never loved them. They were raised to believe that was the most they could expect.

I'd never say that to Gray. There's no point in lifting that particular veil into the lives of Victorian women. He understands the disparity and seeks to mitigate it in his own dealings with women.

"Speaking of marriage, though," I say, "that is actually my question. Why would Ezra and Violet be courting in secret? I can see that if one of them was married or otherwise attached, but they aren't. They're a damn near perfect match."

"I would agree."

I throw up my hands. "So what am I missing? Does her broken engagement make her an unsuitable match? He's an orphan, right? Is that an issue? I'm lost."

"If you wish to know why there would be an objection to the match, you have come to the wrong person. You really do need to speak to Isla. I know nothing of marital suitability."

I sigh. "Because it's a woman's issue, right?"

He pauses, and I think that's my answer, but then I realize he's noticed how close we are to the stable—and the end of our privacy bubble.

He waves me to the side, where we might admire a flowering bush. When we're there, he says, "Marital suitability concerns men, too, as they must understand who they can and cannot court. But it does not concern anyone who has no intention of marrying."

I parse that out. "You don't intend to marry?"

"You sound surprised. Are you truly?"

"I . . ." I shrug. "If you were a thirty-one-year-old unmarried woman, I'd have wondered, but I know it's common here for men to be older when they marry, especially if they have careers."

"My situation is different."

When I don't answer, he sighs. "I suppose if it is not obvious, that is only a mark of how different things are in your time." He looks at me. "Between my bastardy and my skin color, I would not ask any woman to marry me."

"Oh." I fall silent.

He exhales again. "You want to ask more and you are being circumspect. Out with it."

I say, carefully, "I understand those are both obstacles that might . . . limit your choices. But you have everything else a wife could want. Health, money, a good career, stability, and . . ." I swallow, my cheeks heating. "You are kind. You would make a good husband."

"Kind?" His brows rise in mock horror. "Take that back."

He wants me to relax, to smile and break the mood, but I struggle with it and finally say, "I really don't think the situation is as dire as you fear, Duncan. You could marry. Easily."

"To a woman who overlooks my deficiencies in return for stability? For a husband who is unlikely to beat her? No, shockingly, I do not want anyone to settle for me."

"I—"

"And imagine if they did marry me? If they did not fully consider the ramifications of marrying a man whose skin marks him as 'other' everywhere he goes? If they did not consider that their children will most likely also look 'other'?"

"I'm sorry," I say softly. "That was thoughtless, and I apologize."

He eases back and then his lips quirk in a tired smile. "No, that was not thoughtless. You want to think better of people. You know what I endure, and you would like to believe that there are women out there—a bevy of them, apparently—who would want me despite that." His smile lifts a little more. "You flatter me, and I cannot complain about that. Perhaps you ought to marry me."

I laugh, and it's a little shrill and forced as my cheeks heat and I move into the shade of the bush to cover that. "A fine idea."

"Perhaps it is," he says, and there's a note in his voice that's almost serious. "It certainly would solve our difficulties."

"I'm not marrying anyone to 'solve difficulties,' Duncan." Is there a tightness in my voice? A note that should warn him off? Maybe.

"But it would, though." He moves closer, voice lowering. "Marriage would be the perfect solution to our dilemma. We would not need to worry about nonsense like this." He waves around us. "Coming up with excuses to speak together. Sneaking off at night for a picnic and then worrying we have been seen."

"Right. Sure. We'll get married so we can talk more openly while we're on holiday . . . which happens so often."

He rocks forward. "It is more than that. Marriage would resolve many problems. We would never need to worry about being seen alone, and no one would ever question your position as my assistant."

"Because, as your wife, I'm expected to be your helpmeet?"

My sarcasm flies so high over his head that he actually smiles. "Precisely. Also, what if Hugh and Isla married? How would you continue to live with me? You could not." He rocks back on his heels, still smiling. "Yes, marriage is an excellent idea."

Dear God, he's not joking. I watch him, standing there, almost smug, pleased with himself for coming up with this solution, not even considering the possibility I might object? Something roils through me, and I'm not sure whether it's rage or hurt. Both, I think.

"So," I say, not bothering to keep the anger from my voice, "because people think you only hired me to bed me, you'll prove them right?"

"They expect me to bed you, not marry you."

"Then they'll only think you a fool for buying the cow when you could get the milk for free."

He frowns. "Hmm?"

"You'll be the fool who put a ring on it, and I'll be the scheming witch who got what she wanted all along."

"But we know the truth. Those whose opinions matter most also know the truth. It is an excellent idea, Mallory."

"Sure. Since it doesn't seem like Archie and Fiona can get married today, why don't we take their place? Summon the vicar. Make this official."

He finally seems to actually look at me and hear my tone. "You do not want to marry me."

"Don't pull that shit, Duncan," I grit out.

"I do not know what 'shit'—"

"I can see it in your face. If I say I don't want to marry you, you'll take it as personal rejection. It's not about you. I already said you're a damn fine catch. But I am not marrying a man who only wants to wed me to solve his problem."

Does part of me watch his face as I say those words, hoping for some hint that his proposition is about more than resolving issues? Of course it does.

"But it is not only *my* problem," he says. "In fact, I would suggest it is more yours than mine."

I stifle my hurt and call it foolishness. But I can't help pushing on. "Earlier you said it was best for Violet that she didn't marry Hugh. Better not to marry a man who'd never love her. Who only married for duty and responsibility. Is that what you're asking me to do now?"

His mouth opens. Then he shuts it, and he's quiet so long that a traitorous glimmer of hope whispers in me.

"I understand that it is not ideal," he says slowly. "But perhaps, with time, that would change."

I don't trust myself to speak. I don't trust myself to even look at him. I turn on my heel and stride into the stable.

Later, when I'm sitting—hiding?—in a copse of trees, I congratulate myself for having the presence of mind to walk into the stable instead of stomping back to the house. If I'd stalked off, Gray would have followed. He *did* actually follow, when he recovered, but by then one of the grooms stopped him to ask a question. That gave me a chance to slip out, and by the time Gray realized it, I was long gone.

My hands itch to write a letter to my parents. That's how I've been communicating with them. I put letters under the floorboard of my room, and they can read them. Don't ask me how it works—logically, the letters should pile up until the twenty-first century. They don't. My parents can't write me back, but I take what I can get, and what I get is two people I can share my deepest thoughts and feelings with, in a way I haven't since I hit my teen years. Ironic, isn't it? Now that I might never see them again, I open myself up to them again.

Now I want to write to them. Tell them everything I'm feeling, pour out my hurt and confusion. And I can't. I don't even dare retire and write it out for later, in case someone finds the letters. There's been enough of that going around.

So I take as much time in that copse as I can, cognizant of a case waiting to be investigated. I need to find my game face first . . . or as close to it as I can approximate.

What the hell just happened?

Well, it seems that Gray proposed to me.

No, he didn't "propose." He suggested marriage as a business arrangement. I keep telling myself he was teasing. Joking around. That's the way he is, with a sense of humor so dry that most people can't tell he's being funny.

Except I can, and in that moment, he'd been dead serious. Which makes it so much more bizarre. How did he go from discussing a murder investigation to "we should get married"?

Because the issues of our professional relationship have been festering. Haven't I been worrying about that myself? How it affects his reputation, when everyone thinks I'm actually his lover?

Gray has insisted it isn't an issue, but obviously that was a lie, and he's been looking for a solution.

I should have just rolled with it. Teased him and pretended it was clearly a joke. Instead, I'd run off like a goddamn schoolgirl whose crush admitted he "didn't think of her that way."

I've embarrassed myself, and I'm still not sure why I reacted like that. Worse, I still *feel* like that. Hurt. Angry.

Humiliated?

Yes, humiliated, too.

We're supposed to be friends, and this isn't how you treat a friend, cavalierly suggesting an arranged marriage when you know they come from a culture of love matches.

I take a deep breath and lean against a tree.

I'm hurt, and I'm disappointed, but maybe that's on me. To Gray—a Victorian man—this was a perfectly logical solution. He felt comfortable floating it because I'm a logical person. Surely I would see that this made sense, and none of that romantic foolishness needed apply to us. We were above that.

He might be, but I'm not. And I'm just going to need to deal with that.

THIRTY

The short walk to the house might be the longest—and most treacherous—I've faced on this trip. Forget bear traps. I need to figure out how to slip in and act as if nothing's wrong while avoiding Gray, because once I see him, any composure I've found will shatter.

I ease in through the rear door just as Isla is coming down the stairs.

"Excellent timing," she says. "I hope you are ready for your second breakfast of the day, because I am famished and require company." She slows, seeing my expression. "Mallory? What is wrong?"

Yep, my poker face sucks. I lean into it as I shrug. "Just the case. A lot on my mind."

"Where is my brother?"

So much for my perfectly reasonable excuse. I pretend not to notice her tone, which suggests Gray is clearly responsible for my mood. "He was at the stable speaking to Simon. My stomach started growling so I came back. We didn't get a chance to grab breakfast. But I got sidetracked by the kittens, so Duncan may already be back."

"He is not. I saw Fiona on the way down and she said Mrs. Hall saw you both heading to the stable."

"Ah, well, while we should wait for him so Mrs. Hall doesn't need to serve us separately, I really need to speak to you in private. It's about the case. Something Duncan couldn't answer. Any chance of retiring to your room for breakfast?"

She doesn't answer, and I feel her heavy gaze on me. I'm not fooling anyone. In the end, she decides—wisely—not to pursue it.

Breakfast is obviously ready and keeping warm, because we're still settling in when a maid arrives and sets it out for us. What I have to say to Isla must be said in as much privacy as possible, which means we sadly can't dine on the balcony again, where someone passing below could overhear us.

Once the maid is gone, I say, "It's about Violet and Ezra."

"Ah. You have information." Isla leans forward. While there's been zero indication that Violet realizes Isla might be partly responsible for McCreadie breaking off their engagement, it will ease Isla's conscience to know Violet had moved on.

For the second time this morning, I tell the tale of what I discovered last night.

"There was a romantic entanglement," Isla says. "I am certain of it."

"So am I."

"Poor Violet." Her shoulders sag, and she mentally retreats for a moment, contemplating the implications of that. First Violet lost McCreadie. Now she loses Sinclair.

"Was that the question Duncan could not answer?" she says. "Whether you are correct in interpreting a relationship between them?"

"No, he agrees that it seems that way. My question is about the secrecy. Clearly no one knew they were courting. I suppose it's possible they weren't actually courting, in the strictest sense. They could have been having an affair, with no intention of marrying. But does that make sense?"

"With the scandal around Violet's broken engagement, I cannot imagine she would risk an affair."

"But does it make sense to *not* be aiming at marriage. Ezra was a bachelor, right?"

"Yes, at dinner the first night, James teased Ezra about being the last of their trio to wed, and it was clear he was not even courting."

I take a bite of cheese before I speak again. Now that I've relaxed, my stomach really is rumbling. "So there's no impediment to him marrying, and a marriage would rescue Violet's reputation, wouldn't it?"

Isla nods. "It is the best path open to her. I have thought of that, with some dismay. As terrible as my marriage was, I am now free. I may choose to marry or choose to remain unattached, and my reputation would be little affected either way. The best thing that could have happened to Violet would have been marrying a year or so after her broken engagement."

"While Hugh let her go, someone else snatched her up, because she's a prize."

Her nose wrinkles. "I hate to hear women referred to as prizes, but yes, others would see it that way. While one buyer passed on the horse, it did not remain on the market long."

"Ideally, then, she'd have married long ago. Is that the problem? Has she been single so long that Ezra's reputation would suffer if he married her?"

"Hardly. Whenever he married her, his reputation would have risen with the match. She is beautiful, accomplished, and comes with a significant dowry. The problem lies not with Violet but with Ezra."

"Because he's an orphan?"

"He effectively has no family, which is a concern. But even if his parents lived, they would not provide the correct social status. He only attended the same school as Duncan, Hugh, and Archie because he was sponsored."

"And now? He seems well-off enough. Or doesn't that matter?"

"It should not matter."

"But it does. He's an unsuitable suitor."

"Perhaps," she says slowly, "but it is not as if she were courting the valet. One would think—given Violet's age and lack of marital prospects—her parents would leap on Ezra as a son-in-law. They are fond of him, from what I hear. He has a good position—something in business. He would make an excellent husband. At the very least, there should have been no objection to him courting her to see where it led. But I will admit that I cannot answer that with certainty. The Cranstons are in an elevated social class, with the blood of nobility if not the titles."

Like Hugh. That made him suitable for Violet. Old money and blood tinged blue.

Isla continues, "The person I would ask is Annis." Gray and Isla's older sister married an earl, which was a big leap for a young woman of the middle class, even the wealthy end of it. Of course, that wealth is what won her the match.

"I could send her a message," Isla says. "Would that help?"

I shake my head. "It's really more a matter of curiosity. For now, I need to accept that marriage must have been out of the question, for some reason, and that's why Violet and Ezra were meeting in secret."

When I go quiet, she murmurs, "You do not like that answer, do you?"

No, I do not.

Isla and I finish breakfast to discover that Gray and I weren't the only ones getting an early start. When Isla spoke to Fiona, she'd been heading out with Violet to take breakfast to Cranston. They return to tell us that Cranston has agreed to rehire Mr. Hall as gamekeeper. Thus ensues a flurry of activity, as McCreadie and I inform Mrs. Hall while asking her to summon her children from Dundee. She knows these two things are linked, but I think we manage to convey the request in a way that makes it clear we consider Lenore and Gavin witnesses, not suspects. Is that true? Mostly. They *are* suspects, of course. Everyone is.

Mrs. Hall pens a letter, which then needs to be run to Dundee. That's a job for a single rider and a horse. While we'll need a coach to get Lenore and Gavin back home, it'll be faster to send a rider and then hire a coach there. Finding the fastest rider-and-horse pair takes more work—it's not Simon or Folly, which complicates the process—but soon the messenger is off with Mrs. Hall's letter.

All this means I think I've managed to avoid Gray. So cleverly done . . . until he doesn't appear at lunch, and I realize I'm not ducking him. He's ducking me.

How do I feel about that? I can't consider it. I have work to do with McCreadie, as we discuss all the leads and plot our next moves.

McCreadie agrees with Isla. The circumstances do suggest a romantic link between Sinclair and Violet. He doesn't think there should have been any impediment to a proper courtship but agrees that her parents could have dug in their heels. He also adds in another possibility—that Violet and Sinclair were in the very earliest stages of a romance, and the fact that Sinclair was her brother's best friend might have had them proceeding slowly. They also could have been waiting until after Cranston's marriage, so they didn't steal her brother's thunder.

The next step is talking to Nora's family. Because we're setting this up as a condolence call, there's no excuse for McCreadie to go. It'd only tip off

Constable Ross. I can go, though. No one would expect Fiona to pay her respects without a female companion.

Mrs. Hall told us where to find the Glass home. We had to tell Mrs. Hall about the visit anyway, as we were taking a basket and needed food. If she saw anything strange in us deciding *now* was the time to pay a belated condolence call, she doesn't comment. Maybe she just presumes Sinclair's death led to Fiona discovering Nora's death, and a condolence call is a perfectly acceptable way to pass the time waiting for her fiancé to be freed.

As the coach reaches the village, I'm reminded that this is the period when people began abandoning the countryside for the cities. In Scotland, that process was accelerated by the Highland clearances, where people weren't choosing to move to cities—they were forced to relocate. There are also the Irish famines of a few decades ago, driving people into Scotland and its larger city centers.

Cities represent opportunity. That means jobs, but it also means a wider canvas for daily life. I suppose it's the same thing I saw in my own time, where small-town classmates declared they were never moving home. The jobs were in Vancouver. So were the clubs and shopping and dining and all the sports and arts they could want. Housing prices were the highest in Canada, but to them, it was worth it.

In this period, I don't think many people are moving to the cities for sports and theater. They're going for jobs and upward mobility. And they discover, like in modern-day Vancouver, that big-city living comes with a big-city price tag. Most of those industrial age newcomers end up in the slums, entire families squeezed into a place smaller than my first apartment.

In the country, there's more room. That means, at least when it comes to housing, there's a higher standard of living. I see that as Simon drives us through the village. Of course, not everyone is living in adorable cottages like the doctor and his wife. Most are more humble abodes. Then there are the places like the Glass home, a structure that's little more than a shack, with a pen for a couple of sheep and a goat and a few chickens. There is a larger building in the rear, which will be the blacksmith shop. From the sounds of it, Nora's father is hard at work.

As we make our way to the front door, people at a neighboring house come out to openly gape. Fiona nods graciously at them, and I follow her lead. When she raps at the door, a baby inside lets out a squall, and I wince—no one's going to appreciate us waking a little one. Once the door opens, though, the woman standing there is already bouncing the baby on her hip, seeming unperturbed even as sweat rolls down her forehead, another child shrieks inside, and the smell of roasting dinner wafts out.

In my time, women feel that we're expected to do it all, unlike our foremothers, who only had a household to maintain. Try running that household with endless squalling babies, no electricity, and no running water. We've always had it hard and the idea that, historically, women easily managed a household on their own is ridiculous. Even among the lower middle class, as soon as you can afford to hire a "girl" to help out, you do. Otherwise, you hope you have a daughter to enlist once she's big enough to wield a broom or a bottle.

The woman's gaze sweeps over Fiona—dressed in a visiting gown, with elbow-length sleeves and a fitted bodice, a bonnet, and gloves—and she dips in the faintest curtsy. "Good afternoon, m'lady. If it's my husband you need for your horse, you can send your driver around back."

"No, we wish to speak to you. Mrs. Glass, is it?"

The woman frowns. "Yes, miss."

"I am Fiona McCreadie. My fiancé is Archibald Cranston, who recently purchased the estate outside town."

The frown grows. "Do you need a blacksmith up at the house?"

"No, ma'am. I came because I only just learned of your daughter's death earlier this spring. Mr. Cranston is unsure of his place in village life, and I understand he did not pay you a condolence call, so I wished to do so myself."

The woman's face lights up. "Oh, that is very kind of you, miss. Very kind. We did not expect anything of His Lordship."

"Mr. Cranston." Fiona smiles. "He is not a lord, but he is a good man who would have called if he had thought it appropriate." She lifts the basket. "I brought this, but I see you have your hands full. Might I bring it in?"

Mrs. Glass pauses, panic filling her eyes as she looks over her shoulder, doubtless imagining this finely dressed young woman in her home.

Fiona continues, "I understand we have found you at a bad time. I could leave it and return later."

"No, no. Come in. I'll put on a pot for tea. Mary? Come take the baby."

Mrs. Glass ushers us into a main room that's small and shabby but also tidy and scrubbed clean. A girl of about fourteen appears to take the baby, and I see yet another child, a toddler who'd probably been the one shrieking.

"You have lovely children," Fiona says.

Mrs. Glass beams. "Six of them. We'd lost not a single one as a babe. Such fine luck, I always thought." Her smile falters. "But perhaps it was too much. The Lord saw that we had an unfair bounty and took our Nora to keep us humble."

It's an odd sentiment, and an odd way to think of a child's death, but this is a time when six healthy children—none dying in infancy—*would* have been a bounty of good fortune. They might indeed see it as the hand of God setting things right.

"I am deeply sorry," Fiona says as we settle in.

"As am I," I say.

"Oh! Where are my manners?" Fiona sighs. "I will be a married woman within days, and I behave as if I am still paying social calls with my mother. This is my dear friend, Miss Mallory Mitchell."

I greet the family, and then make faces at the toddler as his mother prepares tea. That gets Fiona laughing and it draws the other children nearer, pulled in by the sight of a well-dressed young woman making a spectacle of herself to amuse a child. Another girl, this one about seven, edges closer.

As Mrs. Glass and Fiona talk, I pull out my stock trick for children—I make coins disappear. Then I play the cups game, where I put a coin under one of two cups and move them around. In this case, not wanting to ask for cups, I use my hands. If the child gets it right, they keep the penny, which makes this game a real winner with Victorian children.

The game keeps the kids busy, but also wins some credit with their mother. Because when the small talk with Fiona is done, it's my turn. That, however, doesn't mean I can take over the conversation. Fiona and I discussed how to do this, and I give her the cue by whispering, loud enough to be heard, "You wished to mention Mr. Müller."

"Oh, yes." Fiona clears her throat, as if loath to bring it up. "Mr. Cranston wished me to let you know that Mr. Müller will not be employed with him much longer. He heard what happened with your Nora, and he wished me to convey his sincere apologies for that. There has been some misunderstanding regarding use of the estate grounds, and Mr. Cranston certainly did not expect his gamekeeper to be frightening off children."

Mrs. Glass's gaze dips. "That is most kind of you both. We had told Nora to stay away. The previous owner was clear that he did not wish anyone walking through. But Nora grew up using the grounds, and it was her favorite place to walk. We did not intend any insult to Mr. Cranston."

"None was taken, and he hopes no insult to the village was incurred—he would not wish people to think him an ogre who would drive off children."

"He truly was aghast to hear of it," I add. "Am I correct that Mr. Müller ran her off, shouting at her?"

Mrs. Glass's mouth presses in a firm line. "That he did. Shouting in his own tongue, which Nora could not understand. It greatly perplexed her."

"And frightened her, I am sure," I say.

Mrs. Glass's expression lightens in a fond smile. "No, I would not say it frightened her. Our Nora had the heart of a lioness. Fearless as could be. She knew she was in trouble and ran straight home, but then she had a fine story to tell, how the man chased her, shouting curses in a foreign tongue." She rolls her eyes. "*Curses.* She did love a grand story."

"Did she . . . think he was cursing her?"

Mrs. Glass laughs. "Nay, lass. She knew better, but I took her aside to be sure. While I do not raise my children with such superstitious nonsense, you can never tell what they hear outside these walls. She said she only added that to make it a better story. She understood the man was simply telling her to leave."

"Did anyone else believe he had cursed her?" Fiona says. "If that were the case, we would speak to Mr. Müller and see what he said, to ease any concerns."

"Dear me, no." Mrs. Glass laughs again. "People here do like their superstitions, but it is mostly a bit of fun. Setting out cream for the fair folk and such. They knew the man did not truly curse anyone. It was a story for the children." She straightens, looking startled. "You do not think that we believed her cursed, do you? That we blamed Mr. Cranston—or his gamekeeper—for her death?"

"I heard nothing of the sort," Fiona says.

"I . . . did," I say, feigning reluctance, while shooting Fiona a look as if to apologize for not telling her. Of course, we did tell Fiona about the note, but we wouldn't want Mrs. Glass thinking this was the real reason for our visit.

I continue, "When Dr. Gray and I were in town yesterday, we received a note that might have suggested some responsibility. We did not wish to tell you, Fiona." I look at Mrs. Glass. "Apologies, ma'am. We put no stock in it."

"And you should not. A note you say?"

"Left in our coach."

She shakes her head. "One of the children, then. I did not consider that they might take Nora's storytelling for truth. I will be certain to set anyone straight if I hear talk of curses."

We speak for a few more minutes, with Fiona soliciting advice on how the villagers might respond to a summer picnic at the estate.

Mrs. Glass does not point out that—with Fiona's fiancé in prison, charged with murder—it might be a little premature to plan picnics. She's given no indication that she knows about Cranston's imprisonment. That doesn't mean she's necessarily unaware of it—only that she's too polite to comment if Fiona is proceeding as if nothing has happened.

Before we leave, I take a small wrapped parcel from my pocket. I open it on the table, revealing the ring and embroidered hair ribbon we found in Müller's cottage. Mrs. Glass only looks at them, as if puzzled.

"These were found on the grounds at the estate," I say. "We believe they belonged to Nora."

"Oh," she says. "No, those are not Nora's."

When I hesitate, she calls Mary over and shows her, asking whether she's ever seen them before.

"No, ma'am," Mary says to me. "Those were not my sister's." She picks up the ring, frowning.

"You recognize that?" I say. "It could belong to another girl in the village."

"It looks familiar," Mary murmurs. "But I do not recall where I've seen it."

"We will take them back then," I say. "We do wish to return them to their rightful owner, so if you remember who that ring belongs to, Mary, please let us know."

"We will," her mother says.

THIRTY-ONE

We're having tea on the lawn back at the estate. By this point, even I'm starting to feel rude, separating myself from other guests, eating my meals closeted away in private conference with my friends. I remind myself this isn't like going to a party and monopolizing those I know. There's been a murder, and these are my fellow investigators, and we can hardly discuss the case in the drawing room.

Gray is with us. It's the first time I've seen him since the events outside the stable, and apparently, he's going to act as if nothing happened. He settles into the empty chair and takes a tart from the platter.

Do I notice that he doesn't look my way? Do the others notice? Yes and yes, but McCreadie and Isla are clearly leaving us to work this out on our own, and I appreciate that.

To be bluntly honest, while I bristle at Gray's reaction—or lack thereof—I'm also glad of it. I don't want to get into this now. In fact, I'd be happier if we never got into it. Let his proposal fall by the wayside, as if it didn't happen. If that means it takes him some time to warm up again, at least he isn't giving me the cold shoulder while engaging the others in conversation. He eats and sips his tea and listens, and when I talk, he looks my way. Good enough.

"The items are not Nora's?" McCreadie says when I finish the story.

"They could still be," Isla says. "Perhaps she was not supposed to have them. It could be that a boy gave her the embroidered hair ribbon or ring.

Or she bought them with money her parents did not know she had. It might be better to speak to her older sister in private."

"I thought of that," I say, "and I agree. Her sister recognized the ring, and while she genuinely didn't seem to know from where, she still might know more, especially about any problems with Müller. However, given her mother's account of the incident, my gut says there wasn't any molestation there. Nora returned home bubbling with a story to tell."

"She thought it a proper lark," McCreadie says. "Fleeing the ogre and skipping home to embellish the tale with stories of curses."

"Which no adults seem to have believed," I say. "One of the children must have, and they left that note in our coach when they heard—wrongly—that Archie was dead."

"Except Archie was not the ogre," Isla says. "He was not even there at the estate when Mr. Müller ran Nora off."

"Is it possible," Gray says slowly, "that we have misinterpreted the note?" He shoots me a look and adds quickly, "Not to question your interpretation, Mallory, as it was my own as well. Also, it was not our interpretation at all but Mrs. Rendall's."

"Good point," I say, and he visibly relaxes. "We'll need to take another look at it."

"And find out who that ring and ribbon belong to," Isla says.

McCreadie and I exchange a look. How important is that? Neither of us is sure. It seems more of a mini-mystery, unrelated to the murder. Like the killing of the wildcat. Both of them could be something . . . but both could be just mysteries cropping up at the same time by sheer coincidence.

The wildcat killing is linked if the murder had something to do with Cranston planning to fire Müller. Otherwise, it's just Müller poisoning a cat and staging it to look like the trap got it. Likewise, the ring, ribbon, and piece of bloomers could represent an unrelated crime committed by Müller.

I just don't like how it all keeps coming back to Müller.

"Duncan and I need to speak to Mr. Müller," McCreadie says, as if reading my thoughts. "I say we go in hard and show him what we found, see how he reacts."

"Mallory would be better suited for that," Gray murmurs. "I am a poor judge of such things. She is the expert."

Okay, someone's trying for brownie points.

"I'd happily go," I say, "but how would that work considering the nature of what we found? Part of a girl's bloomers? With two men, Müller might just claim they're mementos of a consensual fling. Would he say that in front of me?"

Isla snorts. "He would absolutely say that in front of you, Mallory. A decent man would not, but I have seen how he looks at you."

Gray makes a noise. "Perhaps I was wrong then, and Mallory ought not to do this."

Isla shakes her head. "It is not *that* sort of look, Duncan. Not one that speaks of genuine interest. It is contemptuous—a man seeing a pretty girl who would never look twice at him."

"He finds Mallory attractive and blames *her* for it," McCreadie says.

Isla's smile beams the delight of liking a guy who notices and understands things like this. "Yes. A man like Mr. Müller will not think twice about claiming the bloomers belong to some girl he has seduced, *especially* in front of Mallory. He will leap at the chance to horrify and disgust her."

"Well, I wouldn't want to miss that," I say. "I guess I'm going to speak to Müller with you, Hugh."

"Would you mind if Isla and I examined the note while you are gone?" Gray says, and his gaze is on me, not McCreadie.

"Knock yourselves out."

He manages the faintest smile, even if it doesn't touch his eyes. "I do not think we need to go that far, but we will do our best."

McCreadie and I leave to speak to Müller. We pass the grazing cows and then hear Müller tramping through the trees. McCreadie heads over, shouting a greeting from enough of a distance that Müller immediately turns on his heel and stalks in the other direction . . . where he meets up with me, after I slipped around to cut him off.

"You," he says, with a twist of his lip that confirms Isla's assessment. His gaze sweeps over me, devouring without pleasure. I am a sweet treat meant for richer men, and he hates me for it, as if I've deliberately laid a trap to tease him.

"Detective McCreadie has not had a chance to speak to you," I say. "He really does need to do so."

Müller's jaw works. He wants to barrel past me, but he also must sense McCreadie coming up behind him, and any departure will seem like he's fleeing. A guy like Müller won't flee from a man as young, handsome, and polished as McCreadie.

In the end, he turns and spits, the gob landing inches from McCreadie's boots.

"What do you want?" Müller says.

McCreadie ignores his tone and launches into the usual array of questions we'd ask of a suspect, most of which duplicate what I already asked. Part of that is seeing whether any of his responses have changed, but it's mostly relaxing Müller's guard.

If Müller killed Sinclair and is worried that we're on to him, this interview allays those fears. It's just standard questions about where he was and what he heard or saw.

McCreadie even gives him a bonus by talking about the wildcat. Not accusing him of killing the beast, but taking another tack.

"Terrible business with the wildcat," McCreadie says.

Müller stiffens. "He said to get rid of the cat and I did. I laid traps, and it was caught."

"I mean how Archie treated you," McCreadie says. "It is obvious that he did not want to upset my sister, and so he tossed you to the wolves, so to speak."

A thin smile. "You saw that."

"I did, and I feel as if I should apologize for my sister. You know women. They can be very soft, and we love them for it, but in matters like this?" McCreadie rolls his eyes. "It was a wild beast. A predator. Not a house pet."

Müller nods, relaxing more. "You understand."

"Of course. The cat had to be dealt with and you dealt with it. I do appreciate your patience with my sister in that, and your time in speaking to me."

Müller actually assures McCreadie it was no trouble and wishes him all the best with the investigation. Amazing what a little empathy can do for someone's attitude. Unfortunately, with McCreadie's wrap-up, the next part falls on me.

Good cop, bad cop.

And, as long as we're going that route, I'll take it a step farther. I walk past McCreadie and start heading back toward the path. He doesn't miss a beat. He joins me, and it's only after a few steps that I say, "Oh, I need to speak to Mr. Müller about another matter. I will catch up with you, sir."

McCreadie nods and continues on, as if completely unconcerned about leaving me with the gamekeeper . . . though I know he won't go far before staking out a hiding spot. To help with that, I walk back around Müller, drawing his attention away from McCreadie. Then I crane my neck to look around Müller, as if being sure McCreadie is far enough away.

"I must ask you about these," I murmur to Müller.

I take the handkerchief from my pocket and open it, revealing the three items. If I had any doubt about who put them under that floorboard, his reaction erases it. Confusion as he tries to see what I'm holding, then recognition as he does, followed by a scowl as his gaze flies to mine.

He doesn't ask how I got them. Doesn't ask what they are or feign confusion. He just looks at me, hate dripping from his gaze.

"I found these in your cottage," I say. "Hidden under a floorboard."

"Why were you in my cottage?" His voice oozes warning.

"I work for Dr. Gray," I say, as if that answers the question. "I found these, but I am not certain what to make of them."

"You think I know?"

"They were in *your* cottage."

"It has not been mine for long. Speak to that girl who lived there. They must be hers."

I lift the piece of cloth. "These come from a pair of bloomers. She would not hide those."

"Would she not?" An ugly smile crosses his face. "As a reminder, perhaps? She was with a boy, having fun, and it was . . ." He bares his teeth in a smile. "Memorable. You would know all about that."

"I do not know Lenore at all," I say, ignoring his meaning. "But I will ask whether these are hers."

"They are," he says. "I am sure of it. Now take your silly questions and go. I have no more time for you, girl."

* * *

It's a quiet walk back to the house. McCreadie glances at me a few times, testing whether I want to talk, but when I don't speak up, he doesn't prod. He knows I'm thinking it through.

We're nearing the house when Isla and Gray come out to meet us.

"What did Mr. Müller say?" Isla asks when we're within earshot.

"May I see that note?" I ask.

Her brows shoot up. "That is not what he said. I am quite certain of it."

She's teasing, but Gray can tell I'm not in the mood to respond, and he hands me the note.

"We believe the misunderstanding comes from the name," he says. "There must be another Nora in town. Do we know what the child's mother's name is?"

I run my fingers over the name. Nora. Or that's what it looks like, but the penmanship is bad enough that I'm only clear on the first three letters.

"What are short forms for Lenore?" I say.

McCreadie lets out a curse. "Of course."

"Her brother called her Len, but are there other nicknames?" I ask. "Lenore isn't a common name in my time."

"Nor," Isla says. "Or Nori."

I nod. "When Fiona and I went to speak to Archie in jail, I mentioned Nora, and he misheard it as Lenore. I didn't make the connection—the similarity in the names—until after Hugh and I spoke to Müller."

I hold up the handkerchief. "Müller says these belong to Lenore. He insinuated she had a fling with a boy and that's why she stuffed the bit of her bloomers under the floor. He clearly recognized the items, but he also told us to show them to Lenore, that they're hers and he's sure of it."

"Bloody hell," McCreadie mutters.

"Now the question is whether we wait for Lenore . . . or we ask Mrs. Hall whether she recognizes the ring and ribbon."

We decide to ask Mrs. Hall. It'll be the independent corroboration we need, keeping Lenore from claiming the ring and ribbon aren't hers. It'll also let us go into our interview with Lenore with hard evidence.

The problem is *when* to ask. It'll be dinner soon, and Mrs. Hall is busy supervising the meal. The question will need to wait. In the meantime, I want to speak to Violet again. Unofficially.

Her late-night meeting with Sinclair is bothering me. I need to speak to her in private, preferably during a casual conversation. In other words, I need an excuse, and I get it when I'm slowly heading up the stairs and sense someone impatient behind me.

I glance over my shoulder to see Violet's maid.

"I am sorry, miss," she says with an awkward partial curtsy. "I need to help Miss Cranston dress for dinner, and I am late."

I'm about to step aside when I see my excuse screaming at me from the girl's anxious expression.

"Your collar is tucked in," I say.

She quickly tugs at it, her cheeks burning.

I lean down. "You also have something in your hair. Straw or grass."

That part is a lie, but her hand flies to her hair, face going scarlet.

"Go on and fix yourself up," I whisper. "I will tell Miss Cranston that you were needed for another task and that I have come to help her dress."

She hesitates.

I lean in again. "I was Mrs. Ballantyne's maid. I know what I am doing. I also know how to ensure Miss Cranston has no idea you were enjoying a deserved respite from your duties."

"Thank you, miss. Thank you very much."

She scampers off, and I smile to myself as I finish climbing the stairs.

I rap on the door to Violet's room. When she doesn't answer, I frown and rap again. Then I hear noise within and realize my mistake. She didn't answer because she presumed I was her maid, only knocking to announce her arrival.

"It is Mallory Michell," I say, and the door opens.

Violet looks behind me.

"Your maid cannot attend you," I say. "She was needed in the gardens earlier, and she must clean herself up before she is in any state to assist with your dressing." Not untrue . . . "I told her I would do it." I move inside and smile. "I help Mrs. Ballantyne all the time. She says no one is better at tightening a corset. Of course, she may not mean that as a compliment."

Still looking uncertain, Violet waves for me to shut the door. She's wearing a day dress, and her dinner gown is laid out on the bed. It's fancier than I expected, but then I remember Fiona announcing they would all dress up for dinner tonight. Get some use of the formal wear they brought. No one was going to argue with a bride on her groom-less wedding day.

I move behind Violet to assist her in removing her dress, and I chatter away, trying to relax her. Off come the dress, crinoline cover, crinoline, and the corset cover. Then she says, "I will need to change my corset as well."

That's to be expected. A formal dress requires a more formal corset.

When I start to unlace her corset, though, she tenses. Is she shy? That's not really a thing with well-born Victorian ladies, accustomed to help dressing. I'd marveled the first time I helped Isla, who'd shed her clothes with a confidence even I've never had in change rooms.

I unlace and help Violet remove her corset. Then I walk around her and start to pull off the chemise under it. I'm pulling it up when her arm clamps down.

"That is not necessary," she says. "This one will do."

I nod, and I'm about to release the chemise when I see her stomach, where I've lifted the chemise. There are marks on her stomach. Odd striations, slightly red but turning a silvery-white. Something in me dimly recognizes what they are, but the answer doesn't come, and I quickly pull down the chemise, knowing that's what she didn't want me to see.

After that, there's no chance of asking any questions. She's tense and distracted, and all I can do is keep up my small talk as I help her dress and prepare for dinner.

Then, as I'm leaving, the answer hits, and I know what I saw on Violet's stomach.

Stretch marks.

THIRTY-TWO

Stretch marks on the stomach aren't necessarily a sign of pregnancy. I need to speak to someone who has known Violet, at least casually, for years. That person also can't be McCreadie . . . for reasons. Nor can it be Isla . . . for reasons.

I also should speak to someone with the medical knowledge to tell me whether I'm missing any possible causes of abdominal marks. That narrows my choices down to one. Yes, I need to speak to Gray. In private. Which I absolutely am not ready to do, but the case takes precedence.

I eat dinner with the others. Then as we are retiring to our separate rooms, men in one and women in the other, I say to Gray, "Sir? Might I have a moment? It is about the investigation."

I say it loud enough for others to hear. I don't want to be seen whispering and shuttling him off. Does Edith still sniff and give me a look that calls me a forward little trollop? Of course she does. Does her husband glance at me and then give Gray a look that calls him a very lucky fellow? Of course he does. But no one else bats an eye, and Gray tells McCreadie and Frye he will join them shortly.

We go outside, which is the only place where we can be sure of privacy, but I lead him around to the south side, where windows from the sitting rooms overlook the lawn. In other words, we'll be out of earshot but in plain view of everyone taking their post-dinner drinks.

When we're far enough away, Gray says, "I wish to apologize—"

"No need," I cut in, and then hear how that sounds and make a face. "I know you were suggesting a logical solution to our problem, and I took undue offense."

"It was not un—"

"I'm still getting used to the culture here. One would think I'd understand, being at this very estate to witness an arranged marriage, but my twenty-first-century Western sensibilities are still horrified. When you mentioned your idea, all I heard was 'marriage of convenience.'" I force a smile. "Which works out so much better in rom-coms."

His brows rise.

I shrug. "It's a trope in romantic fiction, especially comedic. Two people absolutely need to get married for some reason or other."

"That is considered *comedic*?"

"It's different in my world, where the couple always assume it'll be temporary. They'll marry for a few months, solve their problem, and get an annulment or divorce. Except that never happens because, being a romance . . . ?" I trail off with a shrug. "It all works out in the end."

"How?"

That seems an odd question, but his expression is serious. I shrug again. "They get to know each other and fall in love."

"They did not know each other before?"

"Sometimes. Maybe they secretly had deeper feelings."

"Or one party had deeper feelings and the other did not, and the first party hoped to woo the second party, which should properly be accomplished *before* a wedding takes place."

"Uh . . ." I try and fail to parse that out. "I guess so?" I shake it off. "Anyway, the point is that, outside of fiction, a marriage of convenience is never a good idea. Not for me, anyway. We had a culture clash, and I overreacted."

I glance toward the window to see Edith's face turned our way. "And since we have an audience, we should really get on with the case stuff. I have a question about Violet." I pause. "Was she ever larger? In weight, I mean?"

His brow furrows. "Heavier?"

"Significantly."

"I am going to require more context."

"I know, but can you try to answer, please? You've known her socially for a long time. Has she always been roughly the same physical size?"

"I believe she has grown thinner in the last few years, to the point where if I were her physician, I would be concerned, but she has always been slender, so I cannot say she has lost a significant amount of weight."

I tell him then about my scheme to question Violet while helping her dress, how she'd been reluctant to accept help, and what I'd inadvertently seen.

"Stretch marks," I say. "Silverish-red striations on her abdomen, which could signify a sudden loss of weight."

"Marks on the abdomen? As if from . . . pregnancy?" He pulls back, blinking hard, and his gaze shoots to the bank of windows before quickly looking away. Color tinges his cheeks.

"It does happen, Duncan," I say, trying to keep annoyance from my voice. "Accidental pregnancy out of wedlock happens to both men and women. The difference is that guys can walk away without anyone knowing they had extramarital sex. Women can't."

"What?" He looks at me and then vehemently shakes his head. "If you heard censure in my voice, Mallory, that was not what I intended. I am horrified by the thought that Violet had to deal with such a thing."

I relax. "Stretch marks aren't proof positive of a pregnancy."

"In this case, with no history of that sort of weight loss, that is almost certainly what they signify. It would also explain a great deal."

I move to the bench and sit on one end, facing away from the windows. He sits beside me, being sure to leave a decorous gap between us.

I say, "If Violet has stretch marks, then she either had a baby or went through most of a pregnancy. Her parents must have known, and it might explain why she hasn't married. It'd be hard to hide those marks from a husband."

"It would."

"That could explain why marrying Ezra would have been out of the question. But she *did* plan to marry Hugh. Which leads to a very awkward conclusion."

He frowns, and I wait, knowing the answer will hit. When it does, his eyes widen. "You believe Hugh was the father?"

"That's the logical answer, Duncan. She was going to marry him. Then, after he ends it, she goes into what seems like a depression and withdraws from society. I thought that was because of the broken engagement but this fits, too. Maybe even better."

My hands fly up. "Not that Hugh broke it off because she got pregnant. He'd never do that, and it doesn't make sense anyway—if they're to be married, pregnancy is fine. Which is actually my point. They were getting married, so they'd see no problem with an early wedding night or two, and even when she got pregnant, it'd just be a matter of getting married before she showed. But what if Hugh didn't know she was pregnant? If he ended it without knowing, and pride wouldn't allow her to tell him, because she knew he'd marry her, which is a terrible way to start a married life."

Gray goes quiet. He sits there, staring out over the sloping hill leading to the lakes.

"I wouldn't judge him for that," I say softly. "I'm sure he's careful, but mistakes happen."

He shakes his head. "That is not the issue. I am only trying to think of a way to say that I know Hugh was not the father, without sounding as if I am merely defending a friend."

He looks at me. "Is there a *chance* he was the father? Of course. I would be naive to think otherwise. But he had no contact with Violet outside of chaperoned visits. Of course, young couples do find ways around that. However . . ."

He glances toward the house again. "Intending no insult to Violet, Hugh was not a smitten young man, eager to bed his bride. She is pleasing enough that he would have—" He clears his throat, cheeks flushing.

"Not found his marital duties overly onerous."

More flushing. "Yes. But there was no reason *not* to wait. He respected her too much to risk her reputation in that way, and if he wanted such companionship, he found it easily enough."

"So, while there's the faintest chance they had an early wedding night, it's very unlikely."

"Exceptionally unlikely. If such a thing happened, even without a resulting pregnancy, he would have felt honor-bound to marry her."

"Because she was no longer a virgin."

"Yes. It is not as if any future husband would definitely reject her for such a thing. It is exceedingly unlikely one would even realize it."

I look at him. "Realize she wasn't a virgin, yes. Realize she'd had a baby, though, with those stretch marks?"

"That would have been much more difficult."

Gray and I continue hashing it out. If Violet was pregnant—either carrying to term or close enough to have those stretch marks—then she would have needed to go away. Yes, a young Victorian woman going to visit an aunt in the countryside for a few months really is a thing, and I have to wonder how women in the past did legitimately go to visit rural relatives for an extended stay *without* everyone thinking they had a baby.

Abortion is another option. It's illegal, and it'd be hard to find a doctor to perform it, but that doesn't mean it doesn't happen. It has always happened. We know a woman—Queen Mab—who is known for her abortifacients. She prefers to sell birth control methods, but guys aren't exactly beating down her door for Victorian-era condoms. And the only women who partake of her services are sex workers and widows. Young women carrying on premarital affairs don't dare go looking for help . . . until they're pregnant and desperate.

What does happen is women who—having no other options—give birth and then end the baby's life. It's common enough that courts don't necessarily consider it murder. They seem to often turn a blind eye, tell themselves it was a tragic accident, and give thanks for one fewer orphan "draining" the public coffers.

Being upper middle class, Violet is unlikely to have known where to obtain an abortion. She's also unlikely to have been able to avoid her parents discovering the pregnancy. She'd have been whisked off to the country, and if she had a live birth, the baby would . . . go somewhere. Gray is a little fuzzy on the process. It's not something he'd ever considered, being a man. To give him credit, I know—from an awkward conversation with Queen Mab—that he takes all steps to avoid accidental pregnancy.

Gray doesn't know Violet well enough to be able to say, with any certainty, when she might have popped off to the country for a few months. Could it have been recently? Is it possible that *Sinclair* was the father? Maybe that's why they were meeting in secret—if he was the father and her parents had forbidden a marriage. But even if, somehow, Sinclair being the father of her child didn't make the alliance acceptable, Cranston would never have stayed best friends with the guy who knocked up his sister. Sure, it's possible Cranston didn't know, but then her parents would have refused to let her come here, where she'd be with Sinclair.

The baby daddy is almost certainly no one at this party, given that the only remaining possibilities would be Frye or Gray himself.

I put the pregnancy—and how it could be connected to the murder—on the back burner for now. I need to speak to Mrs. Hall, and Gray needs to delicately bring up the pregnancy to McCreadie.

I take Isla to speak to Mrs. Hall. The housekeeper seems to like Isla. I'm not surprised. When I was a housemaid, I don't think I really understood how good a "lady of the house" Isla was. She was an easy boss to serve, and she is an easy guest as well. She's considerate of the staff in a way that others aren't.

Fiona and Violet are kind and gracious, but they also make more demands. They grew up in normal Victorian upper-middle-class households, where the point of having domestic staff is for someone to clean up after you and bring you tea. Fiona and Violet remind me of some friends I had growing up, who'd never think to take their dishes into the kitchen or make their beds after a sleepover.

On the other hand, Victorian domestic staff would be horrified and even offended if their employers did everything themselves. They can be downright territorial. Our housekeeper adores Gray and Isla, but she still bristles if they try to fix themselves a snack in her kitchen.

I will point out that I am just as good a houseguest. However, my odd position means I'm still considered staff, and so I'd damned well better not be ringing for snacks or leaving my room a mess. Being extremely low maintenance doesn't win me any brownie points with Mrs. Hall. It's just proper behavior.

Speaking of proper behavior, Isla doesn't go barging into the back rooms looking for Mrs. Hall. She finds a maid and says she'd like to speak to the housekeeper, at her convenience. It's a testament to Isla's good-guest manners that Mrs. Hall doesn't keep her waiting.

"Thank you so much for coming," Isla says as Mrs. Hall joins us in the library. "I hate to interrupt your evening, but some items were found in the gamekeeper cottage that might belong to your daughter, and we wished to ensure she received them, not trusting Mr. Müller to do so."

Mrs. Hall frowns. "We did an excellent job of clearing the cottage. I cannot imagine what we would have left behind."

"The items are small and seem to have fallen into a crack." Isla smiles. "Or perhaps, as a young girl, Nori—" Her hand flies to her mouth. "Oh! I meant Lenore. That sounded terribly forward of me. I have a friend named Lenore who goes by Nori, and that popped out."

Mrs. Hall's stern face lightens. "No need to apologize, ma'am. Lenore went by Nori as a girl. Some still call her that."

"Thank you for being gracious. As for the items . . . Mallory?"

I take a handkerchief from my pocket and open it to reveal the ring and embroidered hair ribbon.

"Oh! My word," Mrs. Hall says. "Yes, those are Lenore's. The ribbon has been missing for a while now and the ring—" She stops and frowns. "You said they were in the cottage?"

I nod. "That is where they were found."

"Well, then Lenore could not have left them there. I recall her looking for the ribbon, but that was only a few months ago. Shortly afterward I noticed she was no longer wearing her ring, and she said she had given it to a friend. That was after we left the cottage."

"Oh?" I frown. "Perhaps she lost both while walking the grounds and Mr. Müller found them."

Isla nods. "If Lenore lost the ribbon, she might not wish to admit to losing the ring." She lowers her voice, conspiratorial. "I do not doubt Mr. Müller might fail to return them. He seems an unpleasant man."

"Unpleasant indeed." Mrs. Hall's lips compress. "I feel badly for Mr. Cranston, tricked as he was into hiring the fellow."

"Tricked?" I say.

She pauses and then pulls back. "I ought not to say that. I do not know the whole of it, and I should not speak ill of the dead."

I remember Mrs. Hall earlier saying she didn't blame Cranston for hiring Müller, that he'd been misled.

"I know Mr. Sinclair lobbied for Mr. Müller's hiring," I say. "Is there something—?"

"I did not say that, miss." She fusses with the lappet in her hair bun.

I consider, evaluating her body language. Yes, there's more here, and it involves Ezra Sinclair, but if I push, I'll lose any ground we've gained with the housekeeper.

"Well, I would agree poor Mr. Cranston was misled," I say. "Mr. Müller is . . ." I shudder.

Mrs. Hall relaxes and leans in. "That is not the worst of it. Naturally, I am pleased that Mr. Hall is getting his position back, but frankly, he had found work to suit and we would have been fine. My worry would have been for Miss Fiona."

"Fiona?" Isla looks at me. "I have not liked how Mr. Müller has regarded Mallory. Is that the way you mean?"

"It is, ma'am. I cannot imagine he would touch the lady of the house. He wouldn't dare. But it still worried me." She looks at me. "Take care, miss. I know you have been in and out of the house, and you ought to take care around that man."

"Has there been a problem?" I say. "There are several young maids here. Your daughter was one of them."

"He does not turn his attention that way. He likes the lasses—ladies—he cannot have. Not that he could have had my Lenore. But that was never a concern. I watch out for all the girls."

I look at the ring and hair ribbon. "I hate to ask this, ma'am, but given that we found these in Mr. Müller's cottage, I feel I must. You have concerns about his behavior toward young women, and he seems to have had items belonging to Lenore. Is there any chance of . . ." I pause to make sure I have the period-appropriate words and tone. "Any chance he interfered with her?"

I watch for dawning horror. But when she shakes her head, the movement is measured and calm. "No. Lenore would have told me. I believe that you are correct that she lost them and then he found them and could not be bothered giving them back. He is a vile man, and I will be glad when he is gone."

I hand her the ring and hair ribbon. "Please take these and return them. I am glad to hear Lenore was not harmed in any way." I start to step back and then stop. "Oh, Detective McCreadie had a question about your daughter. When exactly did she leave her position here?"

"The beginning of May." She sighs. "I hope she will consider coming back, once we are living on the grounds again."

"Do you know why she quit?" I say, then quickly add, "It will help Detective McCreadie understand the situation here."

"It was nothing to do with the job or Mr. Cranston. She liked both well enough. She'd had a sweetheart, I believe. She would not speak of him and adamantly denied it, but she acted like a young woman in love. Light and happy and glowing. Then it ended, and she was not herself. She left her position here and moped for weeks. She is back to herself at last, and I am glad to see it."

"As are we," Isla murmurs. "As are we."

THIRTY-THREE

The poor woman is wrong," Isla whispers when Mrs. Hall leaves us alone. "Mr. Müller did do something to Lenore. That is why Lenore quit her position and fell into a state of melancholia."

"That's one explanation," I say as I lower myself behind the desk. "But if he did that, would she not have mentioned it? For the sake of the other maids?"

"Perhaps she did not feel the other maids were in danger. And while Mrs. Hall might believe her daughter would tell her, that is not always the case." She plucks at her bodice, as if adjusting it. "I never told anyone about the problems in my marriage. Even my mother, with whom I am extremely close."

"Why didn't you tell her?"

When Isla colors, I hurry on. "That's not an accusation. I think I know the answer, which means this would be a very different situation."

She hesitates and then nods. "I see your point. I did not tell my mother because she could not help. Even in Scotland, it is exceptionally difficult to end a marriage. If I feared for my life, I would have done anything to escape. But it was not as bad as that."

She looks over at me, a wan smile playing on her lips. "I heard that noise you made. You would like to point out that any mistreatment is bad, but you also understand what I mean. My mother could not help me, and I would not put her in that untenable position—knowing I am miserable and she cannot help. Then our father died and Duncan took over the family finances, and he *could* assist me, having seen enough to realize I needed it."

She pauses. "Which has nothing to do with the current situation except that you are correct about it being different. However much I desperately needed my mother's guidance, I hid my unhappiness from her because she could not help. Lenore was not bound to Mr. Müller. Had she told Mrs. Hall, I do not doubt the woman would have found a way to convey it to Archie, who would not have stood for it."

"I agree."

"So you do not think Mr. Müller molested Lenore?"

"Not . . . necessarily." I rise. "But I'm going to need to ask Mrs. Hall something else before I say more."

I speak to Mrs. Hall briefly and get the answer I expected. Then I find Mc-Creadie and Gray outside, still deep in conversation. Seeing that, I pause, but they catch sight of me and wave me over.

"First," McCreadie says, "I absolutely did not get Violet with child. I believe I can speak of such things with you as if you were a man."

"Uh . . ." I say.

Gray arches a brow.

McCreadie gives us both a hard look. "You know what I mean. The sensibilities of your time mean I do not need to act as if I am an un-spoiled flower of male bachelorhood waiting to discover the joys of the marriage bed."

I sputter a laugh. "Yeah, I don't think many single men fit that description. And probably fewer women than Victorians would like to think. But yes, I do not expect you to be a virgin."

"Which I am not. However, I also would never have had premarital re-lations with Violet. That is far too great a risk to her reputation. As we were not in love and I was free to do as I wished before marriage . . ." He clears his throat. "There was no chance we would get carried away while courting. Also, while I liked Violet, I did not feel that way about her."

"Got it, and you understand we needed to ask, just in case."

"I do, and I am horrified to think that someone did that to Violet, that he left her with child." He lowers his voice even more. "It does explain a great deal. While we had long been promised by our parents, no one seemed in any rush to fulfill the obligation. I was only twenty-one, barely out of school, a new police officer. Then, suddenly, things were moving very quickly, and I was told I would be wed within the year, with an increased dowry, supposedly because of my reduced expectations as a policeman."

"Do you think Violet could have already been pregnant?" Gray asks. Then he pauses. "No, the timing would not work."

"It would not. Her parents were in a hurry to solidify the engagement, but the marriage was still six months away. She could not have been pregnant. Also, when I reflected further, I recalled that her parents began to push shortly after she returned from a long sojourn abroad."

"Violet went abroad?"

"Visiting a cousin on the Continent. She was gone for about five months."

"I forgot about that," Gray murmurs.

I swear under my breath. "She got pregnant, was whisked off to have the baby, and then her parents wanted her married as soon as possible. Before you had time to discover why she went abroad."

"I cannot imagine I *would* discover it. They were only making sure the wedding happened."

"Marrying her to the guy she was supposed to marry. Because if you backed out, things would get tricky."

"Yes. Duncan says there are marks on her stomach showing a pregnancy, but I was inexperienced enough that I would not have thought it odd if she wished to keep the lights out and her nightgown on."

"If you didn't marry her, then her parents would also have a broken engagement to contend with. That would have made people look closer. Too close."

His hands clench and unclench. "Which is exactly what I inadvertently subjected her to. I am horrified and shamed, and I cannot even properly apologize because I should not know about the pregnancy."

"Unless it has to come out," I say. "But if it doesn't, then it shouldn't. My sense is that Violet's melancholy wasn't because you ended the engagement as much as a combination of events. The pregnancy, the shame of that, and the fact it meant her marital prospects were limited to the guy she'd been promised to."

"Isla thinks I should still speak to her. Apologize and admit that I did not understand how the broken engagement would affect her."

There's an inflection in his voice that adds a question to the statement. He's hoping Gray and I will disagree with Isla. No one likes to apologize, even when they *are* sorry. There's always the fear of not finding the right words, of making things worse.

Gray and I only nod, and McCreadie deflates, but bounces back with a wry smile. "I really should. I have told myself that I already apologized, but that was for the act, not the consequences. I will do that."

"I have news, too," I say. "I spoke to Mrs. Hall. The ring and hair ribbon are definitely Lenore's, and she did go by Nori when she was young. Putting that aside temporarily, I have a question." I look at McCreadie and Gray. "I overheard Ezra saying he'd been up here more often than Archie. Did he come up on his own?"

McCreadie nods. "Archie was occupied with the whisky business, and I believe there was some arrangement for Ezra to manage his affairs here. Check on the running of the estate while enjoying a holiday, as his current job obligations were not onerous."

"Was it multiple trips? One extended trip?"

McCreadie looks at Gray, who says, "My understanding was that it was two or three visits of a fortnight apiece. Ezra was, in effect, managing the estate. I believe when Hugh says it was an arrangement, he means that Archie paid him for it. As I understand it, they were discussing the possibility of Ezra doing that on a permanent basis, if the whisky business succeeded as well as it seems poised to do."

"If Archie made enough on whisky, he'd hire Ezra to work here and manage the estate in his absence."

McCreadie nods. "It would also allow Fiona to enjoy the estate while Archie was busy. Ezra was glad that Fiona seemed to like the place and suggested to Archie that she could come up more often. Naturally, Ezra would need to move to one of the cottages while she was here, for propriety's sake, but with the staff on site, it would be acceptable."

"Is there any way of knowing when Ezra was here?" I ask.

"I believe the last time was this spring? Early May? Perhaps late April?" He pauses, and then his eyes narrow. "This is not idle conversation. What are you thinking?"

I reach into my pocket and pull out the folded note from the coach.

"'He deserved it for what he did to Nora,'" I read aloud. "We believe the last word is 'Nori,' not 'Nora.' Lenore Hall, who quit her position as maid in early May, after which her mother says she fell into a state of melancholy."

McCreadie's expression goes grave. "Because she had been molested by Mr. Müller."

"That's the obvious conclusion, but we managed to broach the possibility, and Mrs. Hall didn't think it was likely." I lift a hand. "Yes, she's Lenore's mother and might not know, but Isla and I have discussed this. We don't think that's the case. Her mother believed she was courting a young man shortly before that, and she suspects the end of that courtship was the cause of both Lenore quitting her job and becoming depressed."

"All right."

"After Isla and I spoke to Mrs. Hall, I went back to ask her one more question. When Duncan and I went to see Dr. Rendall, a young boy thought it was Archie who died. That made it seem that the note"—I wave it—"referred to Archie. He deserved his death for what he did. But we had to do cartwheels to apply that to Archie. It's possible someone would blame him for a girl—Nora or Lenore—being molested on his estate. But when I went back to speak to Mrs. Hall, I asked whether villagers thought Archie was the victim. She says no, most people realized Ezra was the one who died. Clearly the boy we spoke to misheard the message, but are we sure the person who wrote this note also misheard?"

"I . . . do not understand," McCreadie says slowly. "You believe Ezra molested Lenore?" He rubs his mouth and shakes his head. "That sounds as if I cannot believe someone I know would do such a thing. I should not say that."

"I don't think Ezra molested Lenore," I say. "Her mother believed she had a sweetheart. Someone she didn't want to tell her mother about, but who made her very happy."

"Ezra," McCreadie says, exhaling the name.

I nod. "Maybe they had a fling. Maybe it was just a flirtation. Hell, maybe it was an infatuation and she mistook his kindness for encouragement. I need to get precise dates from Archie, but I have a feeling, when I do, the end of Ezra's last visit will align with Lenore quitting her position."

"She had a romantic disappointment," McCreadie murmurs. "If there was an affair or a flirtation, Ezra ended it. If it was only an infatuation, he told her he did not reciprocate."

"Which means the ring and hair ribbon could be a red herring. Or they could be something else, if there was more than an infatuation and Müller knew of it."

"Blackmail," Gray says, his first word since I started. "He took them to hold what he knew over Ezra."

We need to speak to Müller. It's not yet dark, so we can do that tonight. First we attend to other matters, telling the others where we are going and so on. I take the time to visit the water closet, and I'm leaving just as Alice is coming up the stairs with a bouquet of flowers in each hand and a kitten nestled in the crook of her arm.

Seeing her, I laugh and put out my hand. I mean for her to give me a bouquet, but instead, she slides the kitten into my arms.

"I think she is lonely," Alice says. "Missing her mother and brothers. I have been carrying her about with me, but it is not easy."

"What you need is a pouch, like a mother kangaroo."

Her brows shoot up.

"I will make you one in a moment," I say. "Where are those flowers going?"

"Mr. Sinclair's room."

"Ah."

She means the room where Ezra's body is being kept, and the flowers are not for decoration. Even with the windows open, there is . . . a smell.

I take one bouquet and open the door. With the flowers in one hand and the kitten in the crook of my arm, I head over to replace the flowers beside the bed. I'm halfway there when the kitten explodes, hissing and leaping from my arms.

I bite back a too-modern curse as the kitten's claws scratch my exposed forearm. Then the poor thing lets out a yowl as it falls awkwardly, lacking a right hind leg.

Alice scoops her up and cuddles her, but she keeps hissing. I hurry over to pet the cat.

"It's the body," I say. "She can smell it even better than we can."

I take the second bouquet and set it out as I tell Alice to meet me in the hall. After they're gone, I circle the room, looking for anything else that might have upset the kitten, but I don't see it.

By then, the kitten has calmed enough that we're able to take her back to our room. There, I fashion a sling for Alice to use. Then I realize I've been gone longer than I intended, and I hurry off downstairs. Time to speak to Müller.

I'm in the main-level corridor when Gray catches up with me. He lowers his voice and ducks his head as we walk. "I have just left a note in your room. Under the pillow."

I'm glancing at him, brows raised, when we both notice one of the maids quickly retreating into another room after seeing—and hearing—us.

"My notes on the case," Gray says, louder. "I had them delivered to your room. Please see that they are put in with the rest."

"Of course, sir," I say.

"This is too damnably complicated," he mutters under his breath.

I brace for him to bring up the marriage-of-convenience suggestion again, but thankfully, he only says, "We will find a solution."

"A solution to what?" McCreadie says, coming up behind us.

"The murder," I say. "Fret not, dear detective. The illustrious Dr. Gray and his stalwart assistant are on the case and will solve it for you."

McCreadie makes a rude noise, and we continue to the cloakroom to collect our outerwear.

THIRTY-FOUR

Once we're far enough from the house, Gray says, "I feel I must say something, however disloyal it feels to Ezra."

"It's a murder case, Gray," I say. "We can't afford loyalty. Not to witnesses or suspects . . . or even the victim."

"I know. Which does not prevent it from feeling uncomfortable." He looks over at McCreadie. "Do you remember our last year of school together? When one of the maids was released from her position?"

"Hard for me to forget, given the scandal." He looks at me. "She was let go for having relations with one of the students."

I frown. "How old were you?"

"Oh, sixteen, seventeen? We were hardly children, and such relationships were not unheard of. That is the danger of having pretty girls working around young men. This was a scandal because they were apparently caught, *in flagrante delicto*, by the headmaster . . . who was leading a small group of alumni on a tour."

"Oh my," I say.

"Indeed." He grins wickedly. "The scandal of the year, made even more delicious because no one knew who the young man . . ." He trails off and blinks at Gray. "Ezra?"

Gray rolls his shoulders in discomfort. "I walked in on Archie giving Ezra a proper dressing-down over it."

"A dressing-down?" I say. "Over getting caught?"

"No, Archie was angry with Ezra for carrying on with a maid and getting her fired."

"Oh."

Gray sighs. "Yes, Archie is not the boor I might like him to be. As for Ezra, he was very contrite. Said he did care for the girl. Promised to help her find a new position. It really seemed a youthful mistake."

"One that he might have repeated here," I say. "With Lenore." I remember when McCreadie had talked about Sinclair's popularity with women. Gray had been quiet, as if thinking. He'd also been the one who made sure we kept maids on the list of women Sinclair might have been seeing the night of his murder.

I continue, "Ezra had a past affair—apparently a romantic one—with a young woman in domestic service. He starts another one, realizes he's repeating the error, and ends the relationship."

"But by then Müller knows of it," McCreadie says. "Lenore and Ezra could not carry on an affair in the house, especially when her mother is the housekeeper. There are several unused cottages about, and Lenore would have an extensive knowledge of the property. The same property that is now Müller's domain. He caught them."

"Proving Ezra really *hadn't* learned his lesson," I mutter. "But that might also have been his wake-up call. Müller catches them, and Ezra realizes what kind of trouble he could cause for Lenore, so he ends the affair. But Müller has evidence. Blackmail loot. A ring and a hair ribbon, which Lenore could have laid aside during their liaison and then forgotten in her haste. She might even have forgotten her bloomers. Grabs her dress and what undergarments she can find and misses those."

McCreadie nods. "Müller takes the ring and hair ribbon and tears a piece off the bloomers. He hides them in case he needs Ezra's support."

"Which he does after the wildcat incident," I say. "We've wondered why Ezra stuck up for Müller. This explains it. The question is whether it's connected to Ezra's murder."

I glance at Gray, who's gone quiet again, listening as McCreadie and I hammer it out.

"I believe," Gray says, "that the question is not how it could be connected but how do we sort through all the possible ways it could be connected."

"Good point," I murmur. "This opens up the possibility that Ezra was indeed the target. He could have told Müller he couldn't help him anymore—blackmail or no blackmail. They argue, and as he walks away, Müller kills him. We could also be looking at Lenore. Or her brother, Gavin. Ezra could have been carrying the shillelagh as a walking stick—his prints were on it. Violet also comes back into play—what if they *were* involved? She discovers the affair with Lenore and confronts him. He turns around, and she hits him."

"Violet said the nighttime meeting was to cheer her up," Gray murmurs. "And you overheard him tell Fiona something similar."

"Well, no, I overheard him asking Fiona to do it because he couldn't. But that might have just been a cover-up. Hiding their relationship."

"Whether friends or lovers, they cannot easily speak in private. Also, what if they were also meeting to discuss *his* problems?"

I turn to look at him. "The blackmail. Archie is hell-bent on firing Müller, and that's a problem."

"I am not certain he would tell Violet about his affair with a maid," McCreadie says. "But he could say that Müller is blackmailing him and ask for Violet's advice. Or ask for her help talking her brother out of firing Müller."

"The problem is the note," I say. "The maid's recollection of it is definitely romantic. We need to speak to her tomorrow."

Gray looks over. "What do we know about the maid?"

"Uh . . ." McCreadie says. "Which one is she?"

I roll my eyes. "As a former maid, might I request that you esteemed gents actually ask their names? Learn who is who?"

"I always ask names," McCreadie says. "Which is better than Duncan here. We once spent a week at the seaside, in a house with four maids, and at the end, he was shocked to learn there was more than one."

"They all had a similar mien," Gray says. "Also, while I understand Mallory's point, in our defense, it is not always wise to admit you have remembered their name. It suggests undue and unwelcome interest."

"And we are not Ezra." McCreadie makes a face. "That was unkind and judgmental. A man in his social position might well look to a shopgirl—or even a maid from a good family—for a wife."

Maybe, but Lenore isn't just a maid. She's in her late teens, making Sinclair more than a decade older. That's a double misuse of power. It doesn't mean he realized the imbalance, though.

"The maid's name is Dorothy," I say, getting back on topic. "That's really all I know. In my current position, I seem to float in a strange nether realm, neither fish nor fowl, staff nor guest."

Catching Gray's look of dismay, I hurry on. "Which is useful."

"You are like a governess," McCreadie says. "I once had a flirtation with one, and she said it was much the same for them. They are employees, but of elevated social backgrounds with good educations, and therefore she was not considered part of the staff. Rather more like a poor relation."

"You had a flirtation with your governess?"

His cheeks heat, and he wags a finger at me. "*A* governess. Not mine. Though mine was very pretty. I did notice that. A lad never forgets the first woman who teaches him verb conjugation."

I laugh. "At least you didn't say the first woman who straps him."

McCreadie sputters and then glares at Gray.

"Why are you looking at me?" Gray says.

"As a woman in your household, she is your responsibility. Rein in that tongue of hers, old chap."

"Like to see him try," I say.

McCreadie grins. "That sounds like a challenge, Duncan."

Is it my imagination or does Gray blush?

"I would not attempt it," Gray says finally, "as I value Mallory's help nearly as much as I value my life, both of which I would be in danger of losing if I tried to constrain her. Now, pulling you both back from your fun, the maid we must speak to is Dorothy. She will have finished her shift by the time we return, so that will need to wait until morning. Tonight, we interview Mr. Müller, whose cottage I believe I can see."

I approach the cottage alone. That's McCreadie's idea, reasoning that Müller will probably answer the door for me. Gray *really* doesn't like it. But they stay near enough to intercede.

As soon as I draw near, I suspect all this has been for naught. It's growing dark, but no light comes from inside the cottage. Müller must still be out.

I knock. No answer—or answering noise from within. I knock again and then move to one of the two windows and shade my eyes to peer in. It's dark and empty. *Very* empty. All I see are a table and chairs, with a hearth and wood piled beside it. There aren't any personal items in sight. Either Müller never made this place a real home or he's already preparing to move out.

At that thought, I move quickly to the other window, worry percolating in my gut. This one looks into the bedroom. It's unshuttered, and I can peer inside. I have to find a good angle to see anything, but when I do, I can make out a bed and a dressing table . . . and nothing more.

I take two steps into the forest, and Gray appears.

"This is definitely Müller's cottage, right?" I say.

"Of course."

"You and Hugh searched it. How empty was it?"

"How empty?"

"What is the matter?" McCreadie walks over, undergrowth crunching beneath his boots.

"I can see inside, and there's nothing but furniture. Either Müller is extremely tidy or he's gone."

McCreadie curses and strides around the cottage. He pulls open the door, which isn't locked. Inside, he lights a lantern as Gray and I join him.

I wasn't missing anything from my vantage points. The place is abandoned. We still search, checking in drawers and the single wardrobe.

"He's bolted," I say. Then I glance at the men. "Yes, it's also possible he realized he wasn't going to keep his job, packed his things, and stormed off in a huff, but I think we need to presume the worst."

"That he realized we were closing in," McCreadie says. "At the very least, he heard we had summoned Lenore back. He already knew we had found her belongings here."

"Where would he go?" I say. It's not as if he can call for a cab.

"He would walk to the village and then, from there, get to a coach or train station."

"Is there an inn in town? Someplace he could stay?"

McCreadie shakes his head. "Archie grumbled about that, saying any guests who needed overnight accommodations would be forced to stay an hour's ride away. We will need to check the stables, in case he took a horse. If so, we might be able to catch him."

Müller didn't take a horse. He must have set out on foot. No one has seen him since this afternoon. McCreadie offers to head out for the town with that inn, which also has a train station. But it's not as if he'd find Müller trudging along the road. He'll have holed up for the night.

"We will leave first thing in the morning," McCreadie says. "Duncan and I will travel to apprehend him, and you and Isla will remain here awaiting Lenore's return. That will also allow you to speak to the maid." He pauses, as if realizing he just gave me an order. "Is that satisfactory?"

I smile. "It is."

I've had so many unsettled nights that when I get to bed, my brain is too exhausted to even mull over the implications of everything we've discovered. Gray and McCreadie will need to leave at dawn, and I'll be the sole investigator for most of the day. I need my rest, and so I get it.

I don't know how long I've been asleep when my hand brushes something under my pillow, and somewhere deep in my sleeping brain, a voice whispers that I've forgotten something.

I jerk awake.

Gray said he put a note beneath my pillow. I reach under and pull out the folded sheet.

Then I stop, seeing what looks like a long letter.

I asked Gray to drop the marriage-of-convenience idea. I also asked him not to apologize. It's almost certain this letter breaks one of those two requests, which will only leave me steaming and unable to sleep.

But I also won't sleep if I'm tossing and turning, wondering what he wrote.

I take it to the window and unfold it, braced for a full letter and relaxing when I see it's only two lines.

Mallory,
Meet me at the lake bench at midnight. We must speak.
Duncan

Goddamn it. He really isn't letting this drop, is he?

I want to pitch the letter in the trash. Which, of course, I can't do for fear a maid will find it and misunderstand, especially with the use of our first names. Also if I don't go meet him, I won't sleep. I'll be too busy imagining everything he could say and how much it'll piss me off.

As I think about it, I realize he may not even be there. He wrote this before McCreadie made plans for them to leave at dawn. Gray probably forgot all about the note—and forgot to tell me to skip it.

I check my pocket watch on the bedside table. It's almost midnight. I'll be late even if he is there.

Well, at least that'll mean I won't be hanging around outside waiting for him. I'll quickly get to the lake, confirm he's not there, and come back. Then, tomorrow, when he returns, I'll see what he wanted.

As I'm dressing, the wildcat kitten stirs. I bend to pet it and then I slip out.

THIRTY-FIVE

Gray isn't at the lake. I can see that as soon as I'm on top of the hill. I still pause there, squinting down. Then I check my pocket watch. Twenty past midnight.

Okay, either he forgot all about it or he presumed I'd know our meet-up was canceled, in light of his early-morning trip.

I'm not sure whether to be relieved or frustrated. I don't want to talk about the marriage thing again, but I also don't know for certain that's what he'd wanted to discuss.

What else could it be?

What else did I want it to be?

Damn it, I need to stop this.

I turn on my heel and stalk back toward the house as I fume at myself. I know full well what I was hoping for, as much as it shames me to admit it.

I was hoping for the same damn thing I'd been hoping for when I told Gray I wouldn't marry someone who didn't love me.

I wanted him to tell me he did.

No, I just wanted him to tell me he *could*. I didn't actually expect him to say he felt the same way I did.

A tiny voice in me whispers, *But it would have been nice.*

Damn it. I don't want to be that person. I'm the practical one who knows the most she can hope for is an admission of deeper feelings that could blossom into more.

But I *am* hoping for those deeper feelings. Is that fair to Gray? I've known guys who seemed happy to be friends until they admitted to hoping for more and it hurt. It *hurt*. My friendship hadn't been enough. *I* hadn't been enough.

A few had half joked—even complained—about being "friend-zoned." God how I hated that phrase. As if the only reason men befriended women was in hopes of sex.

Once I made it clear that I wasn't interested, they'd ended the friendship. But that's not what I'd do with Gray, because that is not why I'm in this relationship. His friendship isn't a consolation prize. It's the *main* prize and anything else is a bonus.

Does that make it better? I think so.

I need to be absolutely certain that if I'm angry over this marriage-of-convenience nonsense, I'm not actually angry because he isn't offering more.

I'm walking and thinking when I hear a tiny meow. I almost ignore it. I've been sleeping in the same room as a wildcat kitten. I'm accustomed to meows. Except I'm not in my room. I'm outside.

The meow comes again, small and plaintive.

I stop and peer along the side of the road. The noise comes from inside a row of bushes.

Had we missed one of the wildcat kittens?

Gray and I had followed the mother and her babies, and there'd been three. Had there been a fourth somewhere? Or another wildcat with kittens? Or did one of the two in the barn escape?

These are all valid explanations. Explanations that should have me walking into those bushes to rescue a lost kitten.

Instead, the hairs on my neck rise. I'm thrown back a year, jogging through the Grassmarket in the twenty-first century, hearing a woman in trouble and going to investigate. Because of course I'd try to help.

I'd been lured in by a killer, which is how I ended up in Victorian Scotland.

In this case, I hate to say it, but I'm not hearing a *person* in distress. It's a kitten, and I'm not even sure it's distressed about anything except being lost. There are no larger predators out here. I can head to the barn, check on the kittens, and if one is missing, I'll make a decision then.

I look around. There's no sign of anyone, and I might feel silly being suspicious, but my hand still slides into my pocket for my derringer. I don't even have time to feel around the oversized pocket depths before I'm cursing.

My derringer is in the dress I was wearing earlier, and I'd pulled on a different—darker—one for this nighttime foray.

I do have my switchblade, though, in the pocket of my cloak. I palm it and then resume walking, my gaze and all my attention on that stand of bushes. I get three steps before a crackle sounds behind me, and I realize I'd been watching the wrong damn bushes.

I wheel, knife blade shooting out . . . and find myself staring down the barrel of a rifle.

"Not going to help that poor wee kitty?" Müller says, mangling a Scottish accent.

I say nothing. My brain is whirring as I assess my surroundings. I'm on the road to the house, in a stretch with bushes on either side. The rows of bushes aren't thick enough to make this an inescapable gauntlet, but with the shadows, I can't see a clear way through to the fields beyond.

Müller waggles the gun barrel. "Forgot your little gun, girl?"

I only adjust my grip on the knife, which makes him laugh. It's a dry, raspy sound, raw with contempt.

If this is an ambush of opportunity, he wouldn't have had time to get the cat. Did he know I was coming to see Gray? How? He'd never get in the house to read the note.

Does it matter?

It might. There's a big difference between targeting me and ambushing the first person who steps out of the house alone. A difference that will tell me how to play this.

"I thought you were gone," I say at last. "Your cottage is empty."

"Move." He indicates with the gun. "Back the way you came."

When I don't move, his eyes harden. "I said move, girl."

"Move *away* from the house?"

He sneers. "I do not need you farther from the house. You are far enough. You could scream, and they would not hear."

"You know that for a fact? Because no one heard Ezra Sinclair when you clubbed him?"

The sneer only grows. "I did not kill Ezra. His death has been nothing but trouble for me."

Ezra. He calls Sinclair by his first name. He wasn't exactly respectful when he referred to Cranston, but this is another level of familiarity.

"You were leaving, though," I say. "That says you're guilty of something."

"No, it says I knew your detective friend was going to accuse me of something. Him and that girl."

"Lenore?"

The sneer returns, telling me I guessed right.

I continue, "You knew she was coming back to tell us how her belongings got under that floorboard."

"She would not tell. She knows better."

"Knows better than to admit she had an affair with Ezra Sinclair?"

When his lip curls, my first thought is that we're wrong. But then he says, "That is a pretty word for it. Girls always have pretty words for it. They need to believe it means something when a man wants them. All fancy bows and flowers, ending with a wedding ring."

"Maybe he *was* in love with her."

Müller's laugh is so ugly something inside me hardens. I fight to tamp it down. As long as that gun isn't moving—and he isn't insisting *I* move—that's good enough. Lower his guard while getting what answers I can.

And there's an answer dangling here.

"It wasn't love," I say. "But he did care about her."

"I am certain that is what she will say. She knows the truth, but she will not admit it even to herself. They never do."

"The truth being that he only wanted sexual relations. That's what you presume because you can't imagine anything else. You can't allow for the possibility that he might have cared—"

His laugh answers my question, but I still need to push, and maybe that's for Gray and McCreadie's sake. They want to believe their friend was a good man who saw beyond class and fell in love.

"You sound very sure of yourself," I say.

"I *am* very sure of myself."

"Because you knew Ezra and knew he was not the man everyone thought him to be."

He only smiles. "If I told you the truth about your Ezra, you would not believe it."

"I might."

Müller shakes his head. "Walk. Head down the road. I will tell you when to stop."

"You were blackmailing him."

A pause. Müller's face screws up. "Black mail?" His English is excellent, but he must not know that word.

"Threatening to reveal what you know about him. To tell people what he did."

"Why would I want to tell people?"

"To keep your job. Ezra got it for you, and Mr. Cranston was going to let you go. What you knew about Ezra gave you leverage."

I expect one of two responses. He'll deny it or he'll laugh it off. Instead, his face goes dark.

"Move," he says.

"You—"

"I said *move*."

The gun barrel rams into my shoulder so suddenly that I stumble back. When I open my mouth, Müller slaps me. I reel, hands flying to my face.

"Move!"

I had a chance there, when he took his hand off the gun to hit me. But I missed it. I won't do that again. Stay calm and watch for another opportunity, and do *not* let him catch me off guard again.

I turn around and walk as I think.

Müller is genuinely angry at the suggestion that he'd blackmail Sinclair. I didn't expect that. I'd insulted him, of course, but we'd already accused him of stealing those objects from Lenore. Hell, I accused him of murder, and that hadn't fazed him. This did.

What had he said when I accused him of killing Sinclair? That it wasn't in his best interests to do so, which made sense if Sinclair was helping him keep his job.

I'm missing something.

Clear the mental chalkboard and rethink this.

Lenore had a fling with Sinclair. Müller confirmed it. Lenore thought it was a love affair. It wasn't, and Müller suggested she'd know that, even if she couldn't admit it.

Sinclair was taking advantage of her. Something went wrong—maybe she realized he didn't love her—and she quit.

Müller said she'd never tell. Why?

I mentally shift to the items found under that floorboard. My first thought had been "trophies." It's a classic sign. Predators like to keep items belonging to their victims, as talismans that allow them to relive those moments.

I'd reframed them as blackmail fodder. But Müller's reaction said they weren't. He'd been confused, as if he'd never considered such a thing.

Swing back to trophies then. Trophies of what? The bit of bloomers tells me it's sexual. Did Müller watch Sinclair with Lenore? I certainly wouldn't put that past him. But how would he get those items from her? She could have left the ring behind and lost the hair ribbon, but her underwear?

If I told you the truth about your Ezra, you would not believe it.

Why wasn't Sinclair worried about Lenore talking?

Why did Müller have those items under his floorboard?

These two things are connected. Lenore did something she was ashamed of. Another form of blackmail. One that involved Müller.

A threesome?

I hear Müller walking behind me, his breathing letting me picture the man, and that scenario makes me shudder. Could Lenore have overlooked her revulsion because she was curious? Or because she was in love and her lover wanted her to do this?

If I told you the truth about your Ezra, you would not believe it.

Is "talking his young lover into a threesome" enough to warrant that statement? In my time, I'd laugh at the thought.

But this *isn't* my time, and maybe what Müller meant was that I would be shocked as a young Victorian woman.

"Turn left," he says, startling me from my thoughts.

I glance back, but he only waves the rifle in the direction he wants me to go.

I have a very strong sense that Müller was involved in something sexual with Sinclair and Lenore. That isn't necessarily a problem, though. Not if she consented.

Did she consent?

Holy shit.

Did she consent?

My gut goes cold.

I need to get out of here. Yes, that should be obvious, but my cop brain has taken over, chasing clues dangled in front of me. That's a better trap than a lost kitten, and I fell for it.

I'd been thinking when I need to escape.

Because I do need to escape . . . before Müller does whatever he plans to do.

THIRTY-SIX

I did not say you could stop." Müller jerks the rifle again. "Do you see that bag on the ground? That is where you are going. Now move."

When I squint, I see the bag. Some kind of rucksack.

He's going to put me in a rucksack?

I continue walking toward it.

Be docile. Be cowed. Don't overdo it, but let him think he's in control.

Once we reach the sack, I see it's not big enough to hold me, and there are objects inside. I hold my breath. He's going to open it and take something out, and that will be my chance—

"Open it," he says.

I look at him.

The rifle barrel rises. "Open it."

I calculate and decide this isn't the time. I lift the bag. Inside is a length of hemp rope. Seeing it, something in me spasms, thrown back to how I ended up in this world, strangled by a rope like this. But this is several pieces, and in the next moment, I realize what he has in mind.

"Lie on your stomach," he says. "Place your hands behind your back."

"Wh-what are you going to do?" I say, injecting as much fear as I can into my voice.

"I do not know the custom in this country," he says, "but in mine, when you are released from a position early, you are due a payment. Cranston cannot give it to me, so I am taking it. You."

My reaction must show in my eyes, because he gives a harsh laugh. "Not for that. I said *payment*, girl. I know people who will pay well to take you. I only need to get you to them." His teeth flash. "I am certain they will be very kind to you."

"People in your country?"

Disdain oozes from him. "I do not need to go to my country to find such people. There are enough in yours. *More* than enough."

"People you know through Ezra Sinclair. People who share his . . . tastes."

"Lie down."

"He didn't bring you to Scotland because you're such a wonderful game-keeper. He brought you because you share his tastes."

"Lie *down*."

I lower myself to my knees. "Ezra let you have your way with Lenore. That's what happened, isn't it? You two shared her. Against her will."

"Any woman who would consent to such a thing is a whore. I do not consort with whores."

"What about the wildcat?"

That nearly does the trick. He rocks back, thrown by the seeming non sequitur. But his hands grip the rifle tighter. Then he smiles. "If you mean Miss Lenore, she *was* something of a wildcat. So much fight for a lame girl. You would have thought she would be happy for the attention."

My stomach twists, but I push on. "I mean the wildcat. You poisoned it and put it into that trap."

His face scrunches up. "Did that slap addle your brain, girl? What does the cat have to do with this? And what is this talk of poison? The beast was caught in the trap."

"No, it was placed there. After it died of poison."

More confusion. "I do not know what—"

His grip loosens on the rifle, the barrel dropping just enough. I dodge to the side and grab for the barrel. He's faster, wrenching it away, and I slash with my knife. The blade catches him on the hand. He hisses, but he doesn't drop the rifle, doesn't even loosen his grip.

I pull back my switchblade to stab, but he swings the rifle and the barrel strikes my funny bone. I gasp, my grip automatically loosening on the blade, and my knife starts to drop, but I manage to catch it with my other hand.

That leaves my weapon in the wrong hand. Müller moves, and my gaze is fixed on that rifle barrel, ready for it to swing up. When one hand releases the gun, I lunge to take advantage, which is exactly what he wants, as his fist plows into my stomach.

I fly back, feet scrambling for purchase, but the ground is slick with dew. My boot slips. I go down on one knee, and he hits me again, fist smacking my jaw so hard I fall back.

I twist as I fall, and I manage to flip over.

"Good," he grunts. "Lie on your stomach."

I start to lower myself. Then I vault up, and my brain screams that he has a rifle, and running is the last thing I should do. But it's also the only thing I *can* do, and as I tear back toward the bushes, I veer a split second before I hear the crack of the rifle. The shot whizzes past me.

I keep running, swerving erratically. I'm almost at the bushes when my damn boot slips again. The rifle cracks. Something hits me hard in the back, pain exploding. All I know is that it staggers me but I don't fall.

It's a low caliber rifle. Meant for shooting small game.

I've still been shot. *Shot.*

I dive into the bushes.

Müller fires again, this shot going wild.

I get on the other side of those bushes and then dart across the road to the next row as I struggle to catch my breath. Did the bullet hit my lung?

Keep going!

I dive into the bushes and through to the other side. And on that other side? Wide-open meadow that I can't cross without Müller seeing me and shooting me dead.

I struggle for breath.

The bullet hit my lung, didn't it? I can localize the pain now. It's the right side of my back, about halfway up. Where the bullet could pass through my ribs and pierce my lungs.

Don't think about that. Think about the guy who still has the gun, the one chasing you.

I try for a deeper breath. It hurts, but I manage it. Then I creep along the bushes, knife gripped tight as I look for a spot to hide. I find it just in time, and I wriggle in carefully, all too aware of Müller's heavy breathing only a few meters away.

A grunt tells me he makes it through the bushes just as I get hidden.

I slow my breathing.

Keep walking. Just keep walking.

He doesn't, though. Müller is a hunter, and I have the feeling he hunts more than deer. He knew how to subdue me. He has experience at that and probably experience at chasing prey that has fled his grasp.

He takes two steps from the row of bushes. I can see him there, through the branches, as he looks around.

He knows I didn't run across the meadow. He'd see me if I did. It's too far to the nearest shelter. I couldn't have made it in time.

He looks both ways. I'm in the bushes. He knows that. But to his left? Or his right?

I reach in my pocket for something to throw the other way. There's nothing, and even if there was, I'm not sure I'd dare. I'd be more likely to hit the branches with my swing.

I hold my breath, fingers playing with the switchblade handle. I need to be ready. He will come this way and—

He turns the other way.

I grip the knife even tighter as I weigh my options.

No time, my brain screams. I've already paused long enough, thinking when I need to act. This hedgerow isn't that long. He'll reach the end and come back.

I slide out, breath held, back throbbing. I roll my footsteps as I try to see where I'm placing my boots, but it's too dark and I can only brace, ready for attack if so much as a twig scrapes under my boot.

I have to fight the urge to run the rest of the distance. He's ten feet away, nine, eight. When I hit four, he's too close to the end of the row. He'll turn around at any second.

I charge and slash at the only exposed piece of skin I see. The side of his neck. I don't cut deep enough to kill him. I don't think I could do that unless I was absolutely certain I had no choice.

The blade splits the skin, and he howls. He starts to spin, and I grab the gun barrel. A shot fires, white hot as it rips down the barrel.

I force the gun up. I've still got my knife in hand—no time to put it away—and it keeps me from getting a good grip on the rifle, but blood flows from the side of his neck and panic floods his eyes.

We're locked in a standoff—me awkwardly holding the barrel, switchblade still in my hand, him clenching the gun but all too aware of blood gushing down his neck. When I yank hard, he loses his grip. Then he punches me, another of those no-holds-barred blows that sends me flying. I manage to keep the gun, but my knife falls. He dives for it. The rifle is too big for close-quarters combat. I pitch it aside as far as I can manage.

I get to my knife first. Then he runs for the gun, and I do the same. We reach the rifle at the same time, but my injured back seizes, and I stumble, hissing in pain. I slash at him as he goes for the gun. My blade catches his arm, but he's wearing too many layers for it to do any damage.

I kick the rifle. It's all I can manage. My back is on fire, my stomach screams from the earlier blow and my head pounds from the other two. I can't keep fighting or I will lose. All I can do is kick the gun and then run.

I race for the house. Behind me, Müller fires once, but I'm veering too wildly for him to hit me. At first, his footsteps pound behind me. Then they slow. Then they're erratic, and I risk glancing back to see him staggering, hand clamped to his neck, rifle lowered in the other hand.

I run straighter now. I try to run faster, too, but my entire body is screaming for me to stop. There's a moment when the world seems to dip, and like Müller, I stagger and stumble. As I get my balance, I look back to see the gamekeeper on his knees, both hands to his neck, rifle forgotten.

I slow then. I have to. The world sways, and my head throbs, and my lungs burn.

The house is there. It's *right there*. I can see a light in one of the windows. Someone is up. I just need to get to the house. Another hundred feet. Less than a hundred steps. I can do this. I—

My foot slides. It doesn't even slip. It slides in slow motion, and I fall, hard enough to gasp.

I'm on my knees, pain matched by exhaustion, as if I've run ten kilometers instead of a hundred meters.

Get up. The house is right there.

I can't pass out. It's still the middle of the night, hours before even Gray and McCreadie will be up for their dawn departure.

I rise slowly, pushing with everything I have. I peer at the house. It's only a hundred feet, but it seems an impossible distance.

Just move. One foot in front of—

"Mallory!"

My head jerks up. Someone is running from the house, and I can't see who it is, but I know that voice.

"Duncan?" I croak.

It can't be. I'm hallucinating. He's asleep—

No, the light in the bedroom. That's why it caught my eye. It was his room.

I take one staggering step. Then my legs give out, and I crash to the ground.

"Mallory!"

Gray's voice pierces the fog. I haven't passed out, but I'm dangerously close, struggling to get my eyes open, struggling to speak. His arms are around me, and then he's lifting me, shouting for help as he runs toward the house.

"No," I croak. "Müller."

He slows, and I sway in his arms. "Müller did this?"

"Behind me. Passed out, I think. Might wake up. Escape."

A strangled sound, more gasp than laugh. "That is the last thing you need to worry about."

"Gotta stop him. Not dead."

Gray's voice is tight and hoarse. "If he did this, then he may well wish he were."

A shout comes from the direction of the stable. A groom. Gray quickly tells him that Müller is passed out on the road and to get help to restrain him.

I keep sliding close to unconsciousness and then forcing myself back.

"Needs medical attention," I say. "Cut his neck."

"He will get it after you. If he gets it at all."

"Duncan . . ."

A low muttering. He's walking fast, carrying me, and as I jostle, pain rips through my back.

Shit.

"Shot," I say. "Shot me. In the back."

He stops so abruptly, I nearly fly from his arms. He manages to keep his hold and lowers me to the ground. He puts me down in a sitting position, but I start to fall, and he lowers me gingerly onto my stomach. Then he sucks in breath, and there's a rip of fabric.

I'm wearing a corset, of course. But he doesn't try to remove it. His fingers move over the spot, and he exhales. Is that relief? I'm too woozy to focus. Everything feels surreal. Even the pain from his fingers probing the wound barely registers.

Shock. I'm going into shock.

He says something I don't quite catch. Ribs? That the bullet passed through my ribs? No, he sounds too relieved for that. Did it hit my rib? Is the breathing pain only from the impact?

I dimly feel him turn me over, lifting me to sit again, but the darkness threatens. I want to sleep. Suddenly, all I want to do is sleep.

Time stutters, and the next thing I know, I'm propped against a wall and Gray is crouched beside me, his fingers on my jaw.

"*Mallory*," he says, his voice sharp with panic. "Stay with me."

He said the bullet hit my rib, right? So I'm okay. Just let me sleep.

Another time jump, and now Duncan's in front of me, hands cupping my cheeks, his face so close to mine, I can feel his breath, warm on my lips. My eyelids flutter open to see his dark eyes bright with panic. I want to tell him I'm fine, but I can't form words. My eyelids flag.

"Mallory, *please*. Stay here."

Just need to rest. Give me a moment. I'm fine.

"Mallory." His hands grip me, and I can dimly sense his face over mine. I struggle to open my eyelids and manage to see his eyes, burning with intensity.

"I'm sorry," he blurts. "The proposal. As I said in the letter, I would never trap you like that. I only thought . . . I thought you might come to . . . to care for—"

My eyelids flag. I want to hear what he's saying. I *need* to hear it. But I can't keep my eyes open.

"Mallory. Don't go. Please." His voice cracks. "I do not think I can bear it again."

Bear what? Go where?

A sound in the darkness. A beeping. Familiar, but wrong. I focus on the noise, and harsh light blasts through my eyelids. Then the beeping, slow and steady.

The beeping of a hospital monitor.

I'm sliding back into my old body. The one lying comatose in a twenty-first-century Edinburgh hospital.

I yank myself back so fast I gasp, gulping breath as my heart races.

"Here," I say on an exhale. "I'm here."

His arms go around me, pulling me to him in a hug fierce enough to stop my breath. There's a moment of complete silence, as we stay there, both of us just breathing. Then—

"Dr. Gray?" a voice says.

Gray makes a noise in his throat, lets me go, and turns to a groom asking what to do with Müller.

"Put him in the stables," Gray says. "I will tend to him after I have seen to Miss Mitchell."

"Do you need help carrying her—?"

"No, I do not," he says, and scoops me up and continues on toward the house.

THIRTY-SEVEN

The bullet hit the rib, as I thought Gray said. Only he didn't mean my rib. He meant the rib of my corset. It was a small enough caliber that the main damage is to my corset, which is ruined. The spot will bruise, and it hurts like hell, but the bigger concerns are that blow to my stomach and the ones to my head. Gray will need to monitor me, and he thinks I have a concussion. While I'm in rough shape, I'm in no danger of dying.

In danger of crossing back to my time?

We don't discuss that. At some point, we'll need to, and I'll admit that I really did start sliding back so we can figure out how to handle that.

But not now.

What makes me cross over? The last two times—coming here and then going back again—I'd been strangled unconscious. Losing consciousness from chloroform didn't do it. Does it need to be a serious threat to my life that also induces loss of consciousness? I don't know, but I need to figure it out. I made my choice, and as much as I would love to see my parents again, I don't want to risk not being able to come back here.

Once I'm taken care of, it's time to look after Müller. Gray doesn't want to do that, and I'm not even sure he should, given the murderous look on his face when I remind him.

McCreadie is up now, and he's with us, as is Isla, and they help convince

Gray that he needs to tend to Müller. The man cannot die on our watch, or Constable Ross is likely to arrest me for murder. That gets Gray moving.

McCreadie goes with him, leaving me with Isla, who is under strict instructions not to let me fall asleep. Is that because I may have a concussion? Or because he's worried I'll go back to my own time?

He *did* seem very concerned that I'll go back. I'm groggy, and I can't remember exactly what he said. That whole period from the time I nearly collapsed on the road until he got me inside is only snatches of memory. I remember telling Gray about Müller. I also remember hearing the hospital monitor beeping. I think he said something before that, about . . . a letter? I have the sense that I really need to remember what he said, but I can't.

The important thing is that I remember everything up to the point where I collapsed on the road, meaning I remember what Müller said. Gray hadn't wanted me straining myself as he examined me, so that story needs to wait until they return.

They do, quicker than I expect. Müller lost blood, but not enough to endanger his life. The cut was shallow; the bleeding had already stopped by the time the grooms got to him. He's regained consciousness, and he's demanding to be released, but no one's listening, obviously.

When Gray and McCreadie return, I start my story at the point where Müller ambushed me, only to have Isla cut in with, "You were outside walking alone?" She stops, cheeks reddening. "I apologize. That sounds as if I am blaming you for what happened. I am only surprised."

I sneak a look at Gray. "Duncan wanted to talk to me." I quickly add, "About the case. But he left the note before we realized Müller was gone, and he must have decided against . . ."

I struggle to find a way to word that, one that doesn't blame Gray, but he's frowning at me.

"Note?" he says.

"Under my pillow. You told me you'd left it, and I completely forgot about it until nearly midnight."

"I left you a *letter*," he says. "There were things I wished . . ." He trails off, glancing at Isla and McCreadie before clearing his throat. "Mallory and I had a disagreement earlier in the day, and I wished to respond to it." He looks back at me. "You received the letter and a note?"

I shake my head. "Just the note."

"So the letter . . . ?"

"I don't know where it went."

"You did not read it," he murmurs, as if to himself. "So what I said earlier, when you were injured, it did not make any sense."

"What did you say?" I rub my temple. "It's all a blur."

"Ah." He pulls back, tugging at his tie. "No matter. It is hardly important. Now, about this note . . ."

I pull it from my pocket.

Gray reads it and blinks. "That is not from me. It looks like my penmanship, but I did not write it."

"So Mr. Müller lured her out with a forgery?" Isla says. "But he could not have gotten inside to leave it, and it seems far too coincidental that it appeared when Mallory *was* expecting a missive from Duncan."

"Because it's not coincidental," I mutter. "That maid—Dorothy—overheard you saying you'd left me a note. She took it and copied your handwriting, as well as using the familiarity of first names. She's also the one who allegedly found a half-written note from Ezra."

Isla rises. "I will speak to Mrs. Hall and be sure the maid is detained for questioning."

Once she's gone, I tell McCreadie and Gray the rest. When I get to the part about Sinclair—and what he seems to have done to Lenore—McCreadie pales.

"My God," he says.

"It might not be true," I quickly add.

"But it is not an outlandish lie that Müller told you. It is what you deduced from his words, and he did not deny it."

I nod slowly. I know this is hard to hear. Sinclair was a friend, one McCreadie had admired. Even Gray rubs his mouth, shaking his head.

"It might not be true," I repeat. "We'll need to speak to Lenore."

"Who will confirm it," McCreadie says quietly. "Because it makes sense. Ezra seduced her, and then . . ." He struggles for words. "Gave her to Müller. Against her will. Of course she would not dare tell anyone."

"Because she'd be blamed. She almost certainly consented to sex with Ezra, and so anything else that happened would be seen as her fault because of that. Afterward, she ended the relationship with Ezra, quit her job here, and withdrew."

Silence falls as we all contemplate that.

"This makes it far more likely that Ezra *wasn't* mistaken for Archie," I say. "The question is who killed him."

"I am inclined to say it was Müller and ignore any evidence to the contrary," McCreadie mutters. "I would have no qualms seeing him punished for one crime he did not commit."

"Really? It would never come back to haunt you?"

He gives me a hard look. "Yes. Fine. It would be wrong."

"If I might suggest a course of action," Gray says. "Müller will need to be turned over to Constable Ross for his attack on you, Mallory. If the young man decides—without any help from us—that the gamekeeper killed Ezra?" He shrugs. "It will help keep him out of our way, temporarily."

I nod. "If we say what we suspect he's actually done—with Lenore—Ross might not think it a punishable crime, especially since I doubt Lenore will confirm the story. But if he thinks Müller might have killed Ezra, that gets Müller locked up while we continue to investigate."

"Excellent points," McCreadie says. "I will have a couple of the grooms assist me with getting Mr. Müller to town." He rises. "We will do that now, while you rest."

I don't really rest. Oh, I'm stuck in this damn bed—doctor's orders. But I just set it up as my command center, from which poor Gray and Isla are sent to and fro tracking down answers for me.

The maid—Dorothy—left last night. Or we hope she left, and some worse fate didn't befall her. I presume she was working with Müller. She heard Gray say he'd left a note for me, and Müller must have told her to find some way to lure me outside. She copied Gray's handwriting from his letter and told Müller to expect me at the bench at midnight.

From there, Müller staged the kitten trap. Getting that kitten back was the first task I sent Gray on. He found it hiding in the bushes, poor thing. It's cold and scared, but unharmed. Alice is looking after it.

Why was Dorothy working with Müller? We'd need to get that answer from her. I can't imagine an affair, so I'm guessing blackmail or extortion or even just a hefty bribe.

My fear is that, once Dorothy has served her purpose, Müller did something with her. We have all the remaining male staff out searching the grounds. Her empty clothing chest suggests she bolted, but I don't want to presume anything.

What about the original note, from Sinclair to Violet? Dorothy said she found Sinclair's first attempt in the trash. Is that true? Or more staging? Violet has admitted to receiving a note, but she says it wasn't romantic in nature. Was that the part Dorothy lied about?

I'm working this through with Isla when she says, "We have established that Ezra Sinclair had a predilection for maids."

"So you think that's the leverage he and Müller had over Dorothy? She was Ezra's latest lover? But why would Müller have her tell us about the note?"

"Perhaps that was entirely her doing." When I still look confused, she sighs, as if my blow to the head did some serious damage. "Dorothy is having an affair with Ezra. She discovers that he left a note for Violet, bringing her out in the middle of the night."

"Jealousy."

Isla nods. "By the time she spoke to you, Ezra was dead, but that does not necessarily diminish her hurt, presuming it was a romantic rendez-vous."

"But it *wasn't*. I think Violet was telling the truth about that. But what if Lenore was threatening to reveal what he'd done? He could have gone to Violet as a friend. Told her he was being threatened by a young woman he'd spurned."

"Then Violet learns the truth and kills him?"

"Maybe?" I adjust the pillows behind me. "Lenore told *someone* what happened. Whoever left that note in Duncan's coach knew. My first thought was her brother, Gavin, but he called her Len."

"He could have written 'Nori' to throw you off his scent."

I thump back on the pillows. "I'm missing something."

"Because you are exhausted and injured, and you have suffered a blow to the head. You need to rest."

I open my mouth to argue, but she's right. I feel as if the answer is there, flitting just out of reach, and I'm too tired to grasp it.

"Sleep," she says, more firmly. "We will continue looking for Dorothy, and Lenore will be back later to answer questions."

I wake to the sounds of jubilation downstairs. That gives me pause. Is Lenore back already? I can't imagine her mother being quite so loud about it, and I swear I hear multiple voices.

I rise and put on my second corset, grateful that Isla had gifted me with another. Then I rise carefully, wincing at the pain as I adjust my wrapper. I don't plan to go down—just get close enough to hear who arrived.

I'm making my way toward the stairs when a male voice booms, "Breakfast. That is what I want more than anything. A hot breakfast."

Cranston?

I hurry halfway down the steps to see Cranston in the hall, Violet fussing over him, Fiona standing back, smiling. James Frye pumps his friend's hand as if he just returned from war.

Cranston's gaze rises. "And there she is. My savior." He bows deeply. "If only you did not need to be attacked to see me freed. I am sorry for that, Miss Mitchell." He turns. "Mrs. Hall! Please see that Miss Mallory has a proper room to recuperate in and anything she wishes. I owe her a great debt of gratitude."

"That is very kind," I say, "but unnecessary. I am glad to see you are free."

"For now at least. I have been sternly warned that it might be temporary."

"It is not," Fiona says. "That odious constable shall not have you again."

Cranston bows her way. "From your lips to God's ear. Now, as much as I long for company, I long for hot food and a bath first. You may all join me in the first, but not the second."

A round of laughter, with Violet shaking her head at his impudence. Then, with Cranston leading the way like the Pied Piper, they all file into the dining room to await breakfast.

I change into a proper dress and join them. Over breakfast, Cranston regales us with the horrors of his imprisonment. He exaggerates, but in that booming way that makes it clear he's playing to his audience. McCreadie had only told Ross about the attack on me, but the constable had decided he had a new suspect for Sinclair's murder, which necessitated releasing the old one.

As we eat and listen to Cranston, I take time to think, my brain working better now. I keep circling back to the notes between Violet and Sinclair. Having her waiting to meet him the night he died had seemed a tragic coincidence when we thought Sinclair a fine and upstanding fellow. But now that we've seen his sinister side, I can't help but feel "coincidence" is not the answer.

When breakfast wraps up, I quietly ask Violet if I might have a word. She quickly agrees. I am, apparently, her brother's "savior," even if unintentionally. Gray and McCreadie both glance over, a question in their eyes, but I shake my head. I need to handle this one alone.

We retreat to the smallest of the sitting rooms. With Cranston still holding court in the next room, no one is likely to overhear our hushed voices.

"You know that I was attacked last night," I say as we sit. "What you may not know is why I was out of doors at such an hour. I was lured with a fake note purporting to be from someone I trusted."

A smile tugs at her lips. "Dr. Gray."

When I hesitate, she says, "Your secret is safe with me, though I suspect it is no secret to anyone who sees you together. But I understand the need for discretion, and a response is not required. You were lured out by a note apparently from another."

"Yes, and it got me thinking about your note from Mr. Sinclair. Is it possible that was also false?"

Her answer comes quickly. "I do not think so."

"It was not unusual for him to write you such notes?"

Her cheeks pink but she says, levelly, "We have known each other a very long time. He trusted my counsel."

"Counsel . . ." I muse. "I hate to ask this, but one of the maids swore she saw a discarded version of the note and it was romantic in nature."

Another flush, but accompanied by a firm "No, it was not."

"You were not courting Mr. Sinclair in private? I offer you the same discretion you offered me. It will only help me to understand the circumstances myself, which I do not need to pass along to anyone else."

"Ezra did not write me a romantic note. When you first asked, my brother was imprisoned, accused of murdering Ezra. I would never have concealed something as frivolous as a secret courtship."

"So Mr. Sinclair wanted to comfort you, because Detective McCreadie was here?"

"Yes."

"But you said he trusted your counsel, which suggests he wished to speak to you about something, as well. Seeking your advice. Perhaps about Lenore Hall?"

Genuine surprise slackens her jaw. "Mrs. Hall's daughter?"

"Yes."

She blinks, shaking her head as if to clear it. "No, certainly not."

"Perhaps another one of the maids?"

"No, and this is a very odd line of questioning, Miss Mitchell."

Maybe, but the expression in her eyes looks more like dawning dread than irritation or confusion.

"My apologies," I murmur. "Mr. Müller said something to me that meant I had to ask."

"He said something about Miss Hall and Ezra?"

"Not specifically," I demur. "I am simply trying to piece together things he did say."

She nods, but her gaze has gone distant.

"Is there anything more you can tell me?" I ask.

She shakes her head.

"All right then. Thank you for your time."

THIRTY-EIGHT

I round up McCreadie and Gray and take them outside.

"I think we've been looking at the Violet and Ezra connection wrong," I say as we walk. "I presumed they were secretly courting, but that doesn't make sense. The secret part at least. Violet is adamant that their meeting was not romantic in nature, and I believe her."

McCreadie passes me a dubious look. "I realize Violet is easy to believe. She is not the sort to dissemble. But you may be underestimating how severely she would be affected by a romantic scandal. Also, thanks to me, she has already experienced one. I would not blame her for hiding an affair."

"Yes, but I believe she was being truthful. That she has not, in the recent past, been having an affair with Ezra."

"In the recent past," Gray murmurs.

I nod. "The way she said it—blushing but also firm—suggests there *was* an affair, but she can say, honestly, that isn't why he wanted to speak to her." I look from one of them to the other. "Is it possible that Ezra Sinclair was the father of her baby?"

Silence. Then, McCreadie says carefully, "Had you asked that yesterday, I would have said he would never treat her so shabbily."

"But now?"

He exhales and stops in the shade of an oak. "There was always a closeness between them. I considered it fraternal in nature."

"Her big brother's best friend, who also treated her like a little sister."

"Yes. Ezra was always very attentive. Violet could be shy, and when I noticed him seeking her out at social engagements, I would feel the sting of it—that he was doing what I should have done. Being kind and ensuring she was not alone."

"While he seems to prefer maids, it might be more because they often fit a type he likes. Vulnerable."

"Which Violet was. And she was often ignored by her supposed fiancé," McCreadie says, his voice dropping. "Who did not even suspect that another man's attention might be more than kindness."

"*No one* did. Otherwise, Ezra certainly wouldn't still have been Archie's best friend, treated kindly by their parents." I turn to look at the house. "Maybe I'm wrong about the affair. She said they were friends, that he sought her counsel."

"Because he did not treat her as he treated Lenore," Gray says. "Lenore was . . ." He trails off.

"Disposable."

Gray makes a moue of distaste but nods. "Yes. A relationship between Ezra and Violet could have felt like a romance, which ended when she became pregnant."

"Which seems to have happened before Hugh ended the engagement," I say. "So she chalks it up to a youthful indiscretion on both their parts, and they remain friendly."

"Do we see her as a potential killer, then?" Gray says. "A jealous former lover?"

I look at McCreadie.

"I would prefer not to speculate on Violet as a suspect," he says. "Knowing I ended my engagement to a future murderess would absolve me of a guilt I should not be absolved of."

"But whoever struck Ezra didn't necessarily mean to *kill* him," I say. "Still, I can see what you mean. I don't like jealousy as a motive. What if Violet found out what Ezra did to Lenore and hit him with the shillelagh? I asked Violet about Lenore and Ezra, and she seemed genuinely thrown. But her reaction was . . ." I shrug. "Surprised and yet not surprised. Dawning horror, even."

"As if she did not know of this specific instance, but knew of—or suspected—others."

"Yet Ezra and Violet seemed to get on," Gray says. "Could that have been an act?"

"*Did* they get on?" I ask. "They were polite, but any overtures were made by him."

"As if she was tolerating him," McCreadie says. "Unlike the relationship with me, no one knew about her past relationship with him, so she had to be polite."

"There's one other obvious murder suspect," I say. "If it was Ezra who got Violet pregnant."

"Archie," Gray says.

"Is he, though?" McCreadie says. "The pregnancy seems to have been over a decade ago."

"Fair point," I say. "Also, does Archie strike you as someone who would murder his best friend for sleeping with his sister? For dishonoring his family?"

McCreadie snorts. "If that were the case, he would have killed me long ago for ending the engagement. He didn't speak to me for years, but he eventually admitted that he would not have wished his sister to marry anyone who did not want her. A man concerned with family honor would have forced me to the altar at gunpoint."

"Okay, so shifting the motive back to Lenore makes more sense. Yes, Ezra probably got Violet pregnant, but it seems to have arisen from an actual romance. He reserves his mistreatment for the maids. We've thrown Lenore's brother into the suspect pool, but we also need to throw her father *and* her mother."

"Mrs. Hall," McCreadie murmurs. "What if she *did* know what happened to her daughter? She is a sturdy woman who knows her way around the estate grounds and also had access to the shillelaghs."

"She's been staying at the house," I say. "While the guests are here, she hasn't been going home to her family at night. She could have seen Ezra leaving to meet Violet that night, grabbed a shillelagh and followed."

"Lenore will be here soon," McCreadie says. "I believe we need to hear what she has to say."

* * *

The rest of the morning passes quickly. Having Cranston back changes the tenor of the gathering. They are no longer guests at a canceled wedding, held captive by the investigation. Their host is free, the wedding plans will be renewed—if possible—and there is nothing to feel guilty about if they indulge in whimsical party games.

Cranston himself doesn't participate in those games. He's taking action to fix his mistakes, and Fiona insists on helping him through the social quagmire. Mr. Hall must be told that the gamekeeper position is his if he wishes it. The cottage must be thoroughly cleaned, as if to scour away any miasmic stain left by Müller. Cranston wishes to pay a visit to the Glasses, to personally extend his sympathies on the death of their daughter, and, on Fiona's advice, he wishes to ask Mrs. Hall who they should contact in the village to negotiate a reopening of the grounds to locals.

I rest some more while Gray, Isla, and McCreadie play the party games. Or "resting" is my excuse. Yes, I'm sore and tired, but mostly I want time alone to think about the case.

I'm still missing something. I know I am.

Finally, Lenore and Gavin arrive. They slip in the staff entrance, but their mother brings them straight to McCreadie, who takes Gavin with Gray while Isla and I speak to Lenore.

This conversation requires absolute privacy, so Isla and I take Lenore to that bench by the lake. She seems to expect we're going to walk and talk, but we only ask about her trip.

We're prepared to walk slowly, given her clubfoot, but she clips along. I'm the one who slows us down, still achy. When we reach the bench, I motion for her to sit and she seems to consider standing, but lowers herself onto it. Isla sits beside her while I move closer to the water, gazing out at it before turning.

"We know you were having an affair with Ezra Sinclair," I say.

Lenore flinches so hard it's practically a convulsion, but she quickly smooths her features and fixes me with a stony gaze. "I don't know what you mean, miss."

"You had a romantic entanglement while he was here seeing to Mr. Cranston's interests and you were working as a maid. That ended—badly, I suspect—shortly before you quit."

"I don't know what you mean, miss."

"I believe it ended with Mr. Müller." I lower my voice. "With something Mr. Sinclair coerced you into doing with him."

She goes pale, the pulse at her throat trembling as hard as her hands. She tries to clench them into her lap, but even there, they shake.

"I don't know what—"

"Were you coerced? If you weren't, that's fine. No one will judge you either way."

Her gaze rises to mine, but it's flat, calling me a liar.

"Let me rephrase that," I say softly. "*We* will not judge you."

"We truly will not," Isla says. "I have endured . . . treatment from a man that many would blame on me. At the time, I did not speak of it, though my family would not have judged me. I refused to tell them because I wanted to pretend it never happened."

Tears spring to Lenore's eyes.

"Now that they know," Isla continues, "I wish I had confided in them sooner. As with you, the man who mistreated me is dead, but I still find solace knowing that those I care about realize what he was. No matter how highly others held him in their esteem, my family and my dearest friends know the truth and will never speak kindly of him in my company."

"Or outside it," I say firmly. I look at Lenore. "Mr. Sinclair cannot be punished, but if he is guilty of what we suspect, he should not go to his grave with his good name intact."

Silence.

"As for Mr. Müller, he is being held in custody."

Her head whips up. "Did he kill Ezra?"

"That is for a court to decide. But when he attacked me last night, he hinted at what they did to you."

She shudders, her gaze dropping before coming back up. "He attacked you. Are you . . . all right?"

"He did not molest me," I say. "He shot me, punched me, and gave me a head injury, but I was spared anything else."

"I should have spoken," she whispers. "I know that. I worried about other girls, the maids, and I feel sick for not saying anything, but I knew no one would believe me, not against Ezra. The sun shone on him, and he was adored."

The bitterness in her voice slices through me. She continues, "He had returned to Edinburgh before I quit, and I thought the girls would be safe while others were here, but I was still deciding what to do when he died, and then I did not need to speak up." Her gaze lifts to mine again. "*Were* there others?"

"I do not believe so. Mr. Sinclair would not have acted with Mr. Cranston in residence."

"My mother says he is a good employer. Mr. Cranston." She sniffs. "I do not see it. He is a blustering boor who fired my father and brought in that . . . that man." She looks out at the lake. "But it was Ezra who truly brought Mr. Müller, and Mr. Cranston has been kind to my mother. He told her that if any of his guests interfered with any of the maids, she was to tell him immediately. Perhaps he would have believed me, had I told him. Still, it was his dearest friend."

"What matters is that we have no evidence that either Mr. Sinclair or Mr. Müller interfered with anyone else. So you had an affair, then. A romantic one? With Mr. Sinclair? Or Ezra, as you called him."

Her lips twist. "That familiarity answered your question, I suppose. He seduced me with kindness. Men think it is flattery that will win a girl's heart, but kindness works so much better. I thought I would not fall for that. Many people are kind to me, but . . ."

She inhales. "Outside my family, kindness can feel like pity. For this." She lifts her leg. "To some, the fact I was not burned as a witch is kindness enough. Ezra didn't see a lame girl. He only saw a girl. He talked to me as if I were his own age, his own class. An equal. He spoke of his situation, his parents' deaths, the charity he endured as a child, the shame of that. He said one good thing came of it, though. His lack of family meant he could marry me."

She looks at us. "You think me a fool, don't you."

Isla lays a hand, not on Lenore's but beside it on the bench. "I married a man who claimed to love me and only loved my family's money. I am as educated as a woman can be, raised to think for myself, and I still fell for him. Does that make me a fool? Most women almost have known some man who tricked them in that way."

Lenore looks at me.

"Well, let's see," I say. "There was the fellow who courted me to make another woman jealous. The one who courted me whenever he visited town, and turned out to have a wife back home. And one or two who courted me only to get into my bed."

Lenore's brows knit. "You do not seem old enough for all that."

"Mallory is older than she appears," Isla says. "The point is that we do not think you a fool. We think you human. Women—and men—can be tricked. It is only a matter of finding the right bait for the trap. You are correct that kindness—and respect and consideration—can work far better than presents and flattery."

"We do not think you foolish for falling for Ezra," I say. "We also do not think anything if you were coerced—or even agreed—to what happened with Müller. When you're in love, you agree to lots of things you later regret. As for any impropriety, Isla was only being polite. It's not my age that explains my breadth of experience with men. It's just me."

Lenore sputters at that, even as her eyes glisten. Then she says, "As for what happened with Mr. Müller, I am not familiar with the word you used—coerced?—but I believe it means I was talked into it. There was no talking. I was not in a state to do that." Bitterness sharpens her voice again, even as her hands tremble.

"You were forced into it," I say.

"Can one be forced into something if one is not awake when it happens?"

"Oh!" Isla says.

"I am so sorry," I say, my voice dropping. "You don't need to tell me more if you don't wish to, but I am here to listen if you want."

"Ezra and I were drinking. He often helped himself to Mr. Cranston's whisky, and he would share it with me. I knew how expensive it was, and I would feel fancy drinking it, but I did not care for the taste, so I never drank much. Yet even 'not much' always seemed to be too much, and I would fall asleep. Ezra teased me about that, how sweet I looked when I slept, how loath he was to wake me. I did sleep soundly, and when I woke, I felt . . ." She flushes. "Uncomfortable. Especially in my nether regions. I feared the pox, but Ezra wore something to prevent that and to prevent a child, which seemed to prove he was a good man."

She goes quiet and then murmurs, "A good man. A man who let—" She breaks off. "I woke to find Müller on top of me and . . ."

"Having relations with you," I say.

She nods. "I screamed, and as I was fighting him off, Ezra ran in, panting as if he had just arrived. He said he had stepped out. Only when I first woke, I saw him standing there. He was . . ." Her cheeks go bright red, and Isla squirms, as if wanting to tell Lenore she can stop there. I subtly shake my head. To stop Lenore implies *we're* uncomfortable with where her story is going.

"Watching," she whispers finally, her gaze down. "Ezra was watching. He quickly left and pretended to have come in. He even tried to blame me, outraged that I was so drunk with whisky that I . . . I allowed that." She looks at us. "I did not. He must have put something into the whisky. I thought back to all the other times I fell asleep and I realized what must have—"

She stops and looks out over the lake, and Isla eases closer, her arm tentatively going around the younger woman. Lenore doesn't lean into it, but she does relax.

After a moment, Lenore says, "I confronted Ezra. I told him that I saw him watching. He pretended I was mistaken, in shock, and he apologized for blaming me. He said Müller was a monstrous man who would never come near me again. He did not say, however, that he would see him sacked. I asked for that, testing him, and he blustered that he did not have that authority, and to even attempt it, he would need to tell Mr. Cranston what Mr. Müller had done to me, and I did not want that, did I?"

"Monster," Isla mutters.

Lenore nods. "Ezra gave me money. He said it was because he blamed himself for not protecting me. I knew it was to keep my silence. I took it, and I tried to stay in my position, but I could not. Even when he had left the house, everything reminded me of him. The corners where he would pull me aside for a kiss. The spots in the garden where he would tell me he loved me. That old cottage where we . . ." Lenore shivers. "It was too much."

Isla and Lenore sit in silence as I pace along the edge of the lake, trying to look as if I am calm and reflective . . . and not already leaping ahead to more questions. Normally, I'm the one sitting with the victim, comforting them, and this puts me at an odd remove, where all I can do is hold my tongue and give Lenore the time she needs.

Finally, I say, "Someone knew what happened. We received a note, in our coach, saying that Ezra deserved it for what he did to you."

She tenses. "I know. I heard of the note and that you mistook the name for Nora, and I was not about to say otherwise. The note came from a dear friend. She is a few years younger than me, and suffers from palsy. I used to care for her as a child, and we came together over our shared infirmities. I told her what happened. I had to tell someone, and she would never share my secret. But when Ezra died, her anger got the better of her. She heard Dr. Gray was a famous detective and so she had a village boy put that note in your coach." Her lips twitch. "I believe she was trying to tell you not to bother finding the killer, as Ezra deserved his death. She can be very young and very innocent sometimes. Had she ever thought her actions could lead to my secret being revealed, she would not have done it."

"We may need to speak to her," I say. "But for now, that is enough. I do need to ask about the night Ezra died. We found the stag. We know you were there. Probably Gavin, too, but definitely you, given the use of a bow and the marks of your walking stick."

Her shoulders sag. "I know. We no longer hid the evidence of our poaching. After what Müller did to me, it felt good. I know that is petty, but I couldn't help it."

"You thwarted and humiliated him," I say. "Which he well deserved."

"I am only glad he did not catch you himself," Isla murmurs.

"I was careful. I was always with Gavin, and I was always listening for Mr. Müller. That night, I heard something and went for a look while Gavin saw to the butchering. I saw Ezra, and my mind spun into a tizzy. If he found us, my reaction would tell Gavin something had happened. So I said it was Mr. Cranston himself, coming our way. We grabbed what meat we could carry and left."

"You only saw Ezra," I say.

She nods. "No one else. I know you will ask that, but Ezra was alone. He seemed to be heading for the road right up there." She pointed. "He was walking most determinedly, which made me wonder whether he had heard us. All the more reason to move quickly."

"You grabbed the deer haunches and left."

"Yes."

"Did you hear anything? See anything?"

She shakes her head. "My mind was in too much of a muddle to notice anything amiss, but later, when we heard Ezra had died, Gavin said he heard and saw nothing. He remembered me saying I'd seen Mr. Cranston but that was easy to explain because of the coat."

"That Ezra was wearing Mr. Cranston's coat."

"Yes. But someone was still dead, and we had been out there and had not bothered to disguise that we were the ones who killed the deer. Butchered it a few hundred paces from where Ezra was killed. I was trying to decide what to do when I discovered that my friend had left that note . . . and realized that if you learned it was about me, I would be the obvious suspect."

"So you left."

"I told Gavin that we would be blamed once they realized who killed the stag. We decided to go visit our gran until the matter was sorted. Then I got my mother's letter and knew I had to come back. It is one thing to quietly leave, but another to refuse to return."

"It is."

She looks at me. "I returned because I did not kill Ezra. There were times when I wished I had, and I am not sorry he is dead, but I did not do it."

THIRTY-NINE

Isla and I stay with Lenore until she's ready to return to the house. We've been honest that we need to tell McCreadie and Gray, because it's part of the investigation. And if it turns out that what happened to Lenore was the motive for Sinclair's death, then that also needs to come out. But we're not going to be running to Ross with this new information. No one needs to know unless it becomes critical to catching—and convicting—a killer. Isla does urge Lenore to tell her mother, but only to have someone to help her through the trauma.

We arrive at the house to find Simon outside with McCreadie. Mrs. Hall is nearby, talking to Gavin after his interview. Lenore goes to join them, and Isla heads inside while I stop to speak to McCreadie.

I arrive just as Simon is leaving, tipping his hat to me as he goes.

McCreadie sighs deeply as I join him. "That boy is the height of incompetence."

I blink and stare after Simon.

"No, not Simon, of course. Constable Ross. Simon would be a better police officer. In fact, given his help with this case, I would strongly suggest he apply for a position, so I might scoop him up to assist me."

"Yeah, even in my world, while we have cops with Simon's romantic preferences, they don't have an easy time of it."

McCreadie sighs again. "Of course they do not. Homosexuals, women, people of color, on a police force? Certainly not. They must reserve it for men like me, which means we are stuck with boys like Constable Ross, who tripped into the position despite having no talent for it."

"His grandfather was a constable. It's in the blood. In my day, that's better than any actual skill. Law enforcement is a family tradition. Look at me. My mother is in law, too."

"As a barrister. Defending criminals."

"Made for very lively family dinners." I notice Mrs. Hall walking past and switch to my Victorian voice. "You said something about Constable Ross, sir?"

"Simon is playing spy for me, keeping me informed on the proceedings. It seems that Müller went off on some tangent about the wildcat. He knew it had not died in the trap."

"I fear that is my fault. I told him it had been poisoned first and accused him of doing it." Out of the corner of my eye, I see Mrs. Hall stop. She slowly turns our way.

McCreadie continues, "Well, Müller wishes Constable Ross to know that he did not poison the cat, and whoever did clearly also murdered Ezra. So now Ross is trying to say that Müller poisoned Ezra."

"What?" I say, forgetting my Victorian manners.

"My dear girl, think it through. The wildcat was poisoned. Müller claims the same person killed Ezra. Which means he is clearly confessing to killing both and also must have used the same method. Poison."

I groan. Then I realize Mrs. Hall has stopped parallel to us. While she could have just been eavesdropping, her expression says something in our conversation caught her ear. She looks at me and then quickly continues on toward the house.

"Mrs. Hall," I call after her.

She keeps going, as if she's going to pretend she didn't hear me.

"Mrs. Hall," McCreadie says, and that makes her slow, however reluctantly.

"Yes, sir?" she says, her face impassive.

McCreadie nods to me.

"You were startled to hear that the wildcat died of poison," I say.

She seems to consider denying it, but then says, "Of course. I heard it was caught in a trap."

"Poisoned," McCreadie says. "And then posed in the trap, so it seemed as if it had simply been caught in it."

She shakes her head. "Mr. Müller was not only a despicable man, but a terrible gamekeeper. There was no need to kill the cat. The lads were repairing the chicken coop and that would have kept it out. If the master insisted on getting rid of it, a proper gamekeeper does it quickly. With a gun. Not poison and not traps."

I walk toward her. "But that wasn't what gave you pause, was it? It was something about the cat being poisoned."

When she doesn't respond, McCreadie clears his throat. "In a murder investigation, people must tell us what they know. It is the law. If they do not, and we discover they withheld information, it goes badly for them."

She considers as we move closer. Then she lowers her voice. "I do not know what to make of it, and I fear impugning the name of a man who is dead and cannot defend himself. Particularly as . . ." She looks uncharacteristically uncomfortable. "I did not care for the deceased myself, and others knew it."

That's right. While everyone else here liked Sinclair and thought him a jolly good fellow, Mrs. Hall had been unable to hide her dislike. She'd obviously blamed Sinclair for Müller being here, and she'd flat-out implied he'd tricked Cranston into hiring the man. At the time, that had seemed like misplaced anger. Her husband lost his position because of someone Sinclair recommended, and since she liked Cranston, she had to direct her anger elsewhere.

But now I wonder if it was more. If she was picking up on something we missed. An older woman in service sensing danger in a young gentleman, but not recognizing—or trusting—her gut instinct enough to warn the maids, including her daughter. I ache for the guilt she will feel when Lenore confesses. It's not Mrs. Hall's fault, but she will blame herself. She knew something was off with Sinclair and said nothing.

"I presume you mean Mr. Sinclair," McCreadie says, bringing me back to the conversation.

"Yes. He was in the pantry. Before the wildcat died. I walked in and found him there, and he apologized, saying he was peckish and looking for biscuits. When he left, I found that the rat poison had been moved. I am exceedingly careful with it, and the bag was not where I left it."

"Which suggests the poison came from there," McCreadie says. "What time was this?"

"About five that afternoon."

McCreadie checks with me—his expression asking whether I have questions. Then he dismisses the housekeeper.

Once she's gone, he turns to me. "At the risk of defending Ezra, I cannot imagine he poisoned the wildcat. It makes no sense."

"So he was in the pantry, looking for biscuits right after he took tea with the rest of us? He had a full plate, which I remember, because Duncan grumbled that he took the last piece of cake."

"True. I teased Duncan about that."

A memory flashes. Alice taking the kitten into Sinclair's bedroom. How it had hissed and wanted to flee. Freaked out by the smell of a corpse? Or by the smell of the man who poisoned its mother?

"He was out that night," I say. "I saw him come back. He mentioned hearing the cat. He was also very eager to bury it, though he eventually backed off when we insisted on examining it."

"But *why* would Ezra poison it? He protested its death louder than anyone."

He certainly had. Sinclair had been there comforting Fiona, furious on her behalf, outraged that her fiancé would have allowed such a thing. Why would he . . . ?

Oh.

The last piece of the puzzle finally thuds into place.

When Violet sees me coming, she deflates, but manages the wan smile of one resigned to yet more uncomfortable questions.

"May we step outside?" I say.

"Of course."

I lead her toward the gardens. When she sees McCreadie, she tenses, but I murmur, "He is only ensuring we are not overheard. Dr. Gray is doing the same on the other side."

Her shoulders droop. If she'd had any hope this conversation might not be an unpleasant one, it disappears with my precautions.

Once we are in the garden, McCreadie nods and moves toward the house, getting out of earshot.

"I need to discuss something requiring great discretion," I say. "A matter you will not wish to discuss. I will ask you, though, to hear me out. You do not need to confirm what I am about to say, but let us pretend that your denial has already been registered, as well as any outrage at my theory."

"This sounds most foreboding," she says, struggling for a smile she can't find.

"I saw the marks on your stomach. I know you were pregnant. I strongly suspect Ezra Sinclair was the father, as the result of a youthful affair that has long since ended."

She opens her mouth, as if the denial comes automatically, and then shuts it.

"You do not need to confirm any of that because it is not relevant to what I am about to say. It may become relevant. But at this point, it is not."

She doesn't answer. I take a deep breath.

"I think I know why you went to speak to Ezra that night." I use his given name, deciding to drop the "Mr. Sinclair" honorific. "I do not think it was because he requested the meeting. I believe you intercepted a note intended for another." I look at her. "Intended for Fiona."

She doesn't answer, but the flash of surprise in her eyes tells me I've guessed right. Not so much a guess, either, as a conclusion.

"Ezra had set his sights on Fiona," I say. "He was going out of his way to pay attention to her. That wouldn't seem odd to most. He had a reputation for kindness, and she was his best friend's fiancée. But you noticed it. I did, too, though I chalked it up to a generosity of spirit. Especially when he took her aside, late the first night, to talk about you. To express his concern about you."

She makes a small noise. Oh, she stifles it with a cough, but I didn't miss that noise—a derisive snort.

I continue, "You recognized his wooing, having been the target of it yourself. I then learned that Ezra was making plans for Fiona to visit the estate while your brother was busy. Ezra himself would have been here, to look after her and keep her company. Again, that seemed like an older man's kindness to his friend's young wife. It was not, was it?"

She says nothing, but her mouth firms. She'd heard of those plans, too, and knew them for what they were—a way to get Fiona alone for an extended period.

"Then there was the wildcat."

She looks over, frowning as if she's misheard.

"Ezra poisoned it," I say, "though he made it look as if it had been caught in the trap."

Her hand flies to her mouth. "My God. Why would he . . ." She trails off, as if she's realized the answer.

"To get closer to Fiona," I say. "To position himself as an ally. As someone who understood her and agreed with her sensibilities. Ezra would feign horror at the death of the cat. Feign fury with Müller for doing it—and your brother for allowing it. When Fiona wanted to tend to the kittens—which he knew she would—he would demand she be allowed to do so. That last part didn't work, because your brother was fine with her keeping the kittens. But Ezra still made it seem as if he had won the day."

"For her," Violet murmurs. "He killed the cat so that he could join her in outrage over its death. Show her that he shared her love of wild creatures. I want to say he would never be so manipulative, but I have long feared I did not fully understand the depths of him. The worst depths."

"You realized what he was up to," I say. "Especially when you intercepted that note. You went in Fiona's place to warn him off."

Her mouth twists. "I doubt it was necessary. Fiona had no idea Ezra was interested in her that way. The note would have only befuddled her. I had hoped, when she did not reciprocate, he would give up, but that was foolish. He would never have given up. When I found that note in Fiona's room—I had gone in to get her shawl—I knew I had to act. He would not do to her what he had done to me. I would not allow it. If necessary, I would use whatever munitions I had, including the force of threats."

"To reveal that he had gotten you with child."

She swallows and looks away. "He seduced me when I was sixteen. It went on for three years, and it is not surprising that a child was the eventual result. He may . . . he may even have planned that. He wanted to tell my parents and offer to marry me. I would not let him—I knew they would never agree and I was . . . no longer sure he was a man I wished to marry. The affair ended with that. My parents sent me to visit a cousin in Switzerland. I stayed there while I had the baby. My cousin was married and childless and happily took him."

"So your family knew?"

"My parents did."

"Not Archie?"

She shudders. "Certainly not Archie. My parents did not realize who the father was—I said a young man had seduced me while we were on a seaside holiday. Archie would have uncovered the truth. Had that happened, Archie would have run Ezra out of Edinburgh, perhaps Scotland altogether."

"It must have been difficult continuing to see him socially, as Archie's friend."

She flushes. "When I say the affair ended, I do not mean it ended forever. We would periodically reunite. I was often . . . lonely. Ezra helped me through some difficult times. But that is what he did. He was there when you needed him, offering kindness and sympathy, so when you had cause to question other behaviors, you felt guilty for doing so."

"It didn't help when everyone else saw him as a good man." I look at her. "That's what men like him do. They woo with kindness, and if anything goes wrong, everyone else can confirm they are a wonderful chap who would never do such a thing. Clearly there was a misunderstanding."

"Yes. There was no way I could accuse him and be believed, and his reputation made me feel as if there was something wrong with me for doubting him."

"Yet you did doubt."

She nods, her gaze averted, and she walks a little more before speaking. "Something odd began happening. I would be with him and then it was morning, and I was back in my own bed without knowing how I got there."

A chill slides down my back.

She continues, "He would claim I had fallen asleep and he had snuck me back home, but that seemed . . . odd. Would I not have woken to him carrying me? It made me very uneasy. Then I heard a story about him taking advantage of a maid. I had heard such things before, but by then I had reached the point where I did not automatically dismiss them as tittle-tattle. Four years ago, I ended our relationship for good, which has been difficult. I have always suffered bouts of melancholia. They have become worse, with my mind torn between fearing Ezra mistreated me and then being horrified at suspecting him of such a thing."

"Being here with him could not have been easy."

"It was not," she says firmly. "But I resolved to put a good face on it, and if I seemed despondent, I would let everyone think it was because of Hugh. While that is not an easy situation either, Hugh was always honorable in his dealings with me. Ezra was not."

She walks in silence, and then says, "I have feared that Hugh ended it because he learned of the baby."

"He had no idea," I say firmly. "He ended it . . ." I trail off, not sure where to go.

"Because he loves Isla Ballantyne?" A soft twist of a smile. "Yes, I see that now, and I am happy for them. For both of them, if they can find their way to each other, which I sincerely hope they do."

"That is kind of you."

"Hugh would have made a good husband, but I was in love with Ezra." She looks over. "You are wondering how far I would go to ensure he did not hurt Fiona." She shakes her head. "If I wanted to hurt him, I would have taken away the most important relationship in his life, which I could have ended with a few words."

"By telling Archie everything."

"Yes. I would gladly have threatened that, for Fiona's sake, but I also would have hoped the mere threat would be enough. I would not have hurt Archie that way. For him to realize that his best friend had seduced his sister and aimed to seduce his wife?" She sucks in a breath. "I would not have wanted to inflict that guilt on him."

We walk around the garden one more time, without speaking, before I say, "And your child? You say your cousin took him? I hope he is well."

She lights up at that. "His name is Owen, and he is very well. They are all so happy together, and I have never regretted my choice. I visit every year, and I am Aunt Violet, who brings toys and sweets. I was there just last month, with Archie as a matter of fact." She pauses. "That was difficult, knowing how much Archie would love a nephew, but he still enjoyed Owen immensely." She smiles. "And Owen still got to call him uncle. It was a most lovely time."

She glances over, catching my expression and frowning. "Miss Mitchell? Are you all right?"

No, I'm really not.

Because I know who killed Ezra Sinclair. And I know why.

FORTY

I speak to Gray and McCreadie. I don't tell them my conclusion—just what I've learned. They put that together with what we already know, and they draw the same conclusion, McCreadie seeming to age five years with it.

This was not what any of us wanted. Not even me. A few days ago, I'd have accepted this solution with indifference. Now, knowing the parties involved, I do not.

When we ask around inside, James Frye says he saw Cranston head off on horseback, riding along the road. That's alarming. Maybe not surprising, but alarming.

Perhaps, at this point, we should all mount up and ride to stop our suspect from fleeing justice. Well, McCreadie could. I can barely ride, and Gray is not an expert horseman. But it says something about our reluctance that no one suggests this. We head off on foot instead, as if to say that if Cranston manages to escape, no one is overly keen to stop him.

He's not fleeing, though. He's riding with Fiona, and that's even worse. We hear them in the distance, and she's laughing. Is there flirtation in that laugh? I think so, though Cranston seems oblivious and only responds with a fraternal sort of affection.

When I arrived, I'd been horrified by the thought of this vivacious girl marrying that insensitive boor. But I will admit I'd been wrong, and in their laughter and teasing, it's like witnessing the start of a romance. I see a future here . . . and I'm about to end it.

When McCreadie calls to the riders, they both seem startled, but Fiona approaches, smiling in obvious delight.

"Where are your horses?" she says. "Go saddle some up and come ride with us before supper. Archie has promised to show me a secret path."

"Perhaps later, Fee," McCreadie says. "For now, we must speak to Archie. Alone."

Fiona opens her mouth as if to argue, but Cranston says, "Yes, I suspect your brother needs to have an overdue discussion with me."

"You will make it up to me?" Fiona asks Cranston.

Cranston falters, and that falter erases any doubt. He knows why we've come.

"I will try," he says.

She huffs but makes light of it and rides off. Once she's out of sight, Cranston dismounts and walks his horse to us.

"So, what happens now?" he says. "Back to the constable, I presume."

"You are not going to ask why we are here?" McCreadie says.

"Do I need to?"

"You don't deny it?"

"Is there any point?"

McCreadie's voice hardens. "So you have nothing to say."

Cranston sighs. "I could explain myself, but that will come later, and I doubt it will do me any good. As you are someone whose opinion I value, I will say that I absolutely did not intend to kill Ezra. Yet I did, so that is no defense."

"Tell me anyway."

Cranston looks at him.

McCreadie says, "As a friend who almost saw you wed to his sister, I would like to hear your explanation."

"I presume you've realized Ezra was not the excellent fellow I believed him to be. How much do you know?"

McCreadie looks to me to take over. He's too close to this.

"We know about your nephew," I say. "Owen."

Cranston flinches.

"Did you know about him before that trip?" I ask. "Or did you figure it out then?"

A humorless smile. "The boy looks as if someone painted a portrait that is half Violet and half Ezra. Even then, I presumed he was the unfortunate result of an ill-fated romance. I was upset with Ezra, but not ready to judge him. Ready to dig deeper, though? Yes. I needed to answer my own questions."

Another dry smile as Cranston pats his horse. "I even considered hiring you or Duncan to do it, Hugh, but I could not expose Violet's secret in that way. So I found another man who does such things. What he uncovered . . ." Cranston swallows. "And yet, fool that I am, I continued to deny it. I wanted to think that my sister and my best friend had a youthful entanglement that ended in a child, and that he cared for Violet and never mistreated her."

"What changed your mind?" I ask.

"After the business with the wildcat, I tried to fire Müller. Müller said I would regret it. He taunted me with hints about Ezra and the maids. Lenore for one, and also Dorothy. His hints mirrored the horrible rumors my man had heard, and so I could no longer deny them. Nor could I pretend Ezra had nothing but an ill-considered romance with Violet. He hurt her, and if I did not see that in the way she had withdrawn into melancholia, the way she looked at him now, then I was a blinkered fool, a selfish oaf who saw only what he wanted to see. My sister was in torment being here, not with you, Hugh, but with Ezra, and then he was fawning over Fiona and I realized he had set his sights on my bride, despite the fact she obviously had no interest in him. I feared he might not *let* her refuse."

He inhales sharply. "I saw him leave that night. I took the shillelagh to threaten him. Thump him with it if I needed to. That had never been my way, so I thought threatening physical violence would convey the depths of my rage. Then, as I searched for where he had gone, I saw Violet by the lake, and I knew he was meeting her. She did not notice me, but I saw her, how tormented she looked, and when I found him . . ."

His voice drops. "I came up from behind him, and I struck him, meaning only to knock him down. I did not even think I had hit him that hard."

His lips twist. "I suppose that is what comes from not fighting, when you are as big as I am. You do not know how hard you have struck."

Cranston gazes out over the field, as if seeing himself and Sinclair there. "When he fell, I still did not think I had truly harmed him. I put my foot on his back to hold him down while I told him that I knew the truth and I never wanted to see him again. He did not answer. Did not move. That is when I bent and saw his eyes shut. I even opened his lids, being so utterly convinced that he must be feigning death."

"You *wanted* me to investigate, Archie," McCreadie says. "Constable Ross's case would not have held up in court, yet you did not want him. You wanted me. That makes no sense."

Cranston looks out over the field. "I did not mean to kill him, but I did. There are repercussions for that. I may have teased you, but I know you are an excellent detective. If you did not solve the case, then perhaps Fate decreed my crime did not deserve punishment."

McCreadie growls in frustration. "That is not how it works."

He's right, of course, but in some deep-seated way, I understand Cranston's magical thinking. He felt guilty, and he did not want to get off on the technicality of having the case investigated by an amateur. He wanted some sort of divine absolution, and he didn't get it.

"I understand where you need to take me, Hugh," Cranston says. "But is there any chance you would go back to the house and wait for me there?"

"Allowing you to flee on horseback?" McCreadie says.

Cranston's voice drops even lower. "I will not pull our friendship into this. Nor will I pull in Fiona, and what a murder trial would do to your sister."

"But you *do* mention it."

Cranston shakes his head. "This is about more than me and even your sister. It is about my own sister. There is a chance the courts could set me free. Perhaps even a good chance that I would avoid the hangman. But at what cost? I am asking you to let me face a life on the run to avoid exposing Violet and Lenore and the others to the horrors of a trial. Please. Allow me to run, even if a court might not send me to hang. I will leave the country, taking only the clothes on my back and the few pounds in my pocket. Nothing else."

"No." The voice comes from the trees to our left, and Fiona strides out. "You will also take me."

Cranston blinks. Then he recovers and says smoothly, "You should wait at the house, Fiona."

"I am not a child, despite what you seem to think, Archie."

"Fiona," McCreadie says. "Please wait—"

"Not. A. Child," she says to her brother, and then turns to Cranston. "I heard what you said. I know what you did and while you were vague on the details, I believe I understand what Ezra did. To Violet and other women. What he planned to do to me. In confronting him, you accidentally killed him. So you believe you must flee, and if you do, I will go with you."

"You cannot—"

"I certainly can, being an *adult*. Would you leave me behind to suffer whatever comes?"

"I—"

"You would leave to protect Violet from a trial and from the shame of having an illegitimate child. Yes, that would hurt her. But your leaving would hurt me. People would say that you fled the country to avoid marrying me. What do you think becomes of me after that? Look at your sister for the answer—and in her case, it was a polite parting of the ways, not *fleeing the country*."

"I will ensure no one thinks you were responsible—"

"I do not care. I have the chance to marry a good man, and I do not dare to guess who my parents would wed me to next. You do not wish to marry me? Fine. Take me to America as your sister. As for fleeing with only a few pounds, that is ridiculous. You have money. I have access to money. Leave the whisky business to Violet and she will be taken care of. But we both gather what funds we can before we run."

"Fiona . . ." McCreadie says.

She lifts a finger. "Do not, Hugh. You are my brother, not my master or even my guardian."

I glance at Cranston, who stares at her as if witnessing a transformation.

"However," she says, "as for leaving, I do not think that is necessary." She turns to McCreadie. "Have you not said, repeatedly, that you have no authority in this case?"

"I—"

"You searched for any way that you might be able to take charge, and you concluded there is none. You have no place in the investigation, and

Constable Ross has made it very clear that he does not want your help. So why help him by turning in Archie?"

McCreadie sighs. "Fee . . ."

"Do not 'Fee' me. Do you *want* to see Archie hang?"

McCreadie stiffens.

"Fine, that was unfair," she says. "Do you believe Archie should hang for striking a fiend who mistreated his sister and molested other women?"

"Fee . . ."

She lifts a hand. "Still unfair. Do you believe *anyone* should hang for striking someone who abused others? No, you do not. I know that because I know *you.*"

She moves toward him. "If this were a case you had to investigate, as part of your job, you would need to turn Archie in and let the court decide his fate. You would be uncomfortable with that, but it is your job. You make the arrest. The procurator fiscal chooses the charges, and the judge or jury finds the accused guilty or innocent. But you are not working this case. It is not your job to find the killer."

"I—"

"So you feel ethically bound to take your findings to Constable Ross? Fine. Do that, and if we are not here when you return, that is not your fault. But if you cart Archie off to face justice, you will never forgive yourself, Hugh. Even if a jury decides it was not murder, you will have ruined Violet. Again. Yes, that is not fair, but you know the truth of it."

McCreadie rocks back, pain flashing over his face.

Fiona continues, "At worst, Archie hangs for doing something you could just as easily have done. What if you discovered a dear friend had gotten me with child and mistreated me? And then turned his eye on Isla, planning to seduce and abuse her? You *know* you could have struck him in a fit of rage and fury and hurt."

She glances at Cranston. "Yes, *hurt.* Ezra's betrayal hurt you." She turns to McCreadie, Gray, and myself, as if addressing a jury. "I think we can all understand why Archie hit Ezra. We can also agree, given the tenor of his confession, that he did not intend to kill him. I also heard nothing that sounded as if Archie did not expect to pay for this unfortunate accident, whether by the hangman or by penniless exile. He wanted *you* to investigate, Hugh. But if you follow either of those paths, you will regret it, and

I am offering you a third choice. Not because I do not wish to lose my chance at a husband. As I said, I will go with Archie if he leaves. But I do not wish to hurt *you*."

McCreadie exhales and drops his head forward.

"It will still hurt," Fiona says, her voice low. "I realize that. You will suffer guilt with any choice you make. Turn him in to Constable Ross. Or let us flee. Or step back and do nothing. But which will be the least painful? We are not sentencing Müller to the noose. You are not giving evidence to see Müller convicted of the one crime he did not commit. You are simply letting Constable Ross do what Constable Ross insists on doing. Solving this bloody case himself."

McCreadie says nothing. Oh, I know what he'll decide. The only thing he can. But he's taking his time, and he's making sure not to look at us because this decision must be his.

Fiona continues, "You are not absolving Archie. If Constable Ross comes for him, we will deal with that and you will have no part in it. But let this go, Hugh. Please. I beg you. Let it go."

The silence stretches . . . and then, slowly, he nods.

FORTY-ONE

McCreadie made the only choice he could. I'd have made the same one, and I told him that later, as did Gray and Isla, when she heard the whole story. He will feel guilt. I will, too. Or maybe not guilt so much as discomfort.

I was raised to believe in the righteousness of the law, but that was the viewpoint of a child convinced that her mother only helped free the falsely accused. Of course my mother never claimed that, and as I got older, she answered honestly when I asked whether she'd ever helped someone she thought had committed the crime. That was how the law worked. If you were charged, the prosecution had to make its case beyond a reasonable doubt, and for every guilty person a defense lawyer kept out of prison, there were dozens of innocents they helped do the same.

I was a cop. I still am, in my soul. But that is never—ever—going to mean that I think our legal system isn't fundamentally broken, and I don't mean because guilty people go free. I don't even necessarily mean because innocents go to prison. I mean the way we look at crime and punishment, and all the nuances the law does not see. Justice is blind, and that's not always a good thing. In this time period, it is even blinder, with the specter of capital punishment looming.

Archie Cranston doesn't deserve the hangman's noose. He doesn't deserve life in prison or deportation. He deserves the chance to explain his actions and make an appropriate restitution to society. Fine him with the money going to an orphanage. Sentence him to community service. Make sure he pays in a manner that befits the crime.

But that won't happen. He'll be sentenced to hang or rot in prison or be deported to Australia . . . or he'll be set free. This is a world where women are considered property, even if Scottish law says otherwise. In defending the honor of women under his protection, Cranston defended his property. Either way, McCreadie agrees there's a good chance the court would set him free.

So who would have paid the price? Violet for one. Not only would her illegitimate child become public knowledge, but she'd be faced with the horrifying reality of what Sinclair did to her all those times she fell asleep. For now, she only questions what happened. Hearing Lenore's full story in court, she would know.

Lenore would have paid the price, too, outed as a young woman who had premarital sex. To Victorian society, anything else that happened after that was her own fault. Same goes for any other maids Sinclair targeted.

Even Fiona would come under scrutiny. People would whisper that, sure, she claims she didn't sleep with Ezra Sinclair but that's what she'd say, right? Sinclair was young and handsome and attentive, and she was a silly girl who would obviously have fallen for him.

McCreadie made the right choice, and in the end, he accepts that. We all do.

It's been three days since McCreadie let Cranston walk away. We didn't leave the estate. We couldn't—not without raising eyebrows. After all, there was a wedding to attend.

Cranston wanted to postpone it. I think he wanted to give Fiona time to reconsider her choice, but Fiona didn't need that. Like her brother, she'd made a decision and she was sticking to it. In the end, there was no way to postpone the nuptials, really. Like having us leave, it would only have aroused suspicion. So they'd waited a few extra days, in deference to the death of the best man, but that was all.

So we have a wedding. On a bright and sunny June day, in the gardens of the estate where we've spent the last week.

While the weather is lovely, the universe has given the bride and groom an even more significant gift. It's cleared the specter of Müller hovering over them, and the possibility of Cranston's rearrest. Yesterday, Constable Ross had been transporting Müller to a proper prison, when they'd been beset by masked men, who'd dragged the gamekeeper away.

Cranston wasn't responsible—he hasn't left the property nor sent any messages, being too engrossed in wedding preparations. Had Lenore's family made sure Müller never made it to trial? Or was it the family of the missing maid, Dorothy, who'd turned up at her parents' home in town? From what Müller told Cranston, Dorothy had been seduced by Sinclair, which means she was also certainly blackmailed by Müller. What matters is that Müller's gone, and the case is closed.

Isla and I have finished dressing. After more than two years, she's finally free of her mourning attire and able to dress as she wishes. Her gown is off-white, with lace trim and purple flowers. In my day, it'd be too close to white, but it's perfectly acceptable in an era where brides have only begun to optionally wear that color, after Queen Victoria chose it for her own wedding. The cotton of Isla's gown is ideal for a warm-weather event, while the lace and the tiered skirt make it elaborate enough for a wedding.

My own gown is also off-white, muslin, with blue stripes along the bodice and along the bottom of the skirt. My back still aches from bruising, but my dress had enough give for a slightly looser corset. Also, Gray may have given me something for the pain.

It took us so long to get ready that I'm certain the men will already be waiting impatiently, but we're hurrying down the hall when McCreadie's door opens. He walks out, and I give a little squeal. Then I quickly look around, being sure we're alone. We are. Everyone else has gone outside.

"A kilt!" I say. "You're wearing a kilt." I feign mopping my eyes. "I have been here over a year, and I'd started to think this day would never come. A Scotsman in a kilt."

McCreadie wags a finger at me. "Do not mock. It is a tradition for weddings."

"Oh, I'm not mocking. Where I come from, women love guys in kilts. Totally hot."

McCreadie looks at Isla. "She is mocking me, yes?"

"I . . . cannot tell," Isla says.

"I'm really not. Guys with Scottish ancestry wear them to weddings just for the excuse. There are entire shops on the Royal Mile set up for tourists with even a drop of Scottish blood, who buy kilts for special occasions." I waggle my brows. "And for their ladies in private."

McCreadie's cheeks flush.

I continue, "And that's not even touching the entire subgenre of Highlander romances, where all the guys on the cover wear kilts. They're also shirtless, but I know that's too much to ask for Victorians, so I'll accept the kilt, which looks really good."

"Not 'hot'?" Isla says.

"Er, I can't say that to him. You can, though. Feel free to tell Hugh he looks totally hot, Isla."

Her face goes as red as his.

A door opens behind us. I whirl, grinning as Gray steps out. Then I stop short. "You're wearing trousers."

He looks down and claps a hand to his heart. "Thank God. Imagine the scene if I had forgotten them."

I wave at McCreadie. "Wedding? Kilt?"

"I do not wear kilts."

McCreadie gives a low whistle. "Careful, Duncan. Mallory has just admitted to a fierce fondness for them."

"I have," I say. "And I am dreadfully disappointed. I am not certain I will recover."

"Poor form, chap," McCreadie murmurs. "Very poor form indeed."

"I . . . feel as if I have missed something."

"Never mind." I take his arm. "We have a wedding to attend, and I shall let you escort me, even if you are not wearing a kilt."

The ceremony is held in the gardens. The basics are familiar to me, with a few differences from modern weddings. There are maids and groomsmen, and a bride in her gown, a groom in his suit. Fiona has not opted for white, instead wearing the most gorgeous dress of light blue satin, with an elaborate bustle and equally elaborate flounces down the skirt, all trimmed with ivory lace. Her only jewelry is a sapphire necklace from Cranston and matching earrings from his parents. Both sets of parents walked the bride and groom in. At the front, the parents stood behind, the attendants to the side.

The service is simple, held in the shade of an oak. Isla explained earlier that church weddings are more common these days, but this is still acceptable. Ceremonies are often either morning or late afternoon. This is early afternoon, to take full advantage of the setting and the sunshine.

After the ceremony, we dine at tables in the gardens, eating a feast of chicken croquettes and lamb cutlets with strawberries and cream for dessert, alongside a wedding cake as elaborate as any from my own time.

Once the meal is complete, everyone begins doing their own thing, with musicians playing in one area, a croquet game set up in another, and Cranston presiding over what seems to be a whisky tasting that turns into a loud debate over some trade issue that I couldn't understand even if I wanted to.

I start with Fiona, Violet, and Isla, but then Fiona and I get to talking about the wildcat kittens—the three-legged one can't be returned to the wild, and Alice would like to take it home. Isla has already agreed; now Fiona must do the same. Of course she does, and we're busy talking about how to care for the cat when Cranston whisks his bride off to a dance on the lawn. I turn to look around. Am I kinda hoping to see Gray there, ready to be cajoled into the dance? Of course I am, and of course he is not.

I don't see Isla, Gray, or McCreadie. I wonder whether they're avoiding the two sets of parents. I met them earlier, with Gray, and that was awkward enough. This must be hell for McCreadie.

I've wandered over to the punch bowl and taken a glass when a voice behind me says, "I was going to ask you to dance, but you seem otherwise occupied."

I turn and smile up at Gray. "I could put this down."

"Mmm, you may wish to drink it first, if it is heavily laced with brandy. I am not the best dancer."

"That makes two of us." I turn toward the lawn where Cranston and Fiona lead the dance. "I . . . don't even know what that is."

"A minuet, I believe." He leans down and whispers, "I am not certain either. I know how to do a quadrille and a reel and the Viennese waltz, none of them well."

"I can waltz. My nan taught me."

"Then let us wait for that. Is your back well enough to dance?"

"It is after whatever you gave me."

He smiles and takes a glass of punch. "We shall dance, then. In the meantime, have you seen my sister?"

"No, and I should speak to her. Fiona has agreed to let Alice take the kitten."

"I last saw her walking around the house. Perhaps to the croquet game?"

We head out, sipping our punch and talking. We stay within sight of other guests. That damned propriety again. It's even worse at a wedding, where sneaking off could be construed as being swept away by the romance of the day.

"I do not see her by the croquet game," Gray muses. "Where could she have—?" He stops, and I follow his gaze to a stand of bushes. Protruding from the side is a flower-printed bustle that I'm ninety-five percent sure belongs to Isla.

"What is she doing there?" Gray glances at me. "Did she seem unsettled? The wedding a reminder of her own perhaps?"

"No, she was in a wonderful mood, even while getting ready, which is never her favorite thing. Today she took extra care and . . ." I trail off, as a thought hits at the same time I notice something else.

"She's not alone over there," I say.

"Hmm?" He leans to peer and then pulls back. "Oh."

With the shade of the bush, it's easy to see Isla's pale gown, but her dark-suited companion almost disappears.

I grin at Gray. "When's the last time you saw Hugh?"

He smiles back. "About the same time I last saw Isla."

I glance toward the bush. Isla and McCreadie standing, obviously. I mean, all the power to them if they found a quiet place for something needing more discretion but if so, it'd be more than fifty feet from the croquet game.

When I start in that direction, Gray whispers, "What are you doing?"

I wave a hand. It should be obvious what I'm doing. Spying. I creep toward the bushes until I'm just close enough to see that McCreadie has his hand on Isla's face and she's leaning toward him in rapt, whispered, intimate conversation.

I turn to find Gray right beside me, and I grin, raising my hand for a high five . . . which of course he just stares at, blankly.

"Never mind," I whisper, and hurry in the other direction before we're seen. Then I stop around the corner of the house, where we can be seen but not heard.

"That was what I thought it was, right?" I say. "The start of more than 'just friends'?"

Gray smiles. "It was."

"And that's good, right?"

"That is excellent."

I bounce, barely able to restrain the urge to throw my arms around his neck in a celebratory hug, as if *we* have something to celebrate. We do, though. Maybe we can't take responsibility for the match, but we can celebrate our joy at seeing it.

"Step one accomplished," I say. "Now it's on to a proper courtship and marriage and little Islas and Hughs and—" I stop. "Oh."

I look up at Gray, and see in his expression he's already realized what I have.

If Isla marries, I can't keep living in the Robert Street town house with Gray. If I were the housemaid, it would be acceptable, but tongues would only wag more if I reverted to my former position.

"If they marry . . ." I say.

"Yes." One word. Neither of us needs more.

I worry my lip. Part of me wants to say that maybe they won't marry—or it'll be a long courtship—but of course I hope they find all the happiness they deserve, as quickly as they can.

"We could work it out," I say. "I could get an apartment."

Except I don't want an apartment. I want to stay where I am. Having Isla gone would be difficult, but being away from *everyone*? Living on my own in some empty little room, without the patter of Alice's footsteps, Jack's easy laugh, Mrs. Wallace's snaps and snipes, Simon outside, ready to chat, and Gray. Most of all Gray.

Gray's voice drops. "I know you were angry with me for my suggestion, but this is one reason I made it, Mallory. Isla is out of mourning. Being here helped Hugh overcome what happened with Violet—it reminded him of why he did not marry her."

"Because he loves Isla."

Gray nods. "We will find another way. I understand that my suggestion was offensive to you. I blurted it without forethought, caught you off guard and upset you. I know you did not want an apology, but I still wish to give one. I also wish you to understand that there was no insult intended in my suggestion."

"Is that what you said in your letter?"

He frowns.

"The letter Dorothy took," I say. "The one you left me."

He glances away, and his color seems to rise. "Ah. Yes. The letter. It was . . ." He clears his throat and then nods decisively. "Exactly that. I apologized and attempted to explain myself. Poorly done, of course, and it is best that you never saw it. We will seek other options."

"If we did need to marry, would you wear a kilt to the wedding?"

He laughs softly. "Yes, I would wear a kilt for you." He leans down. "But we are going to seek every possible alternative."

"We have time. I don't think Hugh and Isla are going to be sending out wedding invitations tomorrow."

"Agreed. We *do* have time, and we will use it wisely." He looks up over my shoulder. "In the meanwhile, I believe they are playing a waltz."

I glance over. "Seems like it."

"Well, then." He extends his arm. "May I have this dance?"

I smile and take his arm. "You may."

ACKNOWLEDGMENTS

Once again, thanks to my editor at Minotaur, Kelley Ragland, and my agent, Lucienne Diver, for all their help with this one. As always, it was much appreciated.

And again, a huge thanks to Elli F and Amanda KM, for all their advice on the fashions and culture of the era. As always, any errors are mine.

ABOUT THE AUTHOR

Kathryn Hollinrake

Kelley Armstrong is the author of more than fifty novels in mystery, fantasy, and horror. She believes experience is the best teacher, though she's been told this shouldn't apply to writing her murder scenes. To craft her books, she has studied aikido, archery, and fencing. She sucks at all of them. She has also crawled through very shallow cave systems and climbed half a mountain before chickening out. She is, however, an expert coffee drinker and a true connoisseur of chocolate-chip cookies.